My Darling, My Disaster

LORDS OF ESSEX

My Darling, My Disaster

LORDS OF ESSEX

AMALIE HOWARD
&
ANGIE MORGAN

Entangled Publishing, LLC
2614 South Timberline Road
Suite 109
Fort Collins, CO 80525
Visit our website at www.entangledpublishing.com.

Select Historical is an imprint of Entangled Publishing, LLC.

Edited by Alethea Spiridon
Cover design by Erin Dameron-Hill
Cover art from Period Images

Manufactured in the United States of America

First Edition March 2017

For all the badass princesses out there

Prologue

VOLKONSKY PALACE
ST. PETERSBURG, RUSSIA
SEPTEMBER 1816

Princess Svetlanka Volkonsky moved noiselessly in her younger sister's bedchamber, her hands shaking as she gathered a few articles of clothing and all the jewelry she could find.

Earlier that day, the sound of her uncle's anger had stopped her as she passed the second-floor landing on her way to the music room. Count Volkonsky rarely raised his voice, so hearing it boom from the direction of the hunting room had made her pause. And listen.

What she'd heard told her that she and her younger sister, Irina, needed to get away from St. Petersburg as soon as they could. Out of the country, if possible, and far out of Count Volkonsky's reach.

Because her uncle meant to kill them.

Lana had suspected for years that her uncle had been

selling crown secrets to the French, but she had never guessed that he would be capable of murder…or capable of murdering his own *brother*. Her parents had died months before in an accident, their carriage having overturned and plummeted down a cliff, sending them, their driver, and footman all to their deaths. The blame had been firmly laid upon a faulty carriage wheel, and both she and Irina had been left orphans and wards of their uncle. Now, Lana knew the truth—thanks to what she had overheard earlier that afternoon.

Lana tugged the drapes at the window closed and turned to her sister, who was plucking various items from an open chest and placing them into a small case spread open upon her bed. Lana fisted her hands in the folds of her own dark blue traveling dress. "Only what you need, Irina."

"Where are we going?" her sister asked, her violet eyes wide with fear.

"I…don't know," Lana replied. "But I have sent word to someone who will help us."

Well before he'd died, her father had confided in Lana, telling her that if she ever required aid in an emergency and he was not there to give it, she need only send a note to a particular address. A candle shop, of all places. The note was to be addressed to *LL* and signed with her father's royal seal. *He will come if he is in St. Petersburg*, her father had promised. Lana only hoped that her father's trust in *this* man, at least, had not been misplaced.

"But why must we leave?" Irina cried. "Our lives are here. Everyone we love is here. And why are we leaving in the middle of the night? Will we not say good-bye?"

How could she tell her sister the things she had overheard their uncle saying that afternoon? That in his quest to get his hands on their considerable fortune he had arranged his brother's accident, and now a marriage between Lana and his odious ally, Baron Zakorov. That he and Zakorov would share her inheritance, and soon after the wedding, Lana would not be alive to protest.

If she refused the marriage, her scheming uncle would likely kill her anyway, or turn his attentions to Irina. Lana would never allow either of those things to happen. She shook her head decisively. No, this was the only way.

"Because we must," she answered. "Take any jewels. Anything of value you can find."

"Lana." Her sister's voice caught. "I'm scared."

She moved swiftly across the room to embrace Irina. "As am I."

Lana stared at her sister, who was valiantly trying to hold back her tears, and marveled at the extent of her bravery at the tender age of fourteen. Lana was only older by four years, but she had had more time with their mother and had already made her bow to Russian society. Irina had always been far more sheltered. Still, Lana knew that she should at least tell her a part of the truth. Irina was old enough to understand what was at stake. She took a deep breath and sat her sister on the edge of the bed.

"We cannot trust in our uncle any longer. He means us harm. I have heard him confess it with my own ears."

Irina's eyes widened to huge orbs, and Lana rushed to soothe her. "But you must have faith in *me*. Believe me when I say I will make us safe again."

The tears that had been shimmering in Irina's eyes broke free, coursing down her cheeks in an unhindered waterfall. "I believe you," she sobbed. "But I miss Mama."

"I do, too, but I need you to be strong, Irina." Lana wiped her sister's face with her sleeve. "I cannot do this without you. So dry your eyes, and pack what you can. A few simple gowns, and whatever else you treasure."

She watched her sister rally, and although her fingers shook with every swiftly chosen item she placed in the small suitcase, Lana knew that she could count on Irina not to fall apart. At least not until they arrived somewhere safe, out of the reach of their greedy uncle.

Lana had already canvassed her mother's rooms, untouched since the accident, and emptied her jewelry cases. Gems of every hue glittered among ropes of gold and silver. She hoped it would be enough to get them to safety. Her uncle controlled their inheritance and the small monthly allowance they were given, though Lana had not thought to save a single kopek of it. How could she have planned for this?

Lana lifted the two cases she had packed for herself earlier that evening, one of which was filled with something much more valuable than clothing and treasured memories. When her father had been alive, she had often seen him tuck the small key to his private safe inside a hidden desk drawer. After his death, she had found the key and used it to open the safe.

There had been no money but a number of papers and documents, many of them strangely worded love letters written by her uncle. Curious as to what they said, Lana had kept the documents rather than turn them over to her uncle—a stroke of serendipity, it seemed. They had been an entertaining puzzle to try to sort out while she worked through her grief, and they'd made her feel closer to her departed father.

But now something else her uncle had said to Baron Zakorov that afternoon in the hunting room, about searching for evidence and a cipher, had made her remember them. The papers had to be important if he was looking for them. Lana had hidden the documents in the lining of her own suitcase, determined that her uncle would never get his traitorous hands on them.

The last thing she packed was a small portrait of her family that had stood for years upon her parents' bedside table. Leaving everything else behind would hurt dearly, but it was the smart thing to do. The safest thing to do.

"Ready?" she asked her sister, fastening a heavy woolen cloak similar to the one she wore around Irina.

"I think so."

Hand in hand, they slipped down the narrow back stairs of the house, careful not to make any noise or wake the sleeping servants. Once outside, they hurried across the darkened grounds, making their way by the light of a crescent moon to the far end of the estate. There, on a rarely used horse trail, a plain black coach sat waiting, just as she had requested in the note to her father's trusted, yet anonymous, friend. The horses whinnied nervously beside a hulking shadow of a man. Lana's heartbeat tripped. For a moment, she experienced real fear. What if the note had been intercepted by her uncle? What if this giant was *his* man?

"Princess," the shadowy figure said. "Lord Langlevit bids you welcome."

Lord Langlevit? Lana did not know this man, but his initials aligned with the ones she had written on the note: *LL*. He had come. Just as her father had promised. The terror drained from her body, and with a nod to her sister, Lana let the man help Irina into the waiting coach. She glanced over her shoulder, looking in bittersweet sorrow at her home.

Her birthright.

Lana gritted her teeth at the thought of her devious, conniving uncle. One day, she would find a way to get Volkonsky Palace back and bring her uncle to justice for his crimes—against her family and, possibly, against his country.

For now, her only priority was her sister's safety.

Chapter One

Ferndale
Essex, England
April 1817

Lord Graham Findlay, Viscount Northridge and heir to the title and holdings of the Earl of Dinsmore, rode over Ferndale's western field like the hounds of hell were after him. His chestnut's deep burgundy crest and withers shimmered with every powerful stride, Gray's own blood burning beneath his skin. The exercise wasn't just for his favorite mount, Pharaoh, but for Gray as well. Early-morning rides, while the sky was still rising with color, were the only things that kept Gray from unraveling during the rest of the day.

He spent his nights alone and, without fail, woke each morning with a keen ache deep in his loins. It always hurt worse when he was in London, where his evenings were devoted to dinners with friends, cards at White's, or a more hazardous bit of gambling at one of the gaming hells he'd once frequented far too often. The temptations London held came to him in the most enticing forms—revealing dresses, coy smiles, a hiked skirt to display the shapely turn of an ankle, and at some establishments, much, *much* more than an ankle.

Gray allowed himself to look, but he didn't touch, and for that reason alone he preferred Essex to London, by far.

Here at Ferndale, the ache he woke with every morning, the one he'd come to trust in and yet still despise, wasn't as great. With his evenings spent sedately among his parents and sister, Gray could more easily ignore the fact that he had not taken a woman to his bed in nearly three years. It was a decision he had made for himself, and one he would abide by.

One he would stake his honor upon.

For one reason: Sofia.

The ride with Pharaoh that morning had done more than alleviate the sensation of loneliness. It had strengthened his fortitude to stand by his vow—a private vow, born of a mistake Gray promised himself on a daily basis he would never repeat.

He reined in Pharaoh and turned him to face the ridge of oak and ash trees. The sunrise was a honeyed hue this morning, with large streaks of clouds and blue sky cutting through the gold. Gray took a deep breath and finally allowed his mind to rush forward, into the day that lay ahead of him.

His younger sister, Briannon, would be expecting him in the attics above the servants' quarters shortly after breakfast. It was where they secretly stored their fencing gear, and being situated so high within the manor, the clashing of their foils would not be heard by their oblivious mother several stories below. Lady Dinsmore absolutely forbade her only daughter to participate in anything so active as fencing, the threat of one of Brynn's breathing attacks always there, hovering in the background.

Gray himself did not enjoy indulging his sister's adventurous streak, however he had long ago realized she could not be kept high on a shelf, wrapped in cotton linen. As stubborn as a mule and far too clever by half, she was going to get herself into trouble one way or another. Gray only thought it wise that he be there with her in case her health took a turn for the worse.

This skewed sense of duty was what had led him to teach Brynn how to ride, how to fence, and even how to shoot, heaven help him. The thought made him remember why he was at Ferndale to begin with. The visit had not been planned, but when he had learned that his father's coach had been set upon by the Masked Marauder—the notorious highwayman terrorizing the *ton* from London to Essex—en route to the Worthington Abbey ball, and that Brynn had been accosted by the blackguard, Gray had left Bishop House in London at once.

He had expected to find his family in a state of distress. Instead, he'd arrived the morning before to find only one of them still in a lather: Mother, of course. Brynn had been perfectly well, if a little distracted. His father had been grumbling about the loss of a pair of fine cufflinks but had otherwise appeared unaffected. Gray's hasty departure from London hadn't seemed all that necessary after all, though he never regretted an excursion to Ferndale, and not just to flee the seemingly endless supply of fine women willing to help him crumble his vows of celibacy. Gray looked forward to every visit to Ferndale, and most especially to the neighboring village of Breckenham.

He guided Pharaoh back through the field at a steady trot, unable to suppress the grin stealing over his lips. After an hour or two with Brynn in the attics, he would wash up and make some excuse for missing tea with mother. The Coopers would not be expecting him, of course. He hadn't had the time to send ahead a letter before rushing out of London. He would deliver a note today, announcing himself and requesting a visit, perhaps tomorrow. Gray didn't trust any of Ferndale's servants not to gossip, so he would deliver the note himself.

Discretion was paramount. This he had promised the

Coopers *and* himself.

Gray was still smiling when he dismounted Pharaoh at the estate's stable doors and walked the chestnut in. Hatcher, one of the stable boys, set down a pitchfork and rushed forward for the reins. Gray gave his mount one last affectionate rub against his chin and began for the kitchens. It wasn't a proper entrance for the future master of the house, but it was the most appealing, especially when Cook had breakfast preparations well underway and Gray's stomach was rumbling with hunger.

The kitchens were a vast network of subterranean rooms underneath the first floor of the manor, and it was a place he admitted to knowing next to nothing about. This was not his territory, to be sure, however his nose had been guiding him to Mrs. Braxton's great hearth and stove for as long as memory served. It didn't fail him now. When he slinked into the main kitchen, two scullery maids glanced up from a long table where they were peeling hard-boiled eggs.

He lifted a finger to his lips, and the girls stifled their giggles, their eyes darting toward the cook, who stood with her back to the rest of the room. Mrs. Braxton was a short, lean woman, all bones and sinew—everything most cooks in noble houses were not. The only roundness to Mrs. Braxton was her face, which was the shape of a plump tomato, and usually the color of one as well.

As Gray tiptoed up behind her and reached a hand toward the tray she was busy piling with sausages, he felt like a boy again.

"I know you're there, Master Gray, and so help me I'll rap your knuckles with me fork if you don't—*oh!*"

Mrs. Braxton jumped nearly a foot into the air as Gray swatted her backside, distracting her long enough to pluck two sausages from the tray. The scullery maids burst out with their giggles as Mrs. Braxton swung her fork at him like a sword. He bounded away, holding up his prizes, one in each hand.

"Oh, you scoundrel!" she cried, her cheeks coloring a deeper crimson. She couldn't contain her own grin though. "If that's the way you're treating the young women in London, you'll be a bachelor forever!"

"Or married in a fortnight," he said, winking at her.

Gray laughed and darted out of the kitchen as a new potato came sailing toward his head. Their butler's wife had extraordinarily good aim, and a welt on his forehead was not something he desired, especially if he was going to pay the Coopers a visit tomorrow.

His smile dulled somewhat as Mrs. Frommer came around the corner in the hallway and met him with her usual, dour expression. The strict housekeeper could scatter the rest of the staff under her watch with one glance, and the effect was much the same with him. She bobbed her head, continuing into the kitchen, and Gray made good on his escape.

He was nearly to the top of the servant stairs to the first floor when the door at the landing opened. Brynn's new lady's maid, Lana Volchek, rushed down the first few steps, only glancing up when she had reached the step above Gray's. When she saw him, she didn't widen her eyes the way the two scullery maids had. She didn't gasp or falter at the unexpected sight of a lord in the servant stairwell.

She glared at him, one imperious, dark brow vaulted high. The laughter froze on his cheeks as she regarded him with a disapproving stare far beyond the reaches of her position.

"I know what you are doing," Lana said, her voice low.

Gray looked at the sausages in his hands, one of which was already half eaten. Unfortunately, he had not finished chewing just yet. Hurriedly, he swallowed and licked his lips, concerned one of his ravenous bites may have left behind a drop of grease on his mouth.

"Stealing sausages?" he said.

She rolled her eyes, each bright green iris glittering in the light cast by the stairwell's single wall sconce. "You and Lady Briannon are going to the attics," she said. "Again."

Gray pulled back, this time with indignation. "Did you... Miss Volchek, did you just roll your eyes at me?" he asked, coming up to the same step on which she stood.

She held her chin high and did not blink at his clear censure. Brynn adored her new lady's maid, though Gray could not for the world see why. Yes, she had come highly recommended by the Countess of Langlevit, and her Russian heritage and accent gave an exotic flavor to an otherwise very English staff. But she spoke far too freely, something Brynn rashly allowed. Encouraged, even. Her previous lady's maid, a woman named Nina, had been quiet as a mouse and much more...manageable. She'd also been plain of face and, on the whole, unattractive.

Unlike this girl.

Her eyes. They were what distracted him every time she had the audacity to meet his gaze and challenge him so boldly. As she was doing now. They were a rare shade of green, a color that reminded Gray of the stained glass panels in the family chapel, when the sun would catch the emerald shards at just the right angle and set them aglow. The tendrils of hair that escaped the white cap she wore while on duty was as dark as the thick cocoa his mother sipped every morning, and her skin as pale as the alabaster busts decorating the second-floor gallery. The top of Lana's white bonnet barely reached Gray's shoulder, but she held herself with a confidence that made her appear taller.

No, this maid was not lacking in physical charms.

Gray realized he was staring down at her, his gaze drawn to the gentle flare of her hips. His earlier discomfort, the one he'd woken to that morning, struck again. Frustrated, his grip around one sausage tightened.

He scowled. "You make it sound as if Brynn and I are

going to be plotting a murder up in the attics," he said, refusing to meet Lana's gaze again for fear she would see the raging desires in his.

"You shouldn't jest. You know how she struggles with her breathing. If she works herself up too much, she could—"

"That is enough, Miss Volchek," he cut in, exasperated and suddenly desperate to be away from her. Gray couldn't remember the last time a servant had spoken to him in such a manner. Having dear old Mrs. Braxton throw potatoes at his head was one thing, but enduring the chastising of this maid, who had somehow worked her way so quickly and firmly into Brynn's heart, was something else entirely.

"I know my sister, thank you, and I have things well in hand. There is no need for you to concern yourself." He then thought of something else. "And I do not know how things were done in Moscow, but here, it is wise to address members of the peerage as is suitable to their ranking."

Lana sealed her lips, cutting off whatever she had been about to say, though her eyes flashed with barely contained displeasure. Her sheer impudence astounded him. As if he had insulted *her* by reminding them of their positions in this household, and in society in general.

"Of course, *my lord Northridge*," she murmured, placing unmistakable stress on the proper address that bordered on sarcasm as she bobbed a short curtsy. Gray was far too eager to be parted from her company—and the warming scent of honeyed wildflowers that she had carried into the stairwell—to reprimand her for it.

"Good day, then," he said, and took the last four steps to the servants' door in two bounds. Once he came into the back hall of the first floor, near the dining room and his mother's morning room, he gathered a breath and held it in his lungs.

He'd sounded like a complete brute reminding her of her place, but hell, the chit had deserved it. He only wished he hadn't been coming up from the kitchens at the time — a place he hadn't belonged, either.

The sausages in his hands had grown cold, and damn it if he didn't look like a fool holding them the way he was. Gray walked toward the front hall, and once there, shoved them through the bars of the cage holding his mother's beloved parakeets. She kept the pair in the hallway, believing their bright green and yellow coloring were the perfect foils to the sky blue wallpaper.

"At least you'll enjoy them," he muttered, as their little beaks began to peck happily.

Gray started for the staircase up to his rooms to change out of his riding kit. What did his sister's maid think, that he would push Brynn to the point of breathlessness while fencing? He was not so mindless or careless to risk his sister's health. He still worried over the state of her lungs, even though it had been quite some time since she'd seriously taken ill. Those dark memories from when Brynn had been much younger, the many visits from doctors, and the many days and nights when the whole house would pause, listening to her wheezing and coughing, wondering if she might very well gasp her last breath, had not yet faded from Gray's memory.

Lana had been with their family for several months, and must have already learned that Brynn would not be subdued, not even by her own fluctuating health. He bristled again at Lana's familiarity with him in the stairwell, and he was not proud of how easily his mind had turned to admiring her physical attributes.

Gray swore, aloud this time, as he entered his chamber and kicked the door shut behind him. Damn. He'd been virtuous far too long if he was now lowering himself to eyeing the help. Maddening, belligerent, and far too appealing help.

Sighing, he stripped. A cold bath, it seemed, was in order.

Chapter Two

Lana stroked the soft lilac silk of the evening dress Lady Briannon had discarded the night before, feeling the delicate fabric slip through her fingers. The wave of nostalgia was swift and brutal. She missed wearing such finery and dancing until the blushing hours of the morning. She had owned dozens of dresses like this one, but she had been forced to leave them all at Volkonsky Palace.

It had been nearly eight months since that fateful night when she and Irina had fled for their lives. Eight months living in constant fear that her uncle would track them down and force them to return. But as the days passed and there continued to be no sign of the count or his man, Zakorov, Lana breathed more easily. There was no reason that her uncle would search for them in London, and less reason still that he would suspect the disguise she had undertaken.

She was a lady's maid, a position that was far beneath her true station as Lord Northridge had so clearly pointed out a day past. She smiled to herself thinking of how the arrogant young lord would react if he only knew her secret. That she was one of the exalted peerage he'd spoken about, and that *she*, in fact, outranked *him*. She'd give anything to see his face turn the color of the elegantly tailored plum waistcoat he'd been wearing.

But, of course, Lana kept her mouth shut. Nothing was worth the risk of exposure, not even such satisfaction. Lord and Lady Dinsmore had been more than welcoming, and she and Lady Briannon had liked each other from the start. So much so, in fact, that Lady Briannon had forgiven Lana's dreadful blunders during the first few weeks of her service. Blunders that would have gotten any other maid dismissed entirely—like placing a pair of hot curling tongs on one of Brynn's gowns and burning a hole straight through the linen. As a princess, Lana had known what duties ladies' maids were expected to perform, given that she'd had three of her own, but *how* to perform them properly had been an education. An oftentimes embarrassing one, at that.

Though Lord Langlevit had balked at her plan at first— lowering herself into service was an unconscionable idea for someone of her rank—he had grudgingly agreed that the position was preferable, since ladies' maids in wealthy households tended to have more freedom than most of the staff. So the earl and his mother, the countess, who had not blinked an eye at her son's middle-of-the-night return home with two heavily cloaked princesses, had provided Lana with a spotless letter of recommendation.

She had been transformed into Lana Volchek—the genteel daughter of a respected modiste in Moscow who had come to England under hardships, and with a goal to be in service to a fine family. Irina, however, given her age, had traveled on to Lord Langlevit's little used estate far north in Cumbria and was staying with the countess as her ward.

It was more than either of them could have hoped for.

Lord Langlevit had proved himself to be the trusted

friend her father had claimed he would be. He'd spirited them away from Volkonsky Palace without hesitation or question. Eventually, on their journey to England, he had eased the truth from Lana, why they were in danger—that Count Volkonsky and Baron Zakorov planned to kill her the same way they had killed her parents. She'd imagined the truth would have shocked the earl, but he had simply reclined in his seat on the deck of their ship as it traveled out of the Gulf of Finland and into the Baltic Sea.

"Zakorov. Yes, we have had our eye on him for quite some time," he'd replied, his lack of a reaction startling her.

"We?" she had echoed. "Whom do you refer to?"

"I am not at liberty to say. However, you can be assured that they are people of import."

"Lords like yourself? Members of polite society?" Lana had suppressed a bitter laugh as she'd looked out at the choppy sea. "Not that I am ungrateful for your efforts, but I hardly think a few English lords can stop a brute like Zakorov. Or my uncle."

"You should know by now, Your Highness, that I am more than what I appear to be on the surface," Langlevit had replied quietly.

Lana had not uncovered every truth hiding behind the earl's titled and privileged exterior, but she had since discerned that he was tied to the British War Office, and that his visits to St. Petersburg and Moscow were more than likely of a clandestine nature. He had not admitted it in so many words, but Lana knew what he was. A spy, like Zakorov. Like her uncle. Only he was friend, not foe, and he had the trust of the Russian ministry. Hers as well.

Langlevit had offered to let Lana stay with his mother, the countess in Cumbria, but they had both agreed that it would draw too much attention, especially if she and Irina were seen together. They hailed from a prominent Russian family and couldn't take the chance that a member of the peerage would recognize them. Lana didn't want either of them to get too comfortable. Her uncle was not the sort of man to be underestimated.

Despite Langlevit's generosity and the money she'd accumulated by selling most of their jewels, Lana had chosen to take the lowly position so that she could stay abreast of the movements of the *ton*. Being ensconced in Cumbria with Irina would have made her feel too isolated and vulnerable. She knew firsthand from her own staff in St. Petersburg that servants were veritable fountains of information.

The post had positioned her perfectly to know if and when her uncle or any of his associates set foot on English soil, and as Lady Briannon's lady's maid, her duties were more than tolerable. Lana wasn't afraid of a little work, and she was a quick study. Her days consisted of needlework, hairdressing, and fashion, while Mary, the quiet, young undermaid, took on heavier housemaid duties like cleaning and ironing. It was due to Mary's patient teaching that Lana knew which gowns went where for laundering, which muslins needed starching, and which cleaning solvents were too harsh for certain fabrics. The rest she learned as she went.

Her deft needlework skills allowed her to set a tight stitch and take over most of the mending of Brynn's clothing. It wasn't the same as embroidery, but it was something Lana enjoyed, even if it were as simple as darning a stocking or reattaching a missing button. Sewing had always been calming for her. In fact, whenever she had an altercation with Lord Northridge, she went straight for the pile of mending, which she tackled with uncommon ferocity.

Lana sighed. Of all the family members, only Lord Northridge conspired to drive her to distraction. Lana didn't know why she let him get under her skin, but he was the thorn in an otherwise pleasant tenure. For one, his lightning-swift shifts in temper toward her were impossible to predict. One day he'd be aloof and reserved, and the next he would eye her as if he could barely stand to be in the same space.

Lord Northridge and his capricious moods aside, thus far, the position had served well to keep Lana out of the public eye. Releasing a pent-up breath, Lana returned the lovely lilac silk to the large armoire. She walked to the window in Brynn's bedroom and eyed the empty bed. She guessed that her mistress had gone for one of her early-morning rides before everyone else awake. It was mostly to avoid her mother's consternation, but Lana knew that Brynn enjoyed the freedom and the solitude without everyone fawning over her and worrying for her health.

Though her mistress had only had one minor episode since Lana's arrival, she'd heard enough stories from the kitchen staff of ones that were far, far worse. Mrs. Frommer, the harpy of a housekeeper, did not encourage gossip, but a few of the servant girls were not so inclined. Within days, Lana had learned of all the comings and goings of those who lived at Ferndale, including the terrible lung affliction that had plagued Lady Briannon since birth.

As a result, the girl had been near smothered her whole life. Lana made it a point not to outwardly coddle her, and she knew that Brynn appreciated that. However, Lana *did* worry. She simply could not understand how Lord Northridge could encourage his sister to risk an attack in a dusty old attic, of all places. Had Irina been born with such an affliction, Lana would have made certain she lived happily but *safely*.

Then again, Brynn was a little like her sister, Lana thought—sweet and reserved on the surface, but stubborn and resilient several layers deep. She smiled. Her mistress may have ailing lungs, but she also had a will of iron. Perhaps fencing in the deserted attic had been *her* idea instead of her brother's.

"Who taught you to ride?" Lana had asked one morning when Brynn had returned from her outing, breathless but rosy cheeked.

"Gray," she answered, stripping away the appalling men's breeches and shirt that she favored while riding. These items of clothing, at least, were simple to wash and mend. And if Lana accidentally over-starched or failed to remove a stain, Brynn never complained. "He's the only one who ever teaches me anything. If it weren't for him, I'd be confined to bed every hour of every day."

"That is surprising."

Brynn had stared at her with perceptive eyes. Perhaps something in Lana's tone had carried through what she truly thought of her brother. "Gray takes a while to warm to new people. He may not readily show it, but he's kind and sensitive, with a gentle heart."

Lana had almost rolled her eyes. Kind and sensitive were the last two words she would use to describe Lord Northridge. After eight months, he had clearly not warmed to her. Why, in the servant stairwell the day before, she'd yet again found him to be rude, overbearing, and irritatingly arrogant. As if she were some brainless twit to be scolded at every turn. And as far as him having a *gentle* heart, she'd have to take Brynn's word for it. She had yet to see that he even possessed a heart.

After straightening the bed and laying out a pale blue linen day dress for her mistress, Lana rushed to her room to collect her satchel. She welcomed Brynn's dependable tendency to take morning rides. They allowed Lana to walk the long lane to the entrance to Ferndale, where she tucked her letters to Irina into a slim, deep knot of an oak tree. Lord Langlevit had arranged for a trusted man to collect Lana's letters and ride them up to Cumbria. Upon the rider's return, he would deposit the letters Irina had sent for Lana. They came like clockwork every fortnight.

The earl had gone well out of his way to make sure she and her sister stayed in contact, though they had to be sure to keep their correspondence as vague as possible in case of discovery. Still, Lana loved seeing her sister's girlish handwriting, and treasured each heartfelt, if sparse, letter. She hoped that she would one day be able to repay the earl's extraordinary kindness. As was their custom, she'd written a short message to him disguised as a love sonnet that she'd included with the stack of letters.

The golden morning sun was still cool, just rising over the lush, landscaped gardens of the Ferndale estate. In a way, it reminded her of the rolling hills of her own home, and for a moment she experienced a wave of nostalgia so sharp that it brought tears to her eyes. *Soon,* she vowed. She would find a way to prove that her uncle was a traitor. She would find a way to return home with Irina.

Lana walked the long, curving lane briskly, blood flowing through her veins and filling her body with vigor. She longed to go for a ride, but of course, servants were not allowed such liberties. In St. Petersburg, there'd been so many things she had taken for granted—small things like her horses and her possessions, and bigger things like her family and her freedom. While she missed not being able to ride or attend a ball, she mourned the loss of the latter far more.

As the large oak tree loomed into sight at the crest of the last hill, Lana drew the packet of letters from her bag. Irina had written that she was being tutored in all manner of subjects, and that the countess was seeing to her education as if Irina were to be presented to English society. Lana was grateful if the lessons kept her sister occupied and entertained. Nearing the tree, she pressed a kiss to the bundle and was about to crouch and place it into the hollow when the sound of approaching horses made her shove it back into her bag.

Her heart tripped over itself as a carriage, drawn by four

gorgeously plumed mounts, pulled to a sharp stop a few feet from where she stood. She recognized the coachman as Lord and Lady Dinsmore's London driver, Rogers, and James, one of the footmen, at the back. Stifling her frown, she wondered at the carriage's occupants and why they would have signaled a stop. As far as she knew, Lord and Lady Dinsmore were both still abed. Brynn was otherwise occupied, which left only one other person.

Like the devil himself, Lord Northridge emerged from the midnight blue lacquered coach without waiting for the footman and scowled at her, inducing her own frown to reappear. Her heart sank. Of all the people she might have encountered, it would have to be him. Lana quickly forced her expression into a mask of tranquility, refusing to let his foul mood affect her.

"What are you doing out here at this hour?" he asked.

"Walking, my lord." Her subtle emphasis on the last two words was clearly not lost on him. His blue eyes narrowed at her overbright smile. "And you, Lord Northridge? Taking the air as well?"

Heavens, why on earth was she baiting him?

Lana didn't know the answer, only that it gave her great satisfaction to see the quick snap of his reaction. It was obvious from his formal evening clothing that he was returning from a late night out. His cravat was loosened and his hair rumpled, making her think his night had been one of sleepless scandal. She blinked at the thought and looked away.

"No," he grit out, subjecting her to a baleful stare. "Why aren't you tending to Lady Briannon?"

Lana considered her words with care. She did not want to give her mistress away, but she assumed Lord Northridge already suspected his sister's whereabouts. "It is rather early. She does not require my assistance at the moment, my lord."

He folded his arms across his broad chest, propping

his back against the side of the coach. Lana felt the heat of his stare and finally looked into his heavy-lidded eyes. His deliberate perusal of her person made her uncomfortable.

"Is there something you wish to tell me, Lord Northridge?"

"I find it interesting that you will scold me for fencing in the attic, and yet you let her ride at this hour of the morning." He gestured to the brightening sky. "It is not yet light."

"Let her?" Lana murmured. "You overestimate my sway. I am a servant, my lord, nothing more."

"Why not bring it to Lady Dinsmore's attention?"

She stared at him, realizing that he was now baiting her. She opted for honesty. "I will not betray Lady Briannon's confidence."

He didn't say anything for a long moment, but then he shoved off the coach and closed the distance between them with two short strides. Lana fought the urge to take two matching steps back. She gripped the strap of her satchel and held her head high. "And where were you going at this hour, Miss Volchek?" he asked, eyeing her composed face with a narrowed gaze.

"To the road and back."

"You do know that there was an attack on this very lane not a week ago by a masked highwayman?"

"Yes, of course I know," Lana replied, although she hadn't even stopped to consider the recent attack on Lord and Lady Dinsmore and Lady Briannon.

Lord Northridge's frown deepened. "And yet you venture out here alone, with no thought for your own safety? What if the marauder had chanced upon you? An unaccompanied young woman such as yourself?"

"I am in no danger, my lord," she tossed back, though a prickle of fear inched down her spine. Of their own volition, her eyes darted down the shadowy road, not yet lit by the burgeoning dawn. The shadows seemed much more menacing than they had earlier.

"I see you catch my meaning," Lord Northridge said with a smug note of triumph. "And unless you are carrying a pistol in that sack at your hips, you should not be out here alone." He jerked his head at the waiting carriage. "Get in. I will see you back to the manor."

Lana bristled at the brusque command. "I am fine to walk back."

"I insist."

"And I insist on walking," she countered and then added, "my lord."

His eyes narrowed. "Are you defying me?"

Lana ignored the thunderstorms brewing in those darkening blue eyes. There was that famous temper again, though she remained at a complete loss as to why he only seemed to lose hold of it with her. She was more than capable of sound judgment. She might be a servant in his mother's household, but it wasn't Lord Northridge's business what she did on her own time or whether she chose to put herself in the way of a marauding madman. In truth, she resented the intrusion. Even a lowly maid should be allowed some modicum of privacy.

Her chin tilted slightly as she swept past him. "Of course not, Lord Northridge, I simply prefer to walk."

Lana did not expect the swift, steel grip above her elbow as he steered her firmly toward the coach. Even through her cloak, his fingers burned a brand into the skin at the back of her arm. "Unhand me at once!" she whispered, though it didn't stop the coachman from turning in his seat to ogle them.

"Not until you get in." Lord Northridge's voice brooked no argument, and Lana, mortified by his arrogant high-handedness, relented. She knew Colton—the family's primary coachman—was discreet, but she was not familiar with Lord Northridge's London driver. Humiliated, she climbed into the coach and sat mutinously on one side, her hands clasped in her lap, as Lord Northridge followed.

"Are you quite satisfied, my lord?" she hissed. "Now that you've thrown your masterly weight about?"

Unfathomable blue eyes regarded her. "Yes."

He signaled to the driver to proceed with a quick rap on the roof and then leaned back, one ankle thrown across the opposite knee in a deceptive, relaxed position. She waited for him to speak further, but he said nothing. Instead, he closed his eyes, leaning his head against the cushioned wall behind him, as though she weren't even there.

Lana had been in his presence countless times, and yet something about him in rumpled evening wear with a loosened cravat and a hint of shadow on his cheeks struck her with a blunt force that made her inexplicably breathless. Lord Northridge was an incredibly virile man. Any normal blooded woman would be blind not to notice, and Lana was not exempt, though she knew infinitely better. If the rumors were to be believed, despite looking like a young Apollo and possessing a superbly fit physique, Lord Northridge was more trouble than he was worth.

She counted silently to ten in Russian, her own pulse thundering in her ears. Though the conveyance had more than adequate space, his presence made the interior of the coach seem suddenly half its size. Her breath stuck in her throat at the sight of his long outstretched leg resting inches from hers. One unexpected jolt of the carriage and their knees would surely touch.

Half on edge at the prospect of any part of her body touching his, yet half relieved at his supposed slumber, Lana took the opportunity to study him, watching the way his burnished gold hair curled into his forehead. He had thick, long eyelashes that feathered onto the sharp rise of his cheekbones, a straight nose, and finely shaped lips. Lord

Northridge was handsome, she decided, even though his inner beauty was sorely lacking. He had graceful hands, she noted, with slender, strong fingers. They rested upon the black superfine pulled taut against remarkably muscular thighs. Lana's pulse quickened. Once more, his commanding frame seemed to dwarf the shrinking space.

"Like what you see?"

He had opened his eyes to slits.

A violent flush wicked through her at being caught staring. "I beg your pardon?" she replied in a haughty tone, directing her eyes anywhere but him. "I do not know what you are talking about."

"Don't you?" His eyes remained on her, roving over her face just as she had done with him, but while her perusal had been surreptitious, his was boldly appraising. A wicked smile played along his lips. He knew *exactly* what he was doing, and he wanted her to know it, too.

Lana's blush intensified. Ignoring him, she bit her lip and forced her attention to the small pane of glass on the coach door. Surely, they had to be getting close to the main house. The drive seemed interminable. Or perhaps time seemed to slow when dominated by the devil. Lana almost laughed at the apt comparison. Her companion could be Lucifer personified—the epitome of a fallen angel with his golden hair, blue eyes, and depraved disposition. She shifted, stifling the sudden urge to leap from the carriage.

The interior of the coach felt hot, and she could swear that Lord Northridge's body was closer than it had been moments before. Lana's pulse spiked, every inch of her skin prickling with bright awareness. She had been courted by suitors before and had been the recipient of hastily stolen embraces in the arbor at Volkonsky Palace. But no man had ever made her feel the way she did now—like a fox in a hunt with nowhere to run. Her short nails dug into her palms even as she feigned continued indifference. It was a talent she'd inherited from her mother: the ability to remain tranquil and unruffled in any situation.

But, lord, the man pushed her to the limits of her skill.

Despite her composed exterior, Lana was acutely conscious of him. With each inhale and exhale, she could scent the spice of his cologne and the bite of whiskey and cigar smoke, see the rise and fall of the pulse in his neck, hear the rustle of his clothing against the plush velvet seat. She could feel his hooded eyes settling upon her as if they were hands pressing against her flesh, boldly pushing past the confines of her cloak.

Undressing her.

Refusing to succumb to his debauchery, she met his eyes with cool hauteur, and they dropped provokingly to her lips. He was trying to shock her, she knew. But Lana held his stare, refusing to be cowed by whatever new perverse game he was playing. She swallowed a biting response that would remind him of his place, and hers—Lord Northridge at the best of times was unpredictable, and after a night on the town with liquor in his blood, she would do well to curb her tongue. Lest he force himself upon her like some lovelorn swain.

No, not lovelorn. Lord Northridge would not allow such a common emotion as love to rule him. The art of his seduction, if at all, would be calculated and ruthless...meant only to serve him and no other. Lovesick females fell at *his* feet, not the reverse. Lord Northridge's eyes met hers as if her thoughts had grown transparent, and she flushed when another knowing smirk appeared.

Lord have mercy, he made her want to kick him. Hard.

Flustered, Lana couldn't quite help herself as the coach finally rolled to a sharp stop in front of the manor. "Like what you see?" she asked in succinct tones.

A reluctant smile tugged at the corner of his lips at her

veiled mockery. "Very much."

Lana went still at the candid admission. He looked as surprised as she did. An arctic flush suffused her chest and climbed her neck as James opened the coach door. She slid forward, taking the footman's hand and making her escape with every ounce of grace she could manage. "Perhaps you should endeavor to foist your attentions where they will be better welcomed. Good day, Lord Northridge."

His husky chuckle at what would have been a crushing setdown in any other circumstance followed her all the way to the front door.

Blast the arrogant clodpole to Hades.

Chapter Three

"You are frowning again," Brynn said, inspecting Gray from where she sat on the bench opposite his. The carriage rattled over the country lane, Gainsbridge Manor and the ongoing revelry of the ball well behind them. The hour was late, and Gray longed for quiet.

Though he'd dressed for the masquerade earlier that evening, he'd purposefully tarried, and Lord and Lady Dinsmore had set out for the affair ahead of him. For the next quarter hour, he'd struggled to decide whether to attend as he promised he would, or stay at Ferndale with Brynn, who had been abed all day, resting after a breathing attack that morning.

Damn Archer Croft, the bloody Marquess of Hawksfield. Their scoundrel of a neighbor had chanced upon Brynn during her early-morning ride, and when she'd returned, her cheeks had been flushed and her hair in a wild state of disarray. Brynn had been quick to assure him that the marquess had not been untoward.

But Hawksfield had not caused the breathing attack. No.

That had been due to Gray himself, racing his sister to the manor house like a goddamned fool. It didn't matter that she had suggested the foot race—he had accepted it. Pushed her too far.

Just as Lana had accused him of doing before.

He'd shoved away the thought and sat back against the carriage cushions. He hadn't been in the mood for a masquerade, but Brynn had changed her mind, claiming she felt well enough, and so they'd gone. At least the affair had taken his mind off his disappointing ride to the Coopers the afternoon before. They had not been home, though their butler had said they were expected the following day. Gray had left his card and turned away, crestfallen. It had been a month since his last visit. A month that had stretched on like a decade.

He'd planned to return to Breckenham in two days and had then made the awful decision to pay his old friend Lord Bartley a visit. He'd arrived at Bartley's home in Wharton, an hour north of Ferndale, and found his Oxford mate with a number of other young men. They'd convinced Gray to stay the evening. The carousing had gone on into the early-morning hours with cards and billiards, whiskey, and, quite unfortunately, a pair of buxom young ladies from London.

Their status as ladies was, admittedly, questionable.

Deflecting and resisting their attentions had exhausted every last ounce of Gray's willpower, and by the time he'd called for his carriage and set out for home, he had been in a decidedly uncomfortable state of arousal.

And then he'd seen *her* at the entrance to Ferndale's drive.

His sister's secretive maid had been hovering near the line of oaks that trimmed the long lane, her rich, dark chocolate hair free of the little white cap she pinned into place when going about her duties. She'd appeared nearly ghostlike in the early-morning fog, and Gray had called to Rogers to stop the horses.

"Gray? Are you going to answer or continue to glower at me like I am some repellent creature?" He met Brynn's inquisitive stare as the carriage took them toward Ferndale, and struggled not to remember how Lana had been seated upon that same cushion earlier. Or that he had flirted dangerously with her. The whiskey he'd indulged in all night long had made his tongue loose, and the need to slake the lust stirring in his groin had made him bold.

"Am I frowning?" he replied to Brynn's question. "I blame your dress and those rubies."

Brynn had hidden her revealing gown and the string of rubies, sent to her two days prior by an unknown admirer, with a mink stole until their late arrival at the masquerade. When she'd removed the stole, Gray had nearly suffered an apoplectic fit. If the man who'd sent the damned rubies was in attendance, he'd take the sight of them as encouragement. And what kind of *gentleman* sent such a ludicrous gift anonymously?

"You are right," she sighed now, glancing out the window, her brow furrowed. "It was foolish of me." She drew the mink stole closer around her neck as if trying to cover herself better. Or perhaps she was only chilled.

Gray started to remove his own coat. "Don't think me too harsh. You look beautiful, Brynn, but after what happened this morning with Hawksfield encountering you unchaperoned, and just now with the Duke of Bradburne, who has all but announced his intentions to court you, I can't help but worry. And unfortunately my worry comes across as ill temper."

His sister had swooned and fainted in the middle of the Gainsbridge ballroom when Lord Bradburne, Hawksfield's old rakehell of a father, approached her for a dance. It had given he and Brynn a solid reason to depart for home, but that made two fainting episodes in one day.

"So I've noticed," she remarked with a tired grin.

Gray didn't know why his temper flared every time worry struck—perhaps it was because he knew there were some things he would never be able to control. That no matter what he did or said or planned, there were some things he could never change. Either society wouldn't allow it, or nature would deny it.

For a moment his mind settled upon the Coopers' modest sandstone home in Breckenham. *Tomorrow*. He'd pay his visit tomorrow.

Rogers let out a shout, and the carriage slowed before coming to a halt. Gray tore himself from his thoughts and slid forward to open the door.

"What is it?" he called.

"Up ahead. A carriage in the lane, my lord," came the driver's reply.

Gray glanced at his sister. "Stay here," he said, and then jumped out, landing deftly on the packed dirt of the lane.

There was indeed a carriage sitting still before them, and as Gray approached, he saw why. The horse that had been drawing the conveyance was on its side in the lane. It wasn't moving.

"Bloody hell," he shouted, rushing forward.

"Northridge?" a tremulous voice said from near the carriage. Gray glanced away from the dead horse and saw a man leaning against the carriage for support. Another sat at the edge of the path, his head clasped between his hands.

"Good God," Gray said, recognizing one of his father's oldest friends. "Lord Maynard, is that you?"

He started for the earl's side at once but stopped when he heard the sound of feet behind him. He turned and saw his sister had not heeded his command. He grit his teeth. Lord save him from stubborn women.

"Lord Maynard, what happened here?" Brynn asked as

she approached, followed closely by one of their footmen. He'd thought to bring with him a torch from the side of the carriage. The approaching light began to touch on the earl, and Gray swore under his breath.

"It was the Masked Marauder. He beat Berthold unconscious. Shot my horse! Nearly shot me, too," the earl replied, pressing a handkerchief to his bloodied head. His lip had been split, welts and bruises covered his cheeks, and blood seeped from his nose.

Brynn covered her mouth and started to slump as she took a second glance at the lifeless horse. Gray took her shoulders and led her away, back toward the carriage. His temper flared as he swept the road for any sign of the escaping Masked Marauder, but the bandit was long gone. What kind of ingrate attacked an old man and shot a horse? Gray hungered to chase the bastard down and beat him to a fine pulp.

"Brynn, for the love of all things holy, stay in the carriage, please," he said through clenched teeth, worry again making his voice tight and commanding. "It isn't safe."

This time, Brynn didn't refuse.

An hour later, after the lane had been cleared and the local constable summoned, Gray had driven Maynard to his estate. It wasn't far, just south of Ferndale, but by the time Rogers turned their carriage onto the long lane leading to the manor house, Brynn was nearly asleep upright, and Gray's head ached like the devil.

The Masked Marauder was on the loose in the area, and he had graduated from nuisance highwayman to violent criminal. One more strike to Lord Maynard's head and the Marauder could have cracked the old man's skull. He seemed to be focusing on waylaying conveyances, but what about homes? Would he start attacking people in their own residences now?

Again, Gray thought of the Coopers, and the knot of

concern forming in the pit of his stomach intensified.

"My goodness," Brynn murmured, her voice sleepy. She peered out the window into the lane, lit only by bright moonlight. "Is that Lana?"

Gray sat forward and stared through the window glass. Damn it all to hell. He spotted his sister's lady's maid, wrapped in a dark cloak, once again treading the side of Ferndale's drive.

"Rogers," was all Gray had to growl for the driver to rein in the horses and bring the carriage to a halt.

Gray threw open the door and jumped out. Lana had not yet turned to face him, though she had undoubtedly heard the carriage pull to a stop behind her. Her arms were moving, and for the shortest of moments, he wondered if she might be rearranging the bodice of her dress beneath her cloak.

Oh hell.

Gray glanced up and down the lane. Had she been out here meeting someone? Another servant, perhaps, for a midnight tryst? The tension simmering in the pit of his stomach from the night's events shot to a boil.

"What are you doing out here at this time of night?" he asked, his voice rougher than he'd intended.

Lana finally whirled to face him, her fair skin as luminous as pearls in the moonlight. He registered her look of surprise and guilt at once, followed closely by disappointment.

She *had* been meeting someone.

"Walking again," she said, a touch breathless. "If you recall, I was interrupted on my constitutional stroll earlier this morning, my lord."

His eyes quickly took in the state of her dress. Her black wool cloak covered most of her, so he could not tell if she was indeed in a state of *dishabille*. He was inexplicably more irritated at the thought of her secret rendezvous than the fact that she was out alone with a bandit on the loose. Which was absurd, he knew. The knowledge did little to curb his annoyance.

"Ah, yes, forgive me. It makes infinitely more sense for you to return to your stroll in the middle of the night, along a pitch-dark lane, when there is a violent highwayman traveling these roads." Gray stepped aside and swung an arm toward the carriage. "Inside," he snapped. "I will not entertain an argument."

"Lana?" Brynn called from within. "Do come up. It isn't safe."

The footman riding at the back of the carriage had already set the steps into place, and Lana, hiking her chin, accepted Gray's hand when he proffered it. He had removed his gloves earlier while assisting Maynard, and now, as his fingers closed around Lana's delicate ones, he realized she, too, wore no gloves.

Her skin was warm and petal soft—unusually so for a servant. He'd seen Mrs. Braxton's hands work over the hot stove, and hers were rough and worn. Then again, his mother had explained months before that Miss Volchek hailed from a genteel family that had fallen on hard times, so perhaps she hadn't always had to work. Gray's fingers tightened around her palm, holding on a fraction longer than was proper, his thumb involuntarily caressing the creamy back of her hand.

Lust shot through him, sharp and sweet. An indescribable desire to press his lips to her smooth knuckles took hold of him as his thumb stroked her soft skin again. He felt Lana's arm tense and heard her sudden intake of breath as she set her feet in the carriage. She jerked her hand out of his and took the seat next to Brynn.

As Gray settled into his place and Rogers drove on for the rest of the short ride up the lane, Brynn told her maid all that had unfolded with Maynard's carriage, her voice catching when she spoke of the masked bandit. Lana listened in rapt horror, though she seemed to have lost her ability to form opinions, and she remained oddly silent, her fingers twisting restlessly in her lap.

She's nervous, Gray thought, which begged the question as to exactly what she had to be nervous about. Unless she was nervous about *him*.

They reached the manor, and Gray stepped down from the coach, extending his arm to his sister and then to her maid. Refusing his assistance and not meeting his eyes, Lana quickly descended after Brynn as if the coach were on fire. Her coolness irked him, but he could not fault her for it. Earlier that morning and full of whiskey, he had overstepped when he had all but admitted his attraction to her. Gray supposed some form of apology was in order.

His gaze fell, drawn to a scrap of paper floating from her skirts to the floor of the coach. He retrieved it and turned to hand it to her, but Lana had already started toward the back of the manor. With mounting displeasure, he couldn't help noticing the careful way she cinched the cape closer around her, and instead of returning the note to her as he should have done, he gripped the piece of paper in his closed fist and tucked it into his trouser pocket.

"Don't be silly, Lana, come in with us," Brynn called out, but Lana didn't stop.

"Oh no, I…I must fetch a draught for you, my lady!" the maid replied as she hurried to the side of the manor and the kitchen entrance there. Brynn protested that she didn't need one, but Lana had already disappeared around the corner.

Inside, they were immediately attended to by their longtime butler, Braxton. Gray touched his sister's arm as she started for the stairwell. "Are you certain your chest does not ail you?"

Brynn covered his hand with hers. "Don't fret, Gray. I only need rest. I assure you, my lungs are fine."

His brow furrowed with concern as she proceeded up the stairs with the housekeeper to meet Lana in her rooms. It had already been a long night, and after the events earlier, he was surprised Brynn was still standing. Once more, he couldn't help but worry.

Gray frowned as he loosened his cravat. Lana, on the other hand, inspired another emotion entirely: frustration. Or perhaps, even more so, curiosity. It would take no more than a half hour for her to prepare Brynn for bed, and if Brynn's low mood was any indication, it could take less time than that.

Gray bid Braxton good night and climbed the stairs as well. He knew just the place to sit and wait for Lana to be dismissed. His interest was twofold. The first would ensure that Brynn was indeed only fatigued and not concealing any other underlying symptoms of something worse. But the second was far more selfish—he had to know once and for all what Lana had been doing out on the lane at this ungodly hour of the night.

Recalling the piece of paper he'd shoved into his pocket, he pulled it out to scan its contents. Gray knew he was intruding on Lana's private correspondence, but he didn't care. His sister's maid was acting far too cagey for him to turn a blind, or uninterested, eye. A tiny voice insisted that it was more than that, but he ignored it.

A Heart remains Well Kept,
though it Yearns to See yours.
Soon, my sweet, I promise.
For it Languishes without your Smile,
Hopeful for the day it can be Reunited.
I am Devoted to seeing you Home.

Gray almost laughed aloud at the ridiculous drivel, but his amusement swiftly faded. He'd been correct in his assumption that Lana had been meeting someone, possibly the man who had written this note. She had a beau. A grievously talentless one, but a lover nonetheless. Was he a man from the village? One of the servants at Ferndale?

The sudden image of her naked body tangled up in another man's arms assaulted him, and with it, the tantalizing recollection of her soft, ungloved hand. Gray felt a hot tug in his loins at the sinful thought that the rest of her would likely be as silky and smooth. He stifled his lust with an angry grunt. He was here to suss out the extent of Brynn's maid's indiscretions, not to salivate like a schoolboy over her physical charms.

Pocketing the note, he waited with grim purpose in an alcove off the second-floor hallway, three doors down from his sister's rooms. There was a small bench there, beside a potted fern, and as he sat in the silent corridor, the fatigue of the night before, and the long day and evening, caught up with him. His lids began to droop, and the warmth of sleep began to creep up from the soles of his feet, the way it did when he was exhausted. He closed his eyes just to soothe them from the burn of weariness.

When he felt a gentle nudge against his shin, Gray's lids sprang open. He found his shoulder and head nearly consumed by the large fronds of the fern beside him. He'd slumped over, he realized, and fallen asleep.

"Lord Northridge?"

Another nudge against his shin, only this time sharper. More like a kick.

He straightened on the bench immediately and saw Lana standing before him, a dress and some other articles of clothing draped over her arm. He rolled his shoulders, stretching the kinks out of his back. She shot him a speaking look, and he fought to compose himself. Bloody fine work. Now *she* had the advantage.

"I was waiting for you," he said in a low voice, standing slowly.

She raised one slim eyebrow, the imperious look making her seem more inconvenienced aristocrat than maid. "For me?"

"That is what I said."

She did not rise to his tart reply. "May I help you with something, my lord?"

You can help me to my rooms.

The thought came out of nowhere, and Gray shook his head. He must have still been half addled with sleep. Clearing his throat, he focused on the matter at hand. The note was burning a hole in his trouser pocket, though he couldn't bring himself to admit that he had taken and read it. "What were you doing on the road? And don't bother to answer that you were taking a stroll. We both know it isn't true."

Something flared in her eyes before her lips thinned. She held the clothing in front of her like a barrier between them. "I do not believe that is any of your business, my lord."

"It is my business if my sister's maid is meeting inappropriately with a man."

She flushed at his lewd suggestion but lifted her chin, her voice quiet. "My lord, your question is vulgar, and regardless of what you may assume, what I do on my own time is my own affair."

Ignoring the rise of his temper at her evasive response, Gray frowned at the underlying thread of shock in her voice. She was accusing *him* of vulgarity? He recalled well her numb grip on her cloak, and the poem's verbosely worded desire for a rendezvous. What had she been hiding if not a ripped or hastily laced bodice?

He considered the defiant woman standing before him and changed tactics. She had yet to respond well to interrogation or high-handedness, and she could be a mule when she chose to be. No wonder she got along so well with his sister. He almost sighed at the thought.

"Miss Volchek," he said, gentling his voice and reaching forward. She clutched her skirts as if about to bolt, and he could only react to stop her, grasping her wrist so quickly that two of the gowns slid to the floor. Gray saw a change in her eyes. A pulse of fear. What did she assume, that he planned to harm her? That he was *that* sort of a man? He felt a blow of disappointment and insult.

She froze, though the band of his fingers was not tight. It was as if the mere contact of skin upon skin was the thing holding her immobile. Her wrist felt so fragile in his hand, and as his thumb skimmed the soft underside of it, her teeth sunk into her lower lip. Something hot and unfamiliar sparked between them, making Gray acutely aware of her slim body in such dangerous proximity to his. A matching awareness narrowed Lana's pupils to pinpricks, sharpening the bright, vibrant green of her irises.

Her pulse leaped wildly beneath his fingertips. "What were you doing on the lane?"

"Unhand me at once, sir."

"Give me what I want—the *truth*—and I will," he countered.

She gave him the same answer she'd given that morning, though her voice shook slightly. "I was walking."

Lana's face remained calm, but her eyes, those beautiful, vivid, transparent eyes, told a different story. Shadows slunk in them, hinting at secrets she was desperate to conceal. Gray could see it in their flickering depths. It was something she didn't want him to know...that she didn't want anyone to know. At the sight of her flushed cheeks, he felt an irrational flick of irritation.

"You must take me for a fool."

She jerked her chin upward as he took a step closer, eliminating the gap between them, and Gray had to admire her courage for standing her ground. Her small but shapely bosom rose and fell in bursts beneath the plain serviceable frock she wore, and devil take him, all he wanted was to drag her into his arms and do whatever it was he suspected her of doing with God knows who out on the lane.

Greedily, his eyes roved over her, lingering on the sable curls escaping that white cap atop her head. He ached to pull them loose from their confines and wind his fingers into the thick mass. He wondered if those curls were as silky as they looked, recalling the heavy cascade across her shoulders earlier that morning when she'd been bareheaded.

Her light, floral fragrance filled his nostrils. He'd gone far too long without the company of a woman, and right now, this infuriatingly tight-lipped maid was somehow managing to sing a siren song, luring him beyond the vestiges of his own ruthless self-control. Why shouldn't he succumb? It was not so unusual for society lords to dally with the servants belowstairs, more so the comely ones. And she was more than comely…

Gray caught himself mid-thought and froze.

What in hell was he *thinking*? Dallying with the servants? With his sister's maid, of all people? He must be half-crazed out of his mind.

Self-disgust flooded him, and his mouth tightened as he stepped back with a dispassionate exhale. "I will ask you one more time. Were you meeting your lover? If you lie to me, I will have your position terminated."

Lana's head bowed low, and for a moment, Gray wondered whether his sharp words had frightened her. Her shoulders were shaking. Christ. Was she *crying*?

"Miss Volchek?" His hand released her slender wrist and slid up her arm.

She raised her head and looked at him with such scathing scorn that he almost took a step back. Gray realized belatedly that she was laughing. It was a hollow, haughty sound, devoid of any emotion, that left him cold.

"A *lover*?" she said, contempt dripping from her words. "How like you to assume such a thing, Lord Northridge."

"How like me?" he echoed, stunned at the clipped setdown.

"Not everyone cavorts as freely as you do with the opposite sex. I suppose it is a natural thought for you to assume that others may do the same, and that you would interpret an innocent stroll as a sordid meeting."

Gray's mouth tightened as he took her meaning. She had struck back with a barbed insult, and by the looks of things, she wasn't finished. His hand slid into his pocket, about to display the damning note and indisputable evidence of her tryst. Shame stopped him. He'd purposefully kept and read a woman's private correspondence. Flushing darkly at his own indiscretion, he crushed the parchment between his fingers instead.

"Innocent, was it?" he scoffed weakly.

"Just because you are a known profligate does not mean that everyone else holds themselves to the same despicable standards. Even a lowly maid, my lord."

"I am not a profligate," he muttered. It was all he could manage. He had just been on the receiving end of a blistering rebuke handed down by one of his servants, one who stood before him like an enraged vixen, her color high and her eyes flashing daggers at him. Despite her insolence, Gray felt a hot wash of desire pulse through him. She would be a hellion in bed. That passion he could see simmering just beneath the surface all but guaranteed it.

"Tell that to your mistress," she tossed back, her nostrils flaring as he stared at her in arrested surprise. "However many of them you keep, from Essex all the way to London. You truly are an unspeakable ra—"

Gray couldn't help himself. His mouth swooped down

upon hers and silenced her tirade. The shock of the lush, womanly contact worked a groan from deep in his throat, and he drew her closer, his arms curving around her slim back. He'd forgotten what it felt like to hold a woman, to feel soft curves fitting against his starved body in such perfect accord. The gowns she had not dropped were now crushed between them as his lips teased hers apart, his tongue tracing the soft inside of their contours. With a soft gasp, she clamped her lips shut in response. He craved far more than the brief touch she allowed, but she held herself rigid, refusing to respond to the persuasive pressure of his mouth, and as his reason returned, Gray pulled away.

His heart was pounding in his chest, while she seemed supremely unaffected by the heated, if fleeting, embrace. In fact, she looked downright bored. Her hands were fisted at her sides, her composure stony. If she were a highborn lady, she would be well within her rights to crack her palm across his cheek. Instead, she used the bite of her eyes and whip of her tongue to set him to rights.

"You have proven me right, my lord," she hissed in a low, furious voice. "You cannot control your impulses. You take what you want whenever you want it, with no thought for consequence or whether your actions will endanger others. What if Lady Dinsmore or Mrs. Frommer had been nearby? My position would have been terminated in an instant because of your lewd desires."

Her words stung and were far too close to the truth.

"I've heard the stories about you, about your indiscretions in London, and the trail of broken hearts in your wake. You are a seducer of the worst sort."

Gray let go of her and backed away, the air climbing up between them and chilling his body. "That was before."

She blinked. "Before what?"

But Gray couldn't answer. How could he possibly explain?

Yes, he had been all those things and more. Yes, he'd been a libertine, enjoying the life and pleasures that being one of London's most eligible, titled bachelors afforded him. Women had flocked to him, and he had welcomed their flirtations and charms with open arms. Many, he knew, had wanted marriage, and he had stooped so low as to allow them to believe it possible. He'd offered them whispered nothings and empty promises, and this vexing maid was right—he had left a trail of tears behind him.

And now what he had just done with her was unforgivable. She was a servant…his sister's maid, and he had mauled her like some odious, overbearing, depraved lord of the manor.

Gray took a step back, a wave of renewed self-disgust overcoming him. He stared at the girl standing so quietly regal before him. Most maids would have been cowering. Instead, she had faced his anger, taken both his insults and his advances, and still stood there as if she were the mistress and he the servant. Shame filled him.

He made a short bow, bending to retrieve the fallen garments. "My deepest apologies for putting you in such a position. You have my promise that this will not happen again." Gray placed the gowns carefully on the alcove bench. His eyes met hers—their cool, green depths flickering with surprise—for an instant as he took his leave. "Forgive me, Miss Volchek."

A ride, he thought as he took the stairs two at a time. A ride would clear his head and calm his blood. For as much as he had promised to keep his distance from Lana, his body longed for something more. Her soft fragrance haunted him. Her expressive eyes taunted him. And her sweet mouth…

Blazes take him, he wanted her still.

• • •

Stunned speechless, Lana retrieved the discarded dresses from the bench and clutched them to her chest as she watched Lord Northridge's broad frame disappear around the corner at the end of the hall. Bracing against the paneled wall, Lana let out a pent-up breath, her lips throbbing.

He'd kissed her.

That arrogant rogue of a man had *kissed* her—and dear lord, she'd wanted to slap him and kiss him back in equal measure. Instead, she'd been frozen with indecision and her entire body had gone into some sort of numb paralysis. It had been her saving grace. A few moments more and she would have launched herself at the man like a common lightskirt. Gathering a breath, Lana turned toward the servant staircase, only to see the person she dreaded most hurrying toward her.

The dour housekeeper had not liked Lana from the start. Lady Dinsmore had hired Lana directly, neglecting Mrs. Frommer's official duty as housekeeper to interview all potential household staff. As a result, Mrs. Frommer simply ignored her existence and, it seemed, had instructed most of the staff to do the same. They mostly did, out of fear of incurring the harridan's wrath. Except for a few, the staff treated Lana like a pariah.

Lana knew that in some households, many of the lower servants resented the freedoms of the upper servants, especially the lady's maids. In St. Petersburg, her own maids had enjoyed countless privileges and leisure time, but she'd never stopped to consider the jealousies that would run rampant belowstairs. With the exception of Mary and Mrs. Braxton, most of the other maids gave her a wide berth and whispered behind her back. Lana did not mind, as she could not afford to let her guard down and befriend anyone. Though it was lonely, she often reminded herself that it was only temporary.

As for Mrs. Frommer, Lana had held the onerous

housekeeper at arm's length, employing a distant reserve she'd often used when dealing with difficult young ladies in her previous life. It had been the only way she could endure the woman's constant aggression, and thus far, it had been effective. But everything Lana did was held to an exacting standard. Not that she expected to be treated differently, but Mrs. Frommer was bent on enumerating her many faults and mistakes. The housekeeper seemed to take an unholy delight in all of Lana's failures, though in the last week, she had been busy with the family move to London for the forthcoming season.

Not so any longer, Lana deduced from Mrs. Frommer's ugly expression. Her frown appeared to have been etched with a hatchet as she bore down on Lana, her mouth a disapproving white gash. Lana quickly ticked off her duties in her head. Brynn's chamber had been tidied and aired, her mistress's clothing put away, and her toilette prepared for when she arose from her rest. The pile of mending had been reduced to a few pairs of stockings, and the gowns she held were meant for the laundress.

Notwithstanding the expensive pearl-encrusted evening gown Lana had accidentally ruined two weeks before by placing it in the wrong laundering pile, she hadn't done anything glaring of late, which would give Mrs. Frommer no reason to be displeased.

Unless…

Lana's heart sank. It was her biggest fear come to life, just as she'd expressed to Lord Northridge. If the housekeeper had seen or heard what had happened with his lordship, there would be hell to pay and more.

Lana tensed, her jaw tilting in readiness for the confrontation as the housekeeper approached. She had done nothing wrong. Without a word, Mrs. Frommer grabbed her by the elbow in a pincer-like grip and steered her toward the servants' stairwell.

"With me. Now," she barked, and down the stairwell she went. Lana had no choice but to follow or be dragged the two floors below, into a sewing room.

"Out," she snapped to the two girls working there. Dropping their mending, they scurried past Lana with wide-eyed stares. Once the door shut behind them, the housekeeper rounded on her.

"Just what do you think you are doing?" she hissed.

"I'm not certain what you mean, Mrs. Frommer."

The woman's eyes flashed with rancor as she eyed Lana up and down. "Don't play the innocent miss with me. Don't think I haven't seen what you're about, pretending to be the coy lady's maid while setting your cap at the master. I saw you in the hallway upstairs, his lordship bowing to you as if you were some highborn lady. You, cozying up to him…seducing him with your high and mighty airs. I won't stand for it, not in my household."

Lana blinked. "I assure you, Mrs. Frommer, I have done nothing of the sort. His lordship has no interest—"

Her smile was one of contempt. "Of course his lordship has more good sense than to dally with an uppity tart like you throwing herself at him."

Lana bristled with righteous indignation. Some part of her rebelled at the accusation that she had been the one to instigate anything. She had resisted Lord Northridge's unwelcome advances. If anyone was the tart, it was *him*, not her. Some measure of her pride demanded exculpation for an offense she did not commit, but she remained silent, her body shaking with suppressed anger.

But Mrs. Frommer wasn't finished. She leaned forward and, in a sickly-sweet voice, said, "I must warn you, Miss Volchek, that if Lady Dinsmore were to hear of your lustful designs on her son, you would not be long for this position."

Lana gasped. "Are you threatening me?"

The housekeeper spread her palms wide. "Merely stating the obvious."

Helpless rage and bruised pride warred within her, and Lana hiked her chin, the words rushing out before she could think twice. "Then if I may also be so kind, Mrs. Frommer, as to state that if his lordship does happen to hold me in any regard, it might be in your best interest to keep your opinions to yourself."

The housekeeper spluttered. "Why, you impertinent wretch—"

"I'm merely stating the obvious," Lana echoed as she drew herself to her full height, letting a secret smile play over her lips. She was gratified to see Mrs. Frommer's confidence falter. "After all, if I do find myself under Lord Northridge's protection, as you have despicably insinuated, whom do you suppose Lady Dinsmore would believe—you or her own son? I would think carefully, Mrs. Frommer, as to whether you are certain of what you heard or saw. It would not pay to make such a mistake."

The housekeeper's mouth opened and closed like a fish out of water, but Lana did not wait to hear what she had to say. She bobbed and swept past her, closing the door behind her with a soft click.

The satisfaction lasted all of one minute before Lana was cursing herself in multiple languages as she fled to her chamber. For one, it was beneath her to let the housekeeper believe that she and Lord Northridge had any kind of understanding when they most decidedly did *not*. And two, she had not needed to make a worse enemy of Mrs. Frommer, but that was exactly what she had accomplished.

Chapter Four

The dawn was brightening the sky in pale patches when Lana expertly guided the stallion over the wide gulch at the south end of the Ferndale estate, far out of view of prying eyes. She laughed as the horse thundered toward another obstacle—this one a four-foot-high hedge. Leaning her weight forward, she gripped with her thighs and felt the magnificent animal beneath her gather his strength and leap. The feeling of freedom as her mount easily cleared the jump was incomparable, and one she sorely missed.

"Come, James, do keep up," she called breathlessly over her shoulder to the young footman hot on her heels on another horse.

"Trying!" he yelled back. "You are too fast for me. We've lost Percy."

She'd struck up an unlikely rapport with James and his cousin, Percival, who was a stable boy at Ferndale, and neither of whom were under the thumb of Mrs. Frommer. James answered to the butler, Mrs. Braxton's husband, and Percy to the stablemaster. They were both half infatuated with her, but their company and humor made the days away from Irina and the loneliness Lana endured belowstairs more bearable. And she had to admit she enjoyed learning about cards and sleight of hand, betting, lock picking, and all manner of things that gently bred ladies should never claim to know.

Her hair had long tumbled free of its cap, and even in her mistress's borrowed breeches beneath her dress, Lana couldn't help getting lost in the moment as she gave the stallion its head across a wide meadow. She knew riding was a risk. After all, someone could see, and she had no business being on any of the estate's horses. But when Percival had suggested she and James accompany him while he exercised three of the more energetic stallions, she couldn't resist. For Lana, a hard ride exorcised demons in a way that nothing else could. It was one of the things she did have in common with Lord Northridge, who, like his sister, rode religiously every day.

At the thought of Lord Northridge, her heart raced again, but this time it wasn't fear that provoked it. Something else, hot and violent, set her pulse to a gallop. She still couldn't believe he'd had the audacity to *kiss* her! Lana didn't know what it was about the man that drove her to such insane contradictions—one minute she wanted to strangle him, and the next she wanted to melt in his arms. She'd been shocked at her body's response to his touch, even after his insulting interrogation. She should have wanted to scratch his eyes out for first accusing her of meeting with a lover and then attempting to seduce her himself. Instead, she'd struggled against the flames he'd kindled within her, the embers of which still burned despite her valiant efforts to smother them.

Lana replayed the memory for the hundredth time, not counting the fevered dreams that had plagued her throughout the night. Though she had resisted his kiss, his earthy male scent and the velvet stroke of his tongue had come close to making her senseless. Her dreams, however, had not been so proper, torturing her with indecently erotic thoughts of what could have been, had she but submitted to his desires. Lana's face scorched anew.

Regardless of what she'd purposefully led Mrs. Frommer to believe, engaging in any kind of salacious affair with Lord Northridge would not end well for either of them. For one, she had her reputation to consider. Once this was all behind her, she would return to her homeland and would be expected to marry. And two, knowing Lord Northridge's debauched past, she was certain she'd be nothing but a conquest to him. Obviously, Lord Northridge had no qualms about dallying with servants. Beneath the titled, wealthy, debonair exterior, he was no gentleman.

Still, Lana kept recalling the look on his face when she had accused him of being a libertine. He'd flinched as if she had somehow hurt him with her words. *That was before*, he'd said. But Lord Northridge was a master seducer, and convincing herself otherwise would only be to her detriment. No, she would do well to stop thinking of him as anything but what she knew him to be — a man after his own pleasures, nothing more.

Lana frowned, refusing to allow the man to ruin her good humor. Digging her heels in, she braced low over the horse's neck as he sped across the field, letting her burdens, including the unwelcome thoughts of Lord Northridge, fall far behind. At the end of the meadow, she pulled the stallion to a smart stop and dismounted, handing the reins to an impressed James.

"Where'd you learn to ride like that, miss?"

"My father," she replied. "And you owe me another lesson. I won that race fair and square." She winked jauntily at him as Percival galloped around the bend. "Dice next time, I think. See you lads up at the house. I better get moving before

Mrs. Frommer sends the duns after me."

Lana couldn't wipe the smile from her face as she hurried the rest of the way to the manor house, watching as the two boys led the horses back to the stables. It had been far too long. But her humor evaporated at the sight of a letter awaiting her in the kitchens, upon a tray. She immediately recognized the red-wax seal stamped with a long-eared hare, shown mid-leap. It was not the Earl of Langlevit's official seal, the one he used on regular correspondence. It was the seal he used only for her, and it meant there was a coded message inside.

Mrs. Braxton grinned as she kneaded a large mound of dough. "Well, aren't you fancy? Who's sending you such important letters?"

"It was delivered by messenger not two moments ago," the undermaid, Mary, added in an excited squeak. "Is it from your beau?"

Mrs. Frommer swept into the kitchen, and Mary paled at the sight of the housekeeper's pinched frown. Mrs. Frommer's attention settled on Lana's red cheeks and mussed hair before dropping to the letter already clutched in Lana's hand. Two scullery maids hurried out of her way as the housekeeper's draconian face pulled into an all too familiar scowl that boded ill for anyone within striking distance.

"What have we here?" she asked in a deceptively amiable voice, her question directed to a quaking Mary who stood rooted to the spot. Lana's own temper flared. The woman was a tyrant.

"A letter came for me," she answered, drawing Mrs. Frommer's attention. Lana was relieved to see Mrs. Braxton dismiss the young undermaid out of the kitchen and into the adjoining pantry with a quick jerk of her chin.

Mrs. Frommer reached for the squared edge of the envelope. Her fingers closed upon it. "After your insolence earlier, I have half a mind to burn it."

Lana clutched the letter to her breast and twisted to the side, tearing it free from the woman's pincer-like grip. "It is mine."

The housekeeper's nostrils flared, but she did not attempt to take the letter again. Instead, she subjected Lana to such a venomous glare that Lana was surprised she didn't turn to stone on the spot.

"Where have you been?" The housekeeper's eyes clouded with suspicion at Lana's disheveled appearance. She leaned in, her voice low and laced with hostility. "You may think you are above the rest of the staff, but mind you, I have not forgotten just how inept you were when you first arrived here. I'm onto you, Miss Volchek, remember that." She drew back and raised her voice. "I'll have your position terminated if you so much as put one toe out of line. Do I make myself clear?"

Lana's skin burned with the suppressed desire to put the woman in her place in front of the other servants, but of course this *was* her place. As head of the household staff, Mrs. Frommer had every right to rule the maids as she saw fit. Though Lana had foolishly stood up to Mrs. Frommer in the sewing room, to defy her publicly would be unwise.

She clenched her jaw and assumed a suitably meek expression. "Yes, ma'am."

"Good. Now tend to your duties."

In the stairwell on the way to her quarters, Lana let out a groan of frustration and tore open Lord Langlevit's message. Even if Mrs. Frommer had managed to rip the letter from Lana's hands, she would not have discovered what it truly said. All of her correspondence with Langlevit was written in a simple coded language, and always in the form of love sonnets. They had borrowed the clever idea from her traitorous uncle, who had used similar letters to smuggle secrets to the French.

The reason was twofold: should a message ever be intercepted by anyone—such as Mrs. Frommer, or more dangerously, anyone associated with her uncle or Baron Zakorov—the contents would appear harmless. Silly, but harmless.

Secondly, Lana could not claim family in London. Any letter from them would require a postmarking from Russia. It was more logical to allow the staff to believe Lana had a local beau.

Her eyes devoured the frilly declarations Langlevit had written:

My affection for you is Voracious,
Zinging in my veins.

They had worked it out long before that any capital *V* and *Z* near one another would refer to Zakorov. She read on, her breath hitching painfully.

The sweet Threat shall not abate,
through the Dense Fog of loneliness.
I must be Cautious,
for though I am Hunting my Heart's desire
it remains Elusive.
Fear Not, I will be Faithfully yours.

With a pounding heart, Lana reread the nonsense words, all of which seemed to hint to a lover's suffering and turmoil, but she knew how to read between the poetic ramblings. She isolated the capitalized words, and when she saw Langlevit's mention of dense fog, she felt a shiver of dread.

This letter was a warning.

Viktor Zakorov was in London, and he was searching for them, though it appeared from the earl's carefully chosen sentiments that he was not close to discovering where she and her sister were. Still, terror gripped her. The very fact that her uncle's man was on the same soil as she and Irina made her feel ill.

Lana took a deep breath, attempting to calm the swell of panic, and forced herself to think rationally. There was nothing to indicate that Viktor knew where she or Irina was. He could be here on official business—he was a military man, after all. A Russian diplomat. Why shouldn't he visit London when Parliament was sitting? There was a war on between Russia and France, and England was one of Russia's staunchest allies.

But deep down Lana knew better. Fooling herself with excuses wouldn't do. Viktor was here searching for them and that meant her uncle would not be too far behind.

The correspondences she had discovered in her father's office were important. It was more than intuition that told her so. Why would he have kept them under lock and key had they been simply what they appeared to be: letters from her uncle to an old lover in France? They had drawn Lana's curiosity immediately when she'd found them.

Like Langlevit's words in the letter she now held, her uncle's written sweet nothings had left her feeling dazed and grasping for meaning. Why hadn't her father discarded them? And how had he managed to intercept them? Lana had quickly realized that somehow, her father had discovered what the words had truly meant—and he had been murdered because of it.

Lana hadn't thought twice about handing them to the earl once she and Irina had arrived safely in England. Her father had held Langlevit in high esteem, and after he had gone to such lengths to help them escape her uncle, she trusted him with her life.

"What do you think they are?" she had asked, watching as he'd sniffed the perfumed paper, his brow wrinkling in confusion.

"On the surface? Letters to a woman," he'd said, but his eyes had narrowed as he placed the letters side by side upon his desk. "But see here? The choice of words—*I shall die with desperation before our next rendezvous.*" He jerked his finger to a second line further down. "And here—*upon our rendezvous June hearts aglow.* He uses the word 'rendezvous' again, but the sentence makes no sense. Which leads me to think there must be something more being said between the lines."

"Between the lines?" Lana has asked, frowning.

"A coded message," the earl replied, pausing to stare at her. "You did not find anything else with your father's documents? An alphabetized list? A stencil? Anything that could help us discover what these letters really mean?"

"There was nothing else in the safe. Only a folder containing these two pieces of parchment. Why do you ask?"

"I believe your uncle is working with French insurgents and providing them information through letters like these. Your father had confided his suspicions to me, but he must have intercepted these shortly before the accident. Are you certain there was nothing else? Perhaps a cipher? It could have appeared as a spherical contraption, or a sheet of paper with a strange block of lettering—an alphabet that makes no sense."

"There was nothing else," she repeated, her heart sinking. The earl's words had confirmed everything she had suspected. Her uncle was a spy and a traitor. And a murderer. Her father had grown suspicious of his own brother, and both of her parents had been punished for it.

"Perhaps he had hidden it elsewhere," Langlevit had murmured, running a hand through his crop of sandy blond hair.

Lana had shaken her head. "If he did, then it is still in St. Petersburg, and my uncle will leave no stone unturned. My lord, my father was murdered because he had these documents. My mother…" She could not finish for the hard knot that formed in her throat.

A cold mask of rage had descended over Langlevit's features. Lana had no doubt that he was a gentleman and would never hurt her or Irina, but in that one moment, she'd caught a glimpse of the ruthless military officer he was reputed to be. It hadn't made her afraid. It had made her hopeful.

"I know," he'd ground out, hovering again over the correspondences laid out on his desk. "Count Volkonsky and Baron Zakorov will answer for their crimes. I've no doubt these letters will prove their guilt."

Neither did she. But first they had to know what they said.

"My father must have found a way to translate the letters, or he would not have gone to such lengths to keep them from my uncle. Can you learn what the letters say without this cipher?"

"Possibly." But Lana was aware that it was a false hope. Deciphering the letters without the help of a cipher would be like searching for a single, specific stalk in an entire field of wheat—a near impossible task. Without being able to prove that the letters were indeed treasonous, they'd have nothing. Langlevit had assured her that he had the best agents in the War Office working on it.

Until then, she and Irina would have to stay hidden.

Lana crumpled Langlevit's message in her fist. She hated feeling like a trapped hare. But there was nothing she could do. If Viktor or her uncle found her, they would kill her to ensure her silence. They would kill Irina, too, and that was something Lana feared more than her own death.

Until she had incriminating proof, she was at a disadvantage. She had entertained the idea of luring her uncle in with the promise of the letters and then somehow goading him into a confession with witnesses present. But she knew that it would be a long shot. Her uncle was far too clever to fall into such a trap. Langlevit had confirmed the same and warned her not to be so rash as to engage with Zakorov or her uncle—they were both seasoned in the art of war and would not be deceived by such a scheme. However, the idea had never fully left her mind.

And now the Findlay family was preparing to leave for London for the season. Viktor would be there, mingling among the *ton*, and Lana would have to be ever more prudent should their paths ever cross. Viktor knew what she looked like, though he would hardly expect that she would so lower herself into the position of a maid. Not that a life in service was intolerable. The Findlays treated her like family, and for that she was more than grateful, but she wanted her life back. Not for the fine dresses and balls that went on through the night, or even the handsome gentlemen who courted her with sweet-smelling bouquets and non-coded sonnets. Those things, as lovely as they had been, were not so very important anymore. Irina was. Protecting her was all that truly mattered. What Lana wanted most was the simple luxury of having her sister returned to her.

In her room, Lana held the message to a candle, letting the flame eat away at the parchment. Though written in their secret language, she couldn't take the risk that someone would find the poems, decipher them somehow, and put Brynn or her family in danger. She was already a threat to their safety if Viktor got wind of where she was. They'd taken her in on the Countess of Langlevit's recommendation, and Lana would not wish any harm upon them.

After tending to her mistress's needs, Lana busied herself getting ready and called for a carriage into the village. She composed a hasty reply to Lord Langlevit and gathered her unsent letters to Irina. It was early yet, but she had some errands to run for Brynn, including retrieving some new gowns that had been finished for her trousseau. They were to leave for London at the end of the week.

As Lana waited by the back entrance for Colton to bring the carriage around, she thought of how similar the London season was to the one in St. Petersburg. Full of balls and dinners, theater and music, fashion and politics. The ballrooms would be full of gorgeously dressed dancers, twirling in their finery beneath the flickering lights of the candlelit chandeliers. Dancing had always been her very favorite part of the season. She thought of the sumptuous gowns she had left behind and sighed. They would do her little good here anyway. Perhaps they would be waiting for her when she returned, for she *would* return. She and Irina would go home one day soon.

She closed her eyes and recalled the last waltz she had danced. It had been at the Bobrinsky crush, and Lord Du Beauvoir, a handsome French marquis, had asked for her hand at the end of that very ball. Her uncle had refused, claiming that the man was a fortune hunter. Now Lana knew the true reason behind that decision and the six other suits he had turned down—he'd coveted her dowry for himself. That scheming, murdering knave.

Trembling softly, Lana forced her sadness and anger at bay. She knew she couldn't dwell upon thoughts of her uncle or her previous life in St. Petersburg—not without sending her spirits into a downward spiral—so she turned her mind to the practical errands she would tend to while her mistress and the rest of the household slept in. A trip to the village would also give her a chance to leave her sister's letters in the oak without the interruption of a certain arrogant gentleman. Near the end of the drive, she signaled for Colton to stop the carriage at the gate.

"Lady Briannon wishes for some wildflowers for her room," she said as the horses came to a nickering stop. He opened the door and helped her down. "I'll only be a few moments," she told him, walking toward the oak tree and the sprouts of purple crocus, pink camellia, and bright yellow daffodils. A glance over her shoulder showed Colton checking on the mounts, paying her no mind at all. She breathed out and crouched down, quickly pulling her letters from her cloak's inside pockets. Lana tucked the letters into the hollow near the base of the oak tree before pulling up a handful of blooms.

"Finished!" she called brightly to Colton, who returned to help her into the carriage once again. The tightness in her chest dissipated as Colton urged the horses onward. She'd half expected Lord Northridge to pop out of the woods to catch her in the act as he'd nearly done the last two times. He certainly was suspicious of her—although, now she knew he thought her merely a girl of loose morals.

She sat primly on the velvet cushions. Perhaps he only wished her to be such a girl. Lana easily recalled Lord Northridge the other morning, sitting across from her in this very same coach, undressing her with those bottomless blue eyes. He'd wanted her then. And he'd wanted her when he kissed her in the hallway. Her lips tingled as a warming shiver wound through her. A girl with questionable morals would have given in and let him part her lips to claim her fully.

An aching feeling unraveled in the lowest regions of her stomach, and the moment she recognized it for what it was—a stab of pure, undiluted longing—she shifted her weight and recrossed her ankles. But she could no sooner stop a storm than the deluge of heat spreading to her hips and her breasts at the thought of Lord Northridge devouring her mouth and possessing her with his lips, teeth, and tongue.

Bother!

Mortified at her unladylike thoughts, she refused to think of Lord Northridge and his wretched kissing for the rest of the ride into the village.

Breckenham was a charming little town, its main road as ambling and curved as a hair ribbon that had been tossed to the ground. Shops centered the town, while homes and farms dotted the road both north and south. A milliner's and blacksmith, a cobbler and cooper. There was a tavern and an inn, a livery and a butcher shop, and of course, a seamstress, which was Lana's destination. The proprietor had seen to alterations for a few gowns Lady Dinsmore had ordered for Brynn from London. Lana was in and out of the shop quickly, the seamstress dismissive of her, though not because of her status as a maid. Lana was quite sure her slight Russian accent alarmed the lady, as it did most people. A foreigner in a small village was something to be gawked at it, it seemed.

It didn't bother Lana as much as it had when she'd first joined Lord and Lady Dinsmore's staff. In the beginning, she'd had a difficult time believing her uncle and Viktor had not followed her and Irina out of St. Petersburg, and any attention given to her because of her accent would cause Lana to glance up and around, panicked that she had just been given away. It was silly, of course. But hearing her uncle speak so blithely about her impending murder had chiseled fear deep into her soul and had stripped her of any feelings of safety. Lord Langlevit had given a semblance of that safety back to her, and over the last handful of months with the Findlay family, she'd started to feel even more secure.

Lord Langlevit's note that Viktor was in London had shaken that, however, and as Lana left the seamstresses shop, she found herself searching up and down Breckenham's main road for anyone who looked out of place.

Viktor was a small, wiry man with dark hair and an imperial beard and moustache, and her uncle, Count Volkonsky, had the same tall and broad build her father had possessed. He was a handsome man, her uncle, and clearly a well-trained liar. But there was nothing strange about the village that morning.

Of course there isn't, she chastised herself as she handed off the boxes to Colton. Viktor was in London. He had no reason to come to Essex. Langlevit had covered her and Irina's tracks well. She had to have faith in that.

Colton was busy securing the boxes to the top of the carriage when Lana's eyes caught on a horse and rider emerging from a cross lane. The rider directed his mount to the south, in the opposite direction of the cluster of shops where she stood. Had she not already been eyeing the road for anyone who seemed out of place, she might not have seen him.

Lord Northridge had not glanced up the road, and so he had not seen his own carriage or his sister's lady's maid standing idly beside it. Lana raised her chin, following the sight of his straight back and his mount's proud dock and swishing tail. Curious. There were only homes and farms along the southern portion of the road, and none of the large manors belonging to members of the *beau monde*.

She wanted to know where Lord Northridge was going, though she couldn't quite put her finger on the exact reason why. It had nothing at all to do with the fact that he cut such a fine figure upon his horse. He seemed quite focused on his destination. Lana felt her feet move forward of their own accord, as if to follow him.

She pulled back, though, hesitating. Whatever Lord Northridge was doing, it was his own business. And yet, as he and his horse closed in on the bend in the road up ahead, Lana felt the undeniable urge to know where it was he was going. There could be nothing of interest to a young lord down that way.

Unless he was meeting someone. A mistress perhaps. Exactly the vulgar thing he had accused her of doing, the hypocrite!

If he were indeed meeting someone for a clandestine tryst, she would be livid. How dare he try to shame her so unjustly when he may very well be doing the same thing right now?

Vindication.

That was why she needed to follow him.

"Do you have any errands to see to, Colton?" she asked the driver as he was climbing back down from the top.

He straightened his white wig. "Nothing pressing."

Lana racked her mind for any excuse to delay their return to Ferndale. "I forgot," she said, tapping her chin. "Hatcher said something about a saddle at the tanners. I can't remember exactly, but perhaps you should check and see if there is something there for the stables?"

Colton nodded and started to open the door for Lana, but she put up her hand with a bright smile. "Oh, no, I think I'll take a walk while I wait for you. It's such a beautiful morning. I'll meet you back here shortly."

And without waiting for him to reply or argue, she turned and followed the road south, toward the bend in which Lord Northridge and his horse had disappeared.

Chapter Five

The slate roof and twin chimneys of Sir Gerald Cooper's home came into view the moment Gray rounded the corner along Breckenham's village road. The home was one of the village's statelier residences, with a large yard that ran down to the shallow but wide Brecken Kill river. Sir Cooper and his wife, Constance, were good folk. The finest, in Gray's opinion, among the nobility and gentry alike. As he dismounted and walked through the open gates to the half-moon gravel drive, he was, once again, happy he had found the courage to approach them three years ago.

Gray handed off Pharaoh to Sir Cooper's stable boy and headed for the front door. It opened before he could raise a fist to knock, and he met with the wrinkled face of the Coopers' butler.

"Good morning, Higgs," Gray said, stepping inside and removing his riding gloves. His stomach kinked the way it always did when he paid the Coopers a visit. An annoying mixture of nerves and excitement and, he supposed, a bare measure of regret. Although there was little he could do about the latter.

"Good morning, my lord," Higgs replied, making a swift but short bow. He had to be one of the most ancient butlers Gray knew of, and yet the Coopers had deigned to keep him on. Most likely until Higgs was no longer able to walk—or breathe. Whichever came along first, Gray supposed.

"Lady Cooper is expecting you," Higgs said, and he turned his rail-thin form toward the receiving room to the left. Gray followed his achingly slow lead, trying all the while to refrain from pushing past him.

The sitting room was pristine as usual, its east-facing windows allowing a spread of warm sunshine over the floors. They were a modest gentry family, but as Lady Cooper stood from her sofa cushion to greet him, he was struck again at the elegance she bore.

"Lord Northridge," she said with the pleasant, genuine smile he had appreciated right from the start. "You are well met."

He took her hand and bowed over it. "Lady Cooper," he said before straightening his back and releasing her hand. "I hope I find you well?"

Gray cast his eyes about the small receiving room. It seemed they were alone.

"Yes, indeed," she replied, gesturing toward a chair by the hearth and then bidding Higgs to send for tea.

Gray lowered himself stiffly into the chair as the butler shuffled out of the room and Lady Cooper returned to the sofa.

"I apologize we were not here the other day," she began.

"Not at all. My arrival was unexpected."

"Yes," she said. "I heard of Lord and Lady Dinsmore's misfortune on their way to the Worthington Abbey ball. No doubt that is why you came to Essex? I do hope they were not harmed by this wretched masked bandit everyone is speaking of?"

Gray shifted uncomfortably in the chair, his starched shirt and cravat feeling more inflexible than usual. The mention of the bandit reminded him of something he'd thought of the evening before, after happening across Lord Maynard's carriage.

"They were unharmed, thank you, but I must ask that you be vigilant. The bandit is attacking conveyances at the moment, however homes may well be a future target."

He wanted to ask if they had Higgs lock the doors at night, but it wasn't his place. He had learned to tread lightly here, though it was, at times, a struggle.

"Of course," Lady Cooper replied, another smile tugging at her lips. She was a handsome woman. Gray put her at just over five and thirty, her husband, Sir Cooper, perhaps ten years her senior. That they had remained childless for the length of their marriage had been one of the reasons Gray had thought of them first.

"You worry for her safety, of course," Lady Cooper said, that secret smile growing fuller over her lips. "But you needn't. She is well-kept and cared for here."

Gray sat forward. "I did not mean to suggest otherwise."

"I understand," she said, reaching for a small silver handbell upon the tea table. Lady Cooper gave it a ring and then set it down again. "Truly, your concern is most welcome, Lord Northridge. It makes me happy to know you care so deeply."

His heart started to thud in his chest as approaching footfalls sounded from the front hall.

He sprang to his feet as the sitting room door opened. A young maid entered, her hand guiding forward a little girl with a head full of unruly blond curls. She turned her enormous blue eyes up to Gray, and he expelled the breath he'd gathered in his chest as he drank in the sight of his daughter.

God, she was so small and perfect, and yet she seemed to have grown at least another few inches since the month before when he'd paid his last visit. He stood still, afraid to move.

"Come here, darling," Lady Cooper called, holding out her hand.

Sofia hurried from her nursemaid to the sofa, where she promptly buried her head in Lady Cooper's side.

"Now, now, no need to be shy. You know Lord Northridge. He's come to say hello," Lady Cooper said, pinching Sofia's rosebud cheek gently and working a giggle out of the little girl.

"Hello, Sofia," Gray said, and he dropped into a crouch, resting his elbows on his knees. "I've brought something for you."

He reached into his coat pocket and produced a small bouquet of flowers he'd stopped to gather along the way to town. He had no idea what three-year-old girls enjoyed, but he figured flowers were a decent bet.

Sofia peeled herself from Lady Cooper's side and came toward the bouquet of daffodils and crocuses in his outstretched hand. She looked so little like her mother, he thought, as she reached for the flowers, her fingers closing around the stems and pulling them from his hand. Marianna had brown eyes and hair and had fancied herself Italian, although Gray had often been able to trace the Irish brogue she worked hard to keep hidden. He'd never said anything to her about it. It hadn't mattered to him what her background was. She had been his mistress, and happy with the role.

For a time.

"Thank you, Norry," Sofia whispered, her little nose already stuck in the center of the bouquet.

If possible, Gray's heart swelled larger than before. Norry. It was what she called him, Northridge apparently too difficult for her tongue to work out. He didn't mind the nickname. In fact, he rather liked it. He didn't want her to grow up calling him "Lord Northridge" or "my lord" anyhow. "Norry" would do just fine.

"Papa" would be better, but Gray knew it was an impossible wish.

The Coopers were an upstanding and respectable couple, and Sofia was well cared for and loved here. She would grow to be the daughter of an esteemed gentleman landowner and well-known scholar. Lady Cooper herself had been a fine mother to her for these last three years, and her candor regarding the truth of Sofia's birth had been nothing short of angelic.

No. Gray had chosen his daughter's home well, and the Coopers had never once grown tired of his visits, or seemed put out by his arrival, usually at least once a month. It was never enough, however. Not for Gray.

"Sofia has been under the weather for a short while," Lady Cooper said as the little girl held the flowers aloft for her to smell. She leaned down and took in a deep breath. Lady Cooper then pretended to sneeze, which sent Sofia into a fit of giggles.

"Has she?" Gray asked, eyeing his daughter's pink cheeks. They appeared to have a healthy flush, nothing feverish. "What is wrong?"

"Oh, she's quite well now. Just a cough. Do not worry, we had Doctor Jensen pay a visit to listen to her lungs."

Gray relaxed, though the thought of a doctor listening to Sofia's lungs reminded him too much of Brynn and the many physicians who paid visits to do much the same.

"Thank you," he said, though perhaps unnecessarily. Sir and Lady Cooper loved Sofia just as much as Gray did—why wouldn't they see to her health? But, as always, Lady Cooper was gracious and merely smiled.

"Lord Northridge…" She stopped and turned to the nursemaid. "Thank you, Becky, that will be all for now."

The maid bobbed a curtsy and left, closing the door behind her.

Gray watched as Sofia sat down on the rug between he and Lady Cooper, and her pudgy little thumb and forefinger began to pull each petal off. He stifled a laugh.

"Lord Northridge," Lady Cooper began again. He shifted his attention to her. "You do know that my husband and I are very happy to have Sofia in our family. You've given us something we were never able to give ourselves, and for that, we are eternally grateful. However…I cannot help but think… Well, I know I may be wrong to say this, but…"

The pure joy that fed like a stream into Gray's heart whenever he had the opportunity to visit Sofia turned stagnant. He frowned at Lady Cooper as she struggled to find the words she wanted to say. He feared he knew what they were going to be.

"You do not want me to see Sofia any longer," he said. He had whiled away many idle hours while trying to fall asleep at night with the fear that one day the Coopers may well ask him to keep his distance. For Sofia's sake.

Granted, the excuses surrounding his frequent visits would be more difficult to explain once she grew older. But they had many years yet. And perhaps the Coopers could merely say Gray was a family friend. An uncle of sorts.

I do not want to be her uncle.

He did not want a false status within her heart.

Lady Cooper's lips parted, her expression of horror and confusion plain. "Not see her? Oh my goodness, no! Not at all! Please, never think that!"

Gray exhaled yet again, relieved, though still confused. "Then what do you mean to say?"

She stood from the sofa, her hands clasped before her,

and lowered her voice. "Only that it's so clear how much you adore her. I cannot help but think that you might wish for… something more than your regular visits."

He rose from his chair slowly. "Something more?" He eyed Sofia to make certain she was busying herself with the flowers, and softened his voice as well. "Lady Cooper, do you mean to suggest I should take Sofia from Breckenham? From her home here?"

"Do you not wish for it?" she asked in return.

Gray was at a loss for words. His heart screamed yes, but logic and propriety dictated the opposite. He could never claim Sofia as his.

Marianna had never announced that she was expecting their child. When Gray had started to note her widening middle and fuller breasts during the nights he visited her apartments in Knightsbridge—apartments he kept for her—he had said nothing. He knew better than to tell a woman she was gaining. However, when the protrusion of her belly began to take definite shape, he had asked her point-blank.

He would never forget the way she'd responded. A wave of her hand and a nod of her head, as if he'd asked if it was raining outside.

"Just a few more months. I'll take care of it, darling," she'd said, pecking his cheek.

Just like now, Gray had not been able to speak. Only feel.

"It does not signify if I wish for it or not," he finally said to Lady Cooper. "I am unmarried. The child is…" There was no need to say illegitimate, even though at Sofia's age, she would be blissfully unaware of what the word meant.

Claiming an illegitimate child after he was married would be scandalous. Claiming one before would be utterly ludicrous. He cleared his throat. "Sofia is happy here, and I am grateful for our arrangement. I will make every effort I can to visit."

Lady Cooper nodded, but her frown told him she was not fully satisfied with his answer. Gray suspected she worried that he would have a change of heart and take away the daughter they'd come to love as their own. As much as he dreamed of it, he could not be a father to Sofia without bringing shame and scandal down upon them all. No, she was better off here with the Coopers. In one sense, it would be better if he severed all contact, but Gray couldn't bring himself to do it. He couldn't imagine going without seeing those laughing blue eyes. It was as if she'd lodged herself well and truly into the folds of his heart.

He wondered if all fathers felt this way.

"Perhaps you would like to take her out into the gardens for some fresh air?" Lady Cooper suggested.

"I'd like that very much," he said.

Gray scooped Sofia up in his arms, and she squealed in delight. It had taken her all of five minutes to warm up, her natural childish curiosity winning out over initial shyness. Her chubby arms wound around his neck, and he resisted the shocking urge to nuzzle the crook of her dimpled elbow. It astonished him that he had had some part in creating such a perfect human being. Instead, he breathed in her fresh, clean scent and allowed his cheek to graze the spun softness of the golden curls she'd inherited from him.

He noticed that Lady Cooper, while she had not accompanied them into the garden, kept watch through the open bay windows. The garden itself offered a modicum of privacy, bordered by lush green hedges, and only one corner of it was visible from the road. Gray made sure to keep well away from that side—he did not need to cause any heartache or scandal for the Coopers.

"Shall we play catch?" he said, finding a red ball lying beside a rose bush. Sofia's eyes lit up as he threw the ball. She chased after it, giggling, and tried to hide it behind another shrub.

"Norry, ball," Sofia said.

He supposed he was meant to find the hidden ball and did so to the child's great delight. Their game lasted for a few minutes before she became distracted by a butterfly and ran toward one of the rose bushes at the far end of the garden nearest the gate to grasp it.

A startled wail escaped her lips, her blue eyes filling with tears as she clutched her fingers to her chest. Gray rushed to her side only to discover that she had pricked herself on a thorn. "There, there, Norry's got you, little one."

He wiped the tears from her eyes, dismissing the hovering maid and signaling to Lady Cooper standing anxiously at the window that all was well. Drawing his handkerchief from his pocket, he dabbed the tiny bloodstain and bent his lips to her fingers. He took a perch on the low garden wall before pulling a package from his pocket and opening the wrapping to offer Sofia a sugared date. Her tears disappeared.

Gray smiled. "All better."

Unable to help himself, he pulled the little girl into his arms and sat her upon his knee, where she promptly stuffed the fruit into her mouth and chewed happily. He had never felt such a sense of contentment—the perfection in the moment something to be savored and tucked away for the times he could not see her.

A smile still on his face, he looked up. The smile froze as his eyes clashed with a pair of somber green ones. Time stood still for an endless moment as Lana, standing on the road in front of the Coopers' home, slid her gaze from him to the child in his arms, and then back to him. Gray knew the resemblance between them would be evident, even to a stranger. Once more, he found himself at a loss for words. But this time, there was nothing he could say. His mind was utterly blank.

"Lady," Sofia said, looking through the gate with a winsome wave. Startled, Lana raised her fingers in return and then caught herself. With one last unfathomable look, she hurried away. Gray wrenched his eyes from her retreating form and stood, allowing the child to go to the waiting maid. He swallowed hard.

Damn it all to hell. What had Lana been doing here? Had the incorrigible woman *followed* him? His stomach twisted into a knot, followed by a hot sweep of anger that drained away as abruptly as it came.

She knew his secret. With a sinking heart, he wondered what she would do with the knowledge, and what the price of her silence would be.

Chapter Six

A flood of emotions crashed through Lana as she rounded the corner, out of sight of the pretty manor house and out of sight of what she'd witnessed. Her heart was racing at an erratic pace, and her breath came in short, sharp, painful bursts. She had never had a panic attack—Irina was more prone to them—but she was certain that she was about to swoon. Leaning against a low stone wall in the shadow of a large oak tree, she hauled deep gulps of air into her aching lungs.

She shouldn't have followed him. She shouldn't have been so absurdly curious about his whereabouts. Or let her feelings dictate her actions. She shouldn't have engaged with Lord Northridge whatsoever, or let him get under her skin. Now she'd risked her safety and Irina's just to feel vindicated in her opinion of him. She'd thought he had a mistress, and indeed, she had found him with someone of the opposite sex. Only, it'd been a child. *His* child. Of that, she had no doubt.

She recalled the cherubic features of the little girl. Two or three years, at the most. She was the spitting image of her father, down to the wide blue eyes, the blond hair, the stubborn chin, the full, rosy lips. And if she'd had any uncertainty as to the child's identity, the doting expression on Lord Northridge's face as he held her would have left little doubt.

Lana thought back to the woman she'd glimpsed watching from the window. She'd appeared older, too old to be the child's mother and Lord Northridge's mistress, but Lana claimed no understanding as to the desires of men. Her mind raced with scenarios, but they all came back to one thing: she had just stumbled upon Lord Northridge's secret.

A secret that could put her out of her position, and in danger.

Lana cursed herself savagely. She wanted to stomp her feet in frustration—if only she hadn't been so provoked by the man in the first place, she never would have followed him. But now he would undoubtedly take swift action against her. Lord Northridge was volatile enough to retaliate, even if he *had* kissed her. He'd been angry then, but now… She worried what he'd choose to do. Her fears swelled, threatening to suffocate her.

She was a servant.

She had no other home to flee to.

Viktor Zakorov was in London, and her uncle was most certainly not far behind.

Sweat broke out in a hot wave beneath the uncomfortable bodice that seemed to tighten with each breath. Lord help her, she truly was about to swoon. Steadying herself, her hands gripping the stones behind her, she closed her eyes as her knees threatened to give way.

"Miss? *Miss*? Are you unwell?" The voice pierced through the fog suffocating her brain. Lana blinked, her eyes adjusting to the dappled afternoon sunlight. A young woman's concerned face swam into view as she extended a vial of hartshorn and a fan toward her. Lana declined the smelling salts but accepted the fan gratefully. Her benefactor wore a wide-brimmed hat and light veil to protect against the sun.

"Thank you, my lady," Lana said, bobbing a quick curtsy. Another woman accompanied the young lady, undoubtedly her chaperone. The comely girl was impeccably dressed and bore an unmistakable stamp of nobility. Her manner, however, did not. She was warm and friendly, despite realizing that Lana would be no one of consequence.

Lana held the fan out, attempting to return the item. Sparkling blue eyes behind the veil echoed the unaffected smile stretching on the young lady's lips. "Please keep it. I find myself prone to the vapors on exceedingly hot days. I have a number of fans and will not miss this one."

"Thank you," Lana said with another bob of her head.

After a pause, the woman said, "Are we acquainted?"

"Pardon?" Lana asked, her attention divided. She glanced over her shoulder, expecting to see Lord Northridge chasing after her, but was relieved to see only an empty lane. She did not have the wherewithal to handle him right at that moment.

"I know you."

Lana froze at the three innocuous words that shook her to the core. She exhaled before replying, trying to bring her frazzled nerves under control to deal with the new and immediate threat of recognition. "I do not expect that we socialize in the same circles, my lady."

"Perhaps not, but you remind me of someone. She was someone I met a year ago in St. Petersburg. Truly, you could be sisters, the resemblance is so striking."

St. Petersburg. Lana sucked in a short breath, her back and shoulders tensing with worry and no small amount of fear. For months, she had been so careful. To be discovered now would be frightening, especially with Zakorov so close. Panic set in like a cold chill in her veins. She tried not to show any emotion as she slowly lifted her eyes to the woman standing before her. The lady was frowning, as if still struggling to place her. Her determined gaze swept past Lana's plain navy blue gown and her capped head, and returned to scrutinize her features.

Although she did not recognize the young woman's face, Lana knew that it was a high probability that they could have met if she had indeed been to St. Petersburg.

Lana dipped her head again. "I am afraid that's not possible, my lady. I am from Moscow."

"Moscow, you say?" the lady asked. Her expression then lit up. "Ah, that's it then! You're Lady Briannon's maid! She pointed you out last Michaelmas at Ferndale's annual ball and said that you were from Moscow. I was certain I knew you from somewhere."

Lana forced a smile.

"I am Lady Cordelia Vandermere," the woman went on. "One of your mistress's friends."

Lana's eyes widened in recognition at the name. "It is a pleasure to make your acquaintance, my lady."

She frowned, recalling a previous conversation between Brynn and Lord Northridge that suggested the girl was an unemotional block of ice. She certainly did not seem like one now. Intelligence and humor shone in her eyes.

"Is your mistress with you?" Lady Cordelia asked.

"No, my lady, I am running errands, and I must insist that I return your fan. You are far too generous."

Lady Cordelia smiled. "I won't hear of it. 'Tis only a bit of silk." She looked around as if searching for the Dinsmore carriage. "May I offer you a ride to Ferndale? We were coming through Essex ourselves on our way to London," she added by way of explanation. "I needed a bit of a stroll after being cooped up in the carriage for so many hours."

Lana shook her head. "Thank you for your kind offer, but

my carriage is waiting a few streets away."

"Good day, then."

Lana inclined her head graciously. "My lady."

After Cordelia and her companion continued along the lane, Lana composed herself and made her way back to where Colton would be waiting. She held her breath, wondering whether Lord Northridge would pounce on her at any moment, but her walk to the carriage was uninterrupted.

As they made their way back to Ferndale, Lana knew that she'd had a narrow escape with Lady Cordelia as well. She usually tried to keep a low profile with any guests of the Findlays, knowing that there were decent odds that a visiting aristocrat could recognize Princess Svetlanka Volkonsky. But the likelihood was slim—she was, after all, just an invisible servant. And Lana knew that the *ton*'s view of the help would solidify her disguise.

But the more she thought about Cordelia, the better she could pinpoint exactly when they had met in St. Petersburg, and even recall the burgundy tulle gown that Lana had worn that evening. It'd been in the retiring room at the Bobrinsky ball, one of the few society events she'd attended last season. Lana loosed a shaky breath. She had to be more careful. If Lady Cordelia had come that close to recognizing her, it stood to reason that others would, too.

Worse yet, if Lord Northridge were to terminate her position because of her cursed curiosity today, she would have nowhere to go but to Langlevit's Cumbria estate. Having Irina there was risk enough, but the two of them would surely draw more attention. Lana sank into the velvet seat, her nerves crumbling by the moment.

Perhaps her only option would be to find Northridge and explain that she had only seen him by chance. She shook her head. He'd never believe that. Not when the residence he'd visited had been on the other side of town. He had to know that she had followed him. That she'd been *spying*. No, she had to come up with a better excuse…something, anything that would make him open to her appeal. Lana wondered what it would take to buy his goodwill.

She could lie and say that Lady Dinsmore sent her to find him.

She could beg for his mercy.

I could seduce him.

Lana almost laughed out loud at the last thought. Though Mrs. Frommer had practically accused her of being a harlot, Lana's powers of seduction were rusty at best. Yes, he'd kissed her, but Lord Northridge would kiss a tree if it were willing. Besides, the whole idea was a sad, terrible cliché. Instead of the master titillating the servants, it would be the servant seducing the master. However, *something* had provoked him enough to kiss her in the hallway, which meant he wasn't immune to what little charms she did possess.

"Lana, you are being foolish," she whispered to herself. "If you offered your virtue to Lord Northridge, where would that leave you?"

As the carriage pulled into the lane at the top of the estate, Lana knew that she would have to find another way to convince him. She would not—could not—barter her body for his goodwill. She wouldn't be a maid forever, and she had to think of her future.

Thankfully, Lord Northridge had not yet returned, but Lana moved cautiously for the rest of the afternoon, expecting his looming presence at every turn. To keep herself busy, she spent several hours organizing Brynn's trunks and boxes while creating a comprehensive inventory of every item in her mind. She would be required to unpack everything upon their arrival at Bishop House in London and was determined to keep things as orderly as possible, thus producing fewer hassles arranging Brynn's rooms and closets in town.

Concentrating on the correct placement of every hairpin and stocking, every slipper and chemise, meant Lana did not have any room in her mind for the things she had seen earlier that morning in the village.

Lord Northridge with a little girl on his knee.

His lips kissing away the pain of a small injury.

The pure joy in his smile when he looked at the beautiful child.

Lana shook the images away and realized she'd wrapped one of Brynn's cotton night rails in five layers of tissue. Four more than was needed. She sighed and fixed her mistake, her feet growing weary. Never while growing up in St. Petersburg had she thought in-depth about the tasks her maids and other servants performed with such precision and quiet fortitude. A life of service was no easy thing, and now she knew firsthand. When she returned home and was restored to her old life, she would be sure to never forget the toll such dedication took. Lana didn't know how she would continually thank her staff, but she would think of something.

She pulled out a pair of Brynn's newest dress slippers, purchased this winter, and swore under her breath when she saw three cut-glass beads hanging loose from the floral design on the right toe. She should have noticed them earlier. She glanced at the clock on the mantel. Nearly ten o'clock. Brynn would still be downstairs in the sitting room with her mother. Lord Northridge and Lord Dinsmore would likely be in the billiards room or library. Perhaps a study somewhere discussing Parliament or horseflesh. She would have at least an hour to herself before Brynn retired for the evening.

Earlier, Lana had attended to Brynn after her excursion to the village, listening silently as Lady Dinsmore, seated in a chair in Brynn's bedchamber, announced her delight at Cordelia's unexpected visit.

"She has grown more handsome since we last saw her,

has she not?" Lady Dinsmore asked, her eyes alight with the pleasant thought. "She has slimmed a bit, and the color in her cheeks has improved. I daresay she will be attending most of the functions we've been invited to, and considering it is your coming out as well, Graham will be required to act as your escort."

Brynn had met Lana's gaze in the mirror and rolled her eyes. Lady Dinsmore was scheming, of course, wanting her son to marry and produce the next heir to the earldom. But as kind as Lady Cordelia had been that morning in Breckenham, Lana could not picture her at Lord Northridge's side, as his wife. They didn't suit, though she didn't quite know why she thought so. Just the idea of him falling at Cordelia's feet had left her feeling slightly ill.

Don't think about him, she'd scolded herself.

Fiddling with Brynn's slippers, Lana decided to go belowstairs and sew the beads back into place. She did not want to forget them—the preparation over the next few days would be hectic enough. Her legs were aching and her stomach rumbling with hunger as she took the servant stairs to the basement level. She'd dined with the rest of the staff as usual, but she'd barely been able to take more than a few bites of her meal. The impending departure for London, her discovery of Lord Northridge's deepest secret, and the encounter with Lady Cordelia and her near recognition had soured her appetite.

On her way to the sewing room, tucked between the butler's pantry and the stillroom, Lana snatched a slice of rosemary bread. She devoured it before entering the sewing room and lighting a lamp. The kitchen staff had cleaned up and turned in, and Lana guessed only Braxton remained in uniform and awake to tend to the needs of Lord and Lady Dinsmore.

She sat at a table and rummaged through the sewing box

for needle and thread, her shoulders relaxing as she carried on with the mindless work of repairing Brynn's slipper. She filled the quiet with a song, humming a lullaby her mother had sung so many years before. With it came the memory of her long, graceful fingers running through Lana's hair as she drifted off to sleep. The memory was comforting, and for the first time all day, Lana found herself relaxing.

She was so engrossed in the work that she didn't hear anyone approaching until the floorboard behind her creaked. She gave a start and twisted around in her chair. Her eyes landed on a figure who stood just inside the threshold, his arms crossed over his chest as he kicked the door shut. Lord Northridge's expression was unreadable, adding to her sudden unrest.

"What are you doing here?" Lana blurted out, before becoming aware of a prick of pain growing on her index finger. She looked down and saw blood welling up on the pad.

She dropped Brynn's slipper as quickly as she could, but it was too late. Her blood had already leached into the silk in the center of the beads.

"Oh no!" she cried, shoving back the chair and dropping the needle and thread as well. She popped her fingertip into her mouth, frustrated and ready to scream. She sucked on the pricked skin instead, knowing any outburst would only plunge her into deeper trouble.

"Let me see," came Lord Northridge's voice at her back.

She dodged him, stepping around the corner of the table and picking up a scrap of cloth, left behind from some unknown project earlier that day. She wrapped her finger tightly, her eyes watering. It wasn't so very painful, but she was angry and upset and that always made her teary.

"I've ruined the slipper now," she said, blinking back the mortifying rush of tears. It chafed that she'd damaged yet another of Brynn's possessions with her carelessness. The slipper would have to be replaced, and Mrs. Frommer would not miss the additional accounting.

Lord Northridge picked up the tossed slipper and sighed. "It was my fault. I apologize for startling you."

"I didn't hear you sneaking up behind me. You could have said something or knocked," Lana said, appalled at the whiny, fractious note in her voice.

He set the slipper back onto the table. "Let me see your finger."

"It's fine," she replied. But he followed her around the edge of the table.

"Your finger."

Lana pinched her lower lip between her teeth and swallowed the urge to snap at him. His calmness unnerved her. She removed the strip of cloth and extended her hand. Gray held her infuriated gaze another moment before taking her fingers into his. He flipped her hand so that her palm faced up, and cradled it. His skin was warm and dry and oddly calloused for a gentleman.

He inspected the pricked fingertip, and Lana suddenly felt absurd for having reacted the way she had. The blood was already clotting, and in the dim lamplight, the wound was so small she could barely see more than a red dot.

Lana attempted to pull her hand back, but Lord Northridge's fingers tensed and held on. To her surprise, he pressed his lips together and blew a gust of cool air over her fingers and palm. It shivered up her arm, and she felt it burrow under her skin and into her core. Lana drew a breath and successfully retracted her hand this time.

"You shall see another sunrise, I suspect," he said. His teasing humor poked as sharply as the needle had done.

"I told you I was fine."

He settled his eyes on her again, and she found she could not hold the gaze. She glanced at his crisp white dinner shirt, his jacket gone and his cravat loose, though not undone, and found herself noticing how well the fabric sat upon his broad shoulders. Lana squeezed her eyes shut and when she opened them again, centered them upon the slipper she'd ruined. She reached for it, though she didn't know why. She just knew she had to focus on something. Anything to avoid looking at him.

"This is the second wounded finger I have tended today," he said quietly.

"I am sorry, I shouldn't have followed you—"

"Then why did you?"

There was no anger in his tone, only curiosity, but Lana knew enough of Lord Northridge not to misjudge his moods. He could sway from one to the other in the blink of an eye. As such, she opted for the truth. She set the slipper down again and backed away from him, along the length of the table's edge.

"I thought you were meeting someone." Heavens, she sounded ridiculous. She felt petty and completely humiliated.

He followed her along the side of the table as well, his hand sliding over the tabletop. "A mistress."

She nodded, her ankle striking the table leg.

"And that concerned you?"

"I know it shouldn't have, but..." She struggled not to bungle her words. Her native Russian always wanted to take over when her nerves swelled. "You had accused me of meeting a lover, of having a tryst. Of immoral behavior. And I wanted to see for myself if you were..." Lana lifted her eyes to meet his, though only for a moment. There was a storm brewing in their cool blue depths, and she knew by pressing on she would only bring it closer to her. But she could not back down. "A hypocrite."

She saw his chest rise under his elegant dinner shirt and braced herself for an angry response. One she undoubtedly deserved. However, he seemed to be taking a moment to gather his reply. Resisting his natural desire to eviscerate with words. She had no idea how she knew what his natural desire was—usually they always ended up at sixes and sevens with each other. This time, though, Lord Northridge paused. Her eyes lifted to his once more in surprise.

"And now you have seen the outcome of my own immoral behavior," Gray murmured, his attention riveted to the sewing notions scattered over the table.

The little girl. Lana had known, of course, but hearing it come from him made it all the more real.

"She is yours?"

He nodded once, his hand reaching for a silver thimble. He fiddled with it a moment before setting it down again.

"And no one knows?" Lana pressed gently.

"No one beyond Sir and Lady Cooper," he answered, his eyes finally lifting to hers. "And now you."

He'd kept his daughter a secret from his whole family. From all of those he loved. Lana blinked, unable to grasp how difficult such a task must have been.

"The girl's mother…" she ventured, sensing that he would be amenable.

Lord Northridge tipped back his head and drew in another deep breath. He exhaled and turned on his heel, walking back toward the other end of the table. Lana relaxed a little. The closer he stood to her, the tenser she became, as if his very presence held her hostage.

"A previous liaison," he answered, his back to Lana. Out of his range of vision, she admired the breadth of his shoulders again, and the pleated cut of his shirt, but her stomach turned at the thought of Lord Northridge being intimate with this unknown, unnamed woman.

"We are no longer connected. She chose to give up the child."

Oh. How awful.

"But you did not?"

He faced her, his eyes sparking with offense. "Of course I didn't."

She took a cautious step in reverse. An irritable Lord Northridge was an unpredictable Lord Northridge, and the last time he'd become rattled, he'd claimed her mouth with his. His hands had found their way to places on her body where they should not have touched.

And she had not wanted him to stop.

If he noticed her retreat, he didn't react. His expression went distant again, as if he'd become distracted by his own thoughts. "I am not unfeeling," he said, less force behind his voice this time. "I would never have allowed a child of mine to land in some pestilent foundling home or overcrowded orphanage, or with a family I knew nothing about. The Coopers have taken exemplary care of her. And, until you saw us today, Sofia had been a well-kept secret." With those words, he seemed to lose every ounce of his agitation. His hand rose to his forehead and attempted to rub away some worry or stress. "The truth is I followed you down here to speak to you in private. I need to know I have your confidence in the matter, Lana. Please."

Hearing her given name whispered in his cultured, aristocratic tones gave her the slightest start. Perhaps because he wasn't talking down to her or reprimanding her as he usually did. Or perhaps it was the supplicating look in his eyes that accompanied the request. Lord Northridge had so much to lose should his secret about his illegitimate daughter come to light. And he was asking whether he could trust her. Not ordering. *Asking*.

"I will not breathe a word, my lord," she said.

Lord Northridge stared at her a moment, as if trying to decipher whether or not she was telling the truth. Finally, he must have decided to believe her. He stood taller, bringing both arms straight down at his sides. The tension drained out of his shoulders as if he'd been carrying an enormous weight there.

"Thank you," he said in a gruff, emotional voice. "You don't know what it is like, keeping a secret you would do anything to protect—"

"I understand more than you know," Lana whispered before she could stop herself and sealed her lips. The confession had simply slipped out, and now she wished she could rewind the clock and take the confession back.

He cocked his head and moved a few paces closer to where she stood at the head of the table. "Yes. It would seem that we both have secrets."

Feeling panicked at her blunder, Lana glanced over her shoulder. The door to the sewing room was shut. He'd kicked it closed after she'd startled and stabbed her finger.

"Everyone keeps secrets," she replied, trying to keep her tone light. Instead, it trembled. His sharp and serious stare narrowed in, picking up on her nervousness. He ambled closer, his manner unthreatening, but Lana felt menaced nonetheless. Despite that, she stood her ground. She would not run from him like some frightened rabbit.

"Then what are yours, I wonder? Tell me, Lana, what are you hiding?"

The subtle shift in the way his tongue rolled over her name had her senses on alert. It wasn't soft and beseeching like the prior time. This time, he was testing it…tasting its weaknesses. As if her name held the answers he sought. She swallowed hard as he stepped closer, his eyes and manner unreadable.

"I still think you were meeting with someone."

Lana couldn't outright deny it. She was in hiding, and desperate to stay that way, but she could not stoop to blatant lying, especially after Lord Northridge had been open with her about Sofia.

"You may think what you like," she replied. He finished closing the space between them. Lana refused to retreat another step. "However, you may not *take* what you like."

Lord Northridge's mouth turned up at the corners, as if her stand had amused him. "I take only what is willingly offered."

"I don't recall offering my body for you to paw last evening."

"I hardly pawed," he said with a soft huff of laughter. "Did you truly find me so detestable?"

Lana wanted to say yes. Admitting otherwise felt like a form of surrender. She'd done well pretending to turn to ice underneath his hands and mouth, when inside she'd felt the slow scorch of desire. She hadn't expected to feel *that* during Lord Northridge's surprisingly tender kiss. But she had. For those few moments, she'd forgotten her dislike of him entirely.

"I…did not," she said in a shameful whisper, her fingers tangling together in front of her stomach as she tried to avoid his direct stare. "But I am a servant here."

"Then why is it, I wonder," he began, inching forward, "that you do not behave as other servants do?"

Lana's throat closed off as she felt the bracing heat from his body. She would not cower. She would not scuttle back. He was testing her mettle. He wanted her to back down. And yes, perhaps she should. She was, to him, nothing more than a lady's maid, after all.

But everything inside of her, everything born and bred and royal, absolutely refused.

"I am rather obstinate, I suppose," she said instead.

She felt his warm gust of laughter against her forehead. "You are a mule."

Lana gasped at the insult and snapped her eyes to his.

It was a mistake.

She saw the longing in them. The desire. Even a glint of admiration, unless she was fooling herself.

"You are extraordinary," he whispered. She parted her lips at the unexpected compliment, especially as it rode on the heels of an insult.

"Lord Northridge," she began, and then cut her eyes away, staring instead at his loosened cravat and the barest hint of bronzed skin above it. She felt the oddest desire to press her lips to that hollow, to feel his pulse throbbing there below the tip of her tongue. Stirring, she dragged in a shaky breath and licked dry lips. "I am like any other."

"Gray," he said thickly, focusing on her mouth. "My name is Gray, and I do not want any other. I do not think of any other, not as I have found myself thinking of you."

It was wrong of him. He shouldn't have been saying these things to her. Or asking her—a servant—to address him by his given name. And he should most definitely not have just brought his body to within a scant inch of hers. The air between them shimmered into something reminiscent of a lightning storm, powerful and elemental. She could barely breathe from the longing to have his hands on her. She was mad to want him to touch her again, and yet she did. If she was being honest with herself, she'd wanted their return ever since he'd removed them from her body the night before.

"Only because I am considered forbidden. Only because I am an exciting risk," she said, her chest beginning to strain from the lack of steady breaths. She wasn't sure whom she was trying to convince.

"No. It is something more."

His quiet words were so certain, so supremely sanguine, that Lana couldn't help but be taken in by his conviction. More than what? A fleeting attraction? A desperate tumble belowstairs? She couldn't be so foolish as to hope that he was about to profess his undying love. Men of his station and women of her current one had only one route open to them.

And it did not involve marriage.

It involved ruination. Hers, particularly.

"You feel it too, Lana. I know you do." His hand lifted to dislodge the white cap from her head. She watched it in silence as he placed it on the table. Oddly, the removal felt like he was evening the footing between them, and she had the strangest urge to snatch it to her chest. Her only defense against him was her position, and here he was…discarding it. Showing her that it didn't matter. Her mouth went dry.

"Feel what?" she croaked.

"The connection between us that has been there from the start, from the moment you walked through the doors at Ferndale."

She swallowed a hysterical giggle. "You mean the one that makes me want to pummel you into the next fortnight?"

His lips twitched, but his next words erased the momentary humor. "Physical attraction." Long slender fingers hovered in the air next to her cheek, but he didn't touch her. "Tell me you feel nothing, and I'll leave this room. Say the word, Lana, and I'll go."

His words catapulted through her, bursting through her defenses like cannons on a battlefield. She knew better. She knew better than to trust the aching look in those wide blue eyes or the feeling that this man needed someone to trust, needed someone to hold him. If only for a moment. She could give him that, couldn't she? God knew she was no stranger to loneliness and the need for physical comfort.

But Lana was wary. He was so exasperatingly difficult to fathom. Cold one minute, hot the next. Hubristic to a fault, and then achingly gentle as she'd seen with his daughter. She was not impervious to his looks, but she'd never been the sort of maiden to be swayed by a handsome face. Despite his high-handed nature, Lana found herself drawn to this man. To the tenderness she sensed beneath the surface. She didn't want to think of him like this. So open and vulnerable. No, she didn't want to *feel* anything for him at all, especially when he was staring at her just so. It was a losing battle. He made her want to do unreasonable things. Foolish things.

No, she didn't want him to leave.

Not even when his eyes flared at her silence and he breached the remaining space between them, the moment for retreat vanishing. Panting softly, Lana made no move to stop him when his hand came up and his fingers touched the column of her neck. They slid to her nape and pressed into her skin, sinking up into the mass of her hair.

"Regardless of what I feel, you know nothing of who I am," she breathed, her willpower threatening to dissolve at the touch of his fingertips on her tingling scalp.

"Then show me," he replied before setting his mouth to hers.

Lana's shaky reserve held firm for all of one heartbeat before it crumbled like a fortress built on sand. Gray's tongue drew across her sealed lips, and her mouth, as if governed by another mind, betrayed her. Her lips parted on a tremulous sigh, allowing him entry, and he swept in without hesitation. God, it was even better than what she had imagined so many times in her dreams. Warmer. Hotter. Brighter.

Addictive.

She wanted more. Her hands slid up around his neck, her tongue touching his tentatively. He groaned his approval and deepened the kiss. Lana's entire body trembled at the sensual onslaught as he sought the soft interior of her mouth, drawing her lips between his and coaxing her to respond. Unlike the last time he kissed her, now all she wanted to do was open to him...savor the sleek glide of his tongue, welcome the warm press of his lips, delight in the hard strength of his body. He was all she could feel and taste and breathe, consuming every single rational thought in her head as bursts of heat kindled and ignited along her quivering limbs. Lana moaned into his mouth, lost to the erotic storm he was arousing within her.

Gray swiveled her around, edging her backward until the lip of the sewing table pushed against her lower back. His palms rounded over the curves of her bottom and lifted, hefting her up and settling her on top of the table, even as his mouth continued to ply hers with soft nudges and wet bites. Breaking the heated embrace after an eternity, his eyes impaled hers—so deeply blue and unfathomable, like the ocean she'd crossed to get here, that Lana couldn't speak.

After a long moment, he bent to feather every inch of her face with soft grazes of his lips, as if memorizing every contour and every rise. The aching tenderness of his touch left her speechless. Without realizing it, her anxious fingers had worked their way into the loose linen of his cravat, tugging at it until it fell away, exposing his neck. He smelled of lemon and cedar, and Lana couldn't help herself—she touched her mouth to his throbbing pulse, tasting his warm, salted skin.

"We must stop," she whispered as his own busy lips trailed above her brow and around to her ear.

"Do you want me to stop?" He took her lobe between his teeth, his breath hot. Gray tugged gently, his tongue sweeping out to lick the sensitive skin there. Lana shivered and moaned her answer. *No. God no. Don't stop.*

In response, he slipped his fingers under the cap of one sleeve of her serviceable dress and tugged it down. He brought his kisses to her bared shoulder while sliding down the opposite sleeve. And then, with the fingers of both hands still hooked into the rim of her muslin bodice, Gray pulled again. The top of her dress came down, her chemise with it, and Lana's breasts, completely unhindered, spilled out into the dim light of the single lamp.

She gasped, her breath coming short. But Gray held her panicked eyes, calming her, reassuring her before letting his gaze descend to feast on the sight of her.

"Do you know how beautiful you are, Lana?" he said thickly. "So perfect. I knew you would be. I've never seen such skin like yours, like a luminous pearl."

She blushed deeply, everything falling away—the room, the manor, all of it, until it was only them. Only *him*, and the way he was looking at her.

"Do you want me to stop?" he murmured again, his eyes rising to connect with hers.

Would he? Lana had never been anywhere near this intimate with a man, but she had heard rumors from others. That men could be beasts. That they would simply do as they pleased. She did not doubt Gray's honor, though, not after learning how he had been unable to abandon his child. If she changed her mind in another few seconds, she trusted he would stop.

But the shocking, shameless truth was she didn't want to. Not yet.

Flushing with brazen shame, she shook her head in answer. With a smile, Gray lowered over one peach pink nipple and touched his tongue to the tip before drawing it into his mouth. Gasping at the wicked swirl of his tongue, Lana's back arched like a tightened bow at the instant streak of fire that torched a path from her breasts to her hips. He suckled her, taking her between his teeth and gently tugging. She had never felt anything so sublime, so indecently delicious in her life. As Gray's hands bracketed the span of her ribs and his mouth traveled to her other breast, lavishing his tongue and teeth on that one as well, she couldn't imagine asking him to stop. It felt exquisite. He made *her* feel exquisite.

A clatter down the hallway broke her lust-filled trance. Lana bolted upright, her eyes springing open to land on the closed door. Gray straightened, his gaze following the same route her eyes had taken, his own narrowing with understanding of their predicament. In an instant, Lana saw the peril of their situation—she, spread upon the table in a wanton display with the master leering above her, her breasts swinging free like a common tavern wench.

The utterly mortifying truth of it.

What the devil had she been thinking? She'd let emotion and lust overcome her good sense. She was risking *everything*, and for what? A few scattered embraces with a man who could destroy her fragile house of cards on a whim?

Cursing her stupidity, Lana yanked up one sleeve while Gray slid the other into place. She batted his hand away, covering herself once again and hopping off the table. The distinct sound of footsteps came toward the sewing room door, and Lana's heart tumbled to her feet. Even fully clothed, she couldn't be caught with him like this—she'd be tossed out on her ear with no alternative but to find her way to Lord Langlevit alone, her perfect cover in tatters. Not to mention the scandal that would follow in her wake.

She cursed herself again in several languages. How could she have been so *reckless*?

Wild-eyed, she shushed Gray and shoved him backward, toward the space against the wall next to the door. There was no closet to hide in, no adjoining door for him to escape through. He'd have to hide behind the opened door and pray not to be seen. He stumbled back, his frown telling her he didn't like hiding. But he must have understood what was at risk for her, because he stayed quiet.

The door opened a mere second after Lana caught sight of Gray's discarded cravat beneath the table. She kicked it farther underneath and turned to greet her visitor. She thought she might be ill at the dour face that appeared.

The ever-vigilant Mrs. Frommer had opened the door wide enough to block Gray from Lana's view. Her eyes narrowed on Lana and then canvassed the room in an efficient sweep. Lana felt true fear rise in her chest for a moment as the housekeeper's gaze lingered near the table where she'd kicked the loosened cravat out of view. She held her breath until Mrs. Frommer's cold eyes returned to her person, certain that the housekeeper would see right through the cloud of sin surrounding her.

"I saw the light under the door," she said in a clipped voice, not bothering to disguise her enmity. "I wanted to be sure someone hadn't left a lamp lit."

Lana swiped up Brynn's slippers and shot the housekeeper a false smile, hoping she didn't sound as breathless as she felt. "I was repairing something for Lady Briannon before tomorrow."

Mrs. Frommer kept a hand on the doorknob, remaining in the doorway with one pencil-thin eyebrow raised. "You look flushed, Miss Volchek."

Cringing, Lana licked her lips and gathered her sewing supplies. "It is rather over-warm in here," she replied in as agreeable a tone as she could manage. "But luckily I finished just as you arrived and was about to leave. I will follow you out, Mrs. Frommer."

Though she loathed the housekeeper, if Lana left with her, she wouldn't have to face Gray. The spell his touch had woven through her had lifted just enough for shame to take its place. The throb of her breasts compounded it. Lana nodded at the stony-faced housekeeper, distinctly aware of the virile man hidden not a half step away from her. Her cheeks burned with the scalding memory of his mouth and hands, and her shameless response to them. She was a coward to run, she knew, but it was clear that she could no longer trust herself with Lord Northridge.

With a shaky breath, she reached for the lamp and lowered the wick, extinguishing the flame. She rushed through the door and into the hallway, sighing with relief when the housekeeper closed it behind them.

Chapter Seven

"Lord Northridge," a lilting female voice called out.

Gray turned to see Lady Cordelia Vandermere strolling toward him as he was descending from his coach on St. James's Street in London. At the sight of his sister's friend, he stifled the immediate urge to duck into the entrance to White's. It would be unforgivably rude. It wasn't Cordelia's fault that his mother had chosen her as top prospect for a daughter-in-law—in spite of his own recalcitrant feelings on the matter.

He greeted her nonetheless with unfailing courtesy as she reached him, her maid and chaperone hovering a short distance away. "Lady Cordelia, a pleasure to see you."

"And you." She smiled winsomely, and for a moment, Gray stared at her. Despite her purported frigidity, Cordelia was indeed a lovely girl. His mother was right. She had the right pedigree and circumstances to make him an excellent match, and she certainly was young and attractive. But Gray felt nothing but mild appreciation for her beauty, much the same way as one would appreciate a beautiful portrait. For one, her flaxen hair seemed too pale and weightless. It lacked the supple substance a darker shade might hold. Hair the color of warm chocolate, for instance. Nor were her eyes the kind of bottomless green that made a man want to lose himself in them. Simply put, she wasn't Lana.

Gray groaned inwardly. If he had any sense in his head at all, he would be setting his cap at Cordelia instead of lusting after impossible outcomes with a servant. A servant who deserved better than some lord rutting after her. Common sense, however, seemed to be in short supply, especially where his sister's beguiling maid was concerned. She haunted his thoughts every waking moment.

He focused on the lady in front of him. "I trust you are well?"

"Very well, my lord, thank you." Cordelia nodded, a trifle breathless. "We were visiting the apothecary down the street, and I happened to notice your coach. How is your mother? And Lady Briannon? I haven't seen either of them since our arrival in London."

"They are both well," he replied. "I believe my sister was out shopping with her lady's maid this afternoon for a dinner later this evening."

He clenched his jaw. There had been no reason for him to mention Brynn's lady's maid, but alas, his tongue had formed the words anyhow.

"Ah, yes, the Russian girl," Cordelia said. "I saw her briefly in Breckenham on the journey here a few days ago, and to my great mortification, I quite mistook her for someone else." She laughed, and Gray notched an eyebrow at her decidedly unusual display of humor. Normally, Cordelia was far more reserved, particularly when in the presence of her mother. He glanced to her waiting companion—an attractive young woman not much older than she. Perhaps her mother's absence explained her surprising break from habit. "Well, I shall not tarry longer, my lord, as I expect you are engaged at the moment. I bid you good evening."

"And you, Lady Cordelia."

Gray blinked at his unexpected fortune as she departed down St. James's Street arm in arm with her companion. He'd half expected her to wrangle a dinner invitation out of him or at least convince him to accompany her on a stroll or ride in the park. But then, perhaps, those machinations were her mother's doing, not hers.

White's, he thought as he entered the establishment, was unusually quiet. Only a few members of the private gentleman's club graced its tables, including one who was not known for small talk. It suited Gray's current mood just fine.

"Langlevit," he greeted the earl. "May I join you?"

"Of course."

Nodding politely to the others at the table, Gray settled himself into an empty chair with a large glass of whiskey as play at the table resumed. Placing his bet, he stared distractedly at the hand of cards he'd been dealt, his mind occupied. He'd ridden ahead to London, forgoing a strained carriage journey along rough, rutted roads for a bruising ride on Pharaoh. It had done little to clear his head or his capricious temper. The last few days had taken a brutal toll on his patience.

Signaling a hovering footman for a second drink, he downed the liquor in one gulp as another round of cards was dealt. Notwithstanding his own scandalous behavior with Lana, he'd been forced to endure his mother's herculean matchmaking efforts with Lady Cordelia by singing the girl's praises every half hour. He'd also had to hold himself back from insulting their odious neighbor, the Duke of Bradburne, who seemed intent on pursuing Briannon and procuring a wife less than half his age. Each day following the Gainsbridge crush, the manor house at Ferndale had been filled to bursting with flowers, and it seemed that Bishop House in London was doomed to follow the same fate. He could barely breathe this morning with the scent of lilies in the house. And neither could Brynn, for that matter.

His mother was thrilled at the prospect of her daughter becoming a duchess, no matter that Brynn was as repulsed by the thought of the match as he. Bradburne was old, but that wasn't his greatest fault. He was a lecher, a complete and utter reprobate who collected lovers and mistresses the way some men collected horseflesh or lands. And yet the duke's intentions toward Brynn had been more than clear. They'd been invited to an eleventh-hour dinner that very evening at the duke's residence on Park Lane, but Gray would have suffered a public flogging rather than attend. He'd declined to his mother's—and Brynn's—infinite disappointment.

Unease trickled into his chest and stomach whenever Gray thought of Bradburne or his son, the Marquess of Hawksfield. Both were libertines, though Hawksfield was not as flagrant in his lifestyle as the duke. Gray knew the dark pleasures that came with charming a willing woman in order to satisfy his own base desires. Using, discarding, and then forgetting her, sometimes all within the course of one evening. It was disgusting how much Gray had once had in common with the duke and marquess.

Could a man change?

He'd thought he could. He'd tried. His self-imposed celibacy had been a tremendous test of will. But this last week with Lana had sown seeds of doubt within him. He wanted her with an overwhelming swell of lust, stronger than he could ever remember feeling. And Gray saw the same simmering thirst in the Marquess of Hawksfield's eyes whenever the man looked upon Brynn. He wanted nothing more than to keep his sister far away from both him and his lecherous father. Brynn deserved to be something more than just an object of desire, something that a man fancied for a short while.

So does Lana.

The thought struck him with the force of a mallet. His conscience was merciless, it seemed. And accurate. Perhaps that was at the core of what needled him so deeply—he recognized the debauched, most primitive side of himself in those men. One that Lana had unknowingly awakened. He craved her with a raw need that demanded he satiate his body with hers, consequences be damned. And there would be consequences if he gave in. For himself. For her. For his family.

So maybe he was far worse than Bradburne or Hawksfield.

Perhaps he loathed them because he loathed himself more.

For while either of them could do right by Brynn, there was nothing Gray could offer Lana. Especially marriage. She could only be his mistress. The little he knew of her told him that, despite her heated response to him, she would never accept. And he would never suggest such a thing, not if he wished to maintain some degree of honor. She was a lady's maid. He was a viscount. They'd be shunned by polite society. While the *ton* would tolerate him because of his family's influence, they would publicly humiliate her at every turn.

Gray didn't know what it was about her that bewitched him. She carried herself with bafflingly quiet poise, and though he knew that she was from a genteel family, that innate sangfroid gave him pause. Even compared to someone such as Lady Cooper, Lana possessed a refined self-confidence that surpassed hers. It was something that could not be taught. Lana was a mystery, one that he was determined to unravel.

Gray remembered those slender, unblemished fingers of hers and felt an indescribable need to feel them upon him right at that moment. He'd forced himself not to think about that night belowstairs in the sewing room, but now, it seemed that his memories wanted to torture him.

Her nervous hands sliding along his arms. Her intoxicating

scent. Her mouth. Her sweet tongue pushing against his. Her taste. *God, her full, satiny breasts*.

On cue, Gray's trousers drew uncomfortably tight right there in the middle of the goddamned card room. From a days-old memory. Rattled by his body's untimely response, he composed himself with a rough shake and sat upright in his chair. He focused on the game. And dead puppies. Dead puppies being trampled by a herd of drunken elephants. The resulting appalling image helped. Somewhat.

With a strangled breath, Gray placed a bet and drained the contents of his glass, signaling for another. It appeared that he was doomed to remain at the table for at least the next hand, as standing would invite considerable ridicule from the other men seated around him, all of them barely acquaintances. Growing stiff in the middle of a card game. He'd never imagined he'd be so pitiable.

Then again, he hadn't been with a woman in ages. That probably had much to do with his terrible humor and near-constant state of half-arousal. There were measures he could take to prevent unwanted pregnancies, avoiding the very situation that had befallen his prior mistress, but Gray hadn't felt inclined to satisfy his baser urges. At least not until Lana. Now it felt as if he had a raging mongrel in his trousers every time he thought of her, which was far too often. He adjusted himself again, resigned to the sorry fate he had created for himself.

"Northridge," a cynical voice intoned. "Surprised to see you in town so early for the season."

Gray's head craned in slow motion, although he had already recognized the voice's owner as the subject of his earlier murderous thoughts. His jaw clenched. "Hawksfield."

"May I?" the marquess asked, taking one of the empty seats at the table. He lowered himself into a chair beside Lord Langlevit, receiving a courteous nod of welcome from the earl.

"Suit yourself," Gray replied, his ill humor only slightly dulled by the whiskey he'd consumed. At least the marquess's disagreeable presence appeared to be marginally more distracting than the puppies and rampaging elephants.

As always, Hawksfield was impeccably dressed from the crown of his head to the tips of his polished boots. He wore his arrogance like a second skin, and it rankled Gray like no other. He'd seen the man disappear with Brynn onto the balcony at the Gainsbridge masquerade, and though his sister had insisted nothing untoward had happened with the marquess, she'd been inexplicably agitated upon her return. He'd bet his last farthing that Hawk had overstepped his bounds.

"It's been awhile, Hawk," Langlevit said. "Although, I'm not sure I'm keen to have you divest me of my coin. Northridge has been on a colossal losing streak all night and has fattened up my purse."

"Langlevit," Hawk greeted him. "Good to see you returned from duty in one piece. I haven't yet congratulated you on your promotion. Field marshal, eh?"

The earl shrugged off the impressive new ranking. After so many years of service in the Royal Army, he'd received the highest honor a military man could achieve.

"Thank you," was all Langlevit replied.

"A man of many words," Hawk joked, toasting him. "How is your mother?"

Gray noticed the earl tense but then relax as he answered the question. "Sadly, my mother is unwell of late and has retired to the country for some peace and quiet. I expect it shall be good for her to have a break from a constant stream of guests." He cleared his throat, his expression turning solemn. "Will Lady Eloise be joining you in London for the season?"

Gray eyed him. The earl had danced with Hawksfield's

sister three times at the Gainsbridge masquerade, igniting rumors that he had set his cap at her. Looking at him now, Gray nearly laughed. The man was practically perched on the edge of his seat waiting for Hawk's answer.

"No," Hawk returned. "She is to remain at Worthington Abbey."

Disappointment clouded Langlevit's face. "That is a pity."

"My sister does not enjoy crowds."

"Neither do I," Langlevit said. "Although, at times it is a necessary evil."

Gray frowned at the earl's cryptic words. Just returned from the military overseas, Langlevit would be considered a splendid catch by all the matchmaking mamas of the *ton*. He was handsome, titled, wealthy, and most importantly, unattached. The tendre he'd developed for Hawksfield's sister had come as a surprise to more than just Gray, and not only because of the burns upon Lady Eloise's face, inflicted long ago.

Brynn had always seemed fond of the girl, but Gray had never quite known how to take her. She was kind and had all the right mannerisms, but something about her struck him as…orchestrated. She bore her illegitimacy with the perfect balance of poise and humility. She wore her veils with the perfect amount of grace and courage. And yet, Gray found Eloise on the whole to be somewhat unsettling, as if she were a projection of someone instead of a real person.

Play resumed, along with chatter across the gaming table, though Gray could hardly bring himself to focus. He lost three more hands because of it. He could either go home to an empty house, with the object of his lust far too close in proximity, or he could stay here in relative safety and contribute to everyone else's pockets. There was no choice in the matter. The lost coin was a small price to pay for the retention of his sanity…and what little was left of his dignity.

Lana's indifference over the last two days had been a bitter tonic to swallow. He knew she'd been occupied with the unpacking and beleaguered by his mother's incessant demands to get everything just right, but she'd gone out of her way to avoid being in his presence.

If he entered a room, she vacated it. If he tried to gain her attention, she busied herself with something else. If he tried to corner her, she found clever ways to extricate herself. It was damned provoking. No, if he returned to Bishop House, he would not be responsible for his actions—she would likely find herself on her back with her skirts tossed over her head before she could blink. His erection rose anew. Gray raked a hand through his hair and loosened the cravat at his neck.

"Looks like you are settling in for the night," Hawk noted over the rim of his whiskey glass. "Drowning your devils or your sorrows?"

"I've no better place to be," Gray said mildly, lifting his own glass and ignoring Hawk's question. "What's better than the company of you fine gentlemen?" Toasts of "*hear, hear*" filled the room. "Although I am surprised to see you here, Hawksfield."

"Why is that?"

"I would have thought you'd be at the duke's impromptu dinner tonight. My mother was all aflutter at the prospect of encouraging your father's intentions toward my sister."

Hawk's eyes flew to his. "A dinner, you say."

"At your own residence." Gray paused and smirked. "What, did the duke cut you from the guest list?"

Hawk set his jaw in answer. It was so, then. Bradburne hadn't wanted his son present. Gray could guess why. He was not the only one, it seemed, who had noticed Hawksfield ogling Brynn like a lusty rooster.

"Brynn will be there?"

"Lady Briannon," Gray corrected in a lazy tone, "has the

unfortunate duty of being forced to accompany my parents, seeing as the invitation specifically requested her presence. And, well, one can't refuse a duke, can one?"

Or a viscount.

Gray went cold with the realization. Brynn, who sat only a few rungs below the duke's own ranking, had known she could not deny him without consequence. Had Lana, who was not even within the same social sphere as Gray, felt the same way? Unable to deny his kisses, his advances, for fear of consequence? Had he been fooling himself, thinking she had *wanted* them?

Gray felt sick and had nearly forgotten the other players at the table until he heard his name being mentioned.

"So it's true then that the Dancing Duke is courting your sister, North?" one player, Lord Finton, asked with a waggish grin. "Heard she swooned with delight when His Grace asked her to dance at the Gainsbridge affair."

Hawksfield snorted his derision. "The lady was likely overwrought from the unwanted attention."

"At least we agree on that," Gray said in a deprecating tone, meeting the marquess's stare. "Though, the duke seems to be the only one who is courting my sister *properly*, and perhaps willing to make a legitimate offer."

There was a sudden hush at the gaming table. A muscle ticked in Hawk's cheek.

"Is there something you wish to say to me, Northridge?"

"I just did," Gray answered, though his reply lacked any real force.

They glared at each other with mutual hostility until the marquess pushed back his chair with such force that it tipped over. He stalked from the room without another word. Truly, Gray felt nothing but self-disgust. He was a sodding hypocrite. He had done exactly the same as Hawksfield.

The conversation picked up slowly around the table,

though the others were still eyeing him with wary looks. He ignored them, and several rounds later, White's had become considerably more crowded. The occupants of his own table had shifted as the earlier players took their leave, to be replaced by others Gray knew.

Members and guests wove between tables, stopping to speak and make introductions. One such man approached Gray's table, a smile of recognition lighting his face when he made eye contact. Helmford Monti's crop of thick and wild white hair was his most arresting feature. It reminded Gray of the beaches he'd seen in Crete when he'd taken his grand tour of the Continent three summers ago. Greece had been enjoyable, but it was Monti's home country of Italy where Gray would happily return at the drop of a hat.

"Monti, haven't seen you in a while. Back for the season?" Gray asked as the Italian ambassador arrived at the table.

Monti, who spent more time at social functions than he did at the Court of St. James, nodded and clapped Gray on the back with a lascivious grin. "You know I could not miss the parade of all the lovely English roses."

"Don't they have enough beautiful women in Italy to keep you satisfied?" Gray laughed.

Monti grinned. "Variety, my lord, variety. Besides, I like to share the wealth of my culture. Your English women can only benefit from knowing the fire of an Italian *amante*."

"I assure you our English women are doing quite well without your heavy-handed flirtations," Gray replied, his eyes flicking to an unfamiliar man who had just stepped up to Monti's side. He cut a brutish figure and sported a heavy, dark mustache. The ambassador made a quick, short, apologetic motion with his hands.

"Gentlemen, Lord Northridge, may I present Baron Viktor Zakorov. He is a Russian diplomat visiting from St. Petersburg on urgent business. I managed to convince him to take a respite and enjoy what your gentlemanly establishments have to offer."

Monti eyed two recently vacated seats at Gray's table and quirked an eyebrow.

"Please, join us." Gray answered the unspoken question with the grace expected of a peer, though the Russian appeared too silent and surly to be diverting company. Gray gestured around the table. "Monti, I'm sure you know Lords Marsham, Esterborough, Fintan, and Langlevit."

The others offered their greetings, but Langlevit kept his head down with a grim look upon his face. Gray frowned at his sudden coolness. Strange. The earl was usually a friendly fellow, but he'd become rigid and tense with the arrival of the two men.

"What business are you upon, Lord Zakorov?" Gray meant it simply as polite conversation, but he was unprepared for the swift, icy glare the Russian shot in his direction.

"Confidential." His speech was heavily accented.

"Of course," Gray said with a smile that stayed only on his lips. "Though it is a well-heeded rule that what is divulged at White's remains at White's."

Marsham, Esterborough, and Fintan all chuckled at that, though Langlevit's grim expression didn't change. Perhaps it was the news Hawksfield had delivered about Lady Eloise remaining in Essex for the season that had turned the earl's attitude sour.

Monti clapped Zakorov on the shoulder before lighting a thin cheroot. "Why not tell them?" he suggested. "They may be able to help you. Lord Northridge is a man of many connections, as are the others."

Zakorov looked clearly disinclined to do so, but at the sudden interest from everyone at the table, he nodded after a long pause. "I am searching for two women—Princesses Svetlanka and Irina Volkonsky. They are wanted for crimes against the tsar."

Lord Fintan piped up, "That sounds ominous. Two princesses, you say? What are they wanted for?"

"They are spies for the French, masterminding an assassination plot. My sources say they are here in London."

"Russian princess spies," Fintan mused to himself. "Sounds rather too fantastic to believe."

Esterborough laughed. "Like something out of one of the half penny novels my sisters entertain themselves with."

Zakorov's thick eyebrows slammed together. "This is no trifling fantasy. They are traitors and must be found."

Lord Fintan seemed oblivious to the man's ire, his guileless blue eyes confused. "Even if they were spies, how can two princesses simply disappear? *Someone* must know of their whereabouts."

"That is why I am here." Zakorov snapped the words through his teeth. "To find them."

"I am sure you will be successful in your task," Lord Marsham offered, as if trying to deflect Zakorov's thin-lipped fury. "They are women, after all, and there aren't many visiting Russians in town. And with the season getting underway, two Russian princesses are certain to be on everyone's invitation list."

Gray shook his head, taking Marsham's cue. "I've not heard of any Russian princesses in London."

Esterborough grinned. "Trust me, if Northridge had, his mother would have arranged an introduction to be sure. She is a marriage juggernaut."

Gray smiled around his next sip of whiskey. "Indeed." He nodded at Zakorov, whose hooded gaze met his. "I do not have any information on the matter, but my sister does have a maid from Moscow. I could ask if she has heard of anything."

"Thank you," Zakorov said, "but that will not be necessary. I fail to see how a maid from another city could provide assistance."

"As you say." Gray looked away from the diplomat who had dismissed him and focused intently on his cards, just as Langlevit had been during the whole of the conversation. Like the unwitting Lord Fintan, the earl seemed oblivious to Zakorov's abrasive manner and short temper. Langlevit spoke barely a word the next quarter hour, before standing up and announcing his departure with a curt nod.

Gray played for the better part of an hour until he, too, decided that he'd more than recouped his losses. "Gentlemen, enjoy the rest of your evening." He stood and signaled to the factotum. "Mr. Simmons, please settle my accounts and call for my carriage."

"Yes, at once, Lord Northridge."

Thankfully, the ride to Bishop House was short, for Gray wanted nothing more than to go to sleep. His head was beginning to ache from the copious amounts of liquor he had consumed, and as the carriage made a slow turn into their street, the twinge of pain in his temple sharpened. About halfway around the square, he noticed a hired hack waiting at the curb adjacent to his residence. He wouldn't have paid any extra notice to the coach had it not been for the cloaked female form hurrying up the belowstairs entrance steps of Bishop House, where the servants came and went. She glanced up and down the street, her profile visible for the briefest of moments.

Even in the shadowy lighting, Gray recognized her in a heartbeat. He blinked in disbelief as Lana crossed to the curb and climbed into the awaiting conveyance.

Chapter Eight

Lana knew the minute she stepped into the coach and seated herself across from the earl that something was wrong. Truth was, she'd known the moment the messenger arrived at Bishop House with a man's card, stamped with what she recognized as Langlevit's distinctive coat of arms instead of the leaping hare. There was no flowery language. Only a direct command:

I must see you. Black coach outside. - L.

It was too rushed, too unlike him to risk sending someone to her at so late an hour, and take no steps to disguise the correspondence, but luckily, the family was still at dinner and most of the servants were abed. Instantly panicked, she'd thrown on her cloak and slipped the note into her pocket. She didn't have time to burn it, and she could not risk leaving it lying around the kitchen for someone to find.

Now, all the blood deserted her body at the look on Langlevit's face. Her bones followed suit at his next words.

"I have seen Zakorov."

She swallowed past the lump of fear in her throat, her numb fingers winding into the folds of her skirts. The moment she had dreaded for months was here. Panic threatened to erupt, but she forced herself to breathe and stay calm. "You are sure?"

"I had the misfortune of running into the bastard at White's." He didn't apologize for his language. Instead, Langlevit leaned forward to take her cold palms in his. "He is looking for you."

"Irina?" Her voice almost broke.

"Is safe for the moment. As are you. No one suspects your disguise, but you must be vigilant. Northridge mentioned something about his sister's lady's maid in passing, but I do not believe Zakorov paid him much heed."

Lana tensed. "Lord Northridge was there?"

"Yes," he replied with a frustrated nod. "Your Highness, I cannot caution you enough to remain alert. Although Zakorov will not be looking amongst the servant class, if he sees you, he will recognize you." He squeezed her fingers. "There is something more."

Lana didn't know if she could endure more. She gathered a breath. "What is it?"

"The baron is accusing you and Princess Irina of treason. He says you've both committed crimes against the tsar and claims that he has been sent here to apprehend you."

Lana tore her hands from his. "He is accusing *us* of treason?" She checked her rising voice at the earl's worried glance toward the window. The shade was drawn, and the guttering carriage lamp hanging inside threw shadows over his face.

"He is openly searching for two Russian princesses—he needs to feed some convincing story to those who can help him," Langlevit replied. He reached for her hands again, his white gloves warming her as they closed tightly around her fingers. Lana sighed, grateful for his support. More grateful than she could ever express.

"We both know he is the one who has committed crimes against the tsar. That he and your uncle are the criminals, not you. Not Irina. And when the letters you were wise enough to hold on to are deciphered, everyone else will know as well."

Lana closed her eyes and lowered her head. She felt so defeated. It had been eight months. Eight long, torturous months, and they were no closer to figuring out the coding in her uncle's false love letters. She and Langlevit were certain they contained treasonous information intended for a French contact, but she only had theories regarding how her father had intercepted the letters. Nothing solid.

At least, that is what she thought.

"I didn't want to tell you until I had more to say, but I have been attempting to contact a certain man, formerly of St. Petersburg. Someone who has been known to determine ciphered text and, in some cases, create it. I have reason to believe that this man was an acquaintance of your father's."

Lana raised her face to his, her tears of frustration drying almost instantly. "Do you think he will be able to decipher the letters?"

The earl dragged in a long breath. "I can't be sure, not until I meet with him. And it looks as if he is willing to do just that. Though not in London, and not for another week. There are, it seems, certain figures in town that he would not wish to cross paths with."

She nodded, understanding on the surface. But this level of intrigue was not natural to her. It perhaps was to Langlevit, who, over the last many months, had let it be known that his military tasks were of a sensitive nature. He had seen battle before, on the Peninsula, but these days he aided the Prince Regent in other ways.

"So I am to stay out of sight," Lana said, scrunching up her nose and gritting her teeth. "I was out this morning, on Bond Street with Lady Briannon."

Langlevit squeezed her hands gently. "Had he seen you, he would not have been at White's this evening, looking as though he had been served rancid mutton for dinner."

Lana nodded, certain he was correct, but she would have to be more careful, especially when Brynn requested her presence outside her normal duties at Bishop House.

"I should go," she said, taking her hands from the earl's once more. "You'll let me know how your meeting next week goes?"

"Of course," he replied, rapping the ceiling twice with his walking stick to alert the driver. "And as usual, leave your correspondence for Irina with Mrs. Blakely."

Mrs. Blakely was the wife of a butcher in Knightsbridge who knew Earl Langlevit and was indebted to him. The earl had vaguely explained that he'd helped her son escape a burning munitions bunker but had been reluctant to elaborate further. Mrs. Blakely had promised to help him in any way she could, and collecting Lana's letters and handing them off to one of Langlevit's messenger boys was her pleasure.

"Thank you, my lord," Lana said, her worry slightly soothed by the earl's insistence that all would be well.

"I have given you permission to call me Henry a number of times," he said, smiling.

"And I have given you permission to address me as Lana."

"I could not, Your Highness," he replied with a solemn shake of his head.

She sighed. "Very well, then. Good evening, Lord Langlevit."

He tipped his hat at her, still smiling, as the door opened. Lana accepted the driver's hand as she descended onto the curb. She brought up the hood of her cape and started immediately for the steps leading down from the street level to the kitchen entrance. The hack pulled away a moment later, and the comfort she felt whenever she was in the earl's presence dissipated. He alone knew the truth. He alone knew the danger she still faced.

And now Viktor was here.

Lana paused with her hand on the doorknob. She had to compose herself before entering, in case Mrs. Braxton was still puttering about the kitchen, getting ready for next morning's breakfast.

It was not so out of the ordinary that Viktor would come to London, she supposed. It was a large city, a hub of politics, and he, a diplomat, had every right to be here. She should have expected that he would arrive at some point. She thought she'd be better ready for it, though.

"You will not avoid me this time."

Lana jumped in fright, slamming her shoulder against the door as she turned to see who had crept up behind her. A dark-stamped figure wearing a greatcoat and top hat stood at the top of the stairs, at street level. Though she could not make out his face, she knew his voice. And when he descended the steps toward her, she realized she knew the motions of his body as well.

"Lord Northridge," she said, then hiked her chin. Good Lord. Had he seen her descend from the hack? "I was just going in—"

"You will first answer my question," he said, deliberately placing his palm against the door so that she could not open it. "You were meeting with someone in that hackney cab. Who was it?"

For the love of God, did the man have to turn up at every inconvenient moment? What did he do, wait under rocks and between hedges for her to do something suspicious?

Lana attempted to shrug, though her muscles quivered in her arms. "I don't know what you mean. It's rather foggy out tonight. Perhaps you saw someone else—"

He cut her off again, only this time with his hand curling

around her elbow. "Enough, Lana. You will tell me the truth. No more of your lies. *Now*."

Lana considered launching yet another verbal tête-à-tête, in which she could accuse him of ungentlemanly behavior and maybe emerge victorious. She considered—seriously, and for at least three full seconds—seducing him to distraction. But Langlevit's news of Viktor's presence in London, and his advice for her to stay hidden and safe, had scared her enough to subdue her. Enough to do anything in order to keep her position as lady's maid. Even tell the truth.

"All right," she conceded. "I'll tell you, but not here." Being discovered in the stairwell with Lord Northridge by another servant, or worse, the eagle-eyed Mrs. Frommer, who also seemed to wait in the shadows for Lana to step out of line, would ensure disaster.

Gray exhaled, his grip on her elbow loosening. "Go inside. Come to my rooms—"

"Absolutely not."

Being alone with him there would ensure worse than disaster. And honestly, Lana wasn't certain she could resist him should he make another advance.

"It is the only place we can be certain we aren't disturbed. Or overheard. And I give you my word," he said, inclining his head and placing his gloved hand over his heart in a faintly mocking salute, "I will restrain every desire I have to touch you."

Warmth flooded her lower abdomen. It reached down her thighs and threatened the integrity of her maidenhood.

He wants to touch me.

But he wouldn't. And for that Lana both ached and sighed in relief. For if Gray put his hands or mouth upon her again, she may say things she regretted. Like the entire truth, rather than the limited one she planned to divulge.

She nodded, opened the door, and swept inside.

· · ·

Standing at his window and staring blindly out into the shadowy courtyard beyond, Gray waited in silence. He'd dismissed his valet almost as soon as Harrison had entered his chamber, claiming he could see to his own nightly ablutions. He presumed Lana would have known to wait out Harrison's departure before sneaking into Gray's bedchamber. Once he was dismissed, there would be no one else to disturb them. But as the perpetual *tick tock* of the clock wore on, he wondered if he'd made a mistake in allowing her to go to her room first.

For a moment, he worried Lana wouldn't keep her word—that she'd take any opportunity to escape a confrontation with him. Something she'd become curiously adept at lately. But his instinct told him she wasn't so cowardly. No, regardless of her station, Lana possessed an innate strength and stubborn pride. She'd given him her word. And he had given her his. He would not touch her. He would not give her any cause to feel pressured or forced, and hell, he would make certain she did not run from him, not when she had promised to tell him the truth.

Gray had no idea what that truth would be, though the half-formed presumptions rollicking around inside his mind tortured him. The person she'd been meeting with in the unmarked coach—was he her lover? Had she kissed him? Allowed him to undress her as Gray had at Ferndale? Had this unknown lover sampled other secrets her body had to offer?

Who was he?

The question tortured him, and Gray understood the core reason beneath it. He was jealous…jealous of some unknown man who seemed to have won Lana's trust—among other things. Gray grunted and turned from the window, stalking toward the cushioned mahogany settee beside the lit fireplace.

He stared at the crystal decanter of whiskey sitting on the mantel and had to force himself not to down the entire bottle. For all he'd already consumed, he wanted his wits about him when Lana finally told him what she was hiding. *If* it was a lover, he decided, he would give her the chance to end the relationship.

It had nothing to do with his own feelings on the matter, or the jealousy that still coiled like a venomous snake within him. *Nothing.* No, he would do it to protect his sister. She was sheltered in the ways of the opposite sex, and the last thing he wanted was for her to be exposed to such lewd, scandalous behavior. Though his own reasoning was flimsy at best, he latched on to it with the desperation of a man thrown a life preserver in perilous waters—it was his duty to protect Brynn.

Gray turned from the fire and approached his bed, trying to regain focus.

Despite seeing her descend from the hired hackney cab that night, and the few times he'd caught her walking alone along Ferndale's drive with a convicted look about her person, Gray found it difficult to believe Lana was a woman of loose moral character. Her response to him in the sewing room at Ferndale had been passionate, yes, but her innocence had been evident as well. It had announced itself in her every caress, from the shake of her hands as she'd pulled off his cravat, to the gasp of surprise when his tongue had stroked and parried with hers.

His body tensed at the memory. *Damnation.* He drew a ragged breath and slammed his fist into the solid wooden bedpost, swearing as agony lanced through his fingers. The pain eclipsed everything else—just as he had intended. He'd made a promise to restrain his every desire where Lana was concerned. A daunting task, to be sure, but the fresh ache in his knuckles would serve as a reminder.

Nursing his bruised hand, his eyes flicked to the clock.

Where was she? A quarter of an hour had passed. He whirled on his heel, determined to drag the infuriating girl down by her hair if necessary. Gray flung open the door, and drew to a halt.

Lana stood before him, her hand poised to knock, her mouth parted in surprise.

"Lord Northridge," she said with a nervous glance down the empty hallway.

Gray stood aside. She passed him in a swish of skirts, honey and wildflowers drifting in her wake. Another faint scent followed the first—this one he recognized as the richer odor of cigar smoke. All of his recent rationale regarding her innocence shriveled. With cigar smoke came the certain knowledge that she had indeed been in close quarters with a man inside that hackney. His scent remained on her clothing.

Gray squeezed his injured fist, and clarity returned.

"I didn't think you were coming," he said gruffly, swiftly closing the door behind her.

"I told you I would." She stood with her hands clasped in front of her and eyed him with trepidation. Her gaze slid to the closed door as if considering escape.

Gray forced himself to relax and attempted to remove the scowl he knew had taken up permanent residence on his brow. Lana stood now at rigid attention with her back to the door. No longer garbed in her black cloak, she wore a simple dress and, oddly enough, a butter yellow spencer. As if she were about to go out for a stroll. The cropped jacket covered her arms, neck, and bosom almost completely. *Ah.* She had worn it for protection from his prying eyes.

Wise girl.

Lana's wary gaze roamed the room. She'd likely never been in this wing of the house...or his bedroom, for that matter. He witnessed her eyes flick to the massive four-poster bed that dominated the space. They almost immediately fell away, a rosy blush staining her cheeks.

Hiding a smile, Gray steered her toward the sofa and walked to the mantel. "Please sit. Drink?"

"No, thank you," she said, perching on the very edge of the seat.

Lana looked pale and fragile, the vibrant spark that normally lit her eyes not present. He noticed her shaking fingers and poured the brandy anyway. It would help settle her nerves. After handing her the glass, instead of sitting beside her, Gray took the armchair diagonal from her. He crossed one booted foot atop the other and tried to appear relaxed. She did, at least. The tension had left her shoulders now that he was a safe distance away.

Gray almost didn't want to press her, but relenting was out of the question. Clearing his throat, he leaned forward. "Well? Who were you meeting?"

She stared at him, her green eyes dulled and shadowed. "A friend. Not who you think," she rushed to add. "He is not a lover or a beau, or anything of that sort. He is a friend of my family in St. Petersburg."

Gray frowned. "I thought you were from Moscow." Her teeth worried her lower lip, and he knew she'd revealed something she hadn't meant to. "The Countess of Langlevit said you were the daughter of a respected modiste in *Moscow*."

"I have family in St. Petersburg as well," she said softly, and then took a deep breath. "My sister and I left Moscow when…our mother died. We first went to St. Petersburg, and then our family's friend escorted us here, to England. We wanted a better life here, but…we were forced to separate. My friend is helping me to stay in touch with her. She is with a family in the north."

He wanted to believe her, but he sensed that she wasn't telling him the whole truth. Even if they weren't lovers, he still wanted to know the man's identity.

"This friend of yours," Gray asked. "What sort of man is he?"

Lana frowned. "What do you mean? He is a good man."

"If he has the resources to keep you in contact with your sister in the north, I assume he is well-off? A peer of the realm, perhaps?"

She hesitated before answering with apparent caution. "Yes."

"Then there's a good chance I know him. Who is he?"

"I cannot say."

His mind considered and discarded the possibilities with the speed of a possessed racehorse and then seized upon the Earl of Langlevit. It made sense—it was *his* mother who had referred Lana. But when he recalled the earl's stringent and distant manner since returning from the Peninsula, Gray doubted his own logic. Coming to the aid of a mere servant who was not part of his own household seemed unlikely, even a young and beautiful one. Like Gray as of late, Langlevit was not the type who made it a habit to interact with women.

No. It had to be someone who had designs upon Lana. Someone who wanted her favors in future, he assumed. He ground his teeth in renewed frustration and eyed her. "Cannot or will not?"

"Whichever you prefer, my lord."

Her evasive answer was to be expected, so Gray opted for another tactic to keep her talking. "Why didn't you simply say you had a sister? We, too, would have been more than willing to keep the two of you in contact."

Why had she relied upon this unnamed man instead?

"It was not your burden, nor that of Lord or Lady Dinsmore," she answered with a dogged jut of her chin. "I was more than capable of arranging correspondence with her on my own."

Yes. With the aid of this *friend*.

"The two of you are close? You and your sister, I mean?"

"Yes," she whispered.

Gray noticed something like pain flicker in her eyes. A number of emotions playing out at once. The same ones he suffered whenever he thought of Brynn's illness—love, powerlessness, fear, sadness.

"Is she younger or older?"

"She is younger than I."

"What is her name?"

She swallowed hard, her fingers winding in her skirt as if the mere thought of it was painful. "I…I cannot see how her name should concern you."

Gray stood and crossed the space to sit on the other end of the sofa. Lana stiffened at his proximity but remained still. His gaze locked on hers. "You know my secret," he said gently. "Why is it I cannot know yours?"

"Your secret cannot get you killed." She shut her eyes and sealed her lips, as if her confession had surprised her.

Gray sat forward. "What do you mean?"

She half stood, weaving on unsteady feet, and then sat back down with a strangled sound. It sounded like a sob. "Lord Northridge, I must go. I shouldn't be here."

"Lana—" Gray placed his hands on her arms, and she froze mid-motion, her breath coming in small, short bursts. He kept his voice even and soft. "Please, if you are in trouble, I want to help."

"You can't help," she said without looking at him.

He could feel her entire body shaking beneath the sleeves of her spencer. She was terrified. Of what, he did not know, but he was determined to find out.

A shuddering breath rolled through her, and an unexpected surge of protectiveness overcame him. He rubbed his hands along her upper arms, attempting to soothe her. He wanted to do more…hold her, take her into his arms. He refrained, knowing she would bolt if he came an inch closer.

"I can try," he said.

Damp, jade green eyes rose to meet his, and Gray felt something within him come to a halt. He'd always been struck by her uncommon beauty, but now he noticed other details, like the creamy, fine-grained perfection of her skin, the delicate arch of her eyebrows, and the golden flecks in her irises. He wanted to memorize every freckle and every curve. But most of all, he wanted the defeated sadness in her eyes to disappear. "Whatever it is, we can fix it together, I promise you."

"Why would you bother? This does not concern you. It concerns me and my sister, and involving anyone else would be..." She shook her head decisively. "No. I'm nothing to you."

"You are not nothing. I don't like seeing you unhappy."

Her eyes met his. "Why?"

"Many reasons, one of them being Briannon. Sensing you are unhappy would make her unhappy, and I would do anything to protect my sister."

Gray was unprepared for the fall of tears down Lana's cheeks. He was desperate to comfort her, but he did not move, knowing instinctively it would be the wrong thing to do. She was far too guarded, and that stubborn pride of hers would force her to push him away. So he waited, watching as she fought valiantly to compose herself, but it was as if a dam had been broken, and her walls, now breached, were starting to crumble.

"I am sorry." She wept in earnest now, her head dropping into her palms. "I would do anything to protect mine, too, but I can't. I feel so powerless. So *trapped*."

"I know what you mean." And he did. He was all too familiar with the powerlessness Lana spoke of. "I gave away my daughter to protect her from the ridicule that would follow her throughout her life for being illegitimate, something she had no control over. I handed Sofia over to another family less than two days after her birth, even though she belonged with *me*."

Damn society and its unyielding rules. He'd had no choice, and yet he felt as if he'd abandoned her. And Lana, he suspected, likely felt as if she had abandoned her sister when they'd been separated upon their arrival in England.

Helpless in his desire to soothe her, Gray took a risk and slid closer. He put his arm around her shoulders and tucked her body against his, fully expecting her to flee his touch. But instead, Lana leaned into him, accepting the consolation he offered. She shook as she cried, her tears dampening his waistcoat. She felt small in his arms. So small and fragile. As much as his body craved hers, it was a different kind of need that overtook him right then.

His arms curled around her as a familiar emotion gripped him. It tugged at the very center of his chest. He'd felt it countless times, usually whenever he was visiting Sofia or worrying over Brynn. Gray bent his cheek to the white cap Lana wore atop her head of dark curls. And in that moment, something shifted within him. He didn't care about the man in the hack. He didn't care that she had lied to him to protect her sister.

Gray's fingers brushed her wet cheek and pushed aside a few tendrils of her silky hair. "You can't keep this all inside, Lana. You're going to break apart if you do. I know I've behaved abominably with you, but you *can* trust me."

Her cheek rubbed against his chest as she shook her head. "I can't trust anyone."

"Why?"

"I can't put anyone else in danger." Her words broke on another sob. "You don't understand—I've already put you at risk by telling you this. You don't know what they're capable of."

He gripped her arms again and held her back, so he could see into her face.

"Then help me to understand. Are you hiding from someone?" She didn't answer aloud but nodded. "Who?" he prodded.

She shook her head, refusing to speak.

"A man from St. Petersburg?" he hedged.

Her arms tensed under his hands, and her eyes snapped to his.

Gray frowned, recalling his earlier conversation at White's. It was too coincidental, though the surly baron had been looking for two princesses, not a maid. Still, it niggled at him, especially considering Lana had just confessed to being in St. Petersburg for a time. Perhaps she knew something of the missing princesses? Were the three of them connected somehow? There was only one way to know for sure.

He tipped her chin up with gentle fingers. "Does this have anything to do with a fellow called Zakorov?"

Chapter Nine

Lana jerked her chin out of Gray's hand and stared up at him, the tears she'd been unable to staunch moments ago drying almost instantly. A block of ice formed in her chest at the sound of that name. She no longer felt overwrought. She only felt cold, piercing fear.

Understanding settled on the grim line of Gray's mouth. "I can see you know him. Who is Viktor Zakorov to you?"

The name lashed at her again, cutting through Gray's warm words and the cocoon of safety he'd managed to weave around her. She shot to her feet, furious once more at her apparent idiocy where he was concerned. Her cheeks were still wet and chilled—blast it, she'd been weeping like a babe into his waistcoat! And telling him partial secrets with the hope that he'd leave her be. Only she hadn't bargained on how good it would feel to share some of her burden. Or to be held in those strong, comforting arms. Her fingers fisted at her sides in frustration.

She'd planned out her explanation beforehand as she'd gone from the kitchens to her room and then up the home's main stairwell to avoid passing servants on the back staircases. Her one slip about being from St. Petersburg instead of Moscow had been the first crack in her carefully rehearsed tale. And then, admitting to Gray that her secret could kill her... How foolish could she have possibly been? She needed to fix this, and quickly.

"You're mistaken, my lord. I don't believe I've heard of this man," Lana said, spinning on her heel and trying to move away, toward the door.

Gray's hand on her wrist stopped her. He closed his fingers as securely as a manacle. "Do not insult my intelligence. You recognized his name, Lana. Hell, you nearly swooned."

"Swoon?" She tried to wrest her arm from his grip, forcing a firm note into her tone. "Do not insult *me*. I did no such thing."

He released her wrist, and Lana rubbed at the skin, as if he'd stung her. He hadn't, of course. But any bodily contact with him was a dangerous thing. She'd thrown on her spencer before coming to his rooms just so he would not be tempted to...to...well, lower her dress again. Just the memory of this man's eyes on her exposed breasts, his tongue curling around their tight peaks, made her feel lightheaded.

"Zakorov was at White's tonight," Gray said, slowly circling around her, blocking her access to the door. "He spoke of two Russian princesses who had fled under accusations of traitorous behavior."

Langlevit had told her that Gray had been there, listening, but it hadn't prepared her for being blindsided like this. And Langlevit had also not known that Gray had already caught wind of her secret activities. That he was already suspicious of her.

"What exactly are you accusing me of, Lord Northridge?" she asked, her natural pride slipping back over her shoulders and causing her to stand taller. Acting docile had been a challenge from the start, and now that he knew a sliver of her story and was on the verge of guessing the rest of it, Lana could not suffer another moment of such subservience.

Gray pulled at the cuffs of his jacket sleeves and started to take it off. He kept his eyes fastened on her. "I believe I know your secret, Lana."

She held still as he finished removing his jacket and laid it on the back of a chair. She could disappear tonight. Send a note to Mrs. Blakely and stay holed up in an inn somewhere until Lord Langlevit could come for her. She could go north to Cumbria, fetch her sister, and then continue on to Scotland.

But then she thought of Langlevit's meeting with the fellow who might be able to decipher the letters. She couldn't distract him from that, not to see her up to Cumbria. It was all such terrible timing, and it was only happening because of her and her damned weakness for this man standing before her.

Gray crossed his arms over his waistcoat and stared her down.

"I believe you accompanied the princesses out of St. Petersburg," he said.

Lana realized she hadn't been breathing and dragged in a sharp breath. *Accompanied* the princesses? He didn't know. He hadn't guessed her secret at all. She nearly wanted to weep again.

He saw her stricken look and, likely thinking it surprise rather than relief, came forward. He didn't touch her though. Gray kept his hands clenched at his sides.

"You arrived in England with the desire to be in service, and Countess Langlevit said you had a small amount of experience. Did you enter into service in St. Petersburg?"

Lana said nothing. She'd already destroyed her first pretext, the one Langlevit and his mother had gone to such lengths to perfect. She didn't wish to damage this new one Gray was weaving all on his own.

"You know where the princesses are, don't you? And you're protecting them," he went on. When she again said nothing, he groaned. "And what of you? How are they protecting *you*, Lana? By sending you away the moment they reach English soil? Separating you from your sister?" He cocked his head, suspicion flashing. "Do you even have a sister, or was that a lie?"

"I did not lie about that," she replied. "And yes, I am protecting the princesses. They are innocent! Viktor Zakorov is the traitor. He is the one the tsar should be intent on apprehending."

"Treason is a serious charge, Lana."

"No more serious than the one he has made! What proof does he have? Nothing!"

Gray held up his hands and hushed her. She was losing her temper, and if she continued to shout, she'd chance being overheard and traced to Gray's room. She swallowed her mounting frustration and turned to pace, but found herself standing next to his bed.

It was a man's bed, dressed with a black satin counterpane and pillows. The counterpane had been turned down, exposing blue-black satin sheets. The desire to run her hand over the sumptuous material nearly overwhelmed her. As did the image of Gray sliding between these sheets, wearing nothing at all.

Lana backed away from the bed and sidestepped the viscount, needing more space between them. She'd forgotten for a moment the danger this room posed.

"What proof have you against Zakorov?" Gray asked.

She twisted her fingers together, uncertain if she should mention the letters or not. It may be a mistake, but to say she had absolutely no proof would only make him doubt her more. And that she could not risk.

"Correspondence the princesses' father intercepted,"

she whispered, leaving out any mention of her uncle. Or, the *princesses'* uncle. "It is encoded, and I am not the only one who believes it is treasonous."

She felt him approach her from behind. The floor did not creak, nor did his clothes rustle. Lana merely felt the arrival of his warmth. She sensed him, as if the nearness of his body was an invisible touch.

"Where is this correspondence? Perhaps I could help decipher it—"

"I do not have the letters," she said. It was at least the truth.

"Where are the princesses hiding?"

"I cannot tell you."

Gray took two strides to stand in front of her. His hands cupped her cheeks and angled her face up to his. She saw tenderness, edged with something inflexible, and it made her want to sink into his arms. Into him. "I want to help you, Lana."

She closed her eyes and rubbed her cheeks against his palms. She already had Langlevit helping her expose Viktor, and their break in deciphering the letters was almost at hand. All they had to do was determine what her uncle had been saying, and to whom. What she wanted now was to know that Gray trusted her. Believed her. Even though she wasn't being entirely truthful. It wasn't as though she was deceiving him out of malice. It was only to protect herself and Irina. If he discerned *she* was the princess in question, Lana did not know what he would do. "I want you to believe me," she whispered.

Gray's thumb caressed her cheek, her bottom lip, the soft stroking blissfully distracting.

"I didn't like him," he admitted. Then clarified, "Zakorov."

Lana peered up at him. "You didn't?"

"There is something off-putting about him. But he's determined. He doesn't strike me as the kind of man who simply gives up the hunt."

"That is why I did not wish to involve you," she replied. "He's dangerous, Gray."

She startled at the sound of his given name—his nickname, at that—coming off her own tongue. Lana pulled back, horrified. "I'm sorry, I shouldn't have—"

"Nonsense." He dismissed her apology with a rough shake of his head. "It is my name, and it's only fair, after all. I address you as Lana, don't I?"

"Yes, but my position here…"

He hushed her with a firm press of his thumb against her lips. "Is secure. You have my word."

So long as no one, especially Mrs. Frommer, who needed no easy excuse to send her packing, discovered she and Gray were carrying on in such a manner. His thumb tugged her lower lip, and Lana had the strangest desire to draw it deeper into her mouth, taste the salt of his skin, and torture him as he was torturing her.

Stop, Lana. Focus.

The last thing she needed to do was encourage him, especially with a bed of black satin resting directly behind them. He would kiss her, and she already knew her willpower turned to mist at the first touch of his tongue. She didn't want to imagine what she would do should he try to seduce her here in this room. It would involve things that gently bred ladies shouldn't think about.

"Will you say it again?"

"Say what?" she asked, her mouth's full range of motion impeded by the stalwart press of his thumb. Her breath deserted her at the languid look in those deep blue eyes. As if he could read the heated turn of her thoughts.

He brushed the tip of his nose to hers. "My name."

"Don't kiss me, Gray," she said instead.

"That isn't my name," he teased, his thumb finally freeing

her lip. "But you are right. I gave you my word that I would not."

He took a long step in reverse, putting one arm's length between them. The loss of his hands left her cold. She wanted their return. She wanted more than that. The desire to feel those black sheets at her back, and Gray's warm body against her front, had to be the most scandalous desire she'd ever experienced.

Searching for something to distract herself, she took a gulp of the brandy sitting on the side table. The spirits burned a path to her stomach, forcing her unladylike desires at bay.

"Lord Northridge—"

"Gray."

"Lord Northridge," she said stubbornly. "I should leave. The hour is late."

He nodded and stroked his chin but made no move to escort her out. "If Zakorov is as dangerous as you claim, then I will not rest until he is no longer a threat to you."

He was in earnest, and the vow drew out the needle of fear that had pierced her earlier.

"Your friend, the peer. He has knowledge of Zakorov?" Gray asked next, all business now. She almost preferred the more flirtatious side of him to this grimly focused and solemn side.

Drat it. He'd root out it was Langlevit in an instant. "No."

He quirked his lips into a sly grin. "The next time you attempt to lie, keep your chin down. You always kick it up an inch before you fib."

She scowled at him and started for the door again. It was late. Brynn would be returning from the duke's dinner soon, and Lana hadn't readied her room yet.

Gray stayed where he was, as if he didn't trust getting closer to her again. "I am going to help you, Lana. Whether you wish for it or not."

She paused, her fingers fluttering over the doorknob, her eyes flicking over her shoulder. "I do not wish for it, my lord."

"Yes, you do. You need me."

Lana wasn't sure whether he was talking about his help or something else entirely, and her tongue nearly tripped over its immediate response. "No."

It was a lie.

Gray's answer was a smile because he knew it was, too.

The corridor was empty when she stepped out of his room and closed the door behind her, without another word. She braced against it, her legs wanting to give way beneath her. She forced her hammering heart to slow its fevered pace. His sweet parting offer had almost been her undoing. For an instant, she felt the same tug of warmth on the other side of the door and knew instinctively that Gray stood there. She turned around, her fingers tracing a path on the burnished wood where his face would have been, dragging them across his stern jaw and the firm mold of his lips.

Lana pressed her cheek to the wood as a wave of longing overtook her. In another world or another time, perhaps she and Gray could have found happiness together. Right now, she could only offer half-truths and deceit. And he, though attracted to her, only took the liberties he did because he thought she was a maid. Perhaps he meant well offering his aid and protection. However, Lana doubted he would be so forward with a female of his own station. They would court, and dance, and exchange chaste kisses in the arbor. They would not want to tear each other's clothes off at every godforsaken turn or devour each other with their eyes as he had done moments before.

If she wasn't careful, she could lose her wits to this man. Or much more. He could reach deep into her soul with a single glance, strip her reason away with a whispered word. He made her *want* to trust him. But she couldn't, not when her life—*Irina's life*—hung in the balance. Regardless of her own desires, her sister's safety was paramount. Lana flushed and levered her body away from the door...and from the man beyond it.

Lord Northridge may be a master seducer, but he was also a very proud man. A proud, *honorable* man. If he found out the truth about who she really was and the extent of her deceit, his humiliation would know no bounds.

Which was why she intended to be long gone before that happened.

Chapter Ten

It was late morning when Gray returned to Bishop House. He hadn't slept the night before and had finally gotten dressed and gone out about town just after dawn. First, for a brisk morning ride, to attempt to alleviate the pent-up desire for a certain beautiful, and entirely off-limits, maid. Second, to hunt down information on Viktor Zakorov.

He entered the dining room, where his parents and his sister were finishing a late breakfast. A footman rushed to set another place at the table to the right of Lord Dinsmore. His father looked haggard and pale, and his mother even more so. Her eyes were red-rimmed from crying.

"I should have gone with you," Gray grit out, taking his seat.

His Grace, the Duke of Bradburne and Hawksfield's father, had been found dead in his study during the dinner party the night before.

From what Gray had pieced together from his family's account, delivered when they had returned home after midnight, it appeared that a burglar had broken into the house and been confronted by the duke. A struggle had ensued, resulting in Bradburne's death. Bow Street could not rule out that it had not been one of the duke's own guests, and a full-scale inquiry had been ordered, led by one of their top agents.

The guests from last night had been ordered back to Hadley Gardens that morning for questioning by the Bow Street agent. Gray regretted not having been at the dinner last evening, and he had wanted to be there that morning as well. Then again, had he attended the duke's dinner, he wouldn't have met Zakorov or coaxed Lana to reveal a few of her secrets.

"We weren't in danger, Gray. And as I told you, there was no reason for you to attend this morning," Brynn replied. "Truly, you would have only made things worse."

He snapped out his cloth napkin, offended. "How is that?"

"I fear you would have strangled the inquiry agent," she replied.

"The gall of the man!" Lord Dinsmore exploded. "Wants to make a name for himself. His questions bordered on impertinence. The *gall*! As if one of us could be capable of something so horrific."

Now Gray really wished he *had* ignored his sister's protests and gone with them to the meeting. Instead, he'd gone in search of information on Baron Zakorov.

"The agent was a trifle excessive," his mother conceded.

Lord Dinsmore choked on a mouthful of poached eggs. "Excessive? The man was atrocious. His questions to Briannon were appalling, insinuating that she had visited the duke's rooms, questioning her virtue. The utter impudence!"

Gray set down his toast before taking a bite. "What's this?"

"Papa," Brynn said, her pleading gaze sliding to Gray a moment. "You're going to give yourself indigestion," she said to Lord Dinsmore. "He was only doing his job. After all, the criminal is still at large."

"It really is awful," Lady Dinsmore was saying, dabbing a snow white handkerchief to the corner of her eyes. "They think it was the Masked Marauder."

"It could have been anyone," Brynn was quick to say. "Mr. Thomson isn't convinced that it is the work of the bandit."

Her father's eyes popped with affront. "Well, it certainly isn't anyone we are likely to know. The effrontery of that inquiry agent, questioning us all, even Hawksfield. He is many things, but that boy is not a murderer. I'd stake my title and my fortune on it."

As would Gray. Despite his personal feelings toward Hawksfield, he knew that Hawk had too much integrity to kill his own father. He was arrogant and had an ego the size of the entire country, but he was no murderer.

"Where have you been this morning, Gray?" Brynn asked. She, too, looked drawn. The past night's events had taken a brutal toll on her.

"I was attending to some business matters," he said with an evasive wave. "Nothing of import."

After pacing his rooms all night, and then seeing to his parents and Brynn when they'd arrived home in a furor, Gray's mind had been stretched to its limits. He'd needed sleep, but though he'd closed his eyes and tried, it hadn't come.

Instead, his mind had swung back toward Zakorov at the card table at White's. The other men had questioned him about the princesses. They had tried to make small talk with the visiting Russian. All of them except Lord Langlevit, who'd almost purposefully ignored Zakorov. At the time, Gray put it down to the earl's disappointment over learning Lady Eloise was not in London. But as the first streaks of dawn had reached through Gray's bedroom windows, something continued to feel off about the earl's chilly reception.

He'd taken Pharaoh to Langlevit's house after his morning

ride, on his way back toward St. James's Square. Langlevit had not been available, but Gray had left his card and an intention to return later that afternoon. With any luck, the earl would help him bring the pieces of the puzzle together.

"Perhaps you should rest this afternoon, Brynn," Gray said, eyeing her. She'd barely touched her food, and she seemed listless and distracted.

"We have an appointment at the modiste to be fitted for the appropriate gowns," Lady Dinsmore said, dabbing at her eyes again.

He frowned. "Must you go today?"

"We were lucky Madame Despain could fit us in so quickly." Lady Dinsmore sniffed. "No one was prepared for something like this. Such an unexpected tragedy. And, of course, we are expected to attend the funeral."

The thought of being fitted for gowns at such a time seemed to be as distasteful to his sister as it did to him, if the look on her face was any signal. But it was a necessary evil. He nodded decisively. "Then I shall accompany you."

"Gray," Brynn began. "It really is not necessary."

"I insist."

She shot him a grateful look as she stood. Her hands were shaking, he noticed. Gray leaped to his feet, worry lancing through him. "Do you feel faint?"

"I'm fine," she said, though her eyes did not meet his. Gray knew his sister well enough to know that she was hiding something, but he did not press her. Between last night's events and today's questioning, he'd be surprised if she weren't overwrought. But he knew that Brynn would confide in him when she was ready. "I'm only tired. I promise I will rest when we return."

"Come then," he said, walking around the table to link his arm in hers. "Shall we fetch your cloak?"

The ride to Bond Street was one of the quietest Gray

had ever experienced. Normally, he and Brynn would be amusedly rolling their eyes at each other over their mother's incessant chatter, but today, the interior of the carriage had taken on a somber silence. Brynn seemed preoccupied with her own thoughts, and Gray couldn't fault her for wanting a moment's peace. She had, after all, been in close proximity to a murderer. It would surely test anyone's mettle. His mother, too, seemed cowed. The terrible crime had been too close to home, and if there was one thing she prized most, it was her family.

Upon their arrival at the modiste, Gray escorted his mother and sister into the shop. He bowed to the owner, who knew him by name—thanks largely to his misspent past—and proceeded to ensconce himself in a comfortable chair while two assistants took Brynn into the back of the shop and set to work upon her. Her wan coloring worried him, and after a quarter hour had passed, he stood up and walked toward the partition closing off the back of the shop.

"Brynn, may I enter?" he asked.

"I am dressed," she replied, and he stepped through the open door.

His sister stood in the center of the room upon a small dais, cloaked in a black crepe dress. Madam Despain's two assistants were crouched at her hem. They stifled gasps and grins when they saw him.

Gray approached the dais and reached for Brynn's hand. "Are you well?"

Her skin was chilled, and she looked ready to collapse in exhaustion.

"As I already told you, I am fine."

He did not believe that for a second. His sister could be as stubborn as a pile of rocks when she chose to be.

"You were in the same house as a murderer last evening," Gray replied. "You are not fine."

The two assistants quit their giggling and exchanged wide-eyed looks of alarm. They continued to pin Brynn's cuff, and Gray promised himself that he would bite his tongue and not make a scene.

"Yes, well, I am lucky enough to still be breathing, so I cannot rightfully complain."

Gray let out a sigh and tapped his hat against his thigh. She was lucky. All the guests at last night's doomed dinner were.

"You should not be in here," Brynn said, her eyes fluttering to open boxes containing ladies' lacy unmentionables.

"Don't be ridiculous. I am your brother," he said. "And besides that, I'm furious. Father told me what that inquiry agent insinuated with his questions."

"Mr. Thomson was simply doing his job as investigator."

"That or igniting a scandal," he said.

"There you are, my lady," one of the assistants said, placing one last pin. She turned her eyes to Gray, who did not notice her pointed look.

Brynn sighed aloud. "Dear brother, this is your cue to exit, as I am about to undress."

With an uncomfortable scowl, Gray swiftly left to wait at the front of the shop again. His mind was a jumble of emotions—pulled every which way by his sister's condition, the duke's death, Lana's troubles, and the mysterious and dangerous Zakorov. He wondered briefly whether the two events were connected but discarded the idea immediately. Zakorov was not here to kill a duke, he was here to find two rogue princesses. No, it was likely that the Masked Marauder, terrorizing his way from the countryside to the city, had thought to steal extra coin by attacking homes. Gray would send a warning to the Coopers, though with the bandit here in London, they were likely out of harm's way. Still, he needed to make sure Sofia was safe.

As he stared out at the crowded street, his thoughts wandered back to Langlevit's unnatural demeanor after Zakorov's arrival at White's. Gray wondered if the earl had had previous interaction with the man, which could account for his sudden shift in humor and his stony reception. It was a logical possibility, one his gut supported. Lana had suggested that the princesses were innocent and that Zakorov was the true traitor, and truth was, he wanted to believe her. But he was also a pragmatic man, one who considered all the evidence at hand before acting. A part of him had mistrusted Zakorov on sight, but that didn't make the man automatically guilty. Gray would have to dig deeper. It was the sole reason he'd sought Langlevit out that morning. If the earl knew something of Zakorov, Gray was determined to uncover it.

Gray sat lost in thought until his sister appeared, looking far worse than when they'd arrived. Her face was pale except for the bruised, sleep-deprived shadows under her eyes. Their mother also seemed to notice and rushed over from where she and Madam Despain had been seated, their heads bent together in hushed whispers.

"It is just a headache," Brynn said. Gray took her arm and sat beside her on the window bench.

"You never could lie worth a damn," he muttered. Their mother chastised him for his language and left to finalize the arrangements for the gowns. Brynn seemed to avoid his stare, her attention wandering out the front window instead. Her expression went distant, then distraught. Remembering last night, he figured, or perhaps the morning's questioning with this Mr. Thomson.

"You've lost more color," Gray said, standing up and extending his arm as their mother returned. "I'll escort you to the carriage, and do not even think to refuse."

"I think a rest would be the best thing," Brynn said quietly once they'd settled in and started along Bond Street, the traffic so congested the horses were hardly able to move.

Gray eyed her, even more concerned. Since when did Lady Briannon Findlay capitulate so easily? "I will ask Cook to prepare one of her draughts."

"No, I just want to sleep," she replied.

Gray watched her closely the rest of the ride, but true to her word, Brynn was almost asleep by the time they arrived back at Bishop House. As soon as she was escorted to her chamber by Lana, who did not meet Gray's eyes once, he signaled for Colton to bring the curricle around and took his leave once more. A short drive later, Gray arrived at Leicester Square for the second time that day. Thankfully, the earl was at home. His butler announced Gray's presence after escorting him to the study.

"Northridge," the earl said with a guarded expression. "I received your card earlier. I apologize I wasn't at home to receive you. Did we have a meeting that I forgot? My secretary has bungled a few of my appointments lately."

"No, nothing like that. I wanted to speak on a matter. Is this a bad time?"

Langlevit shook his head. "Not at all. Please, have a seat." He dismissed his butler with a curt nod and then went to the bar. "Is it too early in the afternoon for whiskey?"

"Not so long as it's good whiskey," Gray replied. "And I doubt you have anything but the finest."

Langlevit poured two glasses. "I wouldn't claim my family's distillery produces the finest whiskey," he said, handing Gray his generous dram. "But it certainly is drinkable."

Gray had sipped Langlevit's whiskey before, distilled north of the border, near Dumfries, and it was more than *drinkable*.

"How may I be of service?" the earl asked as he sunk back into his chair.

Gray cleared his throat and cut to the chase. "I want to

know about Baron Zakorov."

"Zakorov?"

"The man at White's last night," Gray clarified.

"What do you wish to know about him?"

"Everything."

The earl hedged, taking a deliberate swallow of his drink and then swirling the remaining contents, an attentive eye on the amber liquid. "What gives you the impression that I know anything about the fellow?"

Gray sat back in his chair, crossing one ankle over his knee. "I've played cards with you for a while now, Langlevit. I know when you're holding a winning hand. You go quiet. You protect that hand by not becoming an object of attention. When Zakorov joined our table last evening, you reacted the same way. I think you would have been content to have disappeared into the chair in which you were seated. You didn't want him to notice you, which leads me to believe you know something of the man."

"Or perhaps I was only holding a decent hand of cards," Langlevit replied.

"You folded, if I remember correctly."

The earl conceded with a laugh. "Very astute, Lord Northridge, but might I inquire as to the root of your interest? Zakorov is not exactly a man in your social circle. I find your interest in him strange after only just making his acquaintance."

Gray had not yet tasted the whiskey in his hand. He brought it to his nose. "He claims he is looking for two princesses who have committed crimes. I may have information, and I would like to know why I should *not* approach him with it."

Langlevit drew his back straight and set his glass upon the desk. His eyes drifted to Gray's before a blank, indifferent mask dropped down over his features. *Like clockwork.* Gray had most definitely played enough hands of cards with the earl to detect his tells. Gray's gut had not failed him. Langlevit did indeed know something about the Russian.

"Zakorov is a dangerous man, Northridge. He is not to be trusted."

Gray sat forward, surprised by the hushed intensity of his reply. "How do you know him?"

"I am an officer in the army. His name is well known."

A vague answer, and Gray presumed purposefully so.

"I suggest keeping your distance from Zakorov," Langlevit continued, pinning Gray with a pointed stare. "Especially if you *think* you have information regarding the whereabouts of these two princesses."

Gray sipped his whiskey, but he didn't taste it. The liquid burned flavorless down his throat, his mind once again slipping back to the conversation with Lana the night before. The promise he'd made her.

He hesitated, choosing his words carefully. "Say I did know something. Say I wanted to help these princesses rather than turn them over to Zakorov," he said, earning an arched brow from Langlevit.

"May I remind you we are allies with Russia? Aiding two women wanted for crimes against the tsar would be extremely poor for our international relations."

Gray watched the earl closely and saw the ghost of a smile twitch at the corner of his mouth. Encouraged, Gray was frank with his reply. "I do not believe they are criminals."

Langlevit took up his glass again, his finger tapping the cut crystal. "Will you tell me what you know?"

He shook his head once. "I have pledged an oath of protection." He would not speak of Lana and risk connecting her to Zakorov or the princesses. "I came here curious to know if you have heard talk of Zakorov himself being under suspicion of treasonous activities."

The earl stood from his chair. "Treason? It sounds as

though you are after information an officer in the Diplomatic Corps might have, not I."

No. Perhaps he would not be privy to such information after all, not even with his newest promotion to field marshal. It was, Gray understood, bequeathed to those who had shown formidable gallantry and valor on the field of duty.

The earl had seen battle on the Peninsula. Rumor had it he had suffered terrible injuries, and though he had returned to London to heal with no visible wounds, he did, Gray noted, often sit and stand with obvious discomfort. "Forgive me, it seems I was wrong in assuming you might know something more discerning of Zakorov." He stood as well, meeting Langlevit's challenging glare. "However, if you can think of anyone else I might be able to call upon—someone, perhaps, who agrees with me that the princesses are being wrongly hunted—I would appreciate your introduction."

Langlevit gave a stiff nod, his hand clenched around his glass of whiskey as he came around his desk. "I wish I could tell you more. From what I do know, you would be wise to keep your investigation as confidential as possible. Alerting Zakorov to your suspicions would only draw the man's attentions. And if it is your desire to protect the princesses—"

"It is my vow," Gray corrected. He had promised Lana to eliminate the threat being made to her and the princesses, as selfish as the two girls may have been for abandoning their maid.

The earl cocked his head. "Is it? Then choose to whom you speak with extreme care. Men who cross Zakorov have a propensity to disappear. Do not underestimate him, no matter your intentions, Lord Northridge."

For a man who claimed to know nothing of Zakorov, he had certainly sounded confident in his warning. Gray held the earl's stare for a moment. Langlevit might have been withholding information, but coming here had not been in vain. The earl had more than verified Lana's claims that Zakorov was a dangerous and slippery character.

"Thank you for your time," Gray said, setting his practically untouched glass of whiskey down upon the desk. "I'll see myself out."

Outside, Gray hesitated as he entered his waiting carriage at the curb. Langlevit knew more about Zakorov than he was letting on, but the man wasn't going to part with anything specific unless Gray returned the favor in kind and confessed the details he knew about the princesses. About Lana. He trusted Langlevit to a degree, though not enough to risk exposing her to his scrutiny.

Without pausing for a beat once he arrived at Bishop House, Gray discarded his hat, cloak, and gloves and strode into the foyer. The house appeared to be deserted. "Where is everyone?" he asked Braxton.

"Resting, my lord," the butler replied, draping Gray's things over his arm to put away properly. "Lady Dinsmore has taken to her rooms and asked not to be disturbed, as has Lady Briannon. Mrs. Braxton fixed her a draught. Lord Dinsmore is…in his study."

Braxton's noticeable pause in explaining his father's whereabouts hadn't been for lack of the butler's knowing. He knew perfectly well, as did Gray now, that the Earl of Dinsmore had settled himself in with a bottle of brandy or scotch. Perhaps both. Last evening and that morning had been taxing. It had seemed to affect Gray's entire family. And yet he could hardly think of anything but Zakorov's austere face and disapproving frown, and what he might do if he sniffed his way to Bishop House and requested to speak to the maid hailing from Moscow that Gray had so idiotically claimed to have.

He could have flogged himself for revealing that. Yet, at the time he hadn't known Lana had been covering her tracks. From here on out, he'd take Langlevit's warning to dig carefully and quietly for information about Zakorov to heart.

Gray climbed the stairs two at a time and turned toward Brynn's room, set at the front corner of the house, with windows overlooking St. James's Square and a side street. He wanted to be sure she was well, especially after her odd concession to rest after the visit to Madam Despain's.

He knocked twice before cracking the door open on soundless hinges. The room was shrouded in darkness. The thick curtains blocked out all but a few rays of afternoon light, causing the form on the bed to appear as nothing more than an indistinct lump of blankets. Gray took in the sight of the breathing apparatus their father had ordered specially made for Brynn years ago, when her lungs were far weaker than they were now. He hadn't seen her wear the contraption in months. The cloth face shield and the rubber tubing connected to a glass bottle that contained Cook's draught. He would have thought she was sleeping if not for the outline of fingers beneath the sheet, drumming restlessly at her side.

"Brynn?"

The fingers stilled. He knew she couldn't speak while breathing in the aromatic brew.

He glanced around her room but saw no other persons present in any of the adjoining chambers. "Is anyone else here? Tap once for yes, twice for no."

Her fingers tapped twice. She must have sent Lana on an errand then, or perhaps belowstairs to wait until she rang for help removing the breathing apparatus. Disappointment bit at his chest, though it was strangely followed by relief. Being in the same room as Lana while she acted as maid to his sister would have only exacerbated his shame.

He was no better than Hawksfield, or the Duke of Bradburne—God rest his soul—whenever he was alone with Lana. A *servant*. He'd known celibacy would not be easy, but hell...he had not thought he'd grow so desperate as to chase a servant's skirts around his own home. And yet, lately, whenever he was with Lana, he found himself forgetting she was a lady's maid. He found himself speaking to her as if she were his peer. And he didn't feel desperate for just any woman's body. He felt desperate for *hers*.

"I'm sorry, I don't wish to bother you," he said to Brynn, lowering himself into the armchair at the side of the bed. He rubbed his temples, the beginnings of a headache gripping him.

A sudden waft of Lana's scent—warmed honey and wildflowers—brought his head up and his eyes focused. The room, however, remained empty except for the two of them. *Hellfire.* Even when she was absent, he could not escape her presence. He ran his palms over the arms of the chair. Perhaps Lana had simply been seated here earlier. He imagined her petite body filling only half the amount of space on the cushion than his larger frame did right now. He then imagined her sitting upon his lap, her legs tucked up, her arms wound around his neck.

The emotion that image wrought, of pure contentedness, threatened to choke him with the impossibility of it.

"Have you ever done something so stupid, so nonsensical, that you wish you could take it back?" Gray whispered, needing to speak, needing to rid himself of his burdens. Brynn was the only one who would not pry for more details than he was willing to give, especially right now, with that mask covering her face.

His eyes slid to his sister's hand. After a long moment, her fingers tapped once.

"But time cannot be regained, can it? Just as actions cannot be undone," he went on. "I have made mistakes, Brynn, and I have sacrificed much of my own happiness because of them. I let go of someone I cared for—deeply—because of the *ton* and their skewed sense of what is right. I obeyed by their rules once before…but I am loath to do it again."

He lowered his voice to a violent rasp. "Why should they hold such power? Why can things not change and evolve?" He huffed a mirthless laugh. "I am certain I'm not the first to ask such questions. Many men before me have found their lot in life and their heart's desire at odds." Brynn's fingers gripped the soft sheets. He swallowed hard and exhaled. He was revealing too much, and his sister was intelligent.

He stared at the glowing embers of the fireplace and rubbed his fingers along the velvet material of the armchair again, another phantom cloud of Lana's scent assaulting his nose. He imagined her fingers lying just so below his on the soft material. He was out of his mind. An utterly lost fool.

"Has anything ever been nearly in your grasp and all you had to do was reach out and take it, but you were too afraid of what the consequences would bring?" It was a rhetorical question, but her fingers flexed and tapped once. He paused, his breathing ragged. She'd said yes, but Brynn couldn't possibly empathize with what he was talking about. How could she? She didn't know about Sofia, and she certainly would not know what he felt for her maid.

He sighed. "Forgive me, Brynn, I know I am speaking in riddles. I should allow you to get some rest." He stood and grasped her slim fingers. They gripped his and squeezed tightly, telling him without words that she loved him. He took comfort from it. "I love you. Sleep well."

Chapter Eleven

Madam Despain bustled into the second-floor morning room at Bishop House, accompanied by only one of her young assistants. The modiste had seemed to become a fixture in the Findlay household, Lana thought, as she stood behind the sofa in which Lady Briannon was seated. First an emergency gown for the duke's dinner, next an emergency mourning dress for the duke's funeral, and now an emergency wedding gown for Brynn's engagement ball.

Lana could still not believe all that had happened in the last two days. One day after the duke's murder, Lady Briannon and Lord Archer Croft, the former Marquess of Hawksfield and the new Duke of Bradburne, had announced their engagement—and all hell had broken loose. To say their betrothal had shocked London was a gross understatement. Screams had filled the halls of Bishop House—those of rapturous joy from Lady Dinsmore, and those of utter fury from Lord Northridge.

Gray.

Lana had barely had enough time to revel in the secret

confessions he'd made to the person he'd believed was a resting Lady Briannon, her face completely covered by the breathing apparatus. But it had been *Lana* lying abed with the strange cloth and metal-framed shield over her face, the tube misting in Mrs. Braxton's minty draught. Brynn had pleaded with her to agree to the farce, saying she had to see Archer, and she must go alone. No one could know she had left Bishop House, and so she'd convinced Lana to take her place, reposing under the blankets and listening for any approaching feet for nearly two hours.

Lana had started to think it had all been for naught when she heard a pair of heavy footsteps coming toward Brynn's bedroom door. She'd barely got the contraption turned on and the cloth shield over her face before Gray had come inside. She'd only been able to make out his figure through the white linen—his hair, tossed into disarray, his muscular shoulders and narrow waist. Lana had lain still, terrified. She had covered her dark hair with a cap, but Lana was taller, with slimmer hips. She'd prayed the piled-on blankets would disguise their differences.

Then Gray had started speaking, asking only for finger taps in answer. Any other man might have asked her to remove the apparatus, but not Gray. He was patient and understanding when it came to Brynn. Protective. Lana had seen that side of him when he'd been holding his daughter as well. Kissing her injured finger, bouncing her on his knee to distract her from the pain. Lana had been subjected to that same care, she'd realized. When she'd confessed some of her secrets, Gray had promised to help her. And he'd kept his word, not touching her in any inappropriate way.

Not that her body had not wished for his touch. It had. *She* had. And while she'd lain in her mistress's bed, pretending to be Brynn and listening to his private admissions of past mistakes and present longings to go against what the *ton* decreed proper, Lana's body had reacted once again. If not for her own sense of self-preservation, she would have ripped the contraption from her face and climbed into Gray's lap. She would have kissed him and massaged the worry from his tensed body in ways no decent lady should ever dream of. And yet her mind had traveled that wicked path.

Madam Despain's voice lanced through Lana's heated thoughts, and she reluctantly returned to the conversation at hand: the designing of Lady Briannon's engagement ball gown.

"You have become the debutante of the season, my lady—every young woman making her bow will be looking upon your person this coming Saturday in different shades of envy and awe. You must give them exactly as they desire, and something more. Something…unexpected."

Lana saw her mistress nod, though it wasn't as enthusiastic as Lady Dinsmore's bobbing head.

"Oh, yes, of course. Something that will leave them all desperate to follow in her footsteps—though, of course, His Grace is the only eligible duke to be had," Lady Dinsmore said with a proud hike of her chin.

Madame Despain was staring up at the ceiling where white doves had been frescoed into the plaster and made no show of having heard the countess at all. "They call him Hawk, I am told. And he is a somber sort of man, yes?"

The modiste looked to Brynn for confirmation.

"It seems you have him made out," Brynn replied in a lackluster tone.

Brynn's argument with her brother after the betrothal announcement had set her back on her heels. She had slipped into a strange state of despondency, but Lana knew the argument wasn't the only reason for it.

Brynn had confided to Lana that the engagement was all a farce. That she and Archer, the former marquess, had been about to become suspects in the late duke's murder—each of them had gone off into Hadley Gardens on their own after the dinner, and neither of them had an alibi for when the duke was killed. Mr. Thomson from Bow Street had sussed it out and…well, Brynn had stunned both Mr. Thomson and Archer by claiming she and Archer had been getting *engaged* at the time.

After the row she'd had with Gray, Brynn had broken down in tears, sobbing that she'd made a mess of everything. Lana's chest still ached for her, and these last two days, she'd shoved aside her own troubles with Zakorov and her uncle to care for her mistress. It had been, Lana admitted guiltily, rather a relief.

"Then you shall be a foil to him," Madame Despain declared, her assistant making furious little notes on a sheet of paper. "Where he is serious, you will be merry. You will shine, my lady, and your glow will shed over your duke as well."

"My glow?" Brynn echoed. "I am afraid I will disappoint you. His Grace is hardly one to…glow."

Madame Despain held up a finger. "You shall see, my lady. Now, let us begin. I think a bright jade satin will do marvels with your coloring…"

The modiste continued to spout her ideas for the gown, pausing only to make sure her assistant had written everything down. Lana tried to pay attention, but as much as she once enjoyed speaking of gowns and fabrics and overlays, trimming and beading and necklines, she could not concentrate on such details right then.

Brynn was hardly paying attention either. She stood up and turned to Lana, her pinched smile looking forced.

Lady Dinsmore clapped her hands, drawing both their eyes. "Oh, while I'm thinking of it, Lana…if Madame Despain insists on a black lace overlay, then I will have you put aside Lady Briannon's blue silk that has a similar overlay. You know the one, I'm sure. We are hosting a dinner on Wednesday, and I would not want her to wear anything that could be too akin to Madam Despain's new gown."

Brynn roused herself from her obvious distraction. "A dinner?"

Lady Dinsmore sighed. "A handful of your father's acquaintances, and not one wife among them. I suspect they'll speak of politics all evening."

"Acquaintances from Parliament?" Brynn asked, her distraction seeming to settle back into place as she took up pacing the rug between the sofa and divan.

"Yes, and a few foreign dignitaries as well. I will be sure to seat you away from the Duke of Bassford—you know how Italians can be." Lady Dinsmore fluttered her lashes. "Though I do wish I'd thought to bring my Genoese lace. Mr. Monti hails from Genoa, you see. No matter. I may place you beside the Russian ambassador instead. According to Lord Dinsmore, the fellow is rather taciturn."

Lana stared at Lady Dinsmore, a quick intake of air scraping down her throat and causing all four women in the morning room to turn toward her with expressions of concern.

"Forgive me..." Lana said, her mind scrambling, her mouth opening and closing like a landed fish. "I...I have a tickle in my throat."

Brynn waved a hand toward the tray of lemonade and cakes a footman had delivered earlier. "Do have something to drink, if you like."

Lana held up her hand. "No, I am fine. Thank you, my lady."

Her arms would shake like a woman possessed if she tried to pour herself a glass of lemonade right then. A taciturn Russian ambassador? It had to be Viktor Zakorov, but of course there was no proper way to ask for the ambassador's name without drawing certain attention to herself.

"Well, you needn't stay, Lana," Brynn said. "I don't believe I'll require your help trying anything on. Will I, Madam Despain?"

The modiste was leaning over her assistant's shoulder, whispering more things for the girl to jot down. "Not until the fitting."

Brynn looked relieved, and Lana felt much the same. For a moment. Viktor was going to be here, at Bishop House, under the same roof as Lana. She felt her color draining rapidly at the thought.

"Thank you, my lady," she whispered, moving toward the door on shaky legs. "I fear I am rather faint."

Brynn came toward her, concern etched on her brow. "Will you be all right? Should I call for anything from Mrs. Braxton?"

"No, please, I'll be fine. I only need a moment," she replied. She needed air and the chance to think. A chance to talk herself away from the edge of panic.

Brynn shooed Lana away, telling her to rest for as long as she liked. On her way down the servant stairwell, she fought the desire to turn around, climb to the top floor, and hide in her room for the next three days. What if Viktor found out that Lord Dinsmore had employed a Russian maid? What if he asked to see and speak to her? He would know her without a shade of a doubt.

Lana would have to be ready to run. She'd send word to Lord Langlevit immediately. Perhaps he could have a carriage waiting outside Bishop House the night of the dinner in case she needed to make a hasty departure.

But then, what about Lady Briannon and the wedding? Brynn trusted Lana. Depended upon her. Lana couldn't just abandon her, not *now*. And then there was Gray. He shouldn't have mattered, but somehow he did.

I can't leave him.

Lana walked through the kitchens and out the servant entrance, stopping to gulp in the late April air. She felt caught between two impossible things. She couldn't flee, and she couldn't stay. Perhaps she could feign illness. But that wouldn't stop Lady Dinsmore or any of the other family members from inadvertently giving too much away should the subject of her employment arise. She would have to let Lord Langlevit know—he'd know what to do. If Lana could get Percival, the stable boy, to deliver a message to Mrs. Blakely, she would see that it got to the earl. Even if he were busy, Percival would make the run for her.

Nodding to herself, Lana turned back into the kitchens and went to the stillroom. There, she tore a scrap of parchment from a roll Mrs. Braxton used to jot down items she needed at the markets. She found a pencil and wrote a hastily coded poem to Lord Langlevit. Once finished, she folded the parchment, tied it closed with twine, and made her way to the stable house.

She didn't pause to notice the meticulously manicured garden with its bright yellow tulips in full bloom as she normally would have. Her mind was too distracted to appreciate the lush arbor and the flowering cherry blossom trees she so loved. The garden was small in comparison to the one at Volkonsky Palace, but it was well cared for, and Lana took every opportunity she was afforded to walk its gravel paths. Perhaps she would take a turn through them to collect herself after speaking to Percival, but not now. She was so intent on her thoughts that she nearly crashed into a person exiting the stable door.

"Oh," she said breathlessly, her heart scattering at the sight of him. Gray looked tired, his blue eyes shadowed. His mouth was a thin slash in his face, and his hair looked as if it hadn't been combed in days. She eyed him, noticing the crumpled shirt and cravat hanging from his fingertips. Gray's disheveled, sleep-deprived, and surly appearance did nothing to alter the startling effect he had on her. Her knees turned to water. He looked haggard, as if he'd slept in the barn. She guessed it was a distinct possibility, given the sharp-edged tension between he and Brynn. "Lord Northridge. I didn't expect to see you."

"That is surprising, considering I live here."

"I meant here at the stables."

Lana awaited a tart and witty response, as she'd come to expect from him, but this time there was only silence. Normally she knew that Gray wouldn't be able to resist a verbal volley with her, but for once, he did. He drew a preoccupied breath and nodded toward the house. "Is the modiste still here?"

"Yes, but they are finishing up," Lana said, watching as a pained frown worried his brow. He was not himself. He hadn't been himself since Brynn's engagement had been announced.

Lana knew he cared deeply for his sister's well-being and, for whatever reason, loathed the late duke and his son. Lana had heard the rumors of the rakish Dancing Duke, of course, but the gossip surrounding his son, the former Lord Hawksfield, leaned toward him possessing a more ruthless temperament than one of carefree debauchery. He was rumored to be as cold as his father had been hot. Still, the ill-fated announcement of Briannon's engagement to the newly seated duke had created a rift between Gray and Brynn. "You do not approve of the match?" she asked.

His eyes turned to frost in the midafternoon sunlight as they latched on to hers. "Would *you* want your sister to be wed to the son of a known rakehell? The fruit doesn't fall far from the tree, and Brynn will be in for a life of misery while Hawk does as he pleases."

Lana wondered whether she should test his temper given his current state of mind, but she couldn't curb her tongue. "You do not know that. From what I have heard, Lord

Hawksfield—I mean Lord Bradburne now, of course—is nothing like his sire, and Lady Briannon seems to care for him. She does not seem opposed to the match."

Gray eyed her. "Has my sister confided this to you?"

"If she has, my lord, it is her confidence to share."

His lips tightened at her soft rejoinder, but he did not press further. "Walk with me," he said. It was not a harsh command, but it was not a request either.

Her gaze slanted to the open stable door. She would likely not have another opportunity to send word to Langlevit before Wednesday's dinner. She'd risk drawing Gray's suspicion, too, especially since he was so focused on knowing the identity of her friend, but she didn't have much choice.

"I need to speak with Percival for a moment," she said, and hastily added, "regarding an errand for Lady Dinsmore."

"I'll wait."

Lana made quick work of finding the young Percival, who was mucking out one of the stalls in the back. As always, he was happy to do her tiniest bidding.

"Yes, miss," Percival repeated. "I'll go as soon as me chores are done."

"Thank you, Percy." Despite feeling a smidge of guilt for taking advantage of his obvious affection for her, Lana flashed her brightest smile as she gave him the directions to Mrs. Blakely's house and handed him the missive. The boy flushed red and bowed halfway.

Just before going back outside, Lana composed herself and ran a self-conscious hand to redirect the curls escaping her cap. Gray was waiting as promised, a booted foot resting upon the side of the building, his jacket slung over his shoulder with casual elegance. He looked so utterly desirable that Lana felt a rush of heat pool in the core of her body. She would never understand why the very look of him had such an impact upon her. He was attractive, but it wasn't the only thing that drew her.

It was the gentleness that lay beneath his topmost layers—the sensitivity she'd glimpsed when he was with his daughter, and the protectiveness that he'd shown when he'd offered to help Lana without knowing the entire truth of Viktor or who she really was. Gray seemed to keep people at a distance with his cool, arrogant charm, but with her, he was different. He didn't hide behind a facade of indifference.

She cleared her throat. "Where would you like to walk, Lord Northridge?"

"Anywhere but there," he said with a nod toward the house.

They strolled in silence, their feet taking them into the garden. Once inside, they paused to admire the blushing roses in bloom. Gray made no move to converse, and oddly, the quiet between them was a comfortable one. Her fingers drew across one velvet petal of a dusky pink rose, and she winced as a sharp thorn caught her on the wrist. "Roses are strange things, aren't they?" she murmured, soothing the scratch.

Gray shot her a sidelong glance. "How so?"

"That something so lovely can come out of a bush full of so many prickles and thorns." Her gaze swept his. "They are worth the injuries one may have to endure."

"Is that supposed to be a metaphor?"

"Do you wish it to be?"

He cocked his head and with a wry expression replied, "Then the Duke of Bradburne is an entire garden full of thorns."

Lana laughed. "Surely not an *entire* garden, my lord."

"Thorns or not, it is a terrible match, although my mother could scarcely contain her delight at having a duchess for a daughter." His lips thinned as they pressed deeper into the arbor and out of view of the house. "The ways of the *ton* disgust me—coveting fortunes and titles like common whores covet coin."

Lana did not react outwardly at Gray's coarse words and bitter tone, though he sent her an apologetic glance. She had heard his whispered confessions one day past when he'd thought her to be his own sister. She knew not being able to claim his own daughter because of her illegitimacy gutted him. How he must have suffered, feeling trapped by his social position. And now he was afraid that his sister had chosen to let herself be swayed by the whims of the *ton* instead of following her heart. His obvious despair made Lana desperate to comfort him.

"You do not mean that," she said gently, her fingers fluttering to his sleeve. Gray froze at the light contact, his eyes flicking to her hand. A muscle jerked in his cheek, and Lana wondered if he felt the same as she did when he looked at her. The inflammatory thought made her tear her fingers away as if she'd been burned, but Gray stalled them mid-flight.

The space between them turned electric as his bare hands caressed hers. "But I do."

"Gray," she began and then caught herself.

"Why don't you trust me?"

She tugged futilely against his hold. "I do."

"Then tell me everything."

"I have already told you." *What I can*, she added silently.

His grip tightened. He drew her toward him, as if he'd understood the unspoken part of her response. It seemed he could read her in ways no one else could, and she'd always prided herself on not being an open book. She tried to resist but took the step that made the front of her skirts brush his trousers. "Lord North—"

"I like Gray better," he said.

"Your mother—" She gasped as his free arm curved around her waist.

"Is busy."

She craned her neck to see around the tall hedge, the shuttered peaks of Bishop House just visible. "The gardeners—"

"Will know better than to follow us."

"Please don't kiss me."

The words were her only defense against him. Against this hypnotic, mind-drugging power he held over her. Even now, her limbs trembled from the merest graze of his body. His blue eyes held hers, his fingers flexing convulsively at her waist. The truth was while she was afraid of discovery, she was more afraid of what giving in to Gray would mean. She had already proven herself to be foolhardy where he was concerned. He made her common sense scatter.

Gray swallowed, his voice soft. "As you wish."

Lana didn't know if it was the simplicity of those three words or the yearning buried within them, but something fragmented inside her. She understood the driving force of his desire—his *need*—because it mirrored hers. He shifted as if to break the loose union of their hands, and of their own volition, Lana's fingers gripped his, stalling him. He tensed as her free hand wandered up to his jaw, smoothing over the stubble-roughened skin and skimming past the underside of his full lower lip. Gray's eyes widened at her bold touch.

"It's not what I wish," she confessed in a whisper, "not truly."

With an inarticulate sound, Gray closed the remaining space between them, crushing their joined palms between their bodies. And when he bent to kiss her, Lana reached to meet him halfway. It wasn't the chaste kiss she imagined that he would experience in an arbor with women of his own set. No, it was a kiss to shame all other kisses—hot, sweet, demanding—and wholly consensual.

Gray's mouth took hers, his lips savoring every curve, every recess, every line. His tongue delved past her parted lips, finding hers, and she offered it willingly. She rose up onto her toes to deepen the kiss, mimicking his movements, kissing him as ferociously as he was kissing her. He groaned low in his throat, his hand skimming down her sides to cup her buttocks and draw her flush against his aroused length.

Lana's body froze at the intimate contact, her eyes going wide at the foreign shock shivering through her. He broke the kiss but held the apex of their bodies together as his gaze met hers. Gray's eyes continued the work of his tongue, seducing her just as easily as his mouth had. They were dark and dreamy with heat, hinting at the sublime promises of things to come. Her center went liquid with simmering want.

Gray released her only when a man's voice pierced through the fog surrounding them. It belonged to one of the footmen. "Lord Northridge?"

"Yes. What is it?" he called out, his voice restrained. She could see him gritting his teeth as he strode briskly to meet the footman before the man could come around the corner of a boxwood and see Lana.

"I have an urgent letter marked to your attention, my lord," she could hear the servant say.

As Gray disappeared around the hedge, she rationalized that the footman, or someone from the main house, must have spied them entering the arbor together. How else would the footman have known to find him here? A chill ran ragged through her, nearly suffocating the heat that had suffused her body over the last handful of minutes. Why was she so weak and impetuous around this man? She was normally so cautious and pragmatic, and here she was alone in the arbor with Lord Northridge. Should they be seen together, it would spark gossip. Lana shuddered at the thought of any such gossip reaching the housekeeper. Mrs. Frommer would not be forgiving if she were made to look the fool in front of Lady Dinsmore. Nor would Lana expect Lady Dinsmore to take it well that her precious son was gallivanting with the servants. And with Zakorov so close, Lana could not chance losing her position or drawing undue attention to herself.

Gray returned a few moments later with an unfolded letter in hand. His face was ashen as his eyes skipped over the writing.

"What is it?" Lana asked, hurrying to his side and immediately forgetting her own worries.

She half expected him to fold the letter and insist she not concern herself. But Gray surprised her. "It's from the Coopers." His voice broke mid-sentence. "Sofia is ill."

Chapter Twelve

"Must you return to Essex right at this moment, Graham? We have been invited to the Hillensbury ball tomorrow, and Lady Cordelia was so looking forward to seeing you."

Gray eyed his mother, curbing his frustration as best he could. She wasn't to be blamed for not knowing or understanding just how swiftly he needed to return to Ferndale and the village of Breckenham. Lady Dinsmore's displeasure was evident, but the letter...it had burned his hands when he'd first read it, and in the half hour since, it had smoldered a hole within his breast pocket.

Sofia's simple cold had developed into a fever. And instead of breaking, as the physician had said it would, it had worsened.

"Surely you are much too busy with Brynn's pending nuptials to be concerned with mine," he replied, his nerves snapping with impatience to be gone.

"A mother's job is never done," she said with an emphatic wave to where Brynn sat in the front parlor, sipping her tea. "And I have two children, not one. Who would blame me to want to see both happily wed?"

His eyes slid to his sister's maid standing quietly in the corner of the room. Lana wasn't looking at him, but at the carpet at her feet. "I am not interested in Cordelia Vandermere or any other simpering debutante on parade this season. I shall go to Ferndale and return with all haste."

So long as Sofia recovered without complication. He could not allow himself to think otherwise and expect to maintain his composure, or at least the facade of it. It was *all* such a facade, and it weighed heavier than ever right then.

Lady Dinsmore shook her head, muttering to herself. "I fail to see how a foaling requires *your* urgent presence. Surely the stable master is capable and can do his job."

"I asked to be summoned," he said, cringing inwardly at the white lie. One of the mares was indeed to foal in a few weeks, though no such request for Gray's presence had been made. However, he'd needed an excuse to go back to Essex, and this one was as good as any.

Lady Dinsmore sighed and capitulated. "If you must. Perhaps this is a blessing in disguise. There is pair of silk gloves that will be perfect for Briannon's engagement ball in my armoire, along with some lace I have been saving for a special occasion such as this one."

Gray's eyes narrowed at the thought of rifling through his mother's possessions. "Anything else? Gowns you may have forgotten? Slippers?"

She leveled him with an unimpressed glare. "No need to take that tone."

"I had planned to ride Pharaoh," he replied, thinking only of how quickly he could arrive in Essex. "But now it seems I shall have to take the carriage."

He could not stuff boxes of lace and silk into his saddlebags and expect them to weather a ride back to London.

"Of course you will," his mother said. She then brightened.

"Take Lana with you. She knows well the lace I am speaking about. Briannon's undermaid shall perform her duties until your return."

Again, Gray's eyes went to Lana, and he knew he was not the only one struck by the surprise of his mother's suggestion. Her gaze had peeled free of the carpet and now fairly goggled between Lady Dinsmore and himself.

"Oh, but I could not, my lady," she said. "This is much too important of a week for Lady Briannon, and Mrs. Frommer needs my help—"

"Yes, it is. Far too important to be falling ill. You were dismissed this morning for not feeling well, were you not?" Lady Dinsmore shook her head. "And Mrs. Frommer will have more than enough help. I insist upon it."

Lana's lips remained parted with shock, and for the briefest moment, Gray imagined the things he could do to them—and *with* them. He felt a dangerous stirring low in his stomach. The very kind of stirring he fought so rigidly to stamp out every morning with vigorous horse rides and cold baths.

"Yes, my lady, but—"

"I cannot see around it, Lana. Briannon's health is far too precarious as it stands. A day or two should put you to rights."

"Mama, *please*, my health is not precarious," Brynn groaned as she settled her teacup in its saucer. But Lady Dinsmore waved her hand and stopped her from insisting she was perfectly well.

"No. I won't hear another word of argument. Lana, ready your things. And don't forget the silk gloves—the ones with the abalone cuff buttons, dear, not the pearls."

Lana managed to hinge her jaw shut and nod obediently, though Gray's pulse continued to thud at the thought of a lengthy confined carriage ride with her. He could barely restrain himself in open quarters where she was concerned, and he had no doubt that such a prospect would be a special kind of purgatory. In the arbor, Lana had responded to him. She had been the one to initiate the kiss. Something had shifted between them, he realized. Something subtle and infinitely hazardous.

It was nearly midafternoon. Leaving now meant they would arrive in Essex well after nightfall. Once he arrived, he would make his way directly to Sir Cooper's home, and damn the late arrival. But that left over six hours in the carriage with Lana. Six protracted hours to endure — *and to do with as he wished.* His mind gorged itself on the possibilities, making his groin clench even as he forced his depraved thoughts at bay.

He would be a gentleman, he vowed. He would have to. For her sake, and his. Gray squared his shoulders, and his eyes met the maid's clear green ones for a scant second.

"Fine. We leave within the hour."

. . .

Lana took the stairs to her small room, tucked high in the eaves of Bishop House. Her ears had not stopped ringing since Lady Dinsmore had announced the order for Lana to travel with Gray to Essex. *Lace gloves.* She was being sent off, practically in the arms of her seducer, to fetch a pair of lace gloves. It was absurd. And yet, it was her own fault. She had claimed feeling faint, and of course Lady Dinsmore would not want to risk Brynn's health during such an important week.

She rubbed her forehead as she hurried along the warm, slightly claustrophobic attic corridor toward her room. They wouldn't be entirely alone at Ferndale, what with a skeleton staff left to oversee the house and grounds during the London season. However, there would not be nearly as many eyes upon them there as there were here.

Then again, his daughter was ill. The prospect of being alone with Lana was most likely the last thing on his mind right now. It should be the last thing on her mind as well. The more she thought of him, it seemed, the less control she had over her own desires.

Lana opened the door to her room, trying to push the kiss in the arbor out of her mind—and came to an abrupt halt. She stared, open-mouthed, as Mrs. Frommer straightened her back, having been stooped over Lana's bed. Lana's valises, the ones she'd taken with her the night she'd fled Volkonsky Palace, lay open, the contents of both in a scattered mess.

"What are you doing?" Lana whispered, her throat bound in a knot of dread. Copies of her uncle's coded love letters, the originals still with Lord Langlevit, were among her exposed belongings, as was the miniature painted portrait of her family, a few articles of clothing, and all that was left of her mother's jewels—a stunning diamond bracelet worth more than five times Lana's yearly earnings.

She had slowly pawned the rest of her mother's jewelry over the last many months, accumulating a small fortune of British pounds and sterling—of which all was divided up and hidden within her room. While she knew Lord Langlevit and his mother would do anything to help her, she also did not want to be naive. There could very well come a time when she had no one to depend upon. Should that day come to pass, Lana would need immediate funds. A large portion of her savings was divided and sewn inside the silk lining in both of her valises, right underneath Mrs. Frommer's nose.

Mrs. Frommer snatched the diamond bracelet from the bed and held it aloft for Lana to see. "Proving my suspicions correct, Miss Volchek. What is a lady's maid doing with such valuable jewels hidden among her things?"

Lana entered her room fully and closed the door behind her, not wanting the housekeeper's voice to carry. Or her own.

"And by whose authority do you dare enter my room and search my possessions?" she asked, her temper flaring alongside her dread, each one urging the other on.

Mrs. Frommer came out from behind the bed, toward Lana, the bracelet still raised and on display in her hand. "My own authority, as I am housekeeper here and in charge of maintaining a decent and moral staff of employees for this household! Now answer me—where did you get this?"

Lana did not shift her stare from Mrs. Frommer's in order to view the bracelet, gleaming in her upheld fist. She could not believe the woman had let herself into this room and gone snooping.

"I don't recognize these as one of her ladyship's pieces. Did you take this bracelet from Countess Langlevit before you left employment there?" the housekeeper spat, her voice rising.

"Of course not!" Lana reacted, both insulted and shocked that the woman would accuse her of thievery.

Mrs. Frommer lifted her chin, bearing down on Lana with a cold gaze. "Then perhaps they were a gift for a job well done? From a certain lord?" She scoffed as Lana's cheeks blazed red. "I know exactly what sort of girl you are, Miss Volchek. The kind that goes panting like a dog in heat around the masters, hoping for castoffs and favors, perhaps even a future set up in the country as a mistress."

Lana's blood boiled just beneath her skin, her heart an unsteady cadence in her chest. This woman was a beast. A horrible, lashing snake. Lana intensely wished for the right to fire her from her position and, better still, the ability to banish her from England!

"I hardly require a setup in the country, Mrs. Frommer," she said through a tight jaw. "And those diamonds are a family heirloom. Not a trinket from any man of my acquaintance. I demand you give them back to me at once."

The housekeeper snorted her amusement and disbelief, her fingers still curled around the bracelet. "There you go again putting on airs, pretending to be lady of the manor. Do you expect me to believe such poppycock? If these are a family heirloom, you wouldn't need employment here. And you will *not* have employment here if I ever catch you dallying with Lord Northridge again!"

She stepped forward, practically lunging at Lana. "Make no mistake, Miss Volchek, Lady Briannon's fondness for you is the only thing protecting you from your immediate dismissal. And with no references, how far would you get? Without my goodwill, you'd be on your back, whoring for coin in Covent Garden."

Lana gasped at the vile words, but she held her tongue. If she opened her trembling mouth, she could not be certain of what would emerge. And she had to be calm. She had to be *smart*, not like the last time the housekeeper had accused her of trying to seduce Gray.

Mrs. Frommer's eyes glittered with malice, as if also recalling their conversation in the sewing room. "You think you are the first girl in this household to turn the eye of Lord Northridge? You are a fool if you think his lordship can secure you anything at all. I'll see you out on your ear before that happens."

Flinching at the threat, Lana's temple pulsed, her patience nearing its limit. She gritted her teeth and held out her hand. "My property, Mrs. Frommer. *Now*."

The woman's thin nostrils flared, her upper lip pulling into a sneer. She leaned closer and hissed, "You have no property here. You are nothing."

She walked swiftly by Lana, brushing against her shoulder. "These, I will keep. One misstep, and I will turn them over to Lady Dinsmore. I highly doubt she will believe your story either. Once you are accused of thievery, you will find no estate in the whole of England willing to take you on."

Mrs. Frommer slammed the door behind her as she left. Lana's skin prickled with unspent energy. The woman had not just stolen from her but threatened her as well. Lady Dinsmore would dismiss Lana in a flash if her trusted housekeeper brought her those diamonds. She knew how it appeared. A servant in possession of such fine jewelry? And if her hidden money was also found… Oh, Lord. One would only have to put two and two together, and she would have no believable defense, not for a mere maid.

Her cover was thin enough as it was; no genteel woman fallen on hard times would have such a fortune at her disposal. She wouldn't be able to send word to Langlevit, and without him to vouch for her in the short term, she would be carted off to Newgate. Once there, it would be easy for a powerful man such as her uncle to silence her for good. Even Gray would not be able to help her then.

Or Irina…

With shaking hands, Lana started to collect her things and stuff them into her valises, remembering then that she was supposed to be packing for her trip to Essex. With *Gray*. Once Mrs. Frommer learned of that…no doubt it would add fuel to the fire, placing her in even more jeopardy. But it seemed that the bracelet had bought her some "goodwill." It was a small price to pay for Mrs. Frommer's silence, but who knew how long that would last? Lana's safety—and Irina's—now hinged on the housekeeper's capricious humor.

It was her own fault. Curse her infernal pride. She should have done whatever was necessary to gain Mrs. Frommer's trust, and now, it was far too late.

Lana closed her eyes, feeling trapped.

Chapter Thirteen

The roads leading out of London and into the countryside, whether one's carriage was headed south to Sussex or Surrey, west to Hampshire, Devon, or Cornwall, or far north to Derbyshire or Yorkshire, were well known as narrow, rutted, and generally painful to travel. After nearly an hour of lurching and jolting along the dirt road that lead directly northeast, toward their country seat nestled in the heart of Essex, Gray was quite certain he could have gotten out and run on foot to Ferndale faster than this godforsaken carriage was managing, and with less exhaustion as well.

His knee would not quit jumping, and his muscles were tight with intolerance for his stationary position upon the forward-facing bench within the carriage. His daughter was ill, for Christ's sake. He should already have been at her side, not riding at a snail's pace to reach her. Not even the beautiful woman sitting opposite him could detract from his restlessness. If anything, she added to it.

Lana had barely spoken a single word since departing Bishop House. As lady's maid, she should have been seated up front with the driver, however Lady Dinsmore had insisted she break from position and ride inside the warm carriage, to avoid catching a chill and worsening whatever ailed her. For that, Gray cursed and thanked his mother in the same breath.

Lana had deigned to remove her bonnet and gloves for the long journey but otherwise sat primly, her back ramrod stiff. She'd seated herself on the backward-facing bench seat, garbed in the plainly cut dress and cloak common to a woman of her position, and had insisted on staring out the window ever since. Not that she could manage to appear plain, even in such practical clothing. There was a graceful *delicatesse* to her, one that lived deep within. Gray saw it in the way she held her chin high and looked down the slope of her pert nose at the passing countryside. A cool, almost untouchable reserve had settled over her features—one that looked entirely at home. It was as though the attentive, subservient expression she wore while tending to Brynn were the mask instead.

The contradiction drove him to distraction. And perhaps, given the current situation, that was not a bad thing. If he had to endure five more hours in this carriage with nothing to think about than little Sofia, feverish in a bed far away, he would go insane. He needed such a diversion badly right now. But the freedom Lana had felt earlier, to speak plainly as they'd walked through the arbor, had been left behind in town. The passion and desire she'd shown him as they had kissed had dried up as well. Instead, as their driver had taken them from the crowded, bustling city streets, Lana had seemed to be practically sinking backward into the squabs. Avoiding him.

No more.

"Are you truly unwell as my mother said?"

He should have asked sooner. These roads were not easy on the hale and hearty, let alone those who were ailing. Perhaps that is why she had grown silent. Yet, he knew deep down that was not it.

Lana stopped gazing out the window, but she did not look directly at him. "No. I'm afraid it was only an excuse to be granted a dismissal from Madame Despain's visit earlier."

"Why?" he asked, crossing one leg over the other to try to cease fidgeting.

Her attention sprang at him, like a cat onto a windowsill. "Have you heard about the dinner Lady Dinsmore is hosting two evenings from now?"

Gray had not. His mother's failure to inform him could mean only one thing: there would be no marriageable ladies in attendance. He shook his head.

Lana's eyes fell to the harsh clamp of her fingers in her lap. "Viktor Zakorov is attending."

He sat forward, his crossed leg coming down hard onto the floor. "Are you certain?"

At Lana's jerky nod, Gray swore under his breath and shifted even closer to the edge of the bench. He wanted to stand and pace, but he was stuck in this cramped box. How the bloody hell had Zakorov secured an invitation to Bishop House? His father hosted dignitaries and men from the House of Lords from time to time, like Helmford Monti, but the timing was too coincidental. Perhaps the Russian had not dismissed Gray's comment about having a maid from Moscow on staff after all. He closed his eyes and berated himself for having been so free with his words.

"I'll be there," he said, his fingers flexing and releasing. "Whatever conversation he attempts to begin regarding the princesses will be smothered. And you will stay tucked away belowstairs, out of his sight."

The warnings Langlevit had given Gray regarding Zakorov had not faded. *Men who cross Zakorov have a propensity to disappear. Do not underestimate him, no matter your intentions.*

Clearly, this Russian was a dangerous man.

Lana nodded but was still strangling her fingers. He slid forward, until his knees were nearly touching hers. "Lana," he began. She stilled, as if sensing what he was about to say. "Tell me where the princesses are. If they are in trouble, in danger of being rooted out by this Zakorov fellow, then they will require adequate protection."

Her mouth remained sealed, her eyes drifting back to the window. "They are being protected."

He sat taller. "By this friend of yours? The peer."

Her lashes flitted a bit, but she didn't face him. Nor did she answer. Gray rubbed his jaw, the bristle his valet, Harrison, had taken a straight razor to early that morning starting to return. The woman was a fortress. How to breach her walls? The question had both his mind and his loins kicking into gear.

He was alone with her, hours of privacy stretching before them. Should he decide to risk it, he knew that she would allow his advances. She had welcomed his kisses in the arbor, and when she'd felt the evidence of his arousal pressing against her, she had been shocked, but not horrified. Not disgusted. Had the footman bearing the letter from Sir Cooper not interrupted them, what more would she have allowed?

Gray craved her willing body in his arms, but he also wanted answers. He wanted to know what she hid from him, and he knew that it was more than just the princesses' whereabouts and the unsupported claim that their father had evidence of Zakorov's own traitorous activities.

"The letters you spoke of," he said, trying another tactic. "The correspondences that require ciphering. You said you don't have them. Do the princesses?"

She shook her head. He considered the tempered response an encouraging victory.

"Where are they then?"

Lana finally turned to face him. When she spoke, her

voice shook. "I am sorry, but the more you know, the more danger you face."

It sounded similar to what Langlevit had said. *Langlevit.* Gray took a measured breath. His time in the Royal Army might have afforded him the ability to cipher code. *Langlevit*, whose mother had recommended her to Lady Dinsmore in the first place. Gray had already discarded the possibility once before, but what if Langlevit did serve the princesses and Lana because of his ties to the War Office?

Could *he* be Lana's ally of means?

He would not get any confirmation from Langlevit himself. His only option was to source it from Lana. And here was the perfect opportunity.

His gaze slid to the woman seated primly across from him. She thought she was protecting him by not divulging what she knew, and her conviction made him feel an odd sense of admiration—he knew several men of his acquaintance who did not have the same force of will and courage as she. It was a noble quality, if unwarranted in this case.

He set his jaw. He'd do whatever was necessary to get her to confide in him. A small part of him acknowledged that if Langlevit were Lana's ally of means, he was far better suited to assisting her than Gray. After all, he was a highly decorated military man and an earl. Gray didn't stop to consider that his interest in Lana's affairs was bordering on obsession...or the why of it. He only knew that he wanted her to trust *him*. Fully, and not conditionally, as she'd done out of some misplaced desire to protect him. She was the one who needed protecting.

He would begin by exploiting a weakness of hers.

"Tell me about your sister."

She reacted to the command with a small line of worry creasing her forehead. "What do you wish to know?" Her voice remained cool, and she quickly smoothed her brow. As if she wanted him to know that she could see through his ploy.

Gray almost smiled.

"What is she like? Is she funny? Smart? Or is she bratty like mine?"

"Lady Briannon is far from bratty, my lord. She knows her own mind, which is a trait most men do not tend to admire in women."

He smiled. "Luckily, I'm not most men. I like a bit of fire in my women." The compliment was overt, and he was rewarded by a slight flush in her cheeks. "So tell me, is your sister anything like you?"

Lana's eyes glinted with amusement then. "No, thank goodness. She's quiet, preferring to read instead of socialize. Then again, she's not yet fifteen. She is sweet and kind, and always has a thoughtful word for others." Warming to her subject, Lana's entire demeanor changed. The tension melted out of her cheeks, and her eyes sparked with humor. "She loves animals. Our home used to be filled with all manner of creatures she insisted needed good homes. Quite a menagerie at times. I fear my parents may have been a bit overindulgent."

"Protective," Gray said. "Sounds like someone I know. Do you miss her?"

"Terribly."

"Perhaps you could visit her. In Cheshire, did you say?"

"Cumbria." She jerked her chin up, her hand flying to her mouth. Frustration and self-disgust flashed in her eyes, and Gray felt a sharp sense of accomplishment. He was one step closer than he'd been several minutes before. Lana's face resumed its shuttered expression, and she glared at him with ill-concealed resentment.

Cumbria. He knew several peers who had estates there. Including Langlevit. The earl was becoming a more obvious choice by the second. He didn't know whether to be relieved or worried. Langlevit's entanglement meant that the princesses' situation, and Lana's, was more than grave. After all, he wasn't a peer looking to collect favors with the Russian tsar, but a man skilled in the art of war. And Lana was caught in the middle of it.

A lump of dread settled in Gray's stomach, wrestling with the nervous worry already pooling there from news of Sofia's illness. It was the sole basis for the brusqueness of his next question.

"Is your ally Lord Langlevit?"

Her expression betrayed nothing this time. "I do not believe I have to answer that, my lord."

"You do."

Their gazes clashed in a fierce battle of wills, but Gray did not give one inch. She more than met his challenge, and the tension in the coach spiked several notches. Grown men had cowered from the deadly look he knew was upon his face, but she did not. Lana set her jaw and stared down the length of her nose with disdain, as if he and his pernicious demands were beneath her. Despite himself, his admiration for her courage rose, along with a mad desire to take her into his arms and kiss the defiant temper from those trembling lips.

"Lana, I only want to help."

He realized Langlevit had likely sworn the same thing, and while his military history and top ranking in the Prince Regent's army would have bolstered Lana's faith and trust, there were also associated risks to only trusting one person with the truth. As an officer, Langlevit could be called away on some obscure duty for the Crown. The man had disappeared time and again in the past, often for months on end. If that came to pass now, Lana would be left unguarded. Unprotected. Gray could not abide that.

"I do not require your help."

Gray did not relent. "Is it Langlevit?"

"I cannot betray such a confidence." In spite of her stony expression, her hands had begun to fidget in her lap. Gray sensed victory within his grasp but knew she would not fall to his trickery again. He only had one other tool at his disposal—one he had no shame employing.

Without breaking eye contact, he lifted himself and settled upon the seat beside her. Apart from the slight flare of her nostrils, she stayed rigid and silent, glowering at him in mutinous defiance, as if she knew exactly what he was planning to do. He closed the distance between them, noting the shift in her breathing and the rapid rise and fall of her chest. She was not immune to him, he knew. And neither was he to her, if his stampeding pulse and the hardness of his groin were any signal. A warning brewed in those transparent eyes of hers, fraught with anger, fright, and desire. She sunk her teeth into her bottom lip, and Gray nearly lost his thin hold on his composure then and there.

He pressed forward until mere inches separated them. Lana sighed theatrically and leaned back. He had to commend her change in tactic. "Must you be so high-handed? May I remind you that your seat is over there, Lord Northridge?"

"I like this one." He hid his smile. Her tells were becoming more obvious. She addressed him properly and with scholarly diction when she meant to fortify herself.

"Then I shall be forced to move." She stood, the skirts of her dress rustling in the carriage, but Gray reached out a quick hand, capturing hers.

Her intake of breath was swift at the contact of their bare hands. She tugged futilely against his grasp, her eyes falling to the discarded gloves that had slipped from her lap. His thumb stroked the top of her knuckles, his eyes never leaving hers.

"Release me," she whispered.

"Do you truly wish me to?"

"Yes."

The pads of his fingers slid around to the soft underside of her wrist, feeling her pulse hammer beneath his touch. "If that's true, then why does your heart gallop so?"

Her chin hiked its customary notch before the lie left her lips. "If you have not yet noticed, this godforsaken road is perilous. I'm simply terrified of falling."

Gray grinned and was just about to release her wrist when the carriage hit a large rut. Lana clutched at his forearm wildly for balance before twisting and toppling right on top of him.

The backs of her thighs slammed onto his lap, and Gray groaned, all restraint forgotten as his hands went to her arms to keep her from slipping off. They slid up to her neck and tipped her chin to the side, and then his mouth closed on hers. She didn't pull away. Instead, she twisted her head to meet him more fully.

Though the position was awkward, they devoured each other, her deliciously curved backside pressing down on his raging arousal. Gray didn't want it to frighten her, but he could no more control himself than he could his desire to explore every inch of her sinful mouth. His palms wandered the expanse of her throat as she arched against him and moaned. She tasted every bit as good as he remembered. Better, even. Bracing her body with his left arm, his right hand curved around her to caress her breasts through the material before impatiently tugging the bodice down to free them.

Gray was grateful that the shades were half closed, although no one would be able see them while the carriage was in motion anyway. Her position, splayed atop him and exposed as she was, was both scandalous and scintillatingly arousing. If he grew any harder, the fabric of his trousers wouldn't be able to hold him. It had been ages since he'd lain with a woman. His self-imposed celibacy had been a trial, even without the warmth of a woman's body pressing against his. Now, his fingers roaming possessively over Lana's breasts and her rounded bottom caressing him with every turn of the carriage wheels, Gray welcomed the sharp-edged torture. He wanted her pert nipples in his mouth, but he didn't want to give up her lips. Not just yet.

"Gray," she whispered. "We need to stop."

Not *you* have to stop, but *we*. He loved that she did not claim to be noncompliant, as if she had no part in what was transpiring between them. It obliterated his earlier worry that she was allowing his kisses only because she did not want to risk his wrath should she reject him. No, she craved his touch as much as he did hers. The knowledge emboldened him. Keeping his mouth firmly locked on hers, Gray's hands slipped down her stomach to tug on her skirts, dragging them up, inch by torturous inch.

"Not yet, Lana," he whispered.

Her body froze above his, her eyes flying open as if suddenly aware of his hands skimming her stockinged thighs. Gray sucked her lip into his mouth, holding her prisoner with his teeth and with his eyes, his fingers climbing higher. He watched her carefully for a sign—any sign—that she truly wanted him to stop. Her hands curled into the sides of her dress, and as his fingers pushed past her drawers, a soft cry of pleasure rushed into his mouth. Her hips arched into his palm with another desperate sigh.

"Gray—"

"Shhh," he said. "Let me touch you."

Her eyes widened as his hand cupped her, and Gray almost spilled himself at the warm, velvety feel of her. She was hot and damp, her dewy skin clinging to his as his center finger moved gently into her core. Lana's head fell back to his shoulder. Gray shifted his body slightly so that he could claim her lips once more, his tongue imitating the indecent movements of his finger. Her hips pushed upward, rocking against him with instinctual need. He adored how responsive she was, holding back nothing.

"Please," she moaned. Gray knew she did not know what she was asking for, but he would give it to her. Even if the wild rocking of her bottom against his erection caused him to burst in his trousers, he would pleasure her.

"Soon, love."

He continued to stroke her, his thumb pressing against the small nub at her entrance, and then her body went still, a stifled cry escaping her lips as she found her release. Gray kissed her, smiling with pure satisfaction at the bemused look on her face. He straightened her skirts and took her lips in one more leisurely kiss before adjusting her to the seat beside him.

He drew an aching breath into his lungs. His own arousal had not abated, but Gray did not care. He kissed the side of her jaw and caressed her arm. He couldn't stop himself from touching her.

"Please. Stop," Lana whispered, turning her head away and dragging her dress up over her bared breasts.

He frowned at her mortified tone. A bright flush suffused the skin of her nape. "Lana?"

"Please, Lord Northridge, I must ask you to…move away."

Move away?

Gray turned her shoulders to face him. The aloof, unreadable set of her features threw him. She'd lost herself to him moments before, and yet now her incurious expression was as impassive as that of a seasoned dowager. He hadn't misread the signs—she'd permitted his touch. She had *wanted* his touch. He moved to take her hand, but she pulled it away.

"I need…I need a moment," she said, and without looking at him, rapped on the side of the carriage. "Colton, please stop. I need some air."

She reached for the carriage door before the conveyance had even come to a complete halt.

"Lana, wait," Gray snapped, afraid she'd shove the door wide and topple out. He reached for her again, but like before, she recoiled.

"Don't! You... We shouldn't have..."

But by then the footman had opened the door himself. Lana sealed her lips and quickly descended into a wooded lane. She disappeared beyond the tree line. As soon as he could be certain his arousal would not precede him out of the carriage, Gray took his leave as well. His eyes stayed on the trees as he leaned against the coach.

He was such a fool. In the heat of the moment, he kept forgetting who Lana was. A lady's maid. And one who did not aim to dally with the lords of the manor. Not that he was one of those lords. At least, he had not thought he was. But Lana was so unlike any woman he had ever met. It was in the way she spoke and the way she carried herself. Perhaps working in the employ of royalty back in St. Petersburg had rubbed off, because in truth, he had to remind himself of the imparity between them.

Regardless of her unguarded response, Gray also suspected she was a virgin. The look of shocked surprise on her face when his hand had coaxed her over the edge hadn't been artifice. Nor had her embarrassment moments before. No man had touched her as he had. The thought pleased him, even though it shouldn't have. There was no future for them, no way for him to do right by her, and if he took her innocence, she would have no future, either. She should expect to marry one day and have a respectable place in a respectable household.

Respectability. He was consumed by its polar and ignominious opposite. It was the last thing he could offer her.

Gray sighed, scrubbing a hand across his face. The woman made him want unreasonable things, the same way his daughter made him want unreasonable things. He wanted, desperately, too many things he could not have. Lana's body. Her trust. Her affection. He wanted her to look at him as she did when she spoke of her sister, to hold him in such esteem.

But he was bound to his station and his duty. And Lana was bound to hers.

After a few moments, she returned, every strand of hair tucked into place and her face serenely composed, as if nothing untoward had happened. Her swollen lips were the only things that hinted otherwise. She did not look at him, and Gray frowned, keenly conscious of the unsatisfied ache between his legs. He'd also lost any hope of getting Lana to trip up and admit who her ally was. But if he were being honest, he'd forgotten his motives entirely the moment Lana had landed in his lap.

Hell. He would ride a while with Colton and take the air himself. Lord knew he needed it.

Chapter Fourteen

Gray stayed with Colton for the rest of the journey, and for that, Lana was grateful. Despite recalling every single moment in excruciating detail over and over, she was in a far calmer state by the time they arrived in Essex past nightfall. She had convinced herself that her moment of lunacy, of pure *idiocy*, had been nothing but a mistake. A ridiculous, foolish mistake. One that she would never repeat. And she could only do that by staying as far away from Lord Northridge as possible.

Lana had no illusions that she'd been seduced by a master. But she also knew that she could have stopped Gray at any time. She hadn't wanted to. She *never* wanted to where he was concerned. The man made her daft, and she feared she'd offer up her innocence without a qualm in the world if he ever touched her that way again. A rush of heat flooded her thighs at the scandalous memory of where his fingers had been, and her breath caught on a silent tremor.

It had felt too delicious for words. Her soul had splintered apart and then smashed back together at the exact point where his hand had pleasured her body. She'd never felt anything like it. The sensations had almost been too much to bear, but Gray had held her so tightly, anchored to him, that she'd felt safe even when she'd fallen apart. Lana blinked. If that was a part of what men and women did in the marriage bed, no wonder her parents' chamber door had been closed more often than it'd been open. They'd always been more passionate than most.

She blushed fiercely. Her parents had been *married*. She and Gray were not. They could never hope to be, either, at least not in her current circumstances. The social rules were the same across the Continent. She was a maid. And he was a lord.

Lana shook her head. She was lying to herself—she was a *princess* dallying with a rake and putting her honor out for the taking.

Good heavens, what was she thinking? Marriage was out of the question. She'd be lucky to make it out of England alive with Zakorov on the hunt for her and Irina. She needed to put Lord Northridge out of her head and not fill it with foolish fantasies of what could be. No matter which way she looked at it, they were from two different worlds.

Furthermore, she told herself firmly, she did not like the man. *You like him well enough,* her inner voice countered slyly.

He was nosy and demanding and overly protective, butting into her private life as though he believed he belonged there. *Yet, you like that he does.*

Touching her in ways that weakened her resolve. *Making you want more.*

He made her want to trust him. He made her want to give herself over to him. *And you do want to, body and soul.*

"Bloody hell," she swore as another unwelcome rush of heat teased her body, and she grinned. Percy and James would be proud of her expanding vocabulary. It thrilled them to teach her words that wouldn't be tolerated in any polite society.

The carriage came to halt, and Lana sat forward. She looked out the window and realized they were not at Ferndale, but in Breckenham. The carriage door opened, and the very man who had been filling her thoughts for the last handful of hours stood within it. She tried to keep her expression one of cool composure, but the tense look upon his face chased away any apprehension she'd had. He was worried for his daughter, of course.

"I'm sorry," Gray said in a low voice. "I can't wait until morning to see her. I'll walk to the Coopers from here, and Colton can take you the rest of the way."

Walk? Understanding was quick as Lana realized the lacquered family crest on the coach would be far too noticeable. Unwanted questions might arise should Lord Northridge be seen visiting Sir Cooper at so late an hour.

She shook her head, deciding in an instant. "No, I'll come with you."

Gray hesitated, but then reached a hand out to her. She took it and descended to the dirt lane.

"Thank you," he said as the carriage started away. "It isn't far."

Gray pulled his hat low, and she followed along behind him. She had no idea why she hadn't let Colton take her the remainder of the way to Ferndale. Hadn't she just promised herself that she would avoid any closer contact with Gray? And yet one glance at his anxious face had her rearing to help.

He hadn't said much more to her other than that Sofia was sick, but Lana guessed that he feared the worst. He'd reached into his pocket numerous times in the first part of their journey to reread the letter that had arrived at Bishop House. He'd wanted to be at his daughter's side even then, and so his swift walk down the darkened road, toward the softly lit windows of the Coopers' fine house, did not surprise her.

Lana's legs were warm with exertion when they finally turned into the circular drive and approached the home's front door. Gray brought down the knocker twice and then stood tall, bristling with impatience, and waited.

"I am sure she is just fine," Lana whispered, wanting only to reassure him. To soothe the glare of worry he was currently burning into the wood of the door with his eyes.

"I do not know what I shall do if she is not," he replied, his voice hoarse and nearly inaudible.

Lana touched his hand, but the door opened and she pulled it away. An aging butler stood aside and permitted Gray in without so much as a blink.

"This way, my lord," the man said. He shut the door as soon as Lana had stepped into the foyer and immediately led them both up the main staircase to the upper floor.

The familiarity and warm welcome so close to a midnight hour struck Lana. They had anticipated Gray's eagerness to see his daughter. The butler led them to a room on the second floor and, with a firm knock upon the door, allowed Gray and Lana entrance.

The nursery was lit by a single lamp and a small fire in the hearth. A little bed, half the size of the ones Lana slept in at Bishop House and Ferndale, was in the corner of the room, and underneath a blanket laid a small bundle of blond curls and pink skin. The child was asleep, her lashes brushing against her over-rosy cheeks. The nursemaid, who had been knitting in a wooden chair beside the bed, stood up quickly, her needles slipping from her fingers as Gray rushed across the room toward her.

"Lord Northridge," the young woman said, jumping out of his way.

He lowered himself to the edge of the bed, careful not to

jounce the mattress and startle the little girl awake.

Lana watched with a breath caught in her throat as he gently pushed a few curls from Sofia's forehead. His hand shook as he withdrew it.

"She is still feverish," he said.

"Yes," replied a voice directly behind Lana, and she spun on her heels. A man in shirtsleeves and breeches entered the nursery. Though he appeared rather rumpled, Lana suspected it was Sir Cooper.

Gray stood from the bed. "Thank you for sending word."

"Of course. I knew you would want to know, and I was correct in expecting your prompt arrival. A room has been prepared for you in the event you do not wish to open Ferndale for your stay." Sir Cooper's eyes found Lana. They were friendly but curious. No doubt he wondered what a maid was doing here as well.

"Sir Cooper, this is Miss Lana Volchek, my sister's lady's maid. She's here on an errand for my mother."

Lana curtsied, and Sir Cooper nodded in greeting. If he was surprised that Gray had allowed his deepest secret to be known by a maid, he did not show it.

"How long has she been feverish?" Gray asked, taking his seat on Sofia's bedside again. "Has the physician been here today?"

Lana saw that the little girl's forehead was dry, her cheeks flushed in comparison to the creamy lids of her closed eyes. A basin and a pitcher of water had been set up on a table, along with a stack of linens. Lana moved toward the table, removing her cloak and draping it over the arm of a rocking chair along the way.

"Four days," Sir Cooper answered. "And yes, Doctor Jensen has been checking in on her regularly. He thought the fever would break by now."

Lana poured lukewarm water into the basin and took

a cloth from the stack. She wet it thoroughly and wrung it out before crossing to the bed and perching herself near the bedpost, next to Sofia's pillow.

"Here," she said, folding the cloth and placing it upon the girl's forehead. She looked to the maid standing out of the way, her knitting now tucked into a basket. "Can you fetch some cold water from the kitchen? The nursemaids my mama always kept on staff folded damp towels and laid them on my head when I had a fever. And the cook would send up yarrow and peppermint tea from the kitchens. Sofia could sip some when she wakes."

Lana removed the now hot compress over the child's tiny forehead before lifting her eyes to Gray. He was staring at her, his brows furrowed.

"Your nursemaids on *staff*? And tea from the *kitchens*?" he echoed. It was then she realized her mistake.

"Yes, well, we did have a large home…when Papa was alive…and well…"

Before she could stammer another senseless word, Sir Cooper interjected, "Both excellent ideas. Becky, can you see that fresh linens and cold water are sent up and the tea is prepared?"

The nursemaid bobbed and darted from the room. Lana avoided looking at Gray, instead staring at Sofia's sleeping figure. She was a beautiful little thing, with round cheeks made for kissing, and an upturned nose that index fingers everywhere would itch to tap lovingly.

"Has there been anyone else in town with a fever like this?" Gray asked.

Sir Cooper shook his head. "Not that Doctor Jensen is aware of. We have not been quarantined for yellow fever or the like, if that is what you are fearful of."

Lana brushed the backs of her knuckles against Sofia's rosy brow, frowning at the heat of the child's skin.

Gray covered her hand with his. "Nevertheless, she could be contagious. Perhaps you should wait in the kitchens."

Lana took the compress and stood, but went to the pitcher and basin instead. "I will stay, my lord." And then with a care for Sir Cooper, still looking on, added, "If I may."

Neither Gray, nor Sir Cooper, argued, and she returned to the bed and placed the cloth on the child's forehead. Perhaps not with enough gentleness, however. The little girl's lashes fluttered, and she made a wakeful noise in her throat.

Lana saw Gray's whole body tense as Sofia opened her eyes.

"Norry?" she said, her voice scratchy. Lana's heart swelled at the nickname for Lord Northridge, but she covered her smile by busying herself with pouring a glass of water.

"Hello, sunshine," Gray replied. "I heard you were feeling low and thought I might pay you a visit."

Again, Lana's heart thudded with emotion. He didn't speak to Sofia with the saccharine tone so many adults took when addressing children. He spoke to her as easily as he would to any other person. Except Lana heard something in his voice that she hadn't before. It was so strange to hear something she had never even noticed was missing: joy. There was a lightness and joy in each word Gray spoke to Sofia.

"Did you bring flowers?" She mumbled her words, still half asleep.

He laughed, and as Lana returned with the glass of water, she could no longer suppress her grin. He looked so pleased, so content, sitting there, holding Sofia's small hand.

"Whatever was I thinking? I have no flowers for you tonight, but I will bring the largest, most beautiful bouquet I can hunt down tomorrow. Are daisies still your favorite?"

Sofia nodded, her head nearly engulfed within the feather pillow, and smiled bashfully at her admirer.

"Good, then," Gray said, his attention lifting to Lana.

He gathered a breath, and Lana heard it rattle. He was still overwrought with worry.

"Sofia, I've brought a new friend," he said, standing up and indicating for Lana to take his place on the bed. "This is Lana."

She sat and smiled at the little girl, whose expression had changed from playfully shy to uncertain. "Hello, Sofia. Are you thirsty?"

Lana helped her sit up and then guided the glass to her lips.

"I'll be back in just a bit," Gray said. "Lana is going to sit with you for now." His eyes pinned her with a puzzled look as he added, "It seems she has had experience with scores of nursemaids in the past."

Lana broke from his thoughtful stare and concentrated on Sofia, who had gulped half the glass of water.

Curse her loose tongue! First, he'd somehow determined Langlevit was her friend within the peerage, then he'd wheedled the truth about Irina hiding in Cumbria out of her, and now Lana had gone and blurted out yet another secret. This one perhaps the most damaging. She was supposed to be from a modest genteel family, and such families did not employ entire staffs of nursemaids and cooks!

Sofia finished her water, and Lana tucked her back in, glad she did not have to meet Gray's eyes again. She had to think of an excuse. Perhaps her nursemaids had been aunts or family friends? Her cook, a helpful neighbor? She smiled at Sofia and waited for Gray and Sir Cooper to leave the bedroom before slumping her shoulders in defeat.

She had known this charade would be difficult to pull off. She'd expected complications to arise. However, she'd never expected that complication to take the form of a man. One she could not resist. One she could not have. Even if Viktor and her uncle were captured and things went back to normal,

Gray would never leave his family… He would not leave his daughter here in Breckenham or take himself so far away that he would never be able to see her, play with her, or tend to her when she was ill. Lana would return to St. Petersburg, and Gray would stay here where he belonged. She would not make him choose.

And if Gray knew the truth, he would insert himself even deeper into this trouble with Zakorov, putting himself at risk. If anything were to happen to him because of her, she would never forgive herself. He needed to be here for his daughter. Lana checked the compress and received a slight grin from Sofia. This little girl, whether she knew him as Norry or as Father, needed Gray, too. Lana would not allow him to risk his own safety.

As soon as she returned to London, she would quit her desperate hiding. Lord Langlevit was supposed to be meeting with someone who might be able to cipher the coded letters, but if that did not turn out as expected, there had to be something else Lana could use. Some other evidence. Perhaps in Viktor's rooms in London, wherever he was staying? Zakorov certainly would not expect her to seek him out. Which meant he might not attempt to hide anything incriminating.

Lana knew it was far-fetched and undoubtedly dangerous, but what else could she do? Continuing on as Brynn's lady's maid was just as dangerous. Gray would attempt to seduce her again, and she knew she would not be able to resist. She'd be ruined. She'd be a doxy at worst, or Gray's mistress at best. Neither was good enough. Not for Princess Svetlanka Volkonsky.

"Rest now. You'll be just fine, princess," she whispered to Sofia, whose lids had started to grow heavy again.

You'll be just fine, princess, Lana repeated to herself.

And she would be.

Chapter Fifteen

Gray studied his valet's handiwork with an approving grunt. Following his return from Essex, Harrison had trimmed Gray's hair and shaved several days' worth of stubble. He looked more human than he had an hour ago. After the last two grueling days at Sofia's bedside in Breckenham, he'd looked worse than a sailor coming off a week of drinking and whoring on the wharves. Not that he'd had any of the latter, but he'd polished off the better part of a bottle of whiskey while waiting—and praying—for Sofia's fever to break. And break it had, partly in thanks to Lana, who had refused to leave the girl's side.

Something stirred within Gray as he recalled the muted sounds of Lana's whispered stories and Sofia's rapt, if drowsy, attention, even as the maid convinced her tiny charge to consume enough broth to make her weak body combat the infection. Lana's vigilant ministrations had been the turning point, Gray knew. With such high, intense fevers, if a child did not have the strength to recover, they would often succumb. Even Dr. Jensen had been prepared for the worst, but Lana had simply refused to give up. She had taken turns with Gray sitting at the child's bedside, alternating between using cooling cloths, warm baths, and offering sips of soothing tea. Her stories had brightened Sofia's eyes in those few moments when the fever lessened.

"You don't have to be here," he'd told Lana, seeing the shadows of exhaustion congregating beneath her eyes. "You should go to Ferndale and rest."

"I want to be here." Her eyes had been unreadable, but something in her voice had tugged at him.

Like him, Lana had not slept a wink. But because of her, Sofia was recovering. Gray was more than grateful—he would forever be in her debt.

He sighed as Harrison straightened the shoulders of his fitted jacket, the thought of Lana all-consuming. It wasn't like before, born solely of attraction and lust. Something had evolved between them…something he wasn't sure he fully understood. Seeing her tenderness with Sofia had made him yearn for something he couldn't quite articulate, even in the privacy of his own mind. He'd felt the grasping need for his daughter and a home where she would be safe and loved.

The Coopers were a loving family of means, but Gray still wanted more for her. He wanted a world where *he* could take care of her himself. But without a wife, that was a foolish dream. And no matter how loving she'd been toward Sofia, Lana was far from an appropriate candidate. Still, the image of her tending to a slightly older Sofia, Lana's own belly round with his child, wreaked havoc with Gray's senses.

Impossible. It was not something even the most liberal of the *ton* would accept.

Gray chuckled humorlessly. As if he cared a whit what any of those asinine highbrows thought. But the shame it would bring to his mother and his sister, who had only just secured her own engagement, was another matter entirely.

Not to mention the fact that both he and Lana would become outcasts, and if he claimed her, Sofia as well. The situation was untenable. Even if he did marry according to his station, no young debutante would want to be saddled with another woman's child.

No, despite his desires, a life with the Coopers was the best thing for Sofia. And for him.

"Thank you, Harrison," Gray said, pinching the bridge of his nose with his thumb and forefinger. He hadn't quite recovered from the lack of sleep. "Please inform my father that I will be down shortly."

"Of course, my lord."

Bishop House was bustling, preparations for his father's dinner well underway, and their guests would be arriving at any moment. He needed a few minutes to clear his head. Viktor Zakorov would be in attendance, and Gray wanted all his wits about him. Perhaps he'd be able to suss out more of the truth about the two missing princesses and figure a way to keep Lana safe.

He frowned, thinking of her offhand comment about having more than one nursemaid and a cook working in the *kitchens*. If her parents had been landed gentry, it wasn't out of the realm of possibility that Lana could have been raised with a household staff. Though it did seem far-fetched that a modiste of modest fortune would keep an entire staff of nursemaids on hand. And Lana had flushed profusely, as if she had made a terrible gaffe by mentioning it. She was keeping yet another secret, and it bothered him.

He could not marry her, but that did not mean he didn't care what happened to her. And that meant keeping her out of the clutches of men like Zakorov. Thankfully, Lana was currently nowhere near the vicinity of Bishop House. She'd left that afternoon with Brynn and Lady Dinsmore. Something about yet another dress fitting for his sister's engagement ball gown. They were supposed to have been back in time for the dinner, but his mother had sent word with Colton that they had run into Lady Cordelia and her mother, Countess Vandermere, and had accepted a last-minute invitation to a musicale at their home that evening.

Gray knew the musicale would entertain the ladies far more than father's dinner, but he did not know if Lana would be joining her mistress and Lady Dinsmore for the evening, or if she had returned home. He'd considered asking Harrison if he knew but had held his tongue instead. He trusted his valet, but displaying an interest in Lana's whereabouts was not a wise move. Most likely Lana had stayed with Brynn and would be occupied elsewhere while the dinner unfolded.

Gray gritted his teeth and made his descent to the dining salon.

"Monti," he called out to the man standing at the foot of the staircase waving a glass of brandy with emphatic gusto. "Good to see you again, although I am disappointed it is not at the tables. I'd hoped to give you a chance to recoup some of your losses."

Helmford Monti threw back his head and laughed. "I am smart enough to know when to fold, and you, Northridge, are a dangerous opponent. Perhaps I shall challenge you with dice next time." He turned to a dour-faced man admiring the paintings along the salon walls a few feet away. "You remember Baron Zakorov?"

"Of course," Gray said as the man strode toward them. Everything he knew about Zakorov rankled Gray, but it was his cold, shallow eyes that worried him. They held no empathy. No warmth. Langlevit was right about this man: he was most certainly capable of terrible things. "Lord Zakorov."

"Lord Northridge," he replied, his rasping whisper free of inflection and just as depthless as his stare. Gray had little doubt that he was in the company of a very dangerous man indeed. "It is an honor to be in your home. Thank you for the invitation."

"Thank my father," Gray said. "He hosts these monthly dinners for the House of Lords. Politics, cigars, and horses tend to be the favored topics of discussion. I trust you will not be too bored."

"I do enjoy a good cigar on occasion."

Gray suppressed a frown, offering only a bland smile in response. Zakorov would not be here without an ulterior motive. He doubted it had to do with Lana, but as he glanced around at the dozen or so guests, there were many powerful English lords and other dignitaries in attendance. He'd stake his title on the fact that Zakorov was here to glean what information he could or perhaps further assistance to his cause.

Gray excused himself and greeted some other men he knew. Though most of the guests were his father's acquaintances, he relaxed when he saw Stephen Kensington, the Earl of Thorndale. Though a few years older than Gray, Thorndale was one of the few men he admired, and even fewer in the circle he called friend. Recently married, to the daughter of a local physician no less, Gray was surprised but glad to see him here.

"Running from the bonds of marriage already, Thorn?" Gray asked, taking a glass of whiskey from a passing tray. "Haven't you only been married a week?"

"Six months," Thorndale said drily. "And I could not refuse Dinsmore's invitation a second time."

Gray nodded to a nearby footman, who replaced Thorndale's empty glass. He lifted his own in toast. "Well, here's to surviving all those months of being shackled."

Thorndale smiled. "I'll be sure to toast you when you are as well-chained as the rest of us. I'm surprised that you aren't off the marriage mart by now. Heard there was rumor of an offer for Lady Cordelia. She's a lovely girl."

She was lovely, yes, but Gray felt cold at the idea of marrying her. No. He would not make an offer. "I intend to defend my bachelorhood for a while more, thank you."

"Tell that to Lady Dinsmore."

"Not a chance." Gray grinned, the light humor lessening his agitation over Zakorov. "You look well, Thorn. It appears marriage agrees with you."

"It does," he said with a broad smile.

There was something more behind it than pure accord. Gray peered at him. "What is it?"

Thorndale's smile increased. "I am not supposed to announce anything just yet, but I hardly consider you a gossip." He lowered his voice. "Christine is with child."

Gray felt a stab of something like envy lance through him at the unbridled happiness on his friend's face. At his friend's ability to make such an announcement.

"Quick work, you old dog," Gray said, clapping Thorndale on the shoulder and swallowing his envy. "Congratulations to you both."

"Thank you." Thorndale paused, staring at him as if the longing on Gray's face was visible. "You'll find your match one day, North."

I already have.

The thought was ensnaring. Absurd. He'd enumerated all the reasons why Lana could never be his, but damn it, he wanted her with a force that was unrecognizable. It tore through him like a storm's wind, leaving him battered. Hell, he was already halfway in love with her. This woman he could not have.

Thorndale's laugh brought Gray back to attention. "Does she know?"

Gray frowned. "Who?"

"The one occupying your thoughts at this very moment."

He considered evading the issue but knew Thorndale would not press for details. "No."

"Time is short, my friend," Thorndale said sagely. "And we must seize the days we have. Don't wait too long."

Dinner was announced, saving Gray from having to reply, and they made their way into the dining room. The men took their seats. To his disappointment, Gray realized the seating arrangements had not positioned him near Zakorov. Instead, he was stuck at the far end of the table, several places away from the man.

"How did your horses do in the last race, Northridge?" Monti asked as the first course of succulent morels simmered in a delicate white sauce was served.

"Not as well as I'd hoped."

"Are you going to race them at Chatham?"

Gray shrugged. "I haven't decided."

And nor did he truly care. He had at one time, but the draw of the races had lost its shine. He could breed the finest thoroughbreds, but he could not control the outcome of each race. That fact used to thrill him. Not any longer. The only way he'd been able to maintain his own rigid restrictions when it came to women was through strict control. Risk introduced weakness.

Lana is a risk.

Gray set down his spoon and picked up his whiskey. He had to put the woman out of his mind and concentrate on Zakorov, who was engaging in quiet conversation with one of his neighbors.

"What of this Masked Marauder tearing through London?"

Gray turned his attention from the Russian and directed it across the table, to a doughy old man whose name he could not recall. "There are rumors that he could be connected to the Duke of Bradburne's murder," the man concluded.

Lord Dinsmore, seated at the head of the table, perked up. "I certainly believe him capable of it, especially after his attack on Lord Maynard. Shot his horse, the bandit did."

In the seat beside the doughy man, Mr. Armstrong, a well-respected barrister and a friend of Thorndale's, entered the conversation. "There seems to be a disconnect between killing a horse during a highway robbery and murdering a duke in his own home. I'm not inclined to believe the two crimes were done by the same man."

As a member of the Inns of Court, Armstrong was a level man, a scholar, and as direct as a fist to the teeth. If he questioned a connection between the crimes, Gray leaned toward believing him. With his mind so trained on Zakorov and Lana, Gray had nearly forgotten about the masked bandit and, as horrible as it sounded, the duke's murder.

"One man or a pair of them, they're bloody blackguards," the doughy man insisted, shaking his head. "My wife is terrified to leave the house for fear of attack. Dinsmore, I heard you'd been questioned by the Bow Street agent. Is it true what I'm hearing—that this inspector is treating every guest at the duke's dinner as a suspect?"

"Bow Street." Gray's father snorted. "Indeed, the offensive man seemed to be sniffing around the possibility that one of us killed Bradburne. Preposterous! As if one of the *ton* would ever be implicated in such scandalbroth. Nonetheless, until the bastard is found and hanged, I've had my groomsmen and drivers take extra precautions. I urge you to do the same."

The discussion grew more agitated as the subjects of self-defense and criminal punishment took over, with shouts of "*hear, hear*" ringing across the table. Gray tuned out, focusing his attention on the Russian. Above the hum of conversation, he studied Zakorov surreptitiously as he ate, noticing his precise, stringent movements. Everything he did was completed with calculated precision—the way he cut the meat on his plate, the way he chewed, the rigid way he held himself as if he were made of stone instead of flesh and bone.

"Lord Zakorov," Lord Dinsmore finally said, catching Gray's interest. "Monti tells me you're visiting us from St. Petersburg. Enjoying your stay in London thus far?"

Zakorov set down his knife and fork, and cleared his throat. "Yes, but I am on official business. I am in pursuit of two fugitives." Conversation around the table flattened as Zakorov became the center of attention.

Gray's father's eyes brightened with interest. "Fugitives, you say?"

"Yes. Princesses Svetlanka and Irina Volkonsky are wanted for crimes against the tsar. My intelligence suggests they are here, in London."

"Two *princesses*?" One of the men, a member of the House of Lords, Lord Calpen, guffawed, only to earn the scathing heat of Zakorov's glare. The laugh petered out, and Lord Calpen stared at his plate in uncomfortable silence.

"Volkonsky. I am familiar with the name," Lord Dinsmore said, tapping his chin. "Do you mean Grand Duke Grigori?"

Zakorov nodded. "His daughters."

"He and his wife died in a carriage accident, if I recall." Lord Dinsmore frowned. "I never met the man myself, but I also recall hearing that Grigori was a friend to both the tsar and to England. Perhaps you are mistaken on the identity of these women."

"I am *not*," Zakorov snapped, adding a terse and clearly forced, "my lord."

Gray leaned back in his chair, his eyes drifting between the downward slant of Zakorov's mouth and his father's offended expression. Dinsmore opened his mouth, likely with the intent of delivering a brutal setdown, but Gray cut him off.

"Lord Zakorov is convinced that these two women are

at the heart of a conspiracy to assassinate the tsar, which I find rather fascinating. What proof do you have of their complicity?" His deliberately insolent tone made the man's eyes flash.

"Letters to the French."

"How do you know these letters were written by the princesses?" Gray asked.

"The letters are stamped with the family seal," Zakorov answered with a flare of his nostrils. "And the elder princess was seen in the company of known insurgents. They will, of course, be given the chance to prove their innocence, even if fleeing St. Petersburg is as good as an admission of guilt." His gaze circled the table. "If anyone has information, they must come forward."

Gray bristled at the acid command. The man antagonized him to no end. Everything Zakorov said was too smooth, too rehearsed, too *oily*. Gray did not believe one word coming out of his mouth. If the princesses in question were found, he knew they would not have any chance to disprove the charges against them. And, frankly, he was more inclined to believe Lana, who had told him the princesses were innocent. She had insisted they had encoded evidence to prove that *Zakorov* was the one consorting with the French. But every instinct told Gray that if this man found them, that proof would have no chance of coming to light.

"Do you have these alleged letters?" Gray asked mildly.

"What good would they be to you? They are in Russian," Zakorov countered. Every pair of eyes at the table was riveted on their exchange.

"You are right." Gray smiled and sipped his drink. "I'm afraid my Russian is rather rusty."

Lord Dinsmore cleared his throat, surprise in his eyes at the strange turn of the conversation, and attempted to dissipate some of the tension. "Perhaps one of our maids can assist. My daughter's lady's maid is Russian."

Zakorov did not bat an eyelash, but a cold smile stretched his lips as his eyes flicked to Lord Dinsmore. "I'm afraid the letters are in not in my possession. However, I would be interested in speaking to the young lady."

"I believe she is out this evening," Gray said swiftly. "With my sister."

"Pity."

The conversation shifted after that, but Gray could feel Zakorov's attention returning to settle on him at points over the course of the dinner. It made him uneasy. Perhaps he should not have been so despotic in his questioning. He cursed the fact that his father had brought up Lana, but that could not have been avoided, and chances were a man like Zakorov would not have forgotten Gray's comment at White's about their Russian maid. He'd unwittingly put Lana in danger that night, and this evening's dinner had certainly only secured Zakorov's interest in speaking to her. Should he request an interview, Lord Dinsmore would see no reason to object, either.

Unless he no longer held any authority over Lana.

If she were no longer employed at Bishop House…if she could not be located…then Zakorov would not be able to touch her. Gray had given her his promise that her position was secure, but why would she wish to stay if the man she was running from was so close to finding her?

Gray could protect Lana—if he could let her go.

Chapter Sixteen

Lana tugged her cloak closer and flattened her body against the mews. Horses whinnied in their stalls behind her, and she drew a shaky breath. This was a reckless, foolish plan, and Lord Langlevit would be livid if he knew what she was up to. He'd received her note about Viktor having dinner at Bishop House, and a reply had been waiting for her upon her return from Essex. Mary had kept it from Mrs. Frommer's wrathful eyes the few days Lana and Gray were away. She'd believed it to be another love note from Lana's secret beau and hadn't wanted the housekeeper to read or burn it as Mrs. Frommer had once threatened to do.

The wax seal had been unbroken when Lana had read the earl's terse reply:

My Strength will Be with you
Even from afar
Ever a watchful Protector
Until my Heart is yours again.
Fear not, Brave one.
We will be Together soon.

She'd deciphered his underlying meaning immediately: Langlevit was leaving for his meeting with the cryptographer, but someone would be watching Bishop House that night. Someone he trusted. Lana knew *Heart* referred to Irina, and Langlevit's coded promise that they would be together soon had settled Lana's nerves, at least a little.

But she couldn't sit by and wait for Viktor to find her. Even now, he was closer than he'd ever been, having dinner at Bishop House. She'd been grateful for the excuse to accompany Brynn to the modiste.

That afternoon, after the dress fitting and Countess Vandermere's impromptu invitation to the musicale, Lana had pleaded illness—again—and asked to be excused. Brynn had taken one look at her fatigued, wan complexion and commanded that she return to the residence. Thank heavens, it would seem, for the few sleepless nights she had endured in Essex. She did as requested and had Colton deliver her to Bishop House, but other than borrowing a worn pair of Brynn's black breeches and a low-brimmed hat, she did not tarry long.

Because she had other plans.

It had been rather simple finding out where Viktor was staying. Her friendship with James and Percy had offered more than just colorful vocabulary lessons. James had been the one to deliver the dinner invitations, and when Lana found him polishing the silver in the pantry earlier that morning, all she'd needed to do was bat her lashes and express an interest in her countryman, Baron Zakorov.

"Who is he?" Lana had asked, feigning awe. "Is he very important?"

"He's a dignitary, isn't he? A toff like the rest of 'em," James answered.

Lana had seen no smooth way around her next question but had attempted ignorance. "Does he live in a place like

Bishop House?"

James had rewarded her. "Nah, he's at the Stevens Hotel in Knightsbridge, where the rest of the military gents stay."

She drew a strangled breath now that she had arrived, struggling for air beneath the bindings of the cloth wrapped tightly about her breasts. She had no idea how Brynn did it, and on horseback, no less. The material itched and felt constrictive, but it had been the only option. The disguise made sense. A man could come and go from the Stevens Hotel as he pleased, but a woman would draw far more attention than was necessary. And she did not have the luxury of time.

In her pocket, Lana fingered the picklock Percy had loaned her, praying it would work. He'd taught her how to use it a few months before, but she'd never tried it anywhere but the stable door. With a determined breath, she walked purposefully down the darkened street and entered through the main entrance. The hall was loud and brightly lit, the armchairs occupied by men smoking cigars and housemaids bustling about, but no one paid her any mind. She didn't think her face particularly manly, but so long as no one looked closely, her disguise would work. She kept her head down and climbed the stairs without incident. At the top, Lana gulped a few relieved breaths. Third floor, last door on the right, James had confided.

The hallway was empty. Most of the occupants would be having dinner at this hour. She hastened to the door and tried the latch. Of course it was locked. Removing the thin lock-picking rods from her pocket, she set to work on the latch, but luck, it seemed, had deserted her. After several botched attempts, she nearly screamed in frustration.

"Aye," a voice asked from down the hallway. "What're ye about?"

Footsteps approached, and Lana recognized one of the buxom housemaids from below. She was young, not much older than Irina. Lana's mind raced even as her heart stampeded like a pack of wild game in her chest. "I am Lord Zakorov's squire," she improvised, lowering her voice and the brim of her hat. "He sent me to retrieve his…cloak."

"The Cossack, eh? How do I know ye ent a footpad off the streets?"

Lana drew herself up to her full height. "How would I have known his rooms? Or his name? Or have a key?" She kept her hand tightly fisted though she waved it in the maid's face. "He sent me to retrieve his cloak, and that is what I am doing."

The housemaid arched an eyebrow at Lana's arrogant tone but then leered at her. "A little scrawny for a squire, ent ye?"

"Not scrawny where it counts," Lana tossed back, forcing back a rush of embarrassment. Where had *that* come from? But then, if she didn't act the part, her disguise would be for naught. Cringing inside, she closed the distance between them. "Maybe later I can show you in person. But Lord Zakorov is not a man who likes to be kept waiting, so off with you, sweetling."

To Lana's infinite surprise and disgust, the young woman winked and obeyed. She couldn't fathom why women let themselves be treated and used in such a manner. But it wasn't like they had much choice—in places like these, such behavior was expected.

She clenched her teeth and went back to work on the lock. After several tries, the mechanism clicked, and the door swung open. *Success!* She let herself into the darkened room and shut the door, locking it behind her. She had to search quickly. There was a chance the maid could return—or worse, Viktor himself.

She lit a lamp and riffled through a small stack of newspapers on his desk, attempting to leave them as neatly arranged as they'd been before. Next, Lana tried the desk drawers. Then the bureau drawers. Then beneath his mattress. Then his trunks at the foot of his bed. A hectic quarter of an hour later, she was beside herself and empty-handed. She had found nothing of import. No personal papers, no letters, nothing. This had been a fruitless errand, and she felt like a fool for believing it would prove otherwise. She was about to leave when the sound of footsteps made her freeze. She listened and prayed they continued past Viktor's door.

They didn't.

"Bollocks," she swore. She was trapped.

With a hushed breath, she shoved herself into the narrow armoire she'd just given up searching. She left the door slightly cracked, considering it couldn't close anyway, not from the inside. She slowed her breathing and listened as the door unlocked and opened. The lamp! She'd left it lit on the desk. Lana cursed herself and clenched her fists as two men entered. She didn't recognize the first man, who wore a heavy-brimmed hat and crossed to the side of the room out of her line of sight. But she did recognize the second man. Tall and beefy shouldered, with dark hair and a thick mustache, both waxed into glossy perfection.

It was her uncle, Count Volkonsky.

The stirrings of true fear curdled in the pit of her stomach. If he was here, then that meant Viktor had summoned him. Because he suspected she and Irina were close? Or did he believe he had found them already? Her heart sank as she strained to hear their exchange from the suffocating confines of the closet.

"It is not like Viktor to leave a lamp burning," her uncle muttered as he approached the desk.

"Let's get on with this, shall we?" the man beyond her vision said, speaking with a heavy French accent. "The baron promised the first payment this evening."

Her uncle turned from the desk, seeming to forget the lamp. "Of course. He sends his regrets for his absence, but he is exploring a new lead. You shall be compensated as agreed—a quarter now, and the remainder when your task is complete."

"You have not told me where I am going," the man said.

"North. A few days' ride at the most."

"How north, exactly?" the Frenchman asked.

"Cumbria. The estate of Lord Langlevit."

A spear of ice plunged into Lana's chest, and she clamped a fist to her mouth to keep from crying out. *Oh God, no.* He'd found her. He'd found Irina.

"Langlevit?" the man hissed. A thread of fear colored the word.

"Do not worry, my sources confirm he is here and not due to quit London any time soon," the count said. "Only his aging mother, a small staff, and a young girl are in the residence. The girl is not to be harmed, but feel free to eliminate any other obstacles should it become necessary."

Lana bit into the heel of her palm. Irina was in danger, as was the countess. She watched as her treacherous uncle opened one of the trunks Lana had searched and came up with a leather pouch. He handed it to the man.

Her limbs started to numb and cramp, but she held herself as still as possible. The man standing with her uncle was a cold-blooded murderer. If Lana were discovered now, she would be taken. And then this man would set out for Cumbria. For her sister.

Hardly daring to breathe, Lana waited for several more minutes while the two men completed their conversation. The lamp was extinguished, and their voices faded as they left the room. Lana slumped to the floor of the armoire, her useless legs collapsing beneath her. She dragged a shattered breath into her lungs as her tears broke free. Never had she felt so alone or so powerless. With Langlevit having just left London for his meeting with the cryptographer from St. Petersburg, there was only one other person she could turn to. One other person she could trust.

She *did* trust Gray. And she wanted to go to him, right then, more than anything. She wanted to run from this wretched hotel, back to the safety of her hiding place as lady's maid at Bishop House.

Only it wasn't safe. Not if Viktor was still there. Lana would have to risk it, though. Viktor wasn't her only enemy in London anymore. Her uncle and the nameless, faceless Frenchman had joined in the hunt.

And it appeared Irina was their first target.

· · ·

"What do you mean she's not here?" Gray stormed.

It was late. Close to midnight, and the last of his father's guests had just departed. Gray had gone directly to his sister's rooms, knowing she must have arrived home at some point during the evening, perhaps while the men were still closed up in the billiards room.

Only he was now staring at his sister being tended to by Mary, the undermaid.

Brynn stared at him with wide eyes that quickly narrowed with suspicion. "Why do you care so very much where Lana is?"

He scowled, realizing he'd been far too transparent. He did not trust Mary not to go running downstairs and relaying the news that Lord Northridge had been asking after Lana. "In case you haven't noticed," he began slowly, forming his excuse, "there's a masked madman running amok about town. I'm merely concerned for her safety, as you should be." Brynn paled considerably at his harsh words, and Gray regretted his outburst.

"She said she felt unwell while we were out and asked to return home." Brynn paused. "Colton drove her back and saw her inside. Perhaps she felt better and went for one of her walks."

Unwell, his foot. She'd used that excuse before, and he was certain that was what it had been this time. "Perhaps."

Gray stalked outside, hell-bent on finding the object of his thoughts. He'd make sure she was *not* ill after all, and then he'd blister her with a piece of his mind for making him crazy with worry. The dinner with Zakorov had left him on edge, and after the men had taken their leave, his only thought had been to make sure Lana was secure. Only she had not been in when Brynn had summoned her, and it was now past the housekeeper's strict curfew. She was out there. Alone, perhaps. His blood simmered anew.

He hurried to the mews, slamming the door open on its hinges so hard it crashed into the wall behind it. He would wake Colton if necessary and find out what the man knew. Someone would have seen her leaving.

Colton and a few of the stable boys and footmen were seated around a card table set up in the center aisle between the rows of horse stalls. They saw Gray enter and jumped to their feet, clasping their hands, still holding cigarettes and cards, behind their backs. Their shoulders went stiff, and their chins hiked with respect, and a little bit of fear. The last thing Gray wanted to do was draw attention to his interest in Lana, but he had to have answers.

"Colton," Gray said. The driver tensed. "You saw Lady Briannon's maid home earlier after their outing?"

"Yes, my lord."

"Did she leave again?"

Colton frowned. "No, my lord. Not that I am aware of."

One of the footmen opened his mouth to chime in. "Is Lady Lana missing, m'lord?"

Lady Lana? Gray's brows snapped together, and he eyed the footman. Tall. Lanky. Young. "James, am I right?"

The boy nodded.

"What do you know?" Gray demanded.

He blinked and stammered the beginnings of a response before uttering something useful. "I didn't think she'd go anywhere tonight, not with the Russian fellow here. Thought she'd be trying to get a peek at him."

Gray's heart fizzled in his chest. "Zakorov?"

James's eyes brightened. "Yes, m'lord, that's the one."

"Why would she want a peek at him?"

James shrugged. "I dunno. She was asking me all about him."

"Why you?" Gray asked. The boy was a *footman*.

"Since I delivered the invitations for the dinner, m'lord. I met him only briefly though, so I didn't have much to tell Lady Lana, o'course."

The invitations. Oh, hell.

"You told her where Zakorov is staying," Gray stated. James nodded.

Good God, she'd gone to find him.

The footman, Colton, and the other stable boys stood in nervous silence, waiting for an order. Gray gave them one.

"Saddle my horse at once."

Gray couldn't wait patiently for Pharaoh to be readied, though. He'd moved in to tighten the girth himself when a slim figure passing by the open mews doors caught his eye. He stopped cold. The person was wearing a heavy cloak and brimmed hat, but it was not a man. He knew the slope of those shoulders so intimately that it wouldn't matter what she was wearing. It was her.

Stark relief flooded him as he ran from the mews and into the stable yard.

"Lana," he called, and the retreating figure drew to a stop.

She turned as he approached, and raised her eyes to his. His relief deserted him. Something was wrong. Terribly wrong.

"You are dismissed," he called to the stable boy, James, as well as Colton, who had followed him into the yard. "I won't need a horse after all."

They slipped back inside the mews and shut the doors.

Lana's eyes were red-rimmed and swollen, and for one terrifying instant, Gray worried that she had indeed crossed paths with Zakorov upon his return from the dinner. In the same moment he realized that if Zakorov had had her in his grasp, he wouldn't have let her go. Gray took her firmly but gently by the elbow and steered her deeper into the shadows of the stable yard, near the brick exterior of the mews. He opened his mouth to speak, but Lana cut him off. "I need your help."

She *was* in trouble, then.

"Where were you?" He couldn't keep the curtness from his voice, his worry and irritation growing in equal measure as he took disapproving notice of the men's breeches beneath the opening of her voluminous cloak. His sister's, no doubt. His frown deepened.

Lana swallowed, inhaling several deep breaths, as if to settle herself before answering. "Gray, please. Just listen. I know what you're going to say, but I couldn't stand by and do nothing any longer." She paused and wrung her hands. "I didn't want to drag you into this, but I don't have anyone else to turn to. I don't have anyone else I can trust to care."

He forced himself to calm, guessing how much it had taken for her to open to him in the first place. "Go on."

"My sister is in danger, and so is the family she is with," she rushed out.

"The one in Cumbria?"

"Yes."

He clenched his jaw. "Explain."

She wouldn't meet his eyes. "I overheard two men talking about going after her."

"Where were you?"

She let out a nervous sigh. "In Baron Zakorov's rooms at the Stevens Hotel."

Ah. Now he understood the reason for her clothing. She'd taken it upon herself to not only find Zakorov's hotel, but to go into it. Into men's lodgings in the middle of London. *Alone.*

As if she could sense his imminent explosion, she placed her small palm to the center of his chest. "I know what you're going to say, Gray, and yes, it was foolish and reckless of me. But I would do it again if it allowed me to keep my sister from harm. These men will stop at nothing."

He fought the emotion barreling through him at the light press of her fingers. "What men?" he asked.

Lana drew a long breath. "One of them was a Frenchman—I don't know his name. The other was Count Volkonsky, the princesses' uncle."

"Are you certain it was Volkonsky?"

"Yes," she answered, her tear-filled eyes dropping to his chest. "I saw him a number of times at Volkonsky Palace."

Of course. When she'd been in service there.

"And they are after your *sister*?" he asked.

She closed her eyes. "We both helped the princesses escape, and these men will use her by any means necessary to get to them. I've been safe here, but she…"

A shattered cry escaped Lana's lips, and a second palm joined the first, fisting into his lapels as if she no longer had the strength to stand on her own two feet. Gray couldn't help himself. He wrapped his arms about her and gathered her close. The strong, proud Lana he knew crumbled into a weeping, broken version of herself. She sobbed in earnest, dampening his shirtfront, her body shuddering with anguish. She'd never fallen apart like this with him before.

She had always kept him at a safe distance, where she could maintain at least a little control over what he knew and how much she divulged. The need to maintain control was something he understood deeply. There had been moments with Lana when he had let go. And now here she was doing the same thing. Asking—*begging*—for his help. He couldn't turn his back on her. Not now. No matter how furious he was that she'd knowingly endangered herself.

"I have a man," he said softly. "I'll send him to Cumbria." Gray tilted her tear-stained face up to his. "Which estate?"

Shadows rushed across her glistening eyes. "The Earl of Langlevit."

Although deep down he'd already known, hearing the name fall from her lips was a blow to the gut. Gray curbed the sudden and unwelcome surge of jealousy. He should be grateful that someone like Langlevit had been helping Lana and her sister. After all, it was because of him that Lana had found employment, and she and her sister had remained safe all these months. It was because of him that Gray had known to take Zakorov's potential danger seriously.

"I'll send someone at once. He will make sure that your sister is protected."

The relief that filled her eyes and her instant sob of gratitude took Gray's breath and wrenched it from his lungs. She tipped her head forward, touching it to his chest, just above where her fingertips still rested. "Thank you."

His fingers rose to stroke the hair at her temple. Lana stirred, as if realizing exactly how intimately she and Gray were standing, but he was unwilling to release his hold just yet. She felt too good in his arms. She rubbed her forehead against him. The gentle nudges from Lana seeking comfort resonated in more than one place within his body. Knowing it was neither the time nor the place, Gray fought for self-restraint, but he could never seem to control himself where she was concerned.

He cleared his throat and inched backward slightly, alleviating the sensual press of her trim body against his. "Lana, if Zakorov is sending someone to Cumbria to fetch your sister, that means he has uncovered your part in the princesses' disappearance. And if he has found your sister, he will find you next—if he hasn't already."

His presence at Bishop House that evening felt even more calculated now. Was he watching the residence as they spoke? Waiting for Lana to show herself?

"I know," she whispered.

"Langlevit is giving aid to the princesses, I take it?" he asked.

She stopped kneading her head into his chest, and a silent moment lapsed before she tried to move away. Again, Gray wouldn't give her more than a few inches of wiggle room.

"Are *they* in Cumbria as well?" he pushed.

"I cannot tell you where they are."

He dug his fingers into her shoulders, wanting to shake her until she saw sense. Until she told him everything. "You trust Langlevit with that information but not me? Why?"

She was ice again, her body rigid and her eyes cast low.

"You dressed as a man and snuck into Zakorov's rooms to do what, exactly? No. Don't answer," he said when she parted her lips to form some pallid excuse. "You want my help but you don't want to tell me the whole truth. You'd rather put your own life at stake than trust in me." He released her arms, hoping his grip hadn't hurt her. "Honestly, Lana, even if I gave you a scalpel, you wouldn't be able to castrate me any better."

She stared at him with both shock and defense. "You don't understand. You can't. I do trust you, and I *want*…"

He arched a brow as he waited out her pause. After a few seconds, he prodded her along. "You want what?"

She didn't answer.

"I'll tell you what I want then," he said, bringing her closer again and, unexpectedly, without resistance. "You won't like it, and you'll definitely argue with me. But you need to hide. Until those letters you mentioned can be ciphered."

Lana frowned up at him. "I *am* hiding."

He shook his head, willing her to remain calm as he said it. "Not any longer. Not if Zakorov knows you are here. Lana, you must leave. Resign your post and go. I have a hunting lodge in Derbyshire, left to me by one of my mother's uncles. You can stay there. It's safe and secluded. No one ever thinks of it."

"No." Lana pulled away. "I cannot run again, not when we are so close to having proof against Zakorov and my—"

She looked up at him as if she'd just swallowed a fly. Yet another drawn-out pause made him arch his brow, *again*. "Your what?"

Lana didn't answer, and she was saved from having to. The sound of an approaching whistle caused her to leap farther away from Gray, but it was only James peeking around the wooden door to the mews. Still, it was opportunity enough for her to take her leave through one of the side doors. *Damn it.*

He'd known she wouldn't immediately capitulate to his suggestion that she stay in his Derbyshire lodge. It wasn't entirely rustic, but it was secluded, as he'd promised. She would not be bothered there. But her own safety was obviously not her priority. Her sister's was. Lana would do whatever she thought she needed to do to protect her. She was headstrong and protective to a fault, but Gray knew that he would do the same if it were Brynn. He scrubbed a hand through his hair and beckoned the footman forward.

James grinned in the direction of the door through which Lana had just disappeared. "Was Lady Lana wearing breeches, m'lord?"

"Never mind what she was wearing," Gray growled.

"Take a walk around Bishop House, James. Come find me if you see anyone unsavory skulking about."

The footman's expression turned serious. "Unsavory, m'lord?" he echoed, and then surprised Gray with a pulse of insight. "Was Lady Lana bothered by someone on her way home?"

Gray eyed James and heeded caution. "Things are well in hand. Just keep a keen eye on your walk around the property."

The footman nodded. "Yes, m'lord. I'm sure they are in hand. Lady Lana has a fine uppercut, if my jaw recalls right proper."

Gray furrowed his brow. "Lady Lana has struck you?"

Lady Lana. Fantastic, now *he* was saying it. Though it did have a nice ring.

"Only while we were sparring, m'lord."

"*Sparring?*" Gray glared at James, who had wisely decided to retreat toward the mews, his eyes going round at the black look Gray knew he had on his face.

"She insisted I teach her how to box, m'lord."

Of all the foolhardy, senseless things! He knew the boy was not at fault—saying no to *Lady* Lana would take a very strong constitution, and Lord knew he found it difficult enough himself to resist any entreaty in those guileless green eyes.

Gray shook his head, his curiosity getting the better of him. "James?"

"Yes, m'lord?" came the cowed response.

"What else have you taught her?"

James shrugged again. "Nothing much, m'lord. Jest some, er, words, and a bit o' lock picking, and some card tricks. Oh, and some horse jumping. Cor, m'lord, like the wind, she is. The gulch she cleared—" He broke off, ducking his head as Gray's jaw dropped.

Swearing, card tricks, *horse jumping*?

If he weren't so irate, he would have burst out laughing. When this was all over—and Gray would see to it that it *did* end—he was going to put that little hellion over his knee.

"Next time *Lady* Lana asks you to teach her anything, find me first."

Chapter Seventeen

Hadley Gardens was a bit finer than Bishop House, and its staff certainly had no qualms rubbing it in. The duke's servants, if they were to be believed, were of a higher class distinction than the Earl of Dinsmore's, and more than one maid and footman had turned their nose up at Lana in the hours she had spent preparing Lady Briannon for the engagement ball taking place that evening. Despite the duke's scandalous decision not to honor the mourning period, in deference to his father's wishes, many people were expected to attend. It was no secret to those closest to him that the late duke wanted his life celebrated, not mourned.

She didn't understand why they couldn't simply ready for the ball at Bishop House, but both Lady Dinsmore and the new Duke of Bradburne's sister, Lady Eloise, had insisted Brynn make herself at home in one of the finer guest rooms. Lana had abided the instructions without comment, more than ready for the distraction of the ball. And more than happy to be far away from Gray.

For the last two days, her mind had been held hostage by

fear and fury. Her uncle's thug was on his way to Irina, but so was Gray's man, whose identity Lana knew little about. Apparently, he worked as security at a popular gaming hell for the demimonde. She would not care if he were a convicted criminal, so long as Gray trusted him to reach Irina before the Frenchman did.

But *Gray*. That arrogant man. He wanted her to leave Bishop House. Hand in her resignation! Lana knew he only meant to protect her, but couldn't he understand that once she was gone from Lady Dinsmore's staff, she would be a duck in open water?

Viktor would have come for her by now if he knew where she was. And yet he hadn't. All had been quiet for the last two days since the dignitary dinner. Too quiet, perhaps. But Lana felt safe at Bishop House. She had the protection of a powerful family of the peerage, though Langlevit would not return from his meeting with the cryptographer for perhaps a few days yet. Without him, she and Irina would have no way to prove their innocence against Viktor's and her uncle's claims.

Gray had cornered her multiple times, insisting she take her leave and flee to the hunting cabin he spoke of. She had refused again and again, not understanding how being alone in the middle of Derbyshire could possibly be safer than where she was now.

And then Gray had finally exploded with a reason. "If you won't go alone, I will go with you. I'll take you there myself and keep you safe, Lana. Upon my word, no one will harm you."

In that instant, she had pictured the two of them in a cabin in the country, huddled together, away from the world. Lana flushed now just thinking about the vision she'd had—she and Gray beneath the covers of an enormous bed, the only light that of a fire in the hearth. Lana, tucked close beside him, feeling safe and loved. And so clearly, and thoroughly, ravished.

What was it about this man that made her lose all good sense? Lana had no illusions of what would happen if she and Gray were in close proximity to each other in a deserted cabin. Her attraction to him turned her wits to gravy—she couldn't think when he looked at her, those eyes caressing every inch of her person. And when he kissed her, she forgot herself. No, she could not go to Derbyshire, and she definitely could not go there alone with him.

Lana's hands shook as she placed the last of the beautiful diamond-encrusted pins into Brynn's upswept hair. The four pins, each one a bird set in different wing positions, had been one gift of many from the new duke. His Grace had showered Brynn with all the requisite gifts, but both she and Lana were still the only ones to know they were part of a grand farce.

Brynn was distraught over it all, feeling she had trapped a duke into marriage—a duke who infuriated her to no end. Lana was not so convinced Brynn deplored her betrothed, Lord Archer Croft, but tonight was not the night to try to make her admit her true feelings. Not with the way Brynn's nerves seemed to be jumping. At least with the craze of the last week, Brynn had not noticed anything amiss with her lady's maid. For that, Lana was grateful.

Even now, Brynn did not notice Lana's shaking hands and pink cheeks from her earlier thoughts about Gray.

"Do you feel ill, my lady?" Lana asked.

Brynn fanned herself. "No. It's a little warm, that's all."

"Well, you look lovely with some color in your cheeks," Lana commented, the bland pronouncement falling hollow even to Lana.

Brynn stood up from the vanity, and Lana could barely feel more than appreciation for the layers of deep green satin and black lace overlay. Madame Despain had created a gorgeous gown, with a low, square-cut bodice, wide bell sleeves trimmed in black lace edging, and a tapered waist that displayed Brynn's trim figure. It was exquisite. And yet, Lana merely smiled the same way she would to a stranger passing on the street.

"I feel like such a fraud," Brynn said, her gloved fingers touching the necklace of diamonds she wore. They had belonged to the late Duchess of Bradburne. "As if I am not here at all."

Lana knew she should say something to encourage her mistress but remained caught on what Brynn had said. She felt like a fraud. Yes. Lana knew that feeling. She was lying to everyone she cared for. Gray had begged her to tell him the truth, to trust him enough to depend upon him, and yet her enormous deception would not allow it. He seemed to believe that the princesses were innocent, but if she told him she was one of them, what would he believe then? He'd only know that she had lied. He might think she had lied about everything else. Despite some of his mistakes, from what she'd come to know of Gray, he was a man who valued honor.

She doubted he would turn her over to Viktor, but he would despise her for deceiving him. Especially when he had told her the truth about Sofia. He'd laid bare his deepest secret, and she had not reciprocated. She had indulged in Gray's kisses, had soaked in the warmth of his passion, all from behind a mask while he had been open and honest.

If anyone was a fraud here, it was she.

"Well, I can see you, and you are lovely," Lana said to Brynn, her throat tight.

She spent the next few minutes reassuring Brynn that she could carry the night off without a hitch and then walked her down the corridor toward the grand staircase that led into the ballroom.

Lana handed her a jade and obsidian Venetian mask, as the engagement ball was a masquerade, and Brynn descended the steps. The entire ballroom had ground to a stop. Only the musicians continued to play their woodwind instruments as the duke's future wife presented herself. All eyes had turned to view her, but only one pair captured Lana's attention.

Gray stood like a stone column at the base of the Palladian stairs, his eyes drifting from his sister to Lana and then back again. He was angry, Lana knew. He didn't wish his sister to marry the duke. He believed she was falling into the shallow role of title hunter, but Lana couldn't tell him the truth of the matter. Yet another thing she was keeping from him. Only, this time, it wasn't her truth to tell.

Brynn joined her betrothed and her family on the ballroom floor, while Lana remained at the landing at the top of the stairs. She wore her usual uniform, a black drop of sobriety among the radiant pond of swirling and dancing colors below. No one looked up at her now that she stood by herself. Even Gray had disappeared into the crowd.

Lana turned from the ballroom and retreated from the landing. The rest of the lady's maids would be hovering near the retiring rooms on the ground floor, simply waiting for a guest who might require her services to mend a hem or replace a hairpin or stained glove. She should be waiting there as well, in case Brynn needed her. Having a duty, even one that put her among other chattering maids whom she had nothing in common with, was preferable to spending hours with her own morbid thoughts and worries.

She took the servants' stairwell, where the music from the ballroom was muted. However, the energy of the ball itself seemed to have permeated the air, and Lana felt the buzz of it as she was taking the steps to the ground floor. Her feet suddenly itched to dance the same way she would have done had she been home, attending one of the balls at Volkonsky Palace or another royal residence in St. Petersburg. She had so loved dancing. The graceful movements of arms and legs and feet, all working to keep the same measured beat of the music. Even the faster dances, like a reel or a country dance, had their charms. To be out of breath at the end of a dance was an indescribable happiness all its own.

Sometimes Lana wondered if she would ever know that kind of happiness again. If she'd ever feel like herself. Princess Svetlanka Volkonsky had become a memory. A shadow. She didn't regret taking the position as a maid, especially since Brynn had never treated her as one, but sometimes she felt that it eclipsed everything she once was. Her memories of her parents and her home, once vibrant, had lost color. Then again, if she'd remained in the role of a princess, she never would have met Gray or discovered what true passion felt like.

Her thoughts flicked to the carriage ride to Essex, and her face grew hot at the recollection. Gray had strummed her body like a virtuoso. No man had ever made her feel the way he did…no man had ever *touched* her as he had. Lana wasn't naive—she understood the difference between lust and love, but when it came to Gray, all lines became blurred. She'd already lost her will to him, and if she wasn't careful, she could lose her heart.

Lana sighed and opened the door that led into a hallway near the retiring rooms. A tall figure swept in front of her and ushered her back through the door, up the first few steps.

It took her eyes a moment to focus on the face staring down at her. Had she conjured him with her wanton thoughts?

"Lord Northridge," she whispered, glancing over her shoulder to be sure no other servant was on the steps. "What are you doing here?"

He had shut the door behind him, and Lana could instantly smell the sharp bitterness of whiskey. Oh, good heavens. He was foxed.

Foxed and dangerously attractive. Dressed in black

tailored formalwear, Lana couldn't help noticing that the sumptuously elegant raven jacket fit his broad shoulders to perfection. She didn't dare look down, but she knew his trousers would no doubt have the same superbly tailored fit. His cravat was slightly skewed, and Lana couldn't help herself—her fingers reached to straighten it. He let her, tensing only as her hands brushed his chest while she deftly rearranged the knot. "There," she said. "At least you're presentable now."

"Who gives a damn if I'm presentable?"

"Clearly, you don't," she replied, emboldened by his irascibility.

"Why must you be so stubborn?" he countered, inching forward to press her into the shadows of the staircase wall.

She huffed a breath, the handrail wedged into the backs of her hips. "I beg your pardon?"

His eyes narrowed. "And why is it that when you feel cornered, the words that fall from your lips could match those from the most highborn of ladies?"

"My mother insisted on a proper education."

"Yes, the modiste with the staff of nursemaids." He paused. "In Moscow. Or was it St. Petersburg?"

Lana tensed. A drunk Gray would be untempered by the voice of propriety that she'd seen rear to life within him from time to time, as if attempting to subdue his natural tendency toward mischief. He had a conscience, Lana knew, but that wild current inside of him flowed just as straight and strong.

"I don't know what you mean."

"Always evading," he murmured, his hand lifting to stroke her cheek. "Such a temptress. You drive a man to distraction."

"Lord Northridge," Lana whispered. His light touch ignited a scorching trail of fire that shot to her breasts and to the deep place between her thighs. She swallowed hard as his knuckles grazed her chin and slid down her neck to the stringent collar of her uniform. For once, she was glad of the high, scratchy neckline, even if her memories of the things he had done to her in the carriage made her tremble.

Lana grasped his wrist. "What are you thinking? Anyone could see us, and the servants here are not like at Bishop House. Please, you need to go back to the ball."

Gray twisted his hand to capture hers, holding it between them. "Why? To see Hawk parading my sister like she is nothing but an expensive prize? He seeks a fortune, and she a title. I never thought she could be so shallow."

Lana wanted to slap him for insulting Brynn. She cherished Gray and he her. "That's not true, and you know it."

"We're all bred to do our duty, aren't we? Born into it and bound to it." He closed his eyes, his body swaying slightly. From the look and smell of him, he was more than well into his cups. The odor of drink rose up, tainting his clean, spicy scent. The one that usually made her want to press her lips to his throat. Oh, this man. Why him? Why now?

"Gray," Lana said firmly, detaching her hand from his. "Let me fetch you some water. You need to sober up and support your sister. Her heart is aching because of whatever has happened between the two of you."

"No," he said, blinking as if coming out of trance. "I came here to tell you of my decision."

"Decision?"

"I'm coming forward to Lady Dinsmore with the truth."

Lana's stomach dropped, and she pressed back against the wall. *The truth*? He would betray her confidence? She felt the first thread pop, and after months of trying to keep everything so tightly sewn, Lana's world started to unravel. All the lies she'd told, the lurking fear she'd worked so hard to suppress, the worry for Irina's safety…all of it. "You can't."

"You've left me no choice," he said.

She tucked her fingers into her palms, her nails biting

into her skin. "Lady Dinsmore won't understand. She'll go to Zakorov, she'll tell him where I've been hiding—"

"No," Gray said, his unfocused eyes blinking rapidly as he gripped her shoulders. "Not that. I'd never tell her or anyone about your involvement with the missing princesses. I want to keep you safe from Zakorov. That is why I must do this."

Lana shook her head. "But you said you would tell her the truth."

"Yes." He angled his body closer now that he had his hands upon her again. "The truth of my attraction to you. That your position at Bishop House has become an inappropriate inconvenience." His eyes fell to her tightening expression at what the loss of her position could mean. "I would never leave you in dire straits, Lana. I would see you well cared for, you can count on me for that. A house, money, whatever you need. You would be safe."

An inappropriate inconvenience? Lana's fear turned into fury, and her rage made her see red. The desire to rip the cravat she'd just fixed from his neck and strangle him with it overtook her, but she kept her fingers tightly fisted at her sides. "Keep your promises! I never should have trusted you," she hissed.

She hated herself for being so weak. So foolish. She hated *him.*

"You've forced my hand, Lana. If you can't see that you'll be safer far from London—"

"This is not protecting me! You're throwing me to the wolves."

Gray released her shoulders, a muscle beginning to tick in his cheek. "You will be out from under Zakorov's shadow. That is the only thing that matters right now."

"No," Lana said through clenched teeth. "You're drunk. You don't know what you're saying. You're not thinking clearly."

He kept his hands at his sides, but Gray's direct stare stroked her just the same. He loomed over her, his focus sharpening. "I cannot stand by and do nothing. Not where you are concerned." His eyes smoldered with purpose as he closed the inches between them. "I only know that I will do whatever I must to keep you safe, even if it means forcing you to see reason."

He smothered Lana's gasp with his mouth. Tasting of whiskey and mint, his tongue drove in, his mouth possessing hers utterly as his hands took hold of her hips. Gray's thighs ground against hers, the hard thrust of him leaving her in no doubt of his desire. And Lord help her, the wicked, wanton part of her that he'd awakened wanted more of what he'd given her in the carriage. At the shameful thought, Lana's breasts, flattened against his chest, tingled as hot need pooled low in the crux of her. Helpless against the deliberate storm he was arousing, Lana moaned as he coaxed her tongue into his mouth. She gave it to him for one sweet, forbidden instant before gathering all the force she could muster and shoving him away.

Breathing hard, she glared daggers at him. Heavens, the man could seduce a saint—his gold hair was tousled, his eyes dark with passion, and his *mouth*. She dragged her greedy gaze away before she could throw herself back at him like a lusty barmaid.

"Stay away."

"You know you want me," he said, his arrogance and husky voice as effective as his lips had been.

Want. If that single word encompassed all the liquid heat running rampant through her, then of course she wanted him. But not at the expense of what he intended: for her position to be terminated. She steeled herself, remembering what was at stake. "The only thing I want, Lord Northridge, is for you to keep your distance."

"Lana." He leaned in purposefully, but she anticipated his movements and pushed past him, rushing up the stairs.

When there was a safe amount of space—at least a half dozen steps—between them, she turned, her voice cold. "If you take it upon yourself to tell Lady Dinsmore anything, I will be forced to betray *your* secret."

His eyes widened as he took her meaning. Lana would never do such a thing, but *Gray* didn't know that, and if her threat stopped him from exposing her, then so be it.

"And sober up before you embarrass yourself, Lord Northridge. No one likes a drunk."

· · ·

Gray stood on a balcony of Hadley Gardens. The lush landscape below, lit with small lamps and glass globes, did nothing to distract him. All it made him think about was dragging Lana into that shadowy arbor, tearing every inch of clothing from her sumptuous body, and doing all manner of indecent things with his hands and his mouth until she screamed his name. He shifted uncomfortably at the mental image, his body still half-aroused as he inhaled several gulps of cool, evening air. He could still taste her on his lips, mingling with the whiskey he'd tried to drown himself with.

She was a siren who would drive him to madness. To destruction.

Gray sighed, thinking of her parting threat. He didn't believe she would tell anyone about Sofia, but he couldn't take the risk. Lana was as fierce and determined as she was vulnerable, and she very well *could* retaliate if he followed through with his own threat.

Announcing to his mother that Brynn's lady's maid was in danger of his untoward attentions would have been humiliating, but he would have done it. At least he would not have been lying. The attraction between them was real and compulsory, even when she was furious, as she'd been in the stairwell.

She'd bewitched him.

"Graham, what are you doing out here?"

He composed himself before turning around to face his mother, who stared at him with thinly veiled consternation as she swept through the balcony doors. He'd found another glass of whiskey somewhere between the servants' stairwell and balcony, and, looking at it now, found it nearly empty.

"Jus' taking the air, mother."

"Lady Cordelia has been waiting patiently for you to ask her to dance, and I've taken it upon myself to traipse this entire residence to find you." Her disparaging gaze swept him from head to toe. "And here you are, shockingly in your cups. Come, make yourself look respectable."

He eyed her, squinting at her blurry face. "Shouldn't you be busy crowing to the other mamas about your daughter's splendid match?"

Her mouth tightened. "Don't be rude."

Gray bent to kiss her cheek and nearly lost his footing. *Damn*. He truly was bashed. "Apologies. I'll be in shortly, and I'll make it my sole purpose to find Lady Cordelia and sweep her right off her privileged feet."

Lady Dinsmore frowned. "What has gotten into you, *other* than too much drink?"

He knew too bloody well what—no, *who*—had gotten into him.

"Nothing." He took her arm with a gallant bow, but the effect was spoiled by an undignified burp. "Allow me to accompany you back inside."

Gray escorted his mother to the refreshment room, paying close attention to his every step and attempting not to stumble. As soon as they arrived, he quickly made his escape from the throngs of matchmaking mamas settling their avaricious gazes on him. He signaled to a nearby footman to bring him another glass of whiskey. Where had the other one gone? He couldn't recall setting it down anywhere.

He knew he'd promised to dance with Lady Cordelia, but in his current state, it would be a disaster. Lady Cordelia was far too well bred and far too poised to tempt him to stray from being a proper gentleman, no matter how intoxicated he was. She didn't incite his blood the way Lana did. No woman did. No woman ever would.

No. It was the safety of Lady Cordelia's toes he worried for. He drained the contents of his glass and decided to take his leave, to hell with the whispering that would follow such an early retreat.

He pushed through the crowd, intent on finding the ballroom's damnable exit, when the pointed rise of conversation stopped him. Something about someone fainting. He didn't know how, but he was certain it was Brynn. His sister had fainted. He'd known something had been amiss. She'd agreed to this farce out of fear, or something else. The bastard had coerced her into marriage. The thoughts were racing through his muddled brain too quickly to make sense, but he knew he had to find her.

Gray snagged the arm of a passing footman. "Have you seen Lady Briannon?"

"I don't know, my lord. Perhaps Heed can be of service." The footman nodded to a white-haired man standing off to the side in front of a pair of closed doors.

Gray's eyes narrowed as he strode toward the butler. The old man said something. His lips moved. His white-gloved hands lifted to stop Gray, but he plowed past him and shoved the doors open.

"Where is she?" he snapped, his eyes taking in the occupants of the room, including Hawk and Brynn, seated side by side upon a chaise. Both looked at him with surprise and vexation, which only fanned his ire.

They were not the only ones in the room.

His eyes fluttered to Lana as she appeared in his vision, barring his approach. She stared him down like an enraged governess. "She is upset enough, Lord Northridge."

"Get out of my way, Lana."

"I will not allow you to make her worse."

God's teeth, she provoked him beyond reason. "I am not here to endanger my sister," he said through a clenched jaw. "Now let me pass."

"You are drunk."

"And you forget your place."

Her eyes flashed her fury at him. "Do I?"

Brynn was the one to interrupt the escalating tension between them, requesting that Lana wait outside. After raking him with a glare he felt to his bones, she did as Brynn asked.

"Gray," Brynn began. "I know you're upset, but this is not the time nor the place."

"It is the perfect time," he seethed.

"You're foxed," she said. "His Grace and I—"

"His *Grace*," Gray hissed, his eyes sliding to the silent, imperious duke standing at his sister's side. Though they used to be friends as children, Gray could not fathom the aloof man as a match for his gentle-hearted sister, not if all the gossip about his coldness and ruthlessness were true. Hell, he had struck his own father in anger. What kind of husband would he be to Brynn? No, she deserved better.

As did Lana.

Gray's breath faltered, the latter half of the thought demolishing him.

At least Hawk would give Brynn a life of luxury. What could he offer Lana but ridicule and ostracization? A union between them would not be tolerated by society, and though she was a maid, she deserved so much more. He'd wanted to protect her, but it'd only been his own whims he'd been serving. He'd wished to be the hero…her savior, but it had only been to satisfy his own vanity and the way he wanted Lana to see him. Not to truly help her without any thought for recompense.

He was contemptible.

His self-disgust found an easy target in Hawk, whose cool, unflappable expression ignited the furor in his own wretched heart.

Gray sneered at him. "The man has looked down his nose at all of us for years, preferring to spend his time in a stable than in his own house. It was a surprise to everyone at large that his father claimed him out of all his other bastards."

"That is enough!" Brynn gasped, a shocked look on her face.

"I won't give you the thrashing you deserve," Hawk replied in a low, arrogant tone that only served to fuel Gray's rage. "If only out of respect for your sister, soon to be my wife. I will offer you the chance to leave of your own free will."

"Your wife," Gray repeated, rocking unsteadily as the bright sweep of the liquor coursed through him. "What did you do to get her to agree to your proposal? She would never marry you. Did you compromise her honor? Did you?"

"Gray! Stop this. He did no such thing." Brynn flushed to the roots of her hairline, and Gray's fury erupted. He could see that she was lying. That lying miscreant had seduced his innocent sister.

The same way I've seduced her innocent maid.

He swayed on his feet with the sudden awareness. He'd seduced Lana. She may have kissed him in return, opening herself to him and allowing her own passion to burn high, but he'd still abused his position of authority the same way Hawk and the late duke both had. Gray recoiled.

"Name your second, you bastard," he growled, his loathing for Hawk and for himself blurring into one monstrous thing.

He threw his arm out in a wild swing that missed his target by a wide margin. Hawk caught him by the collar of his jacket and dragged him out to the balcony.

"Go home," Hawk said. "You're drunk, and you're making a scene."

"I demand satisfaction," Gray shouted. "Do you hear me, Hawk? At the point of a pistol. You forced my sister into this. She is obviously terrified of you. So terrified that she nearly fainted in your arms at the thought of sealing this betrothal. Don't you think she knows that you were questioned for the late duke's murder? Everyone knows you are no gentleman."

The words, they wouldn't stop. They came to his tongue and jumped, wanting only to injure. *You are no gentleman.* No, Hawk wasn't. Neither was Gray. But at least Hawk didn't try to hide what he was.

"Enough," the duke warned, a muscle going wild in his jaw. "Or you will have exactly what you want. I assure you I am an excellent shot, and where will that leave your beloved sister? Without a brother?"

"Without a bastard of a husband," he replied, but he felt the fire leaving him. He looked to the glass-paned doors, catching sight of Brynn's anguished face. Regret surged through him. It was her engagement ball, and here he was, a drunken idiot, ruining everything. His mind clouded as the whiskey loosened the strength of his legs. He slumped to the ground, leaning against the railings.

"I assure you my parentage is as unsullied as yours," Hawk said. "You may dislike me, but I am still marrying your sister. And unless you are truly willing to die to stop this wedding, I suggest you return to Bishop House and sleep it off. This is what she wants. What we both want."

"You will only hurt her." Gray hiccuped quietly and saw

Lana's figure moving within the room with Brynn. "Everyone knows of your proclivities—and the type of women you favor."

The types of women Gray himself used to favor.

"It would break her, and she doesn't deserve that," Gray said, feeling the bluster leave his body. "She deserves a chance to be happy."

That was all he'd ever wanted. Brynn's happiness. And Lana's. The moments Lana had seemed happy were so limited. When she'd been speaking about her sister. When she'd been whispering tales to Sofia. Gray wanted her safety, yes, but he also wanted to see her smile more.

"You are right. She does," Hawk said. The silence stretched between them as Gray studied the stringent man standing above him—the boy who had once been his childhood friend. Brynn's, too. "I'll do everything in my power to ensure it," Hawk said after a long moment.

Gray nodded, sensing something like sincerity in the duke's tone. He might not love Brynn, but he would make sure she was taken care of, that much he knew. "Brynn's heart is special. I want your word as a gentleman that you promise to do right by her."

"You have it."

Gray accepted the hand that Hawk reached down to him. He nodded again, though mostly to himself. "Tell her I'm sorry," he murmured. "I'll take my leave now, Your Grace."

Passing unseen through the side gardens, Gray hailed a hackney. He'd leave the carriage for his parents and Brynn, not trusting he wouldn't be sick all over the floor as it rocked over the roads back to Bishop House. His head was spinning from the effects of all the whiskey when a voice penetrated his foggy senses. His eyes focused on a woman striding toward him, a cloak and hat in hand. *Lana*. She still looked furious, but something like compassion shone in her eyes.

"What are you doing out here?" he asked.

"Lady Briannon insisted that I see you safely home."

He frowned, feeling chagrined. "I do not require a chaperone."

"It is my lady's wish."

She signaled to someone behind her, and his family coach ambled into view with Colton at the helm. Gray swayed, nearly tripping at the curb and crashing headfirst into the waiting carriage, when Lana's firm grip steadied him. Her lips twitched as she helped him into the conveyance. "Don't worry. I promise your virtue will be safe, Lord Northridge."

He stared at her as she arranged herself primly in the seat across from him. "Ah, but will yours?" From the rosy color tinting her cheeks, he knew she was recalling the last carriage ride they had shared. "I give you my word that I will stay in this seat," he said, crooking an eyebrow. "Unless, of course, you wish to join me."

"You are stewed, Lord Northridge," she whispered.

"And you are beautiful." He grinned. "Too beautiful for your own good. And mine."

Lana blushed, lowering her eyes. "I am still angry with you."

He blinked against the fog encroaching on his brain and leaned back into the velvet squabs. "Yes, well, it seems I have no control when it comes to you. I am completely at your mercy. And I'm truly sorry I angered you. Whiskey, it seems, is good for dulling one's wits, drowning one's misery, and not much else."

"Why would you consider saying such a thing to Lady Dinsmore?"

"I only want you…to be safe."

"I am safe here."

He closed his eyes, his voice turning to a harsh whisper. "If anything were to happen to you, I would not be able to—"

He stopped himself. Just as he'd felt when he'd received that letter from Sir Cooper, stating Sofia was ill, a wild beating of panic took flight in his neck and chest at the thought of Lana falling prey to Zakorov.

"To what, Gray?" she prodded.

"Live with myself. Live at all."

The question was soft, as if coming from a great distance away. "But…why?"

"Sweet Lana." His response was a slurred, barely audible whisper. Gray inhaled deeply, the smell of fresh wildflowers filling his nostrils. He'd never known a scent to stir his blood so deeply. His eyes felt so heavy, the rocking of the carriage lulling him into a quiet stupor. The sounds around him faded into silence as he gave in to the fog. But first, he had to finish his one thought. "Surely you must know by now."

Chapter Eighteen

Lana pinned a last curl into submission and stood back from Brynn, inspecting her in the mirror. "You do not look ready to receive visitors," she said with a shake of her head. Brynn had insisted on a plain dress and ordered Lana not to fuss over her hair. A simple bun would do.

"It's not yet nine in the morning. No one will be out and about at this hour to pay a visit anyhow," she replied. Lana knew she was right. The engagement ball had run into the small hours of morning, with dawn just about to peel back the night when Lord and Lady Dinsmore and Brynn had returned to Bishop House.

By that time, Gray had been unconscious in his bed, placed there by both Braxton and Harrison. They had dragged Gray's inebriated body up the stairs from the foyer moments after Lana and Colton had seen him inside the house.

Surely you must know by now.

They were the last words he'd said in the carriage before passing out, and they had haunted Lana the rest of the night. They had ricocheted around her mind when she'd woken from a light sleep to help undress Brynn and get her settled into bed at three in the morning. They had echoed when she'd then roused herself at five to start the day's duties. And even now, they taunted her as Brynn dismissed her with a grateful smile.

Surely you must know.

Know why he could not live with himself if anything were to happen to her? Why he felt a responsibility to protect her? Gray was attracted to her, yes. He'd insisted time and again that he could not control his longing for her, and the times they had been intimate he had clearly been just as affected as she had been. But he couldn't feel more for her than lust and some misplaced responsibility for her because of it.

Could he?

Lana took her leave from Brynn's rooms and quickly hurried to the kitchens. She sat at the table with a few other maids but couldn't eat. Her stomach roiled with misgivings, and with the lingering worry that Viktor or her uncle would appear at Bishop House and drag her away at any moment. Their Frenchman would be arriving in Cumbria any time now, as would Gray's man. She hated not knowing what was happening. And where was Langlevit? Shouldn't he have been back from his meeting by now?

Avoiding Mrs. Frommer's evil-eyed stare, Lana's hands shook as she excused herself and stepped out the back door of the kitchens into the stable yard. What if something had happened to the earl? Her uncle or Viktor…what if they had led him into a trap? They knew where Irina was. They must have known Langlevit was involved somehow. Why hadn't she thought of this before? She'd been so wrapped up in Gray and his threats to see her released from service that she hadn't stopped to consider it.

A horse and rider trotted into the stable yard, stealing her attention. Gray turned his horse into the mews and dismounted, dismissing Percival with a shake of his head. He wore no hat, and his hair was a tousled blond mass, his cheeks flushed as he strode into the mews to care for his own mount. Lana's feet moved of their own accord, taking her across the stable yard and into the mews before she knew exactly what she was going to say to him. This was what he did to her. Gray stole all intellect and rationality from her mind and replaced it with the single need to be near him.

"Lady Lana," Percival said, popping out of a stall and startling her. "Are you and James going for a ride again?"

She shook her head and glanced down the row of stalls. Pharaoh's door was open, and she could hear Gray tending to him.

"No, that's better done at Ferndale, I imagine. I have a message for Lord Northridge," she lied. "From Lady Briannon."

The stable boy only nodded and returned to his work.

She entered Pharaoh's stall, stopping within the entrance and watching as Gray removed the saddle and hung it on its hook. He kept his back to her.

"I owe you an apology," he said, hanging on to the leather saddle a moment longer than necessary. He then returned to his mount's side, his eyes on his task and not Lana. His face was pale, his eyes dark-rimmed. He certainly looked as if he still felt ill from the night before.

"You've already given me one," Lana said.

"I have?" he asked, starting to glance over at her. He changed his mind at the last moment and jerked his eyes back toward relieving Pharaoh of his traces.

"In the carriage," she explained.

"I don't remember much of the ride."

Did that mean he didn't recall saying he couldn't live with himself if anything happened to her? That by now, she should know why?

"You owe Lady Briannon an apology also, I believe."

He nodded, kneading his eyes after he hung the bit and traces next.

"She knows you were only trying to protect her," Lana added, taking a few steps farther into the stall. From the spotless look of things, she gathered that Pharaoh lived well. "But, my lord, you cannot protect people from their own decisions."

He dropped his hand and faced her, with a brooding and salty arch of his brow. "We are no longer discussing Brynn, are we?"

Lana shook her head and bit the inside of her cheek to keep from grinning. He looked so chagrined. So boyish, standing there, the ankles of his riding breeches splattered with mud from what she imagined had been a vigorous ride through Hyde Park.

He let out a long sigh and started to rub Pharaoh down. He worked thoroughly, his attention and care evident in the gentle caresses of his left hand as his right brushed the horse's fine coat.

"I told my man, Hurstley, to send word the moment he arrived in Cumbria and had presented himself to the countess," he said, his voice strained from his work. "Meanwhile, I put another man on Zakorov."

Lana straightened her shoulders, her lips parting in shock. "You did?"

He hadn't told her this before.

Gray nodded, switching to Pharaoh's other flank and meeting her gaze briefly. "You thought I would not keep eyes on him?"

She should have thought of it herself.

"What has he been doing?" she asked, fearful she was about to hear that he had been loitering around Bishop House or getting close to Lord Dinsmore.

Gray lowered the brush. "I met with my man this morning. Zakorov has disappeared. He quit his rooms yesterday and hired a carriage to take him from London."

Her pulse hammered out a warning. "Where did the carriage go?"

Gray shook his head. "The last my man saw he was headed southeast."

Lana braced a hand against the wall, her heart's pounding rhythm high in her throat. At least he had not been going north. But she should have asked Langlevit for specifics on where he was planning to meet the man who might cipher the letters. As it stood, all she knew was that they were meeting outside of London.

"What if he's left to find Lord Langlevit?" she asked, the edge of panic making her breathless. "Zakorov must know he's involved. He could be in danger."

"Langlevit is no stranger to that. He can take care of himself," Gray replied, setting down the brush upon a shelf and walking toward Lana. "And let's not forget that Count Volkonsky has not been seen in public at all. There are no rumors supporting his presence here, just your account from when you saw him in Zakorov's rooms. Which means he's slinking around town like a snake."

Lana pushed off the wall. "Or he is gone as well."

Though it had not sounded as if her uncle had intended to go up to Langlevit's estate with the Frenchman. Where else would he have possibly gone?

"I'm not inclined to let our guard down," Gray said.

She rubbed at her temple, which had started to throb. "Then what do we do? I'm going mad with worry over Ir—" Lana bit her tongue before she let Irina's name slip. That was the princess's name, and Gray knew it, just as he knew Svetlanka was the other princess. She was surprised he had not yet made the connection between Svetlanka and Lana, and lived on the edge of knowing he could, at any moment, unravel her web of lies.

"Over irrational things," she finished, unable to look him in the eye.

Gray swept his feet through a pile of straw and came closer, lowering his voice. "What do *we* do? I take it then you are finally accepting my help?"

She parted her lips and lifted her chin, prepared to bite back with a retort that she could take care of herself well enough, thank you. But the way he'd pinned his lower lip with his teeth in an amused grin stopped her. He was only needling her. Only wanting to make her smile.

Gray took her elbow. The simple touch softened her shoulders and the muscles along her back, aching from sitting up all night in bed, sleepless.

"There is little we can do until Langlevit returns," he answered. "Or until we hear from Hurstley."

Waiting. Always waiting. Sometimes it felt to Lana that she would never retrieve her old life. That she would forever be stuck hiding, kept apart from Irina and her home in St. Petersburg. That Viktor and her uncle would emerge triumphant.

"So tell me," Gray went on, his fingertips traveling from her elbow up the back of her arm. "What do you like to do for fun?"

Lana startled, thrown by the change of subject. "What?"

"What do you like to do for fun?" he repeated slowly.

"I…" She paused. For fun. How long had it been since she'd thought about having fun? "I don't know. I'm…not used to thinking about diversions."

That, at least, was a truthful statement, both for Lana the lady's maid and Lana the princess in hiding. This was not, as it turned out, an acceptable answer.

"Say you were used to it," Gray replied. "Say you had all

the time between sunrise and sunset to do as you pleased. What would you most like to do?" He grinned. "Besides lock picking and horse jumping."

Her cheeks turned the fiery tones of the sunset. "James told you?"

"Don't worry, your secrets are always safe with me. So what else do you enjoy? What would you choose to do if given the chance?"

She huffed and shook her head, immediately thinking about chores and duties and tasks she performed for Brynn. Airing out and selecting fashionable clothes, working out stains, running errands on her mistress's behalf, mending hems and cuffs, learning new hairstyles for Brynn to wear so she could be *au courant* because Lord knew she did not give a whit for it. Her hours were filled from sunup to sundown and—

Lana stilled her head.

And she was exhausted. She'd known exhaustion as a princess, but that had been different. That had been due to late homecomings after a soiree or hours of shopping. How she longed for that sort of exhaustion again.

She shrugged a shoulder, suddenly feeling timid. "I suppose I would like to dance."

Gray dragged his fingers back down her arm, raising the small hairs on her nape. "I think I can arrange that—if you're not put off by the lack of musical accompaniment or having me as a partner."

"You don't mean here? Now?" She turned, half expecting Percival to be standing there, listening.

Gray slid his fingers along her wrist and pressed his hand into hers. "Yes, here. Yes, now. Though…" He went to the stall door, pulling her alongside him. He listened for what Lana imagined to be a sign that Percival was close by. All she could hear was the thrum of her pulse in her neck. She hadn't danced in ages. And there was no music. How could one dance without music?

"Come," he said, and before she could protest, they were darting across the center of the mews, toward an open stall door directly across. Gray winged her inside, and she came to a halt, the urge to giggle stuck in her throat. The floor was clean, the trough empty. No straw or grooming implements. There was nothing but open space.

Gray closed the stall door, the hinges well-oiled and silent, and he turned to her. And bowed.

He swept his arm out to his side, as if he was greeting a queen. *Or a princess*, she thought. Innumerable men had bowed to her in the past. It had been required of them. Demanded. But this man...he bowed now because he wished to. He wanted to make her smile. When he straightened his back, her grin was already in place. She covered her cheeks with her palms and laughed quietly.

Gray extended his hand to her. "Do you care to dance, Lady Lana?"

Lady Lana. It was what James and Percy called her, though she couldn't fathom why. Perhaps it was her accent. Perhaps they thought she sounded regal because of it. When they called her Lady Lana, it felt like an adorable pet name she chose to endure. But Gray did not sound teasing when he said it. He was as somber and polite as the dance floor at any London ball required.

Lana's legs trembled as she curtsied in answer and then slipped her fingers into his waiting hand. He'd removed his riding gloves before rubbing down Pharaoh. His skin was warm and firm, calloused by the reins and what she knew now was a tendency to care for his own mount.

"What music are we pretending is playing?" she whispered.

He pulled her to him, settling his hand on the small of her

back, their joined hands straight out at their sides. The front of her dress brushed against his riding kit. Her breath caught.

"The waltz?"

She exhaled. Of course he would choose the waltz. It was the only dance that would bring their bodies into such close contact.

He peered down at her, not yet having moved his feet. "You know it?"

"Yes, of course," she answered, hasty to add, "Doesn't everyone here?"

Gray began to move, taking the lead and sliding his feet to the side and back. Lana's feet stumbled, but as they started to twirl through the open barn stall, they remembered what to do and how to move.

It was awkward at first, what with no music to keep in time to, and being alone in the stall without a dance floor filled with other couples. Lana closed her eyes and let Gray lead her, feeling her light steps upon the barn floor, springing and gliding. She fell into the pattern of their steps, the ever-shifting box their feet were tracing out. Lana felt the rhythmic sway of her hips as she moved backward and forward and side to side, and it wasn't long before the euphoria of the dance, the predictability of it, started to consume her.

There was no music, but she could still hear the distant strings in her memories. There were no other dancers, but she could hear their chatter, the roar of conversation and laughter, the tinkling of glass and silver. Lana leaned her head back and turned her face upward, toward memories of lit chandeliers, swirling round and round until she was dizzy with laughter.

Her feet ground to a stop, but Lana's body still tried to move. She stumbled, and Gray broke their waltz positioning and caught her by the shoulders. He stared down at her, a strange slant to his eyebrows.

"Where did you learn to dance like that?" he whispered.

Lana couldn't think of an excuse right then. Her body was still humming from the movement, her cheeks still aching from the grin she must have been wearing.

Gray shook his head, as if to clear it. "You amaze me, Lana."

He kissed her smile, his teeth raking along her lower lip and tugging it. The heady sensation of falling endlessly, like a leaf spiraling down from the highest branches of a tree, had cleared her mind and drowned her worry. All she wanted to do was kiss Gray back.

So she mimicked him and took his lower lip between her teeth. After a gentle nip and a flick of her tongue, Gray moaned something incomprehensible. He liked that, Lana determined, and so she licked his lips again, her tongue running along each one before delving past and inside. He captured her mouth, and his tongue teased hers. Like in the waltz, he took the lead, driving her feet back until her heels struck something. A wall? Her eyes were partly open, but all she could see, all she wanted to see, was Gray.

His hands cupped her backside and lifted, taking her feet from the floor and settling her atop something solid and wooden. A bench of some kind. She only knew, only cared, that Gray then positioned himself squarely between her legs. Her skirts only allowed so much range of motion, and so Gray batted the front of her skirt up until her stockinged knees brushed against his outer thighs. The soft wool of his riding breeches gave her a jolt of unexpected pleasure, and she couldn't dream of protesting. Her lashes fluttered, and she took a quick glance at the stall door. Still shut. Lana wished there was a bolt to throw as well.

"You're tensing," Gray whispered against her lips, hitching her chin higher. "I'm being careful, Lana. Trust me."

She did trust him. And she didn't want this moment to end, precarious as their hiding spot was. Lana nodded, and

Gray kissed her again. He kept his thumb hooked under her chin, and the new angle allowed him to stroke his tongue deeper into her mouth.

Every plunge and retreat of his tongue started to feel less and less like a kiss and more like…a promise. Like an allusion to what Gray wanted to happen between them. The hardened bulge of his arousal pressing into the center of her cotton drawers didn't shock or frighten her as it had when she had been sitting upon it on the carriage ride to Essex. With the jounce of the carriage and her position on his lap, her backside had been pressing and grinding against it. She'd felt it swelling beneath her then, and now as well. Though this time, it felt—different. As she met every thrust of Gray's tongue she felt it jut and withdraw as well.

Lana whimpered, his assault on her mouth as exquisite as it was overwhelming. She didn't want him to stop, and yet she couldn't breathe, she couldn't think. There was only his lips and tongue, his powerful hold on her neck to maintain the angle needed to make love to her mouth—and then the hardness between her legs, every thrust more frantic than the last. More overt. One of her palms slipped off the wooden bench.

She didn't think.

She only reached.

Lana touched his erection through his trousers, sucking in a shocked breath at her own boldness.

Gray moaned into her mouth before breaking the kiss. His expression was dark and tight, a pinch of what looked like pain between his brows. Heat flooded her cheeks, and she started to release him, certain she'd done something wrong. But he stilled her hand.

"Don't," he whispered, that tormented expression still ruling his face. "Don't stop. God, Lana."

And with his hand still clamped over hers, he guided her

hand down, along his stiffened length. His riding breeches were a snug fit, and while they were looser near the fall, movement was still restricted. He hissed and swore an oath under his breath as she stroked him again, her blush riding high on her cheeks, especially when he would not look away from her. He held her stare without shame, as if relishing the intimacy between them.

"Lana," he breathed. And then his clamped hand turned to steel, arresting the next stroke. "Enough."

She jerked back her hand, releasing him, and watched in confusion as he hunched forward, as if he'd just taken a fist to the gut. Gray turned himself slightly away and stepped out from between Lana's tossed up skirts.

She gasped at the sight of her bared drawers and shoved her skirts down. And then, taking stock of her surroundings once more, she saw that she sat upon a wooden saddle horse.

Lana leaped down, her heart racing, her body hot and pulsing.

"I'm sorry," she said, her voice tremulous. "I shouldn't have—"

Gray spun toward her so fast she nearly toppled back onto the saddle horse. He pulled her to him, but he didn't kiss her. He shook his head, his breathing coming fast. "You did nothing—*nothing*—to apologize for. My God, Lana, you have no idea how incredible you are. How incredible that felt."

She shook her head. "It seemed like I...like I hurt you."

He laughed, his chest rumbling as he tried to keep it soft. "You did the absolute opposite. I think you brought me back to life."

She went quiet at those words. They were beautiful. They were also terrifying. What had she really done to him? If she hadn't hurt him, then she must have given him pleasure. The same soul-splintering pleasure he'd given her in the carriage? Her breath caught at the realization, something responsive tingling deep within her. She still felt hot and full in the space between her hips.

Her eyes skipped down to where he'd been swollen just a minute before. A darker spot on the fall of his charcoal gray trousers caught her attention before he nudged her chin up with his thumb.

"That's rather embarrassing," he said, and he did look slightly shamefaced. Though he couldn't stop his grin. Understanding hit Lana, and she widened her eyes. Oh. *Oh.*

A crash from out in the stable yard broke Gray's hold on her chin. He pulled away, and Lana quickly adjusted her skirts. She'd been away far too long. Brynn could be looking for her.

Voices rose from the courtyard next. It sounded like something had broken, and she could hear Percival rejecting the blame for it.

"I'll go out the front doors," Gray said, leading her to the stall door. "You should go through the back."

She nodded, nervous she'd be spotted. Worried about the potential rumors it could stir.

But then...not rumors. Anything the servants gossiped about would be the truth. She was carrying on an affair with Lord Northridge. Meeting for trysts in barn stalls and carriages and dimly lit stairwells. Good Lord, she was well on her way to ruination.

As she watched him straighten his jacket and rake his fingers through his hair before walking back through the mews, Lana could not help the secret smile that graced her lips. She could not regret it. For this single moment, she would allow herself one forbidden luxury.

Chapter Nineteen

Gray handed his cloak and hat to the attendant at White's. His eyes roved past the lavishly appointed foyer of the gentleman's club—a fair step away from his earlier outing at The Cock and the Crown gaming hell where he'd met with Croyden, a French hazard dealer and a piece of hired muscle and eyes when he was paid well. Gray had filled that requirement handsomely enough for Croyden to follow Zakorov, and now he'd secured Croyden for a second task: to locate the missing Earl of Langlevit.

"Good evening, Lord Northridge," a bespectacled man said, bowing low. "A pleasure to see you again so soon."

"Mr. Simmons," he said with a shameful grin. He nodded to the factotum as he made his way into the crowded establishment. "Too soon, it seems."

"Your usual table, my lord?"

Gray shook his head. "No, thank you, Simmons. I found the man I've come to see."

He strode to the back of the club, where a group of men sat around a felted royal blue table, a staggering pile of chips at its center. From his vantage point, he could see the Earl of Thorndale, the Marquess of Bates, and the Duke of Bassford. The other two had their backs to him. They all wore identical looks of concentration as they frowned at their cards, with the exception of one man. Hawk. His sister's betrothed. The ill-fated engagement ball seemed like weeks ago, though it had only been yesterday.

Gray sighed and pushed through the crowds of dandies standing between the tables. He'd come to White's to apologize, especially after he'd learned that the new duke had paid a visit to Bishop House earlier that morning when he'd been in the mews.

With Lana.

His blood stirred at the mere thought of her. He hadn't expected dancing in a horse stall without music to be enjoyable, but once again, something involving Lana had surprised him. She'd waltzed with effortless ease, much as she seemed to do everything else, but what had happened next had been as much of a shock to her as it'd been to him.

Gray considered himself an experienced man, but his lack of sexual release had obviously taken its toll on him. He'd embarrassed himself like an unschooled buck, the innocent stroking of her fingers along his erection sending him hurtling over the edge like a runaway horse. She hadn't held back or been frightened of him. No, she'd been the one to reach forward. Her open passion had been gratifying and arousing. The memory of Lana's natural sensuality and naive inexperience made his body tighten with instant lust.

Gray composed himself roughly and focused on the task at hand. His trousers were fitted enough as they were. As he walked closer to the table, he recognized the high-pitched tones of his friend Monti. And the man at his side, with austere posture and black, glossed-back hair, was none other than Zakorov. The man turned to say something to the

Italian ambassador, throwing his profile into clear view. Gray clenched his jaw and slowed his pace.

Croyden had reported that he'd left London earlier that morning, heading southeast. Gray trusted his man, which meant Zakorov had obviously returned. And that he had not gone far from London. But for what purpose? Did this have anything to do with Langlevit?

With the same sense of unease that had been intensifying all day, Gray suspected the two were connected. Lana had said that Langlevit had gone out of London to meet with someone. It had been days, and she had had no word from him. Gray's frowned deepened. He and Langlevit were acquaintances, but Lana's relationship with the earl was clearly something more. She'd depended upon him for months, and he had gone to great lengths to protect her. A strange beast stirred to life inside his stomach right then. Appreciation and jealousy in equal measures made a confused monster. Langlevit was a good man, and for Lana's sake, Gray wanted to get to the bottom of where he was. He hoped Croyden proved as useful as he had while tailing Zakorov.

Thorndale looked up from his cards and grinned as Gray approached the table. "Speaking of, here is the lady's brother himself," he said loudly. "Northridge, wonderful to see you, old chap." Thorn indicated the last open seat at the table. "I see you are back for another sound whipping." He grinned as Gray found himself the focus of everyone sitting there, including Zakorov. Thorn was having far too much fun at Gray's expense to notice the grim set of his jaw, or the glint of interest in the Russian's expression.

"Northridge made the mistake of coming here before your engagement ball last night," he went on. "I doubt he will remember much of it, other than leaving with sadly empty pockets."

Gray had known he was there last night at some point

before the ball, but he could recall little of it. His eyes met Archer's, and he inclined his head. He'd intended to apologize, but this was too public a place to discuss what was now a family matter.

His idiocy had led to some overzealous reporter publishing a piece in the *Times* about the nature of Hawk's and Brynn's relationship that had been suggestive and incendiary. Apparently, he had overheard the entire argument out on the terrace. Gray regretted having so much drink. He'd acted foolishly and irresponsibly. And worse, he'd hurt Brynn in the process. He'd apologized to her first thing that morning before leaving to ride his frustrations out with Pharaoh, but he feared it would take more to mend things between them.

"Thank you for the offer," he said after a moment, careful not to meet Zakorov's direct stare. "But I think I'll favor the dice tables tonight."

With a nod to Thorn and the others, he walked into the adjoining room. After his father's dinner, Gray had counted himself lucky that Zakorov had not returned with a request to speak to Lord Dinsmore's Russian maid. He hoped the man wouldn't dredge up the notion now that he'd set eyes on Gray, and Gray was determined to avoid any sort of conversation as well.

He passed the time on a few rounds of hazard, his attention drifting toward the cards room time and again. Zakorov had not yet left his seat, but on his next glance, Gray saw another one of the players had.

"Northridge," a loud voice said as Lord Marcus Bainley, son of the aging and wealthy Marquess of Bates, clapped him on the back. "Didn't you suffer enough losses last evening? I heard you got well and truly fleeced."

"I am aware you heard, Bainley, considering you were seated at Thorndale's table when he said as much," Gray replied, keeping his tone bored. He stared at the man, taking in the ostentatious jade green jacket, matching pantaloons, and his needling grin. Bainley was tolerated by many because of the influence of his mother, the Marchioness of Bates, his considerable fortune, and the title he would inherit. Soon, it would seem, if the murmurings of the marquess's failing health were true. Unfortunately, Gray was not in any mood to tolerate the fop's irritating tendencies.

Nodding to the factotum, he collected his winnings. Unlike the night past, he'd accumulated a sizable pile in the short time he'd been at the hazard table. Not that any of it could help solve his current problems.

"Wise decision, though it disappoints my pockets to see you leaving us so soon," Bainley said. Gray wanted to smash the sly grin off his pompous face.

In any other circumstance he would stay just to teach Bainley a lesson, but he shrugged lazily instead. "While I would love to recoup my losses at your expense, sadly, I do have a previous engagement."

Ignoring Bainley's insulted look, he turned to leave. His eyes went to Thorn's table, and a spike of alarm pounded through his veins. The dour-faced Russian was no longer seated there. He wasn't at any table in sight. Gray walked quickly through the room, worrying that the man had slipped away to visit Bishop House while Gray was preoccupied. Lana would be summoned. She'd have no one there to protect her.

He swore under his breath, turned the corner for the coat check—and crashed into a man coming from the other side.

"Ah. Lord Northridge," Zakorov said in his thick accent, his sleek eyebrows rising.

Gray's alarm tempered, and he attempted to compose himself. "Lord Zakorov." At least the odious man wasn't trying to weasel his way into Gray's home at the moment. He nodded in parting. "If you'll excuse me."

Zakorov held up his hand. "A moment of your time, if I

may."

Damn.

"Both Lord Dinsmore and yourself have mentioned a Russian maid in your employ."

Yes. And Gray would kick his own arse for it if that could have been physically possible.

"What of her? She is a servant. Hardly worth discussing," he said, the arrogant lie leaving a sour taste on the back of his tongue. *She is worth everything.*

"Perhaps. But it seems that my sources have confirmed that she spent some time in St. Petersburg. I wish to speak to her."

His *sources*? What bloody sources? Was there someone in Bishop House feeding Zakorov information? Another servant perhaps. And if that was the case, the servant may have even delivered the rumor that Lord Northridge and the Russian maid were involved. The blood in Gray's veins turned to ice. Not because of the gossip. He simply did not want the man anywhere near Lana. "Your sources are mistaken. My sister tells me she is from Moscow."

The baron inclined his head. "Perhaps."

"If you'll excuse me," Gray said, stepping around Zakorov's short, rangy figure. "I have an appointment elsewhere."

Zakorov bowed. "Of course."

Gray didn't waste any time returning to Bishop House. He wanted to find Lana and make sure she was safe. If Zakorov's source was not another staff member, perhaps there was someone skulking about the house, watching her from afar. It made him think of this Count Volkonsky fellow Lana spoke of. The princesses' uncle. Croyden hadn't been able to locate Volkonsky, so he was either hiding well or no longer in London. Zakorov's short jaunt outside of London didn't bode well either. Gray supposed he would have to wait and see.

However, two more days passed without any word from Langlevit or Croyden. It worried him, though, he was more concerned for Lana, who seemed to be losing hope by the day.

"My lord," Braxton said, meeting him at the door to Bishop House and handing him a note. "This arrived for you."

Gray frowned and opened the letter, his mind remaining stuck on reassuring Lana. The handwriting diverted his attention though. The letter was from the Coopers.

His pulse beat out an uneven flash of panic, until he'd finished reading the first two sentences to see that Sofia wasn't ill. The Coopers were merely at their home in Kentish Town just north of London and had invited him to visit with Sofia. His heart lightened at the prospect of seeing his daughter again so soon but then grew tight as he thought of Lana. He did not want to leave her alone, not with the threat of Zakorov and the count. But she already knew Sofia. Perhaps he could convince her to accompany him.

"Thank you, Braxton. Please ready my curricle."

He took the stairs to his sister's chamber two at a time, only to find it empty. He frowned. Perhaps they were downstairs. He should have asked Braxton instead of racing up here like an impatient fool. A noise caught his attention as Lana moved into view from the side of the armoire near the windows to sit on the window bench. Out of her customary uniform, she wore a simple muslin dress, but the pale lilac color suited her to perfection. Tendrils of hair spilled from the pins holding them in place. His frown grew as Gray noticed the slim book in her hands. He squinted at the cover. French poetry. She was reading aloud, her lips moving as she spoke the words flawlessly.

"You speak French?"

Startled, she looked up at him, the book slamming closed. A flush tinted her cheeks. "As I told you, my mother insisted on a proper education. May I assist you with something, Lord Northridge?"

Gray cleared his throat, the welcome sight of her making his chest ache. She looked beautiful. And tired, despite the becoming blush on her face. He wished there was more he could do to put her at ease. Perhaps an outing would serve a dual purpose.

He looked around. "Where is Brynn?"

"She is out for the afternoon, my lord."

Perfect. "The Coopers are in town with Sofia and have extended an invitation to visit. Would you consider accompanying me? If you are not busy, of course."

"I am not." She stared at him, something oddly like relief appearing for a brief moment before it disappeared. "I would be delighted. It would be lovely to see Sofia again. Lady Briannon has no need of me this afternoon." Gray had expected more of a fight—some refusal or anything but such quick agreement. He stared at her at a loss for words. She paused and added softly, "Though Mrs. Frommer is altogether another matter."

"I'll deal with her."

Lana's brows drew together. "How? She's unaffected by your charms."

He grinned. "You think me charming?"

"To *anyone's* charms."

"Trust me, I can be very persuasive when I need to be." He enjoyed the lovely rise of color in her cheeks at his meaningful words. "We will leave as soon as you are ready."

"Oh, but…the others. If anyone were to see me riding off with you…"

He blinked and remembered, with a pang of annoyance, that Lana could not simply hop in his curricle and ride away. "At least one of us is thinking," he murmured. "Take a stroll to York Street. I'll come by and fetch you within the half hour."

She smiled in relief, and Gray headed back downstairs to advise the housekeeper that Lana needed to run an urgent errand for Lady Dinsmore, which did not require much persuading on his part. Mrs. Frommer would do as she was bidden. Gray had little appreciation for the housekeeper's complete lack of personality, but she ran a tight household and kept his mother happy. However, he did understand Lana's worry about not drawing unnecessary notice.

Before departing, he took the stairs to his chamber to change into less formal clothing. The chances of being recognized this close to London were much higher than in Essex. By the time he was dressed, James had readied the curricle with a matched pair of chestnut horses he had recently acquired. They snorted and tossed their glossy heads impatiently. Gray couldn't have agreed with them more.

He drove anxiously toward York Street, his eyes sharp on the sidewalks. Sure enough, a lithe figure in a simple lilac day dress and a cream-colored spencer came into view. She strode along the sidewalk, moving with measured grace. He could have watched her stroll for much longer, admiring her all the while. But Gray steered his curricle to the side of the street ahead of her and climbed down.

Gray bowed to her and tipped his hat in greeting, though it was mostly a show for the others passing by on the sidewalk. None of whom he recognized, thankfully.

"It feels as if we are doing something illicit," he said softly as he guided her up into the curricle.

"I believe in the eyes of many, we are," she replied.

Gray took the reins again, eager to be off. "I think that is the problem with this town. The sheer amount of eyes."

They took Highgate Road toward Kentish Town, making one stop along the way. Lana was quieter than normal, but she had a half smile on her face, as if thoroughly enjoying the experience. He didn't want to ruin the moment by bringing up Zakorov, so he settled for passing the time with bland conversation instead. Only, with Lana, nothing was ever truly bland. Her natural animation threaded through her tone as they discussed the countryside, the weather, and Sofia's exploits, making the journey pass quickly until they arrived at the Coopers' home.

"Norry!" Sofia squealed, throwing her tiny body into his arms as the Coopers welcomed them in the foyer. Gray could not describe the depth of the emotion slamming through him at the sight of her. It grew more powerful each time, filling his chest so much that it felt like it would burst.

"Sofia, my darling," he said, kissing her rosy cheeks. "You remember my friend, Lana, don't you?"

She nodded and greeted Lana shyly, retreating behind Lady Cooper's skirts. She nudged forward though once she saw the huge bouquet of daisies in Lana's hands. The flowers had been Lana's idea. It had touched Gray that she'd remembered they were the child's favorite.

"She has been eagerly awaiting your visit, Lord Northridge," Lady Cooper said. She nodded to the kitchen. "I hope you do not mind, Sir Cooper and I are heading into town. Cook has prepared a picnic for you in our garden. It is very private," she assured him. She looked like she had more to add, but when she merely smiled and stepped back, Gray figured he'd been wrong.

"Thank you, Lady Cooper."

It was a perfect day for a picnic with not a cloud marring the bright blue sky. After the Coopers left, Sofia led them out to the garden with the picnic basket. Gray was familiar with the garden, but it had filled out in the last few months. A tall hedge and thick shrubs protected the garden from curious eyes. Fragrant rose bushes adorned the perimeter, adding splashes of bright color. It was a charming setting, and Gray felt the tension of the morning melt from his body.

The Coopers' staff had been well compensated by Gray to turn a blind eye to his frequent visits, but as he stared at his daughter spreading a blanket on the grass with Lana, Gray knew that that could not last much longer. There were eyes in London. There were eyes *everywhere*, and the resemblance between he and Sofia was becoming more pronounced by the day. Eventually, someone who wasn't paid for their silence would notice.

"What has Cook prepared for us today?" he said, stooping to unpack the basket.

"Jam samidges," Sofia shrieked, rushing to assist him. "Lem'nade."

"My favorite," Lana said, although Gray kept his thoughts to himself. He preferred something a little heartier. Luckily, Lady Cooper had also included some fruit and cheese with fresh-baked crusty bread. He grinned as Sofia proceeded to get strawberry jam all over her face, but Lana was quick to wipe the little girl's cheeks clean. "My sister and I used to have tea parties with jam sandwiches and lemonade all the time," Lana told her. "Cook sometimes let us put a dollop of cream on the top as a special treat."

Sofia paused mid-bite, her blue eyes bright. "May *I* have cream?"

"Next time, I promise," Lana said as Sofia resumed munching happily on her sandwiches.

"You're good with her," Gray commented softly.

"I love children."

Even those not your own?

The thought was lightning quick, but Gray couldn't help himself. It was obvious that Lana cared for Sofia. It showed in the gentle way she spoke to the child and how tender she had been in her ministrations while she'd been ill. He wondered whether it was because she loved children in general or if it was because Sofia was his. His pride hoped for the latter, but he knew it was likely the former. Servant or not, there was no doubt in his mind that Lana would be a wonderful mother. He watched them, their heads bowed together, one dark and one light, as Lana showed Sofia a tiny ladybug on her finger.

"Lana, swing!" Sofia shouted, discarding the remains of her lunch and running toward a garden swing below a spreading oak. Gray smiled. Obviously Sofia adored Lana, too. Normally, he would be the one she dragged to the tree swing. Sofia's giggles and squeals filled the garden as she decided they should switch places and she was pushing Lana. Gray joined them.

"Push Lana, Norry," she told him, and after he obliged, she proceeded to pursue a butterfly.

"She is lovely," Lana murmured.

"Thank you."

"She looks so much like you."

"Yes," he agreed.

"Have you thought about what you will do?" she asked quietly. "Later, when she is older."

"No." Gray walked around to the front of the swing so that he was facing her, his hands resting above hers on the sides of the rope. More of her hair had escaped their pins. Gray wanted nothing more than to release the rest of the heavy mass and run it between his fingers, but he kept his hands firmly on the ropes.

Her eyes met his, compassion swimming in them. "You're her father, Gray. She should be with you."

"It would be a scandal." He sighed. "My mother—"

"Would love her," Lana interrupted. "I think you should give Lady Dinsmore more credit. She loves you and only wants for your and Brynn's happiness. And Sofia deserves to know her family."

"But the *ton*—"

She pursed her lips, drawing his attention there. "You

think other men in the illustrious *ton* haven't gotten mistresses pregnant? You are the decent one for looking after your child instead of sending her away and pretending she never existed." She bit her lip as if worried that she'd been too forward. "Where is…her mother?"

"She doesn't want her."

"Does she want you?" Lana's whisper was nearly inaudible.

His hands slid down the ropes to rest upon hers, his fingers stroking in between the gaps. The warm contact of her skin electrified his blood as much as if he had bent to press his lips to hers. "No. I haven't seen Marianna in years, and she has no claim to Sofia. I made certain of it before placing her with the Coopers."

Lana licked her lips, and Gray found himself leaning forward, mesmerized, before a small body hurtled between them and plunked herself in Lana's lap. "Push, Norry!"

"Very well," he said with a grin and a sharply inhaled breath. Kissing Lana in a garden with strange servants around was not a smart idea. "I am honored to serve my two special ladies." The words were out of his mouth before he could stop them, but he could not deny their truth. The emotion threatening to spill out of his chest was not only because of Sofia; it encompassed Lana, too. The devil take him, he wanted to laugh. He had an illegitimate daughter, he was in love with his sister's maid, and he could not be more deliriously happy than he was right at that moment. Fate, it seemed, had a curious sense of humor.

The hour flew by, and soon the Coopers returned. As they said their good-byes and Lana hugged and comforted a tearful Sofia, Lady Cooper sought him out.

"Lord Northridge," she said. "May I speak with you for a few moments?"

He frowned. "Certainly."

Once they were ensconced behind the closed doors of the morning salon, she blurted, "Sir Cooper and I are expecting a child."

His frown turned into a wide smile. "That is wonderful news. My congratulations."

"Thank you." Lady Cooper paused, her hand fluttering to touch his sleeve. "We adore Sofia and are honored to have her in our family," she began. "She asks for you every day, you know. It seems that deep inside, she knows who you truly are. The other day she pointed to her face in the looking glass and said 'Norry.' I think she knows that she is connected to you in a way that we are not." She drew a long breath. "Children are far smarter than most expect, and I suspect that it will only become clearer for her as she gets older."

His chest ached with pride at the image of Sofia staring at her face in the mirror and recognizing his.

"What are you saying?"

"That we only want what is best for her. And if you decide that her place is with you, we would not disagree."

Gray felt the floor drop out from below him. A barrage of feelings assaulted him, though he didn't know which was strongest. Hope? Fear?

Lady Cooper must have seen the confusion upon his face because she rushed to assure him. "And should you decide her place is here, we are happy for that also. We love her as our own, and she is a part of our family. However, sooner or later, you will have to tell her the truth."

Or stop seeing her.

She didn't have to say it. Gray knew the complications his presence would bring, especially if the resemblance grew as she became older. She would be better off knowing only the Coopers as her family...without visits from the family friend who happened to look so much like her when she looked nothing like her own parents. But he couldn't fathom

AMALIE HOWARD AND ANGIE MORGAN   265

the thought of not being able to see Sofia...not being able to laugh with her, not being able to *hold* her. He couldn't conceive of never being a part of her life. Of not having her know *him*.

"I will consider what you have said," he replied after a while.

Lady Cooper released a pent-up breath. "That's all I ask, my lord."

Chapter Twenty

Lana stared at Gray's solemn profile as he guided the horses on their way back to London. He looked troubled—it was evident in the slant of his mouth and the frown that seemed to have taken up permanent residence upon his brow the moment they'd left Kentish Town. He'd seemed lighter in the garden with Sofia, but now, he was preoccupied.

"Is something amiss?" she asked quietly.

His eyes flicked to her, surprise registering in them, as if he'd forgotten she was there. He sighed and nodded. "Yes and no. Lady Cooper is with child. Like you, she thinks Sofia's place is with me."

"And you?" Lana asked. "What do you think?"

He turned his eyes from the road to stare directly at her. "I love her, and I want her more than anything."

Lana drew a shaky breath. Of course he did. He loved his daughter. What father wouldn't?

"Then you should do everything in your power to get her."

He held her gaze prisoner. "I plan to."

Lana's breath shuddered in her chest. She wasn't sure he was only talking about Sofia. As she tore her eyes away from his, she saw a large log blocking half of the road. "Gray! Look out!"

He jerked wildly on the reins, forcing the pair of horses to run off the road to avoid hitting the limb. Lana clutched at the side of the curricle as he tried to get the conveyance and the startled pair under control before they veered into a thick copse of trees. He swore loudly as the branches swept into their faces and reached one arm to block them from hitting her.

The reins were wrenched from his fingers, and the horses were off and running, dragging the curricle behind them like a broken wooden toy. The crack of the wheel was like the shot of a pistol as the axletree split in half, and Lana was thrown to the right. She landed in a wet patch of mud, all the wind knocked out of her. She gasped for air and sat up, the dampness soaking into her dress and mud caking every inch of her. Fortunately, she didn't seem to be hurt, although her clothing was ruined. A huge rent ran up the side of her skirt, exposing her muddied stockings.

"Lana?" Gray called.

"I'm over here," she said, breathing hard.

"Are you hurt?" he asked, limping into the grove. His eyes went wide at the sight of her, and Lana imagined how frightful she must appear. She was lucky to be alive. They both were.

She shook her head. "Not that I can tell," she said and then frowned, noticing his awkward gait and the flowering red poppy on the hem of his white shirt. "What happened?"

"It looks worse than it is," he assured her. "A small gash, nothing more."

The crimson stain at his side was spreading. "Even so, we need to get that cleaned before infection sets in. Where are the horses?"

"They stopped a bit ahead." He stood at the edge of the mud pit and reached a hand down to her. "Can you walk?"

"Yes," she said, pulling herself up. "But my skirt is ripped." Gray's eyes dipped to the tear in the material, and Lana held the torn edges together, blushing fiercely. Gray drew a breath, running a mud-splattered hand through his hair. "Neither of us can show up at Bishop House looking like this." He studied her. "Can you ride?"

"I think so."

"We can unhitch the horses and ride them to The Cock and the Crown. It's not far from here."

"The *what*?"

"The Cock and the Crown." Faint color flushed his cheeks. "A gaming hell."

"Oh." She'd heard of such places and the types of men who visited them. Gray claimed not to be that sort of man any longer, and she wanted to believe him. But doubt surged nonetheless. She nodded, her voice cooling slightly. "Very well, my lord."

He avoided her eyes as if embarrassed. "I know it's not a proper sort of place for young ladies, but I know the owner. We'll be able to get cleaned up and find you some clothes. And I can send a messenger to Bishop House. Colton and one of the footmen will have to retrieve the curricle." He glanced at her, lines of concern pressed between his brows. "I'll ride back with them. The Crown has a number of conveyances available to its members. I'll see to it that you're settled into one and returned safely. None of the staff at Bishop House will ever know you were with me."

Lana knew it wasn't shame over being caught with a maid that had Gray carefully working out a solution to their current situation. It was attentiveness to her reputation among the staff, and her very position as lady's maid, and assuring her that he would protect them both. For that, she was thankful.

A few paces away, the horses were still joined to the remaining half of the curricle, and the team stood grazing quietly. Gray stopped short and swore under his breath, his frustration evident. "We have no saddles."

Lana grinned, deftly unhooking the straps of the horse closest to her. She wrapped her fingers in its mane and pulled herself on top of the horse, tucking her frayed skirts beneath her limbs. Gray's jaw practically dropped to the ground, and she laughed at him from her perch. "Saddles are for the weak."

"You surprise me, though by now you should not," he said, unlatching the second horse.

"Lead the way, Lord Northridge."

They rode at a decent pace toward the north end of London, Lana keeping pace easily with Gray, despite her torn clothing and no saddle, a fact that he couldn't seem to comprehend if the glances he sent her were any signal. She grinned. She forgot decorum and rode astride, the way she much preferred. Of course that was better achieved in trousers as opposed to skirts, something she shared in common with Lady Briannon. Although she would never admit it. Brynn didn't need to be encouraged in her exploits.

Lana's eyes widened as they rode through the narrow, filthy streets of the north end and approached the imposing, greasy exterior of the gaming hell. Gray kept his mount close to hers, and she was grateful for it. They dismounted, and Gray tossed the reins and a few coppers to a boy standing nearby. He then ushered Lana through a side entrance, where he introduced her to a fox-faced man named Dunworthy.

"This is Miss Volchek," Gray said, offering no other explanation.

Dunworthy inclined his head. "Miss."

"We ran into a spot of trouble on Highgate." As Gray continued to fill Dunworthy in on what had happened, Lana took measure of her surroundings. It was unlike anything she'd ever seen, not that she'd ever been in a gaming hell. The place was dark and cavernous—all red and black carpeting with deep mahogany walls. It was showy and not tasteful in the least. The sound of chatter and laughter drifted through the heavy drapes at the far end, and occasionally she could see a flurry of movement. Her curiosity was well and truly piqued.

"Go with Frieda, miss," Dunworthy was saying to her, and Lana blinked as a buxom redhead approached. "She'll help." Gray nodded, and Lana followed the woman up some narrow stairs to a set of apartments at the top.

"You must have taken quite a tumble," Frieda remarked, her eyes kindly. "You look a fright. Not to worry, we'll get you cleaned up in a tick."

She led Lana into a room that appeared, if possible, even more cave-like than the entrance room below. Baize green walls, dark wood paneling, and a four-poster so thickly carved it could have held a sleeping giant. A fire was already in the hearth, a copper tub close.

Frieda peeled Lana's muddy clothes off inch by inch, wrinkling her nose at the smell. Two housemaids entered to fill the tub with ewers of hot water, their eyes averted from Lana, her body wrapped in soft toweling as she waited. Once the maids took their leave, Frieda helped her into the small tub. "We'll have you right as rain in no time."

She soaked for no more than a quarter hour before the water turned cold. Frieda wrapped her again in the soft toweling and sat her before the fire while choosing a dress. Pulling on a worn but clean chemise, Lana flushed at the fact that there were no drawers to be had, but there was nothing to be done for it. Hers were ruined. Lana frowned when Frieda held out a gown. The bodice was low and narrow. Much too small for Lana. "That will not fit."

Frieda winked. "What do you think God gave you those bosoms for? North won't be able to tear his eyes away."

"It's not like that," Lana said, flushing deeply, but Frieda only grinned knowingly as she tied the strings on the corseted back of the dress. She then tackled Lana's mass of damp hair, tugging and brushing and pinning with industry, if little finesse. "Does...North come here often?" Lana asked after a while.

"Not as often as he used to. There, have a look."

Lana turned to the looking glass and stopped short. Her hair was part up, part down, cascading over her shoulders. And the vibrant green dress left precious little to the imagination. Without stays, her breasts swelled over the lace edges of the bodice, and the material clung to every curve from her waist to her hips. She looked nothing like herself. Oddly enough, it made her feel confident, a bit daring.

Which was why when she finally came face-to-face with Gray in a private salon on the main floor, she held her head high. The shocked look on his face was well worth the time spent under Frieda's coarse ministrations as his eyes roved her greedily from head to toe. "You are a witch," he whispered, taking her hand in his and drawing his lips across her knuckles.

"A witch?" she shot back, insulted.

"An enchantress."

"In that case," she said, blushing as he handed her a glass of sherry. "Thank you, my lord."

She saw that he, too, had had a bath and was dressed in clean clothing with no sign of a bleeding wound. Gray noticed the direction of her stare and patted the side of his torso. "Good as new."

"So what do we do now?" she asked, her eyes perusing the small but lavish room. A small fire burned on one side beside a cozy sitting area. It was intimate and private, and Lana realized with a start why it was so. It was a room, no doubt, where gentlemen went to meet with their paramours. Although she knew that she and Gray were here for the sake of privacy instead of…whatever it is those other men did, she couldn't help the shot of panic that sent heat to her chest and cheeks. She sipped her drink, hiding her sudden malaise.

"I've already sent a message to Colton, so we will wait until his arrival. The less we are seen here, the better. As such, I hope you don't find my company too dull."

Lana froze. "Colton is to meet us *here*? Together?"

"He won't see you," Gray said, raising his hands as if to settle her. "Dunworthy has already sent word to have one of the Crown's carriages readied for you. It should be no more than an hour, and I shall follow later, whenever Colton arrives." Gray eyed her. "What would you like to do while we wait?"

"What does one do in a gaming hell?"

His eyes dropped to her breasts, and Lana flushed. He cleared his throat, his voice tight. "Cards. Dice. That sort of thing."

"Shall we play cards, then?" she suggested, taking a seat in the armchair set beside a matching sofa.

Gray nodded and sat in the seat opposite. His face looked strained as he explained the rules of *vingt-et-un*. Lana didn't let on that she already knew how to play, and Gray only realized it himself after he'd lost three hands.

He shook his head with a resigned grin. "Let me guess. James?"

"He's a good teacher."

"Perhaps we should up the stakes with a bet." His eyes dropped to her lips. The way he was looking at her made it hard to breathe, as if her body was about to ignite on each inhale. "If I win, I claim a kiss."

Her heart thumped unsteadily in her chest. "And if I win?"

"Claim whatever you like."

Perhaps her mind wasn't in the game, or deep down she wanted to lose, but she drew too many cards, going over twenty-one. He won with a paltry twelve. Lana's mouth grew dry at the look in his eyes.

"I claim my kiss." Gray pushed back his chair purposefully. Each step he took toward her made her body tremble, until he leaned over her, his arms pressed on either side of the armchair. He didn't hesitate—his mouth took hers in a hard, demanding kiss. His lips and tongue were the only things anchoring her to him, and Lana strained upward, scraping his lower lip with her teeth. She knew she was being wanton, but she didn't care. She drew her tongue along the inside of his lip, and Gray growled low in his throat. He ravaged her mouth until they were both breathing hard.

He pulled away abruptly, and without another word, turned and resumed his seat. The only signs that anything untoward had just happened between them were the rapid rise and fall of his chest and his storm-pressed eyes. Lana composed herself as best she could, despite her overheated body. Every part of her tingled, like tiny wicks of flame were singeing the underside of her skin. Lord, one kiss and the man set her afire.

"Shall we play another round?" His voice was husky.

Lana downed the contents of her glass and nodded weakly. Gray dealt and then stood to refill her drink. Her body thrummed at his proximity, but he made no move to come any nearer to her before returning to his chair. Lana's hands shook as she held her cards. Sixteen. She knew she should stay—the odds were in her favor—but she asked for another card. She held her breath as Gray dealt it. A five. A natural. She had won, unless Gray held a natural, too.

"Twenty. I lose," he said, his gaze heavy-lidded as she turned over her cards. "What do you claim?"

Lana stared at him, her pulse racing like a runaway horse. Her breath deserted her. It would be so easy to claim a confession or a coin for her winnings, but those things wouldn't satisfy. She wanted the same as he did. As he'd just *done*. She wanted his mouth on hers. His hands on her body. The dress and the gaming hell made her bold. Impulsive and reckless.

She licked dry lips and answered before she could stop herself. "I claim…you."

He remained absolutely still but for his pupils constricting and a short, indrawn breath. They were the only signs he'd heard her before she stood on trembling legs and walked to his chair. She sat on the edge, her own breath coming in shallow pants. She leaned down and grazed her lips across his. Emboldened by another softly indrawn breath, she slid her tongue along the crease and pushed tentatively inside. Gray sucked it deep, grasping her arms and pulling her into his lap in one motion. His teeth ground against hers as he possessed her mouth completely and utterly. This kiss was nothing like the first. It was all heat and burning passion, threatening to ignite them both. And ignite it did. Her breasts ached, and the space between her thighs felt molten with want. Lana could feel his erection pressing into the backs of her thighs, and it only made her feel more empowered.

"I want your hands on me…as they were in the carriage to Essex." She heard her own brash words and hid her overheated face in his neck.

Gray leaned back with a sharp gasp, resting his forehead on hers, his eyes closed. "You should not say such things, Lana. I am weak when it comes to resisting you."

"As I am with you," she admitted softly, her thumb rising to trace the contours of the lips that had taken hers with such urgency. She pushed her thumb into his mouth, and he sucked on her finger. White-hot sensations streaked from her breasts to her thighs.

Lana knew what she was doing was imprudent. She was inviting ruin, but the truth was she didn't care. She wanted a sliver of happiness. With this man before her. Now. She wanted him. *All* of him.

For all she knew, she would be dead in a week—if her uncle and Zakorov had their way. What use would her virtue be then? She had no way of proving their guilt, and they would stop at nothing to silence her and Irina. And if by some miracle Langlevit came through with decrypting the coded letters, she would be able to go home. She'd leave England forever.

Leave *Gray* forever.

It was something she did not want to consider, but her virtue seemed a small price to pay for the piece of him she would keep with her for a lifetime. This was her choice; he'd made that clear. Even though he thought her a maid, Gray would be honorable no matter what. She could act, or she could stop.

She had no intention of stopping.

She masked her nervousness with a laugh and pulled his head down to hers. She kissed him with unconcealed urgency, looping her arms around his neck as he scooped her up without breaking the kiss. Gray took her with him to the sofa, laying her down and pressing open-mouthed kisses to her throat. He nipped lightly at her skin as he traced a hot path to her swelling breasts. Lana arched backward, pleasure coursing through her from the feel of his hands skimming her sides and the tortuous, teasing track of his mouth.

"This dress is sinful," he muttered as his teeth tugged on the lace edge of the bodice. "And the sight of you in it even more so."

Gray pulled her bodice down with a satisfied grunt, laying her bare before him, and Lana blushed. She may have felt daring, but she was far from experienced. As his mouth closed over the peak of her breast, she almost expired from the wild burst of pleasure. He turned his attention to her other breast, his hands moving restlessly along the sides of her legs. Gray made every inch of her feel alive, and she wanted desperately to make him feel the same way. She knew she'd given him pleasure in the mews by touching him. Her hands slid down his tense stomach, brushing against the narrow fall of his trousers.

"Lana," Gray said, going still over her.

She drew her fingers along his rigid length with a shuddering breath. Heat saturated her skin, and blood pounded through her veins at the hard feel of him. Gray raised his head, his eyes dark with passion, and stalled her tentative stroking with his hand. "Lana, enough," he gasped. "I won't be able to stop myself."

"I don't want you to."

His hungry gaze snapped to hers. "What are you saying?"

She smiled through her sudden vulnerability, and the twin look of it in his own eyes. "I won that last round fair and square. Don't try to renege now, Lord Northridge. Fulfill my claim."

"Lana—" he said with a groan. "You do not know what you are asking."

"I do." She shook free of his hold and gripped him boldly. "I know what I want. Please, Gray."

He covered her lips with his.

Chapter Twenty-One

She meant it. She wanted him. And as he held himself over her, Lana's hair a tumble of loose silken curls on the velvet sofa cushion, her eyes sharp with determination, Gray wished she would push him away. Tell him to stop. That this wasn't right. Something, anything, to argue against what his body and soul was yearning for. *Her.* He wanted to touch and kiss every inch of her skin. He wanted to bury himself deep inside of her and claim her as his own.

Gray's fingers trailed down her side, his eyes taking in the sight of her breasts, high and free of the bodice of that sinful scrap of a dress.

"Have you been with a man before?" he asked, his gaze skipping back up to meet her reaction.

She bit her lip and shook her head. He'd suspected as much, and a shot of pleasure accompanied the knowledge that she wanted to give herself to *him*. A virgin. This would be new territory for Gray. Territory he knew he should not traverse.

"We are in a gaming hell," he whispered. The dark purple

sofa they were on suddenly felt like a bed of coals. "I should not take your innocence in a place like this."

Lana's fingers grazed his cheeks, her thumbs pulling on his lower lip. "It doesn't matter where we are. Place means nothing, I know that now. It is who you are with that matters, and Gray"—she lifted her shoulders from the sofa and kissed him lightly—"I would give myself to you anywhere."

He closed his eyes and groaned, her words pulsing more blood and desire into his already agonizing erection. He pictured her in all manner of places, her body open to him, wanting him.

"I made a promise," he heard himself saying around the images. "To myself. To never risk—" *Another mistake.*

That was what he had meant to say, but it didn't feel right. Or honest, not anymore. Sofia had, at one time, felt like a mistake. But that had been before her birth. Before he'd held her for the first time.

Lana had heard it anyway. "You don't want to get another woman with child."

He nodded, his nose brushing the soft swell of her breast. His tongue moved without a command from his mind. Lana whimpered as he suckled her nipple, the delicate pink skin tight and hard under his tongue.

"There is always—" She gasped as his palm kneaded her breast and his teeth nipped at her flesh. "Risk," she finished, her hips rising in an instinctual thrust. The pressure against his swollen length had him nearly ready to free himself. Ready to shove up her skirts and take what he wanted. Give her what she claimed to want.

"Not if you resist," he replied, angling his hips so that hers could not push up against his again.

Lana stilled beneath him. Her eyes cleared, and she pushed up onto her elbows, causing Gray to move back another few inches. "You mean you...you've resisted?"

He nodded once.

"For how long?" she asked, blinking her surprise.

He thought of their encounter in the mews and how the mere pressure of her hand against his length had been enough for him to spend himself in his smalls. It had been mortifying, but understandable, considering the amount of time that had passed since he'd last bedded a woman.

"Since Sofia," he answered.

Lana sat up farther, nearly pushing Gray back onto his haunches. "Do you meant to say you haven't—" Lana stopped, her lips still parted, a second blush rising to her cheeks. "That you've been alone for *three* years?"

His eyes went to her breasts, still bared and so full and tantalizing. "God, you're the most perfect thing I've ever seen."

"Gray."

"What?"

She touched his chin and made him look her in the eye. "Three years?"

He covered her hand with his and kissed her palm. "There's been no one."

Just the aching, never-ending monotony of solitude. Seclusion. The temptations had always been there. Beautiful women. Willing women. But they had been faceless and nameless, and when he'd resisted their advances he had not felt remorse. He hadn't felt as if he'd lost anything at all. But with Lana... He kissed her palm again and knew that without her he would feel adrift. He wanted to stay with her.

He wanted to make her his.

"Oh, Gray," she whispered. The tenderness in her voice was his undoing.

He took her mouth in a kiss that pushed her back upon the cushions of the sofa. His hand was at the fall of his trousers, freeing himself, when he felt Lana's slim fingers joining the task of pushing down the fitted waist. Gray allowed her to take over, not wanting her to feel the shake of his own hand. He'd longed for her, dreamed of her, and knowing that she wanted him as much as he did her would make it extremely difficult to move slowly. Gently. But he would. It was salacious enough that her first encounter with a man would be in a gaming hell. She didn't deserve to be rutted like an animal as well.

Gray pushed up her skirts to find a soft lawn chemise, edged with lace around her upper thighs. His palm caressed her bare thigh, paying close attention to Lana's hands. If she touched him again, he would be finished. His fingers reached past the sheer fabric in an upward search for her drawers, but Lana made a small noise in her throat. It reverberated along his tongue, which was currently entwined with hers. Gray broke the kiss, certain she would now push at his chest and tell him to stop. But once again, Lana surprised him.

"I am not wearing any," she confessed in an embarrassed rush, her lashes brushing her bright pink cheeks. Gray's fingers stalled in their ascent as he clutched the folds of the chemise in his fist. Her innocent, provocative words nearly made him spend then and there.

Inhaling raggedly and willing his rampant loins under control, Gray's knuckles traversed the hot, velvety skin of a trim thigh. She was so soft, so warm. So *bare*. He cupped her uncovered womanhood and groaned at the hot, lushly feminine shape of her that fit snugly into his palm. Lana sighed, arching into his touch. His finger slid into her wet warmth, and with another push, he felt her close around his finger. She moaned her pleasure at his touch.

"Lana." He swallowed, his throat tight, need filling him everywhere. "I don't want to hurt you."

She rolled her head side to side, her hair tangling underneath her. "You won't. You never would. I trust you, Gray."

Lana thrust up against his hand, and he couldn't endure another moment. He removed his hand from her center and aligned himself, his erection painful. He must have winced, because Lana, alarmed, lowered her gaze. She dragged in a sharp breath, her eyes going round and anxious.

"Shhh," he said, knowing what she must have been thinking. That he could never fit within her. "Our bodies are meant for this."

She nodded but still eyed him with trepidation.

"Lana," he whispered, dipping his head to interrupt her stare. "It will hurt. But only for a moment. I promise you."

He wanted to bring her pleasure, not pain. Which meant he had to fight his desire to pound into her, the way his inner carnal need was screaming for him to do right then. He could not change the surroundings, but he could control *how* they came together. He slowed himself. He had to make her first time special…and something worth remembering, despite the entirely unsuitable ambiance.

Gray took her lips in a hungry kiss, leaving no inch of her mouth unexplored. Her fingers gripped his shoulders, her head falling back as he licked and nipped his way down her throat to her cleavage. His hands were as busy as his mouth and tongue. He reached forward, her core hot and damp and ready. Lana's undiluted responses to his caresses excited him more than anything. His fingers stroked expertly, making her breaths shorten to tiny gasps as his mouth grazed over the bud of her nipple, drawing it deep.

"Gray…"

Lana's entire back arched, her eyes going wide at the release he knew was rocketing through her rigid body. As her shudders crested, he slid into her, inch by agonizing inch, grinding his teeth and holding her stare, her expression shifting between bliss and discomfort. He nudged against the wall of her innocence and held himself steady.

"Is that...all?" she whispered.

Gray wanted to laugh, but it hurt too damn much. "God no."

He thrust forward hard and seated himself completely. Lana cried out, but she wasn't alone. Gray's own groan of satisfaction rent the air of the private salon.

He wanted to give her time to adjust to him. Wanted to be patient as her pain subsided. But Gray had to move. He needed to feel the sweet friction of her body around his length before he came.

"Does it hurt too much?" he asked, his voice strained.

"N-no," she gasped. Gray made a small, testing thrust, and Lana's gasp dipped in octave to a moan. "No," she said, more clearly.

Her fingers threaded through his hair and gripped the back of his neck, and Gray broke.

He withdrew completely and thrust back inside without hesitation. He rocked into her again and again, each time seating himself deeper and deeper. Lana's body gripped him as he retreated and parted for him as he returned, and he felt himself hurtling forward, toward a bliss he hadn't realized existed. He took her with him, watching her eyes dilate from the sensations possessing her as thoroughly as they did him. He would hold himself back if it killed him.

And it just might.

It wasn't only that he was finally bedding a woman after being so long without. It was *her*. He was making Lana his in the truest way possible. He wanted to keep her this close for always. He wanted her in his bed every night and every morning. Hell, every afternoon. He pictured her writhing beneath him in the midnight blue silk sheets on his bed, whimpering his name the way she was right then. He shifted position, and she clutched his shoulders, crying out from the force of her pleasure as her nails scored his skin.

Gray's climax rushed up on the wake of hers, a deluge of pain and pleasure and raw need.

Stop.

His conscience had a weak voice, but he heard it nonetheless. He withdrew from Lana's trembling core and spent himself. He couldn't see. Couldn't breathe. His body thrummed with life and the desire for more of her. But he held himself away, taking deep, steady gulps of air.

"Gray?" she whispered. His vision returned, and he stared down at her. Lana's eyes conveyed confusion. He knew why.

"To be safe," he explained.

She nodded, her eyelids heavy with satisfaction. Her pink cheeks bordered on crimson. He kissed the apple of each cheek and then her lips.

"You've made your claim, it seems," he said, attempting humor. But his voice shook, and Lana did not smile.

She stared up at him, her breasts rising and falling on each quick breath, and Gray understood he'd made his claim as well. Lana was his. This beautiful, bewildering woman who he'd had no business at all making love to, was his.

And he would not lose her. He *could* not lose her.

Conversation was limited as they hurried to ready themselves after a brisk announcement from Dunworthy that one of the Crown carriages would be there shortly. Gray blotted the dampness from both he and Lana as best he could with his cravat before tossing it into the fire. She blushed the entire time. And as they waited for Dunworthy to summon them when the carriage arrived, her cheeks remained rosy, her eyes bright. Her lips were still swollen from his kisses, making him want to possess them again.

He stirred to life in his trousers, and Gray almost

chuckled out loud. The effect she had on him was astonishing. If she didn't have to return to Brynn's side and if he hadn't committed to the damned Kensington ball that evening, he would have whisked her away in a heartbeat.

"Did I hurt you?"

Her flush deepened, but she shook her head. Lana held herself primly, but there was no regret on her face—nothing that would suggest she held doubts about what had happened between them. But he could see the tension mounting in her fingers as they pressed into the folds of the gown.

"Gray," she began, and then paused. "This doesn't change what I am or who you are. We cannot…I cannot lose my position." She looked away. "And Brynn cannot know."

He eyed her, amused by her efforts at formality. What had happened between them changed everything. But Gray knew the root cause of her anxiety. Any gossip would ruin her standing with his parents as Brynn's lady's maid, especially Lady Dinsmore, who had high hopes of making another *splendid* match with her only son and heir. He rolled his eyes inwardly. If his mother caught wind of where his true feelings lay, she would be appalled. And furious.

And Lana would be out on her pert little bottom without a farthing to her name and without a reference to find another position. He would support her, of course. Keep her well as his mistress. But she did not want that, he knew. What did she want? He knew only her immediate desires: for Zakorov to leave her and the princesses be. Justice for the princesses. For herself. And Lana wished to be reunited with her sister. But what more after that? A life of service?

Until he could navigate a solution, their relationship would have to be kept secret. And Gray was good with secrets. After all, he'd kept a monumental one for three years with no one the wiser. What was one extra?

Gray nodded. "As you wish."

"Thank you."

Her relief was obvious, and he left her to her thoughts just as Dunworthy rapped his knuckles against the door to their private room. Gray saw her into the carriage and watched her leave, feeling something unfamiliar tugging in the pit of his stomach when the carriage drew away, as if they were somehow still connected. He'd never felt like this after being with any woman...the urgent need to keep her lodged at his side. It was curious. And surprising. Then again, the more he knew of Lana, the more he came to realize just how uncommon she was. Gray recalled her unaffected kindness as she'd thanked Dunworthy and Frieda for their assistance. Even in a place of ill repute like this, she seemed to remain untouched by its underlying vulgarity.

Gray took his own leave when Colton arrived fifteen minutes later. He thanked Dunworthy and left him in possession of a hefty sack of coin. As they neared Bishop House, Gray sighed. He couldn't be arsed about going to some ridiculous ball, but he'd promised Thorn he'd be there. In truth, he couldn't fathom anything worse than being surrounded by elaborately coiffed maidens vying for a title and a fortune. He'd happily give up both for any chance of a future with the woman he'd sent ahead earlier. Lana was more of a lady than any of those simpering debutantes could ever be.

Striding purposefully to his chamber, he called for Harrison. The hour was already late, and he'd catch hell from his mother if he didn't at least put in an appearance. Harrison outdid himself, putting the finishing touches on his kit within the hour, and Gray was on his way downstairs when a commotion at the front door drew his attention.

A man's voice was shouting, "The road was closed! He came upon the carriage. Hit me in the head!"

Gray frowned. It sounded like Beckett. Which was odd. He should have been en route with Brynn to the Kensington crush. Sure enough, Beckett's thatch of red hair loomed into view. Blood dripped down his face from a gash in his head, and Gray's stomach dropped. He took the stairs four at a time, nearly crashing into the small crowd of servants surrounding the coachman. They cleared a path for him, his fear solidifying at the terrified look on Beckett's face.

"What happened?" he demanded. "Where is Lady Briannon?"

"He took her—" Beckett broke off as Gray grabbed his lapels.

"What do you mean? Who took her?"

"The Masked Marauder, my lord." Sobs broke from the man. "I woke up, and they were gone. She was gone."

Gray's heart stilled. The Masked Marauder had already been taken into custody. Or *someone* had. "Are you certain it was the Masked Marauder?"

Beckett nodded. "Yes, my lord. I'm certain of it."

"Where? Which street?"

"Near Orchard Street, my lord."

"Oh my God, Lady Briannon!" The agonized cry was from Lana, who had just arrived, her hands clasped to her mouth.

"My lord." Braxton stepped forward, his steadfast composure visibly shaken. "I do not know if it will help at all, but His Grace, Lord Bradburne, called upon Lady Briannon shortly before she departed for the Kensington affair."

Gray peered at him, a scowl fixed upon his face as his mind grasped for answers. "They left together for the ball, then?" He shot a look at Beckett who quickly shook his head.

"No, my lord," Braxton answered before the driver could speak. "His Grace left mere minutes before Lady Briannon."

Gray's knuckles ached from the tight fists he'd formed at his sides.

"Why the hell wouldn't he have gone with her?" he asked.

"Why let her travel alone?"

He didn't have time to pick apart all the answers. Gray started for the door, but Lana's hand landed on his forearm, halting him.

"The Bradburne diamonds." Her voice had dropped to a strained whisper, and when Gray turned back to her, he saw her eyes were distant, as if she was piecing together a memory. "She spoke so much about those diamonds. She told everyone she planned to wear them tonight. It was so unlike her. My God, I think she *wanted* to attract the criminal." She shook her head, her eyes going wide with alarm. "So this is why she wanted me to—"

Gray's stare narrowed on her. He dispersed the rest of the servants with a quick word, issuing clipped orders to Mrs. Braxton to take care of Beckett and for Colton to ready the carriage. He'd hunt the man down to hell and back. But first, he had to know what Lana had been about to say. He drew her to the nearby salon and closed the door, noticing briefly from the ends of her damp hair that she, too, had bathed and changed.

"What did Brynn want you to do, Lana?" he asked urgently.

Indecision flicked across her face before she drew a shattered breath. "She said she wanted to go to the ball alone, without you as an escort, so she asked me to distract you for the afternoon."

Gray's temper spiraled. "Distract me? Why?"

Lana was wringing her hands, as if shouldering some of the blame. "I thought she wanted a few stolen moments to meet His Grace. I didn't think anything of it." She glanced at him. "You have had a tendency to be overbearing when it comes to the duke."

But why wear the diamonds? And why would she want *him* out of the way? Gray considered the facts he knew.

Rumors of Hawk's impending arrest had been circulating the *ton* before Bow Street had managed to get some unnamed gentleman in custody. He frowned. If Beckett were right and the Masked Marauder had attacked Brynn's carriage, then that meant the man in custody was the wrong man. What on earth had possessed Brynn to draw the Masked Marauder out? The little fool!

He ground his teeth. It wasn't Lana's fault, he knew, despite wanting to throttle the pair of them. "Did she say anything more?"

"No." Her voice shook. "I didn't think she would do anything so rash."

"My sister is the master of asinine plans." Gray frowned. "If she met with Hawk before leaving here alone, he might know something more." Whether Hawk had next gone home or to the Kensington Ball was unknown. Surely he wouldn't have known of Brynn's harebrained scheme? "My first stop will be at Hadley Gardens, and then I'll try Thorn's home. I swear, if this bandit has laid one finger on my sister, I'll put him into the ground."

"I am coming with you."

"No, it's far too dangerous."

Her chin jutted forward. "As dangerous as a gaming hell in north London?" she asked in a silky voice. "I am coming whether you allow it or not. I will follow on horseback if I have to."

"And if I forbid it?" he said tersely, a muscle jerking in his jaw.

Lana met his stare. "That will not stop me."

He knew it would not. The woman was as insufferable as his sister.

"Fine. Do as you will." He pocketed his pistol from Lord Dinsmore's gun case and strode to the front door, where Colton was waiting. "Summon the constable," he told

Braxton. "If we are not back within the hour, find my father."

They rode to Hadley Gardens in stony silence, each occupied by their own thoughts. When Gray got his hands on Briannon, he was going to make sure she didn't sit for a week. He didn't wait for the carriage to come to a stop at Hawk's residence before leaping out. "Do not for one second consider leaving this coach," he snapped to Lana, the warning in his voice little more than a growl. She nodded, an eyebrow vaulting at his tone.

Gray ran up the steps and knocked loudly, waiting impatiently until the butler opened the door. "Good evening, Lord Northridge."

"Heed," Gray said. "Is the duke at home?"

"No, my lord, he left for Lord Thorndale's function two hours past."

Two hours? Gray's head spun. Was he at the Kensington Ball, then, none the wiser that his betrothed was in danger? Again, Gray's fury and confusion ran rampant. Why would Hawk not have escorted her himself after calling in at Bishop House? Had they quarreled? "Thank you, Heed. If he returns, please send a messenger to my residence at once."

"Of course, my lord."

Gray nodded and returned to the carriage, mapping out possible routes. Beckett had said they had been forced to stop at Orchard Street because of a blocked road. It was odd. The Masked Marauder did not kidnap victims, and yet, Beckett had insisted the bastard had *taken* Brynn. He'd drive toward Orchard Street on his way to Thorndale's. He would need more help if he was going to find his sister.

Gray took one step onto the carriage rail when a muffled *crack* rang out from behind him. He froze. It had sounded close and too much like a pistol shot. Lana's terrified face appeared in the carriage doorway, and he reassured her with a tight smile. "It's probably nothing, but I'm going to have a look. Sounded like it came from the direction of the mews."

Lana placed a hand on his sleeve, her heart in her eyes. "Gray, please be careful."

"I will." He glanced at Colton. "Are you armed?" The coachman nodded. "Good. Shoot anyone wearing a mask who comes near this coach. Guard her with your life, do you understand me?"

"Yes, my lord."

Unable to place the exact location of the shot, he took off at a cautious run through the back lawns of Hadley Gardens, making his way through the shadows and expecting to be waylaid by a masked bandit at any moment. His pulse was racing. He knew what he'd said to Lana, but it was too much of a coincidence. Gray combed his way through the hedges until he came to a courtyard. Houses lined either side of it, and before him were the mews. He could see shadows moving from the lamplight.

That had to be it.

He was already preparing himself for the worst when he heard a distinctly female voice coming from the depths of the stables. "We were never friends," the voice was saying. Gray frowned. He knew that voice.

He edged forward, keeping to the darkness, and peered through a crack in the window. He almost rushed in at the sight that greeted him: Brynn stood in a torn dress, a bruised and bloodied Hawk at her side, with Eloise, the duke's half sister, pointing the short barrel of a gun toward them. Gray had always suspected Eloise was a bit unstable, but here was the undisputed truth.

He inched closer to the stable door, Hawk's raised voice masking his approach. Gray was steps away from her.

"Shut up!" Eloise screamed. "Or I will drop your precious love like a fly."

His heart pounded at the threat to Brynn, but here

was his opportunity. Eloise was angry and distracted. Gray slid forward in one quick movement, raising his own pistol to Eloise's temple and divesting her of the gun in the same motion. "I'll take that, thank you."

"Gray, how did you find us?" his sister said, locking her wild eyes with his.

"Lana told me everything, and Hadley Gardens was my first stop to find you when I heard the shot." With his free hand, he managed to relieve Eloise of her gun, but she was too quick and whirled out of his grasp.

"Don't hurt her," Hawk said, even as Gray kept his pistol trained on Eloise, where she now crouched behind a saddle stand. "Get Brynn out of here," Hawk added, pushing Brynn toward him. "I will take care of it."

"I have Lana in the carriage outside. Come," he told his sister.

"No, Archer," Brynn cried out. "I won't leave you."

"It's over, love. She can't hurt anyone now." Hawk's face was pained as he walked toward them to kiss Brynn on the temple. His eyes met Gray's, and Gray nodded, handing the duke his pistol before ushering his sister out of the mews.

Gray wrapped her in his cloak, holding her trembling body close, and then scooped her into his arms. He wanted to put as much distance between them and the stables as possible. Lana's eyes were wide when they arrived at the carriage and Gray tucked Brynn into the seat beside her. As Gray made her more comfortable, Brynn explained what had transpired—that *Eloise* had been in league with the masked bandit.

"Did Eloise hurt you?" he asked Brynn, anger rising in him at the bruised welt on her temple.

"I'm fine," she whispered. "Archer—"

"Hawk can take care of himself, Brynn," Gray assured her.

He was floored by the naked emotion on his sister's face. He hadn't believed that she loved the man, but he knew it now. Her feelings for him were written all over her. As Hawk's had been in the mews.

Gray's eyes met Lana's over Brynn's head, and something terrifying took him in its grasp. He couldn't fathom what he would do if anything happened to either of the two women sitting across from him. If it had been Lana standing at the end of a gun, he would have moved heaven and earth to protect her.

Thrown himself in front of the bullet if he had to.

Gray closed his eyes. There it was: the simple and irrefutable fact. He loved her.

Chapter Twenty-Two

The next handful of days unfolded at a slug's pace and yet somehow also like a summer tempest. Lana did not leave her mistress's side as they prepared for their retreat from London. It had been decided quickly that Lord and Lady Dinsmore and Lady Briannon could not remain in town after Lady Eloise's funeral. Not only would they be made to weather the scrutiny revolving around Lady Eloise's death and that of the Masked Marauder in the Hadley Gardens mews, but also the very public and very humiliating retraction of Archer and Brynn's betrothal in the *Times*.

Brynn had shrugged it off. Lana knew the engagement had been a farce, intended only to protect Archer from being considered a suspect. But that night in the mews, when a second gunshot had split the night, Brynn's fear that Archer had been killed had nearly driven her to hysteria. Gray had needed to restrain her from rushing back into the mews, the light of a building fire flickering inside. And when Archer had finally emerged, shouting for Gray's help to extinguish the flames that Eloise had set, Brynn had sobbed with relief.

She loved Archer, but she was not going to marry him.

Lana understood entirely and shared in the solemn pall that hung over Bishop House the next few days. As she folded and wrapped each article of clothing, every accessory, every shoe, Lana thought of what had happened at that indecent gaming hell. On that decadent purple couch. Underneath the most exasperatingly handsome and charming man she had ever known.

At that moment, Brynn swept into the room from the adjoining bath chamber, where Mary had been assisting her in her morning ablutions, and jerked Lana from her heated thoughts. Lana ducked her head, hoping to hide her flushed cheeks, but of course, that did not escape Brynn's notice.

"Is something amiss, Lana? You haven't been yourself lately." Brynn shook her head. "Not that any of us are, but... you do seem distracted."

Oh, it's nothing, Lana imagined herself answering. *I simply can't stop thinking about how your brother made love to me in a gaming hell a few days ago.*

Lana nearly smiled at how ridiculous and wrong it all sounded. And yet, being with Gray hadn't felt wrong at all. He'd said something to her when she'd taken in the sight of his impressive, and a bit alarming, length with a shiver of fear. *Our bodies are meant for this.* They were meant to come together. To share in one another. They had, and it had been an exquisite union. Now she couldn't get the notion that her body had been meant for his, and his body for hers, out of her mind.

She had given herself to him. Her body. Her trust. And, though she felt like a fool even thinking it, her heart. She didn't regret a moment of their time at The Cock and the Crown. She didn't regret any moment with Gray at all, come to think of it. The only thing she regretted was not being able to stop herself from falling in love with him.

She was in love with Gray. And it was going to be a disaster.

Not that she could tell Lady Briannon any of this.

Mary curtsied and took her leave while Lana put aside the folding. She then retrieved a comb and the hot iron for her mistress's hair. "Don't trouble yourself, my lady. I'm sure I'm just a little shaky from my interview with Mr. Thomson yesterday."

Brynn, Archer, Gray, Lana, and Colton had all been interviewed, but Mr. Thomson, the Bow Street inquiry agent, had felt he could press Lana and Colton, as servants, more than once with questions where he could not with the others.

"That atrocious man," Brynn grumbled, sitting in her chair before the vanity mirror. "When Gray heard he'd been in the kitchens asking you more questions, he nearly boiled over."

Gray. Lana had seen him in passing, but they had not been given the opportunity to be alone or talk.

"Did he?" she asked. Then, with a forced shrug, added, "I suppose Lord Northridge only wanted to be sure I didn't stray from the story."

Brynn peered at Lana in the mirror's reflection. "I feel terrible about asking you to lie, Lana."

"Do not be silly," she replied. "It was necessary to protect Lady Eloise's reputation."

In the rushed moments between Archer and Gray extinguishing the flames in the mews and the arrival of the constable, the four of them had concocted a timeline of events that would shield Eloise's memory from being stained.

As it now stood, the Masked Marauder had set upon the carriage taking Gray, Brynn, and Lana to the Kensington Ball. Archer had chanced upon the attack, and they had all been forced back to the Hadley Gardens mews. There, they'd been bound and gagged while the bandit scoured the main home for the loot he'd had to leave behind on his last visit—the visit where he had shot and killed the Duke of Bradburne.

Eloise, they all agreed to say, had interrupted the bandit in the mews. She had been shot, while Gray had wrestled free of his restraints, gotten a hold of the bandit's second pistol, and then shot the bandit. A lit candle, they agreed, had set the stable on fire.

Lana was nearly finished with Brynn's hair. She was leaving to call upon Lady Cordelia, though Lana knew she would rather stay in and brood.

"You are wonderful, Lana. Truly. We are so lucky to have you with us."

She smiled, though it was shaky. "I am the lucky one, my lady."

"Are you disappointed to be leaving London so soon?" Brynn asked as Lana released a lock of her mistress's hair from its coil around the hot iron. It bounced free and perfect next to Brynn's ear.

"Not at all, my lady," Lana replied, hoping her anxiousness to be gone from town had not sounded as apparent to her as it did to Lana. She wanted to be anywhere Viktor was not. It had been well over a week since she'd last heard from Lord Langlevit, and she'd started to seriously consider that something might have happened to him. It was all her fault. If he'd been harmed in any way in his attempts to clear her name and protect her and Irina, she would never forgive herself.

Adding to her frazzled worry was the fact that Gray's man had not yet sent word, or returned, from his trip up to Cumbria to protect Irina from the Frenchman her uncle had deployed. It would have taken four days, five at the most, to reach the Langlevit estate. Not knowing what was happening was maddening. At the very least, Essex would be closer to Cumbria.

"The funeral service is tomorrow," Brynn said, though

needlessly, as Lana tied her stays and helped her into a pale green muslin day dress. The entire household had been riding the swell of a black wave toward the event all week. "Mama wishes to depart for Ferndale immediately after."

"Yes, my lady."

Brynn sighed. "I don't know why Mama thinks both you and Mary need to be attached to me every single second. I'm perfectly fine. I'm not going to faint at the funeral or expire at the sight of His Grace." Her voice shook slightly on the last, but she tossed her head. "It's all well and good that the farce is over with. Now the duke can move on with his life, and me with mine."

Lana didn't answer, but she knew exactly why Lady Dinsmore wanted her at her daughter's side. Despite the fetching hairstyle and lovely gown, the gauntness of Brynn's face spoke volumes, as did the broken heart she tried so valiantly to conceal. Lana's heart wept when she saw Brynn's red-rimmed eyes each morning, but there was little she could do other than be there for whatever Brynn needed, which, at the moment, she insisted was nothing.

Lana couldn't imagine what Brynn had gone through—not knowing whether she was going to live or die, losing everything she loved in one fell swoop. It made her stomach clench painfully, because all she could think about was Irina, and what would happen if she ever lost her. The horrific events last week had been an epiphany. She had to make sure her sister was safe, no matter what. Irina had to come first, above all else.

"After the funeral, I should like you to go to Ferndale with the rest of the staff beforehand," Brynn was saying. "There is no need for you to ride with me to Essex, and I would hate to have you perched on the driver's seat with Beckett the whole time. Mary will do in your stead, and I think she would not mind a little time with Beckett."

Lana set the iron down in a porcelain bowl to cool. She hadn't expected the sensation of relief that filled her just then. Not for the fact that she would be able to ride inside a carriage with other servants, but that she would be escaping London one day sooner than anticipated.

"Thank you, my lady," she said, but Brynn touched Lana's arm as she drew away to remove the bowl and iron.

"All will be well, Lana, you'll see," she said earnestly. "I know you worry for me, but it's better this way. Truly."

Her heart aching, Lana curtsied. "If you say so, my lady."

Brynn departed a few moments later, and Lana made her way belowstairs. The kitchens were being scoured and the perishables put on ice and crated for the journey back to Essex. As much as Mrs. Braxton liked to complain about the unexpected departure back to Ferndale, Lana knew she was happy to be rushing around, clucking like a hen. Mrs. Frommer, on the other hand, wore her usual pinched expression as she barked orders to the scullery maids.

Avoiding the housekeeper, Lana slipped through the commotion, wanting only to sit and not think. Not worry.

It wasn't to be.

She sought a brief respite on the bottom step of the servants' staircase. She couldn't stop thinking about Irina. And about Gray. About what she wanted to do, and what she *had* to do. As much as she cared for him, Lana knew they had no future together. He needed to be with his daughter and his family, and she needed to be with hers. She had to end it with him…and the sooner she did so, the better it would be for everyone.

Suddenly, Lana understood why Brynn insisted on being so strong through the cancellation of the banns. The duke needed to move on with his life, just as Gray did. And as it stood, Lana was in the way. Gray had a future—he was the heir to an earldom. People would depend on him. Whatever

misguided sense of honor he felt for her was simply that…
misguided. She would not take him away from his family and
all that he loved. Lana rested her head on the paneled wall of
the narrow staircase and stifled a gut-wrenching sob.

The church for Lady Eloise's funeral service was not overly
full, Lana noted. From the little Brynn had told her about the
duke's reclusive sister, she did not have many acquaintances
so it was mostly family in attendance. A handful of people, if
that, filled only the first three pews.

Curious, Lana glanced around from where she sat,
farther back, near the end of the sixth pew. She recognized
Lady Cordelia as well as a few familiar faces she'd seen in
and around Bishop House, including Lord Thorndale with a
petite woman Lana expected must be his wife. It was certainly
not the number of people who had turned out en masse for
the late Duke of Bradburne's funeral. Then again, he'd been
well loved. Lady Eloise had been tolerated as his eccentric
by-blow.

Lady Dinsmore had requested Lana stay close at hand
during the service, in case Brynn took a turn for the worse.
Lana had seen no reason why Viktor would attend the funeral
services, so she had gone without much worry. However,
Brynn seemed fine, if quieter than usual. But Lana suspected
that had to do with seeing His Grace, the Duke of Bradburne.
Lana couldn't help noticing the duke's hard, implacable
expression, though it had softened imperceptibly when he'd
greeted Brynn. Even now, he sent her surreptitious glances
from time to time. Despite what Brynn had said about her
betrothal being a farce, it was obvious that the duke cared
about her. Perhaps when everything settled, they could still
have a chance together. Lana wished very much for her

mistress to be happy.

Her gaze slid to the man sitting at the end of the second pew, and her heart stuttered. Gray had not wanted to attend the service, which was no surprise given the truth of what Lady Eloise had done. He had only come under duress from Lady Dinsmore and to support his sister in her hour of need. His opinion of Bradburne had changed, too, but Lana suspected that had to do with what had happened in the mews when the duke had risked his life in order to protect Brynn.

She had missed seeing Gray these past few days. He'd accompanied the Coopers from Kentish Town back to Essex to see Sofia safely returned to Breckenham. Lana did not fault him at all for wanting to see his daughter after the ordeal in the Hadley Garden mews. It was the heart of why she needed to focus all her energy on Irina. Lord Bradburne had lost his sister so unexpectedly. So violently. The fear of losing Irina the way the duke had was entirely mind-numbing.

And it wasn't completely out of the realm of possibility.

With the threat of Viktor on their heels, and Langlevit gone now for well over a week, Lana felt powerless. She couldn't help feeling that a noose was cinching tighter and tighter about both their necks, urging them into a looming trap that they would not be able to escape. She had to *do* something. She had to get to her sister.

If Langlevit's cryptographer contact had fallen through, or, heaven forbid, if something had happened to the earl himself, then she and Irina would have to run. There would be no hope for deciphering the letters and no one to be their ally. She and Irina would always have to stay one step ahead of the baron and their uncle. Perhaps she would take Irina to Egypt or India. Or even the Americas. It would be a new start for both of them. And far enough away that they would be safe.

The only problem would be Gray. He wouldn't let her go, not willingly. If he followed, if he tried to come with her and Irina, she would be putting him in danger. And she would never want him to leave his family for her. She swallowed past the boulder-sized lump in her throat.

She had but one course of action: she would have to *make* him let her go.

Out of the corner of her eye, Lana drank in the sight of him, committing the shape of his face to memory. She devoured the image of his proud brow, graced with pale blond eyebrows. Her breath caught at his full lips, so perfect in profile, as were his straight nose and the strong jaw that framed them. She'd dreamed of that face for a thousand nights, and she'd savor it now for the nights to come.

In that same moment, as if sensing her stare, Gray shifted his head a fraction to the left. His blue gaze drilled into hers. She felt that look to the tips of her toes. It mirrored everything she was feeling and more. Tearing her eyes away with a harsh breath, Lana focused on the closing moments of the service, folding her trembling hands in her lap. The blatant yearning on Gray's face would do nothing to change her course. She couldn't afford to let it. For Irina's sake. For his, too.

Steeling herself, Lana vowed to tell him her decision as soon as she could.

It turned out that *soon* came far sooner than she'd expected.

As Lady and Lord Dinsmore ushered Brynn through the church and out the door, to their waiting carriage, Lana stayed near her pew. Once the rest of the lords and ladies had left, she would follow in a coach with Lady Dinsmore's maid, who had also accompanied the family. Lady Dinsmore was nothing if not prepared. As Lana approached the church doors, however, a hand shot out from a shadowed alcove and wrapped around her elbow. She was drawn forcibly into the alcove, where carved stone steps led up to a turret.

Warm fingers clamped over her lips, trapping the scream

billowing there. "Hush, Lana, it's only me."

Gray.

"My lord! What are you doing?"

He buried his face in her hair, his arms going around her. "God, it was torture sitting there watching you, not being beside you. You have no idea."

Conscious of the people just on the other side of the archway, Lana tried to push them both deeper into the alcove, behind the twisting stone stairs. "Stop, someone will see."

"I don't care." His lips caressed her forehead, her cheeks, her nose while his scent spiraled around her like another, less tangible, embrace. Her body thrummed at his touch, wanting to fold into his, to take strength from him, but Lana knew that if she gave in, all would be lost. *She* would be lost.

"Gray, please." Lana's fingers curled into fists against his jacket, and she shoved away from him with all her waning strength. It was futile. He didn't budge.

"I don't care who sees us, Lana." His warm lips grazed her ear, making her knees weaken as they traced a path down her jaw. "Let them look. Let them stare. It's you I want."

"I care," Lana said, turning her face away from his meandering lips. If he kissed her, she would not be able to think, much less do what she meant to. And if she had to do it here, so be it. "Please, Lord Northridge."

A frown puckered his brow, but the formal address made him pause. "Lord Northridge?"

"You must stop. This can't go on."

Gray finally took a step in reverse, though he was still touching her. He looked at her with a pointed, uncertain expression. Lana forced herself to hold his gaze, though she longed to look away. She didn't want to hurt him, but she felt something closing in on her. An inescapable truth. One that she had been ignoring every single time she saw Gray, spoke to him, kissed him. *Given* herself to him. She had been living a lie for the last eight months, and everyone she'd met during that time had been caught up in the tangles of it. Even him. *Especially* him.

Their entire relationship had been built on lies and half-truths. *Because of her.*

Lana fought the flush creeping up into her cheeks, but he still saw it.

"It is too late to stop, Lana," he said evenly, and just like that, she was picturing him above her on that velvet couch, his body joining hers, claiming her in every way.

She shook her head. "You know as well as I that there is no future for us."

And if Lord Langlevit did not return from his meeting with the cryptographer…if things took a turn for the worse, she had to be prepared to leave England with Irina. Leave without the threat of Gray coming after her. Inhaling deeply, she took a half step back, until her shoulders were pressed into the stone wall, but it was enough for his hands to fall away. Silence hummed between them, heavy and fraught.

"I can't do this anymore," she said.

"What, exactly?" His voice was guarded, but Lana heard the thread of hurt beneath it. She pressed forward, strengthening her resolve.

"Us. We do not belong together. You are a lord, and I am a maid."

He eyed her, a muscle along his jaw tensing. "We have already been through this. Let the rest of the blasted *ton* think what they will. I don't care. All I care about is you, Lana."

"That's just the problem. You should care," she said gently. "You should care for Sofia's sake, and for your family's. For Brynn's."

Gray shook his head, his resolve showing in the rigid line of his shoulders, but he leaned forward to gently grasp her elbows. "I will not allow other people's opinions to rule my heart. Or my decisions. I allowed it once—"

"With Sofia, yes. Because *you knew* there was no other way. You would have been skewered. Your family, scandalized. You thought of them first then, and you should think of them now."

"I am," he muttered. "I do think of them."

Lana steeled herself for what had to come, for the pain she would cause him. But it had to be done. "Do you, Gray?" she asked pointedly. "When you leave Sofia in the care of strangers, are you truly thinking of her well-being? When you try to protect yourself at her expense, are you thinking of her? Or are you just hiding from responsibility?"

His mouth parted on a soundless exhale, as if she'd just knocked the wind out of him. "That's not fair."

"Sadly, my lord, life isn't fair, but we cope as well as we are able. My sister needs me, and your daughter needs her father. Your family needs you."

"And you don't?" he asked.

"No." She shook her head, her heart breaking into tiny pieces at the betrayed look in his eyes. "You don't even know me, Gray. I have a sister, and a family in Russia. That is where I belong. Not here. And not with you. I was a passing flirtation, nothing more. You have to marry to your station, and I have to…return to my life. We must say good-bye."

"Lana, why are you doing this?" he asked softly. "Is it because you're afraid? I'm afraid too, but we can make this work. You're right. I need to take responsibility, to be a better man. I can make this work. With Sofia. With you. With my family. Just let me try, please, that's all I am asking. One chance."

Oh, God. He was begging. Pleading. Gray's hands stroked hers, sliding up her arms and pulling her toward him. She could barely steel herself against the look in his eyes as it was. Lana grew desperate, swallowing the battered joy rising like a geyser in her chest. She should have known he would never give up that easily. Her eyes burned with unshed tears, but Lana held on to her fading composure with every shred of strength she had left.

Irina, she reminded herself. *Irina* was the only person who mattered.

She had to make him hate her.

Lana's heart would mend and so would Gray's. The horrendous lie she was about to speak nearly choked her, but she forced it out. "I can't. I have to tell you something. Before we left Russia, my uncle arranged for my hand in marriage to a local boy."

It was as if all the air was sucked out of the room. Her chest rose and fell with frantic, gasping breaths, but Gray only stared at her, his eyes disbelieving. *Agonized.*

"Marriage," he repeated, his voice flat. "To a local boy."

"Yes."

He took a breath. "You are betrothed?"

Lana nodded, unable to speak.

"Then why did you…" He raised his chin, fury cresting in his injured glare. "Why in hell did you give yourself to me at the Crown?"

She flinched, her eyes drifting from his as she dug deep, to the layers of cool reserve drilled into her from birth—the ability to hold one's composure no matter what. For the first time in months, she reached for the hidden princess buried underneath all the layers of the servant.

"I had heard so many rumors about your prowess in the bedroom. Can you fault me for being curious?"

Lana was grateful for the cool tones of her voice that conveyed the despicable words, meant to flay him to the bone. They succeeded. Gray released her elbows, and they dropped to her sides, heavy as lead. He stared at her, stunned disbelief warring with confusion in his eyes.

She delivered the final blow with an insouciant shrug of her shoulders. "What is it Lady Dinsmore always says—a girl can't do better than to catch a duke? Well, I didn't catch a duke, but I had a part of you. And you didn't disappoint, Lord Northridge. You, a viscount, an English lord, the heir to an earldom. In truth, you were…a pleasant novelty for a mere maid like me."

"You're lying," he whispered.

Lana strained to meet his stare. She had to make him believe, even if it gouged out her heart. "I am not," she said, keeping her voice calm and steady. "I only wish I had made myself plain before now. Once Lord Langlevit helps me bring Zakorov and Count Volkonsky to justice, I plan to return to Russia with my sister and marry the one of my uncle's choosing. I have no desire to stay here in England. With you or any man of my acquaintance."

More lies.

Lies built upon lies. An entire fortress of them.

She held herself entirely still, her expression cast of stone. One flicker of emotion, and she would crumble. A small, quiet part of her screamed for Gray not to believe her, to argue and force her to admit the truth, to dispute every ugly word trespassing her lips and violating her heart. But she had been too exact…too perfect in her cold, ruthless performance.

"Any man of your acquaintance," he said dully. "I understand now."

Lana longed to correct him…that he had been—*he was*—the only man, but she couldn't lay it all to waste now. She had to cut him loose for good. "Perhaps I am more like Marianna than we both knew."

A muscle flexed in his cheek, and Gray stepped to the side, his eyes falling away from hers. His lips were parted, as if he wanted to say something. He licked them and then flared his nostrils as a sweep of pain and humiliated anger transformed his features.

"Of course. How lucky am I to have been your entertaining diversion while Langlevit fixed all of your problems. Go home, then, now that you know what it is to lie with a lord. Go marry your pauper boy." He flexed his hands into fists and brushed past her, pausing only to add, "You will be forgotten in a fortnight."

He stalked out of the alcove, and Lana's heart went with him, stretching and ripping, completely destroyed. She closed her eyes and braced herself against the cold twisting stone stairwell. God, he hated her now. But she had done what she'd needed to do. He would not come for her. He would stay where he was needed, with Brynn and Sofia and his family. He would stay safe.

Unlike what Gray had promised her, she would not forget him in a fortnight. She would never forget him. Never stop loving him. How absurd, how cruel, that *this* had been the only way she could show it.

Chapter Twenty-Three

Perhaps I am more like Marianna than we both knew.

They were the most damning words he'd ever heard. Worse, because Gray had never thought to even compare the two women. Their only commonality had been their humble origins. But he'd been wrong. Lana, as it turned out, was far worse than Marianna had ever been. At least Marianna had been truthful about not wanting Sofia.

Lana was a liar. A schemer. A fraud.

She had hurt him worse than Marianna ever had.

"That will do, my lord," Harrison said, with a satisfied nod at his handiwork. Gray scrubbed a hand over his face as his valet finished the last touches on his cravat, completing the intricate knot with a diamond stickpin. The man in the looking glass looked exactly like the man from the night before—pressed evening clothes, clean-shaven jaw, not a strand of blond hair out of place. He looked like his normal self. The arrogant aristocrat without a care in the world. Which was what he intended.

"Thank you, Harrison. Please send for my carriage."

"Already done, my lord. Rogers is out front."

Descending the staircase, Gray entered the waiting coach and sat back on the velvet squabs. He did not want to go out, but he would go insane if he remained another minute within the empty walls of Bishop House. The rest of his family had departed for Essex days before, leaving him with Harrison, a cookmaid, a footman, and his driver. The only reprieve had been that Brynn had taken her maid with her. Gray didn't know if his heart could handle the sight of her, which was why he'd chosen to remain in London. To clear his head.

It hadn't helped a whit.

She haunted him everywhere he turned. He couldn't play a hand of cards without thinking about her sprawled on that sofa at the Crown. He couldn't go into a garden without smelling her fragrance. Hell, he couldn't even close his eyes without seeing her face.

So, tonight, he was trying something different. He would attempt to *replace* her face with another. Not a courtesan—he'd tried that but couldn't bring himself to do it, not after years of celibacy that he'd only broken with Lana.

No, he'd replace her with something more.

Be responsible, as she'd leveled at him. Marry to his station. Do his duty. A wife would do nicely.

The King's Theatre was crowded, glittering under the flickering gaslights. He'd invited Lady Cordelia Vandermere to his private box at the opera, choosing it for its exposure. It seemed like all the young ladies he was acquainted with longed for the chance to be seen at the opera with a prospective beau, and if he remembered something Brynn had once said, the opera was one of Lady Cordelia's favorite pastimes.

But as he walked through the crowded foyer of the King's Theatre, the thought of sitting in an enclosed box with only the young lady and Mozart's *Don Giovanni* for company made him feel ill. Not that he was anything like Don Giovanni, a notorious libertine and seducer of women, but the subject matter felt too close for comfort. He couldn't help noticing the fact that the last woman of his intimate acquaintance had been promised to another and he had taken her innocence.

He clenched his jaw. He hadn't taken *anything* that hadn't willingly been given.

Cordelia had arrived with her parents and stood at the far end of the hall. He grasped a glass of whiskey from a nearby footman and drank it in one gulp. For fortitude. Determinedly, Gray made his way toward the lady and her parents, even though his feet wanted to flee in the opposite direction. He stopped to converse with a few people he knew, though it felt as if he were in some sort of waking dream. Like his body was a wooden puppet with someone else controlling the strings.

"Lord Vandermere, Countess," he said with a short bow to her parents before taking Cordelia's gloved fingers in his palm and pressing his lips to the silk. "Lady Cordelia, how lovely you look."

"Lord Northridge, what a kind thing to say," she said graciously and inclined her neck as her parents offered their greetings and pleasantries.

His smile felt plastered on, but Gray had to admit Cordelia looked beautiful. The ice blue gown set off her figure to perfection. Her skin glowed with radiant health, and her flaxen curls framed sparkling eyes the same color as her dress. On the surface, she was everything he *should* want: cultured, poised, beautiful, and blue-blooded. She would make an excellent match. His mother would be ecstatic, but Gray felt nothing but hollowness in the pit of his stomach as he escorted her to his private box.

Her parents went to theirs, but Cordelia's quiet chaperone—the same young woman who'd been with her in front of White's—trailed a few steps behind them and sat unobtrusively in the corner once they arrived. Her presence, dictated by society, was a necessity.

"I must admit, Lord Northridge," Cordelia said, flicking open her fan. "I was surprised when you called upon me the other afternoon."

"Why is that?"

She inclined her head. "I had heard the rest of your family left for Essex shortly after Lady Eloise's funeral, and I suppose I expected you to return as well."

"I had business in London."

She smiled from behind the pleats of her fan. "Of course."

Their conversation faded into silence as the first act began, but as the opera wore on, Gray found that he couldn't concentrate. He shifted in his seat, his knee shaking with restless energy. His eyes swept to the woman at his side, and he saw, to his surprise, that she was looking at him instead of the stage. He arched an eyebrow, uncomfortable at the odd, incisive look in her eyes.

She flicked her fan open again. "You don't enjoy the opera?"

"Not particularly," he admitted.

"Then why did you ask me?"

"Because it is what you like."

The corner of her mouth tipped upward into a half smile as she stifled a laugh. "We have known each other for years, Lord Northridge, and never once have you cared a hoot for what I like. What has changed?"

Surprised, Gray stared at her. She had never struck him as anything less than icy, but now he saw something else: a deep intelligence and a sly humor. He appreciated her bluntness and answered equally so. "I suppose it is time I chose a wife."

A faint flush shimmered over her cheekbones, her fan gliding into motion. "Though I am flattered, what makes you think I would be interested in such a suit?"

Gray blinked. "Isn't that what all young women want?"

"Not all women, Lord Northridge."

She surprised him again. But this time, something in her voice tugged at him. It contained wistfulness. A resignation to a fate not wished for. He recognized the feeling intimately, and Gray was curious to know what she meant. He turned to face her. "And what is it that you want?"

She angled her head toward the stage and took her time before answering. "I wish for freedom."

"If you marry the right man, you'll have it," he said, frowning.

Her laugh was hollow. "Come now, Lord Northridge, surely you don't believe that. I mean freedom from this." She waved a gloved hand, her voice low and intense. "From expectation. From what *should* be done. Who says I must marry?"

He tented a slow eyebrow. "You don't wish to?"

"Not if I can help it. How do you think I've managed to stay free for three full seasons?" Cordelia laughed. "I am as skilled at avoiding unwanted suits as I am at attracting them."

"And your parents?" he asked, starting to realize that her icy demeanor had been an act.

"They only want for my happiness. My father married a governess after all, though it's remarkable how well the *ton* chooses what it wants to remember."

Gray sat back in his chair. Had he known that Lady Vandermere had been a governess? He couldn't recall any gossip of that nature, though it would have been twenty years ago.

"Who says I must be a dutiful wife to some lord?" Cordelia's slender shoulders rose in a shrug. "Become a broodmare for his heirs? I wish freedom from it all. To be who I want. To love whom I want."

Gray's eyes narrowed at her. "Love," he repeated.

"The thing we live for...the one we breathe for." Almost

as if she hadn't meant to, her eyes flicked over her shoulder to the woman seated in the corner of his opera box. The chaperone met Cordelia's eyes only briefly, but it was long enough. Gray drew in a clipped breath. He shook his head, convinced he had misinterpreted the look of longing, but then Cordelia smiled and tipped her head to the side. "We want who we want."

Gray couldn't help it. He laughed. For the first time in days, he laughed. She—the icy, unflappable, prim and proper Lady Cordelia Vandermere—had shocked him.

"You are right," he agreed.

She leaned toward him, her eyes sparkling. "And it's evident, Lord Northridge, that you do not want me."

Gray went silent and then swallowed, his eyes returning to the final act unfolding on stage. "You are right, but what if the young lady in question is promised to another?"

"Do you care for each other?"

His breath stalled at the blunt question. He'd thought they had. But Lana had well and truly shattered that illusion. Gray flinched at the biting recollection of her words. But then he took a breath and pushed past the dull ache to recall her face. Her eyes, glistening with unshed tears. The unhidden agony in them.

He'd been so consumed with his own that he hadn't seen hers. He knew what had happened in the mews had affected her greatly and that she worried for her sister. Gray frowned. Had she said what she had out of some skewed notion of protecting him? Was there even a man waiting for her? Or had she said it all to push him away? To protect him.

Oh, Lana.

"Yes," he answered in a hoarse voice. "I think so."

Cordelia smiled at him. "Then why are you here courting me? Go, Lord Northridge. Find happiness. There is no cost too great to pay. Trust me on that."

His chest felt tight as he stood and bent to kiss her hand. "Thank you."

"Think nothing of it, my lord," she replied with an airy wave. "After all, we free-spirited souls need to stick together."

"If there is ever anything I can do for you, Lady Cordelia, please do not hesitate to ask," Gray said, and meant it. "I shall take my leave. My apologies for not seeing you home. Should I escort you back to your parents?"

Cordelia hid a secret smile behind her fan. "I think I shall stay here a few minutes more, if that suits you, Lord Northridge. Precious few moments like these are not to be wasted."

"Please, stay as long as you like."

Gray left the box, drawing the curtains closed behind him. The sound of soft laughter reached his ears through it, but he had other things on his mind—his own happiness, as it were.

With renewed purpose, he strode down the plush carpeted steps to his waiting carriage but was halted from climbing into it by a man shouting, "Milord! Lord Northridge!"

Surprised, Gray turned to see Croyden, the man he'd hired to keep an eye on Zakorov, riding toward him. Gray frowned. Croyden was grimy and covered in filth, what looked like globs of crusted blood stuck to his face and clothing. "What happened to you?"

"The baron, milord," the man wheezed, sliding in a bone-weary heap from the saddle and clutching his middle. "Caught me and young Tommy tailing 'im. Thrashed me to within an inch. Dumped me in the river and left me for dead, he did."

Gray felt his insides turn to ice as he gripped the man's shoulder. He knew all too well what a brute like Zakorov was capable of. "Do you know where the baron is now, Croyden? Is he still in London?"

"No, milord." Croyden shook his head. "Tommy followed him. North. His carriage rode north."

• • •

The darkening clouds closing in on Ferndale worried Lana. She'd helped Brynn prepare for an early-evening ride less than a quarter hour before, and by the looks of it, her mistress would be caught in a downpour soon. Lana sat upon a chair just beyond the kitchen entrance, a bucket of soapy water at her feet. The cool breeze had been too delicious to pass up, so she had thrown on her black cloak to shield against the chilled air and taken the bit of laundry she had for Brynn outdoors.

She scrubbed a few spots of dark red wine from the left half of a pair of delicate kidskin gloves, hoping to lift the stain. Lana's mind wandered, her scrubbing intensifying as it touched on everything she did not wish to think about. Her sister and whether or not the Frenchman, or even Gray's hired man, had reached her in Cumbria. Lord Langlevit and the now undeniable knowledge that something untoward had happened to him. There could be no other reason for his prolonged absence. Her uncle and Viktor's whereabouts were up in the air as well, now that Lana had been in Essex for nearly a week.

And Gray. She thought of Gray and winced at the cruel things she'd said to him. The lies she'd uttered in order to push him away and keep him safe. The pain of it still pricked her soul whenever she remembered the look in his eyes as she'd torn out his heart—and her own.

"Lady Lana?"

She stopped her scrubbing and looked up. James, the footman, was approaching her chair, which she'd dragged out from the kitchen and placed in the swaying grass. The breeze had kicked up a notch, and even the winter cloak she wore felt insufficient against the raw cold. James held out a slim letter. "This just arrived for you."

No one sent her letters. No one except the Earl of

Langlevit.

With her breath caught in her throat, her pulse pounding with hope, she took the letter. She let out a near sob of relief when she saw the waxed seal with the usual jumping hare.

"Is anything wrong?" James asked, frowning with worry. Lana set the glove down and jumped to her feet.

"Oh no. Nothing at all," she said and, thanking him, darted inside the kitchen.

She hurried toward a back corridor and dipped into the stillroom. It smelled of herbs, dried fruit, and the sharp scent of liqueur, but Lana paid no attention to that as she ripped the letter from the envelope. She instantly recognized the earl's hand, though the contents were not coded.

Deepest apologies on my absence. Followed a lead to Cumbria after finding my cryptographer contact dead. Did not wish to alarm you. No choice in matter now. Your sister has been taken. On my way to Essex. Reason to believe that is their destination. You are in danger. You must remain in London. Entrench. Request Lord Northridge's help. He will give it, I am sure. Trust me to retrieve your sister.

Your servant, as always, L.

The edges of the parchment crumpled in her hand. Her arms shook, a hard, hot sob lodged in her throat. Irina. The Frenchman had succeeded. He'd taken her. After so many days of only imagining the worst, it had come to pass.

Lana let out a whimper and squeezed her eyes shut. Tears stung them, her heart shuddering madly in her chest.

She'd failed her sister. She'd said she would protect her, and she hadn't. No, she'd been tucked away in London and Essex doing Lady Briannon's hair and falling in love with a man she had no right loving in the first place.

Love. She loved her *sister.* And she needed to get to her.

Langlevit didn't know what had happened, clearly. The letter was dated four days prior, first sent to Bishop House, then redirected to Essex. He hadn't known Eloise had died. He had no idea she and the family had returned to Ferndale. Though if he'd been on his way to Essex four days ago, he had likely arrived.

She left the stillroom, her pulse a staggered beat, her mind whirling. Where had Lana been when Irina had been attacked and stolen? Swinging in the Coopers' backyard? Dreaming of an idyllic life with Gray and his daughter? Lana felt so guilty. So wrong. And angry.

Viktor would not harm her. Lana wouldn't let him. Langlevit had advised staying in London and seeking out Gray's help, but it was too late for that. She was already in Essex, and she most certainly couldn't go to Gray now, not after what she'd said to him after Eloise's funeral. She knew he'd remained behind because of her, and she'd been grateful for it. She'd been happy to not be tortured by his presence at every turn. But now, Lana couldn't help but wish he were here. He would know exactly what to do...what to say. But Gray was gone.

And now, so was Irina.

As she climbed the servant staircase, her tears fell hot and fast, and she swiped at them furiously. What good would they do for Irina? Tears, like hopeless wishes, were useless. Lana reached her room in the attics and threw off her cloak. She placed Langlevit's letter in a ceramic washbasin and, striking a match, lit it on fire. As Lana watched it burn to cinders, she dried her eyes and tried to steady her breathing.

The knot of worry that had settled in Lana's stomach grew heavier with every passing moment. The earl had ordered her to stay put. It was something she could not do.

His Essex home, Hartstone, was only a fifteen-minute ride from Ferndale. With the skies about to unleash a torrent of rain, Brynn would most likely be returning from her outing very soon. Lana knew she should stay at Ferndale. It was her duty to see to her mistress. However, those rules weighed nothing compared to the duty Lana felt right then to her sister. She could no longer stay where she was, hiding and waiting.

Lana made up her mind. She would see if the earl was in residence at Hartstone. At least it would be something to *do*. Resolute, she forwent her heavy woolen black cloak and donned her green cape, a lighter material and better suited for both rain and a fast ride through the countryside.

She then took a circuitous route to the stables in order to arrive there unseen.

Percival was in the stables, tending to the horses. He thought nothing of Lana's request to take one of the lesser mounts out, though he did express concern about the coming storm.

"Just a short ride," she told him, making sure to smile widely and flutter her lashes a bit. She felt like a fool, but it was worth it. "You know my skill, Percy," she added with a playful tap to his shoulder.

The boy's ears went pink, and he helped her saddle the bay. Within minutes, Lana was streaking down Ferndale's lane, through the village of Breckenham, and onward to Langlevit's estate.

Anything at all could have happened in the four days since he'd written Lana. She prayed he had Irina with him and that the Frenchman her uncle and Viktor had hired was now in custody. Or dead. It was a heartless thought, but yes, she wanted the man dead. She wanted any person who threatened her sister's safety dead.

I should have been there to protect her.

It was the thought that would not quit playing in her mind as she rode, the first drops of rain striking her heated cheeks. Of course, she knew nothing could be reversed. She'd thought she was doing the right thing—the best thing—for them when she'd taken a position as lady's maid.

Hartstone was not as large as Ferndale, but it was stately just the same. Its many windows were dark, and with the storm eclipsing the last bit of sunlight in the sky, the house looked eerie. She would have believed it was vacant, had there not been a few windows along the ground level dimly lit by firelight. She turned up the long, straight drive to the front courtyard. It was indecent, really, a servant showing up unannounced at this time of night. But Lana could not have cared less. What did it matter now? Her secrets were crumbling out from underneath her. If they had found Irina, it was only a matter of time before they found her, too.

She tied her mount off on one of the posts and went straight to the front door. Her pounding knock was answered almost immediately by none other than the earl himself.

He stared at her, a clicking sound coming from behind his back where he held his arm hidden. When he brought his hand into view, she saw a pistol.

"What the devil are you doing here?" he hissed, grabbing her elbow and pulling her inside the foyer.

"Where is Irina?" she asked, her eyes jumping to the stairs and the balustrade above the foyer. She saw no one. Heard no one. The place was utterly dark, except for a receiving room to the right. In there, she saw the flickers of a fire in the hearth.

"I told you to stay in London," he said, ignoring her question. She supposed it was only fair. She'd ignored his, after all.

"I was already at Ferndale when I received your note. We left London shortly after—" She broke off and shook her head, not wanting to explain about Lord and Lady Dinsmore's early departure from London. There had been talk, Lana knew, among the servants, that Eloise had become of an interest to Langlevit. If he did not yet know of her death, Lana didn't want to be the one to inform him. Selfishly, she didn't want him distracted either. "Never mind why, I'll explain later. My sister. Where is she?"

Langlevit muttered something underneath his breath and locked the front door, throwing the bolts and placing the pistol's barrel into the waist of his trousers. The weapon did not bode well.

"She's not here," he answered, his tone rich with impatience and exasperation. The stony knot in Lana's stomach grew larger, and she bit back tears. "I've only arrived tonight," he said, gesturing for her to enter the receiving room. "I've sent my staff away as a precaution. I can't put them in harm's way should anyone unsavory arrive." He slanted a look at Lana. "Why have you come here, Princess?"

"My uncle. He's in London. It's not safe there. And after learning Irina might be here—"

"I should never have written to you. They are using her as a lure! Don't you understand that?"

A part of her had, yes. Dangling Irina's life or death over Lana's head would certainly entice her to come out of hiding. Viktor and her uncle both must have known to what extent Lana would go in order to protect her sister. They had to have known that she would give herself up in an instant. But the impossibility of it still lingered. Irina knew about the letters. She knew Viktor and Count Volkonsky were spies. So did Langlevit. They were all in danger no matter where they were.

"She depends upon me!" Lana cried. "If anything should happen to her—"

She couldn't finish the sentence. She didn't know how. A world without Irina was not a world she wanted to live in. Irina was the only real family she had left, and she could not lose her. Lana shook her head again, trying to dispel the tears brimming in her eyes. Frustration and fear bound her tongue, and she couldn't speak.

Langlevit stepped forward and took her shoulders in his hands. They gripped her firmly, and when she dragged in a breath and opened her eyes, she saw the earl's head cocked to the side, his eyes boring into hers. Firelight danced on one half of his face. He was a handsome man. Stately, like his home. As trustworthy as its walls and as strong as its foundation stones. Lana relaxed under his steady gaze.

"I gave you my promise in St. Petersburg, Lana. Your father was a trusted friend, and I will not allow any injustice or harm to come to his daughters."

Hearing him address her by her given name for the first time surprised her. Oddly, though, it made her feel even more at ease in his presence. With a shaky nod, she placed her hands upon his chest. He wore his shirtsleeves and waistcoat, his collar unadorned by a cravat. His hair was rumpled and his jaw unshaven. Of course. He'd let his valet go to protect him. The same way she'd pushed Gray away in London in order to protect *him*.

Distracted by thoughts of Gray upon thoughts of Irina, her fingertips frantically worked the small, embroidered pattern of ivy on the earl's waistcoat, a dry sob catching in her throat. "I know. And I'm so grateful. I truly can't thank you enough for everything you've done."

"Stop," he said, and gently pulled her closer, into a brotherly embrace. "I want no thanks, not until I retrieve Irina. And I *will*," he added, pulling back so he could see her fully. "Even without me, you would have other help. Northridge, for example. I know that he is suspicious of Zakorov."

Lana dropped her eyes, her distraught fingers stalling out on the embroidery.

"If anything should happen to me, Lana, you must go to Northridge. He's a good man. You can trust him."

She gathered a breath, the calming pressure of Langlevit's hands on her shoulders making her swirling thoughts be still for the first time. "I know. *He* knows," she said, her voice soft. "About me, I mean."

Langlevit let go of one shoulder and nudged Lana's chin up so he could look at her, incredulous. "What are you saying? He knows you are the princess?"

She shook her head quickly, her chin trapped in Langlevit's hand. "No! Not that. He thinks I'm the missing princesses' maid. He knew something was off about me, and he now knows Zakorov is searching for them—I mean, *me*—but he doesn't know it, and…oh! I didn't know how to explain it to you. And then you were going to meet with your contact about the cipher, and Gray wouldn't stop pressing me to tell him the truth—"

"*Gray?*" Langlevit said, interrupting her incomprehensible rambling.

She sealed her lips, her eyes wide. She shouldn't have called him that.

The earl opened his mouth to speak again when several loud bangs on the front door cracked through the silence. He released Lana and stepped away, drawing the pistol from his waist. He held out a hand to her. "Stay here," he whispered, then pointed to the hearth. "Take up a weapon. Hide."

She stared at the iron shovel and poker that hung on a stand next to the fire, her heart in her throat. The next knock on the front door practically shook the house. She heard the person rattling the locked knob, trying to get inside. Lana raced to the hearth and took up the heavy iron poker as Langlevit called out to their unexpected visitor.

Chapter Twenty-Four

Gray slammed his fist down upon the entrance to Hartstone. He seethed with fury, his roiling temper seconds away from overwhelming his ability to think. And thinking was all he'd been doing for the last twenty-four hours, ever since Croyden's arrival outside the King's Theatre. Worrying that Zakorov would be headed straight for Essex. Straight for Lana. Even if she'd been telling the truth about a betrothal, which he now suspected she wasn't, Gray didn't want her in any danger, especially at the hands of Zakorov.

It had been close to midnight, and setting off on the north road out of London at such an hour would have been asking to be robbed at gunpoint, stripped of his horse, his coin, and very possibly, his life. So he'd paced Bishop House, his muscles tense and his mind roiling with unease, waiting restlessly until the first drop of dawn's light lit the sky. He'd taken off for Essex, nearly riding Pharaoh into the ground that first hour on the road.

When Gray had finally reached Breckenham in the waning daylight as a ceiling of foreboding clouds settled overhead, he'd pushed his lathered mount up Ferndale's long drive, muttering a slew of curses. He'd avoided the front door, and ultimately his parents, and had gone straight to the kitchens in search of Lana. The other servants had shaken their heads with alarm. She had not been seen for some time, they'd said. James, the footman, had said she'd received a letter and had rushed off to read it.

Gray had chucked every last shred of propriety out the window and climbed the four flights of stairs to the servants' quarters. He'd gone into each and every room, not knowing which one belonged to Lana until he'd found it. He recognized her scent the moment he stepped over the threshold. And her familiar black cloak had been tossed without care onto the floor. He'd stepped in and picked up the cloak, only to find a folded white card slipping from its pocket.

Gray had read it, and his blood began to boil.

I must see you. Black coach outside. - L.

The bloody handwriting. It was the same from the poem he'd found on the floor of the coach when he'd been convinced Lana had been meeting with a lover. He'd memorized every silly line, laughing to himself that women could find such nonsense appealing. He'd thought the poet to be some local swain in Breckenham. He couldn't have been more wrong.

Langlevit was the author of both.

God, he'd been so blind. So goddamned gullible.

Lana had told him herself she didn't want to be with any man of her acquaintance. Yet, in her hour of need, Lana had gone to one of them. She'd trusted *Langlevit*, not Gray.

I must see you.

He'd crumpled the note in his fist.

Gray's heart clenched in agony—clearly, having a betrothed hadn't been her only secret. How often had she and Langlevit met like this in the past months? How many times had they written such sonnets of undying love to each other? Was it before or after she'd lain with Gray? He'd never figured the earl for a poet, but apparently love turned men into colossal fools.

It certainly had turned *him* into one.

Gray thought of that night in London, when he'd spied Lana slipping into a waiting carriage, not knowing then that the earl was within. She'd promised that there was nothing untoward happening between her and her anonymous peer protector…and Gray had believed her. And even when he'd discovered Langlevit's note, a small part of him had hoped that Lana's feelings for the earl had been in the past. Before him. Before Gray.

But he'd never been more wrong.

He'd come to Hartstone and, through the wide windows, had seen Lana looking up into Langlevit's face, his fingers caressing her jaw…holding her in a lover's embrace, their bodies so close together that not an inch of space remained between them. Her profile had been lit partially by the firelight, and the devoted look in her eyes as she'd gazed at the earl had made Gray nearly stagger to his knees.

She'd stared at him with the same trust before. The night in his bedroom, when she'd admitted to needing help with Zakorov. When she'd broken down in panic outside the mews upon learning her sister had been found. When she'd won her hand in *vingt-et-un* and claimed her prize. She'd gazed at him with rapturous certainty when her luscious, deceitful body had been splayed beneath him.

Gray drew a ragged breath. His hand shook as he raised it again to slam into the mahogany panel of the door. Rage and jealousy consumed him, incapacitating any ability to think clearly. Had she given herself to Langlevit as well? Had she also wanted to know what it was to lie with a goddamned earl? None of her words at the funeral service had been lies after all. He'd just been too blind—too infatuated—to see it.

"Who is it?" A man's voice. Muffled and cautious. Gray's fury simmered anew. Of course the bastard would be cautious. Lana had come to his home in the middle of the night. For what, comfort?

"Northridge. Open this door."

"North? What are you doing—"

The door opened far enough for Gray to get enough leverage with his shoulder to smash his fist into Langlevit's face. Grim satisfaction overtook him as Langlevit stumbled backward, a pistol clattering to the floor as the earl clutched his bleeding mouth. Gray kicked the door shut behind him, only partially taking in the lack of lighting and the absence of any staff. The other part of him saw Langlevit's state of half dress. Gray's lewd imaginings took flight like a provoked swarm of bees.

"I know she is here," he growled, advancing toward the double doors that led to the salon Lana and Langlevit had been standing in moments before.

Langlevit swiped at the blood flecking his lips and spit a mouthful to the polished marble floor. His voice was calm. "For Christ's sake, Northridge, what the hell has gotten into you?"

"A healthy dose of the truth, it would seem," he answered before pushing the doors open wide.

"Gray?" The soft voice came from a shadowed corner of the salon. She came forward, her feminine form taking shape out of the darkness. He couldn't stop the immediate stutter of his heart at the sight of her and gritted his teeth in disgust at his body's weak response.

"What are you doing here?" she asked, the poker in her hand falling to her side.

Gray took in little details, like the heightened color in her cheeks and her tousled hair, half of the dark mass hanging loose as if she'd only just tumbled out of bed. His anger escalated. He drew his eyes along her person and flared his nostrils, annoyed at the emotion knotting his throat. How could a woman look so angelic and be such a scheming opportunist at the same time? She was a wolf in sheep's clothing. A chameleon. And he'd fallen for every one of her lies. "The question, love," he drawled, "is what have *you* been doing?"

Her eyes widened as she took his meaning. "No, Gray—" She broke off, looking past him with a stricken expression to Langlevit, who had entered the salon. Gray felt nothing but numbness spreading across his body as she dropped the poker and held her hands out to him. The same numbness he'd nearly drowned in when Lana had speared his heart in that church alcove. "Lord Northridge, it isn't like that."

"Why so formal, sweet?" he said, pain and anger causing his voice to pull low.

"You don't understand," she said.

"I'm afraid neither do I," Langlevit interjected from behind Gray. The earl sauntered into Gray's view, the pistol he'd dropped earlier back in his hand. Though his grip was relaxed and the barrel pointed at the floor, Langlevit's eyes blazed with suspicion. They flicked between Lana and Gray, his mouth a grim slash.

Gray withdrew the card he'd found in Lana's room from his pocket and flung it to the floor. "Does this help jog either of your memories?" His eyes went to Lana. "How long has he been sending you love letters?"

"Love letters?" she said, her hand rising to her throat.

"Poems," he snarled. "I found one weeks ago on the coach floor. You'd dropped it. The handwriting on the earl's card is one and the same. I must say, Langlevit, I expected better from you. They were truly atrocious. The one question I have for my sister's lovely maid, however, is whether she was as careless with her favors as you were with your words."

The earl's eyes narrowed on him. "What have you done, Northridge?"

"*I?* Oh, that's rich, you bloody hypocrite. It seems rather clear to me that we've sampled the same waters."

"Gray!" Lana's cry was a hoarse whisper of disbelief.

"You bastard," Langlevit muttered, his lips barely moving.

"Henry," Lana begged, as if to quell the skyrocketing tension between the two men. She blinked in mute shock, as if realizing what she'd called him. "Lord Langlevit, *please*. Explain to him—"

"Henry?" Gray interrupted, his attention revolving back to her. They were on such familiar terms that she could call him by his given name?

The memory of Lana dropping his title and addressing him as Gray for the first time struck him. He remembered how it had felt, hearing his name on her tongue. Her voice moaning it as he touched her. Something hot and wild consumed Gray then—a jealousy so unhinged that it made him feel like he had the strength and the rage of a thousand men.

"*Henry* has no need to explain. I understand him perfectly. He likes the water he's sampled." Gray's eyes bored into Lana's, the desire to hurt her stemming from a place that revolted him, and yet he did not stop. He *could* not stop. He wanted her to break as he was breaking inside. "He simply doesn't like the idea of sipping from a public fountain."

Langlevit moved like a bullet, crashing into Gray's torso and slamming them both to the floor. The gun clattered to the floor a second time, and Langlevit used the free hand to pound his fist into Gray's stomach.

Gray fought back with every shred of force in him, but his anger had risen so high and hot that he couldn't think. He struck out at Langlevit, his fists glancing off muscled flesh. He couldn't land a decent strike, even though they were fairly matched in size. Langlevit had skill and experience on his side, and it wasn't long before Gray felt the earl's arm cinch around his throat. He'd maneuvered him into a chokehold.

"Don't hurt him!" Lana cried out.

"Stop struggling," Langlevit warned as he swung around to twist Gray's arm up the middle of his back. "I don't want to break your arm."

"Break it," Gray grunted.

Lana stooped beside them. "Stop this! Both of you! Lord Northridge—"

Gray smiled through the agony. Not because of his arm, the bone currently straining toward a fracture. It was his heart, cleaving into two as he looked up into her beautiful, treacherous face.

"Not Gray, as you so tenderly called me at The Cock and the Crown?"

Lana clapped her hands to her mouth, her horrified gaze riveting not on him, but on the earl whose hands viciously tightened. Gray's shoulder felt like it would rip out of its socket at any second. "You. Took. Her. Where?" Langlevit's hissed words at his ear were blunt and lethal.

"It's not his fault," Lana rushed to explain. "We had a carriage accident, and the gaming hell was our only option. Release him, please. It's time he knew the truth."

Gray frowned at the clipped, aristocratic tones. What truth? There was more to her deception?

"I will not, unless he agrees to yield," the earl replied.

"Fine," Gray snapped. "I yield." He would listen to whatever new lies she came up with, and then he would take his leave. The sooner he put this scheming seductress and her lover out of his life, the better. The thought carved a deep gulch in the center of his chest.

Langlevit released him slowly, and Gray scrambled backward, rotating his aching shoulder. The earl stood and walked over to the mantel, where he poured himself a liberal glass of whiskey. He offered a second glass to Gray, who took it after a moment and downed the drink, feeling it burn and fill the hollow spaces within him.

"My apologies for the lack of staff," Langlevit said as he refilled Gray's empty glass.

"Your apologies are wasted on me," he replied, ensconcing himself in an armchair and throwing one booted foot over his knee. He turned to Lana. "By all means, Miss Volchek, take your time declaring yourself. I trust it's not another surprise betrothal."

Flinching at his tone, Lana cleared her throat as she perched on the embroidered sofa opposite him. The threading shimmered in the firelight like gold. Hell, it could have been gold for all Gray knew. Langlevit was not lacking in fortune. Perhaps she had thought him a better diversion than Gray. One without an illegitimate child tied to him.

The little that remained of his battered heart shriveled into a ball as he steeled himself and looked at her. He instantly wished he hadn't. She'd never looked more heartbreakingly beautiful. All he wanted to do was pull her into his arms and salve his misery with her body. Love made people want to do foolish things, it seemed—like turn to the ones who had broken them in the first place.

"I didn't mean to lie to you," she began.

"And yet you did." He sipped his whiskey and smiled politely at her. "When did the lies begin to pile up and become too much to navigate—before or after our afternoon at the Crown?"

A glass crashed down onto a countertop, shattering pieces of crystal everywhere as Langlevit turned to them with a murderous look on his face. "Exactly what happened between the two of you at that gaming hell?"

Gray lifted an arrogant eyebrow, the insinuation obvious.

It was amusing that Langlevit was now the one who was jealous. He frowned and reassessed the thought as his eyes met the earl's. Langlevit did not look jealous in the least. He looked shocked. And protective.

Gray's grin was as humorless as his rejoinder. "Perhaps you should read some of your poems if you lack sufficient imagination."

"Do not test my patience—" Langlevit ground out.

"Enough." Lana stalled the earl once more with a flick of her palm, color blooming in her cheeks. "Those poems were coded messages, Lord Northridge, about the baron. Nothing more." Then she turned to Langlevit, her voice quiet. "I am a grown woman."

"But, my lady…"

My lady? Gray's frown deepened as Lana stood and walked to Langlevit's side.

"You've been a good friend, and I thank you for everything you've done, but my choices are mine alone. I do not wish to speak of what transpired at the…Crown."

She hadn't wanted to use the word cock, Gray noted with a spike of bitter amusement as she turned back to him. Just like a lady. Lady Lana…just as the besotted stable hands and footmen called her. They were no worse off than he. Infatuated, foolish, and wrecked beyond belief.

Lady Lana.

He noted, once more, what they must have seen: the regal slope of her shoulders and the tilt of that imperious chin. He heard what they had as well: the precise diction and the gentle command of her words.

Gray would have stumbled if he hadn't been sitting.

Time drew to a stuttered halt as he saw what he'd been utterly blind to before. How many times had he noted how differently she carried and conducted herself from other maids? Now he understood Langlevit's sudden and protective reaction…and the appalled look on his face earlier.

Because Lana wasn't a maid at all.

The realization was slow at first, but then it gathered speed like a rock rolling downhill. Gray swallowed. "You're the missing princess."

She nodded, her heart in her eyes as Langlevit crossed the marble floor toward them. His voice was only slightly mocking. "Lord Northridge, allow me to present Princess Svetlanka Volkonsky."

Gray sat forward, the whiskey glass in his hand slipping. He caught it, though barely, his fingers having turned to air. "Svetlanka," he repeated dully.

"Lana for short."

Everything stilled in that moment as all the pieces crashed together—all the hints and the clues he'd refused to see. The way she talked. The way she held herself. She was a bloody *princess* acting as a maid.

And *hell*. He'd taken her innocence. In a damned gaming hell.

Not a breath was drawn in the explosive silence until the front door to Hartstone slammed into the wall.

Langlevit dove to the mantel, reappearing with his pistol, while Gray leaped to his feet.

"Not one move," Zakorov warned, striding in. He was followed by three burly men. They were all armed, and the earl lowered his weapon. "Your Highness," Zakorov said in an unnaturally loud and jovial voice to Lana. "It's good to see you alive and well."

She showed no fear at all. "Where's my sister, you piece of scum?"

"Now, now," he said in a falsely sweet tone that made Gray want to break his teeth. "That's no way to talk to your betrothed."

Gray clenched his jaw. *This* was her betrothed? Not a

pauper boy, but Zakorov?

"I will never marry you," Lana hissed.

Zakorov smirked. "I have a feeling you will soon change your mind."

"Where is Irina?" Lana demanded, her eyes flicking toward one of the three men standing behind the baron. "You're the one my uncle sent to Cumbria. What have you done to her?"

Gray could hear the tremor beneath her words. The man she'd been speaking to, a tall and greasy-looking fellow, smirked. "To your sister?" the man asked, his French accent strong. "Nothing at all. However, I was forced to take care of the blundering brute that was on my tail. What was his name? Hurst?"

Hurstley. Gray ground his teeth. *Damn it*! He'd gotten the man killed. Gray wanted to put a bullet between the Frenchman's smiling teeth for it, too.

"Your sister is safe," Zakorov agreed, waving his arm. "For now. But her continued safety depends entirely upon you. You will need to come with me."

"She will not," Gray said, his arm rising to bar Lana from taking a step forward.

Zakorov smiled at him. "She has no choice, Lord Northridge. After all, her young sister's life rests in her hands."

A thousand emotions stormed across Lana's face. Gray knew she would acquiesce, if only out of loyalty to her sister. "Lana, no."

"He's right, I have to go with him. For Irina." Lana nodded to Langlevit before pushing past Gray's arm. He tried to catch her elbow, but she wrenched free. She looked up at him, her voice low so that only he could hear it. "I'm sorry that I lied to you about who I was. And I said terrible things to you last week. Dishonest things. I only wanted to keep you away from this." She shook her head. "*Nothing* else was a lie. I hope you believe that."

Gray wanted to catch her arm and haul her back behind him, but the pistol trained at his head from one of Zakorov's men kept him still. He didn't trust himself to speak but did anyway. "I'll find you."

As Lana disappeared from view, Zakorov's voice filtered back before the door slammed shut. "Kill them."

Gray and Langlevit exchanged a single look before the earl exploded into motion, his gun firing as he dove simultaneously to the second gunman. Gray tackled the Frenchman, who stood nearest him, as another gunshot rent the air. He felt the bullet whizz by his face, narrowly missing him, as he collided with the man. They went rolling across the floor, knocking over a marble bust. Gray grabbed a chunk of the broken marble, slamming it into the Frenchman's head, again and again, until he went still.

"Bastard," he grunted, and then stood, panting. He watched Langlevit make quick work of the second man. The first was dead, Langlevit's precise shot now a gaping wound at the center of the man's forehead. The earl raced to the door, but Zakorov had already disappeared.

They stared at each other in the charged silence. Langlevit was the first to speak. "You love her."

"What?"

"You love her." It was not a question.

Gray considered lying but knew Langlevit would see right through him. "Yes. I do."

"Good." The earl smiled, but it didn't reassure Gray in the least. "I didn't want to have to call you out at dawn. We both know I'm a better shot than you. We will settle this later, and mark my words, it will be settled to my satisfaction. For now, the princesses are in danger, and Zakorov has had a decent head start. Their uncle, the count, plotted with Zakorov to murder their father. Lana has letters in her possession that will incriminate them both."

"The coded ones?"

Langlevit stared at him as if surprised Gray had this knowledge. "Yes. Which means he will go back to Ferndale to retrieve the letters." The earl paused. "This is not a game, North. I will understand if you wish to remain here."

Gray felt cold resolve settle into his bones. "Not on your life."

· · ·

The gunshot had made Lana's blood run cold, but Viktor's firm grip upon her arm kept her from lurching away, back toward the house. "Into the carriage," he snarled, all but tossing her in before climbing in after her. Her attention was arrested by the tiny female figure cowering on one of the seats.

"Lana!" Irina's face was tear-stained as she threw herself into her sister's arms.

"Oh my God, you're alive!" Lana held her sister close, her own tears breaking loose. Her eyes flicked to their uncle, sitting at Irina's side. "Did they hurt you?"

"No." Irina shook her head. "Lana, I was so scared that something had happened to you. I was out for a walk in the gardens, and a man came out of nowhere, forcing me to go with him. The next person I saw was him." Her head jerked to the stern-faced count watching them. "He…he said they would kill Countess Langlevit if I didn't tell him where you were, but I didn't know the name of the estate."

Lana raised cold eyes to her uncle. His smile made her want to tear it off his face. "Lovely to see you, Svetlanka. You've been busy, niece."

"You're no family of mine," Lana snapped. "You deceiving bastard."

The count *tsked*, studying her down the length of his

prominent nose, his mouth curling with displeasure.

"How did you find us?"

"We followed Lord Northridge," Viktor interjected, his voice mocking. "I knew something was amiss when he tried so hard to deter me from speaking with you. And the connection with Langlevit was too coincidental not to investigate further." He grinned, waving the pistol. "And I was right, wasn't I? He led me straight to you."

Lana ignored him, staring at her uncle and trying to conceal her loathing for the man. "What do you want?"

"You know what I want. The documents you stole."

"I stole nothing. They belonged to my father." Her mind was racing. She'd noticed the driver and one other man out front, but only Viktor in the carriage displayed a weapon. Perhaps she could distract him and then snatch the pistol. The thought, though satisfying, was not without its risks. What if the gun went off and Irina was hurt? What if her uncle had a pistol hidden under his coat? And no matter how quick she was, her uncle wouldn't stand by and let her gain the upper hand. No, she could not take that chance. She'd have to wait until they arrived at their destination and hope for an opportunity then.

But what if he had more men? What then? Her thoughts passed to Gray and Langlevit, and the gunshot that had echoed as they'd left the house. She refused to consider that either of the men were dead. Langlevit was far too seasoned in the art of war to have been taken down in such a manner. And Gray... She didn't even want to consider it. The odds hadn't been in their favor—not with three of the men holding weapons. But she'd just seen Gray and Langlevit square off against each other, and based on that, she knew neither of them would have gone down without a fight. She clenched her jaw. And neither would she.

"Where are you taking us?"

"Your place of employment." Viktor chuckled at his own joke. "Of course."

Ferndale. Her heart sunk. Lord and Lady Dinsmore and Brynn were there. The house was fully staffed. She knew all too well what this man and her uncle were capable of. If they could kill a Russian grand duke and his wife, what was stopping them from murdering anyone who happened to be in the way?

Her gaze slid to Irina, who sat immobile at her uncle's side, her fingers twisting in her lap. Lana was proud that she displayed no fear, even though one of his hands was tightly manacled above her elbow. She sent her a reassuring smile.

"Let's get down to it, *niece*," her uncle said, his sarcastic emphasis on the last word evident. "I believe you have something of mine."

She lifted her chin. "Did you kill my parents?"

The man actually had the audacity to smile. "My brother got himself embroiled in a situation that was beyond him, but what happened in that carriage was a tragic accident. Didn't you read the newssheets?"

Lana drew a sharp breath, contempt for the man who called himself her uncle filling her. "He found out you were selling crown secrets to the French, so you killed him."

The count's eyes narrowed, his lips thinning. "Where are the documents?"

"Not until you admit the truth."

Lana was unprepared for him lurching forward or for the backhand that cracked across her face. Her sister's cry was the only thing that kept her from fainting. Hot, white stars swam in her vision as warm blood seeped into her mouth. Her teeth ached as if they'd been loosened. "Don't provoke me," he snarled. "Where are the papers?"

She swallowed a mouthful of blood and squared her shoulders. He wasn't going to allow them to live, not after she handed over the papers. She'd risk another blow to her cheek for the one thing she'd been craving for months: "The truth."

Her uncle moved to the edge of the seat, sitting nose to nose with her, his hatred oozing out of every pore as his eyes bored into hers. "Grigori deserved to die. And yes. I killed him. Now, tell me where my documents are before I slit your darling sister's throat."

Even though Lana already knew what he'd done, hearing the cold, unrepentant confession from his lips brought a wave of pain so agonizing that she almost doubled over. She vowed that she would find a way to make him pay, no matter the cost and no matter how long it took. And, if not in this lifetime, then in the next. She would never rest until he was punished for what he'd done.

"Harm one hair on her head, and it will be the last thing that you do," she snapped through her teeth. "The papers are at Ferndale."

Her mind was working furiously. The only thing she had to bargain with were the documents. Langlevit had written that the cryptographer he'd found had met with an unexpected end—no doubt at Viktor's hands—and without being able to decipher the letters, she had no proof to use against either of the men. She didn't care much for her own safety, but she worried for Irina's.

"I will give you the letters in exchange for Irina's freedom," she said as they pulled into the deserted courtyard at Ferndale.

"Lana, no, not without you," Irina blurted out.

Her uncle laughed in her face. "You do not make terms."

"You should know that I have copied the letters, and that Lord Langlevit is not the only man at the war office who has seen the originals," Lana said coolly. "One set is at Ferndale, and the other is elsewhere, safe and awaiting my word."

He froze in anger. "You are lying."

"That is for you to decide, uncle. It is your choice whether you live in constant fear of discovery or agree to my proposition: Irina's freedom for the letters, including the hidden copies. I will send a message for them to be destroyed."

His expression shifted again, this time into something carefully blank. "What do I care? To anyone else, these are nothing but love letters."

"Until they are deciphered," she replied, undaunted. "And you and I both know what they will say then. Do you really want to invite such risk, keep such a threat hanging over your head, ready to fall when you least expect it?"

The count's gaze flicked to Viktor, who hadn't uttered a word since their arrival. A sadistic smile worked over his face. "Irina's freedom and your hand in marriage to Viktor."

Everything within her recoiled at the base suggestion. It was what her uncle had been planning all along—he wanted the Volkonsky fortune, and a marriage to the odious baron would ensure it. She couldn't fathom becoming that man's wife…having him touch her as a husband would…having him touch her as Gray had. The mere thought revolted her. "No, I will not."

"I thought you would say that." The oily voice was Viktor's. "So I wish to provide some incentive. My man has been looking into yours and Lord Northridge's activities, and your recent foray to north London. We have a lovely new guest with us."

"What guest?" Lana asked, her blood turning to ice in her veins.

"A precious little thing with beautiful blond hair," Viktor said. "She looks so much like her father, I must say."

Lana's breath stalled as her hands curled into powerless fists at her sides. She leaned toward him and stopped short. "If you've hurt her—"

Viktor's smile was triumphant, as was her uncle's. "She is

safe and sound in London, Princess, and awaiting our arrival. Her continued safety, too, depends entirely upon you. Agree to marry me, and she will be returned safely home."

"You are despicable." Helpless rage filled every part of her as she eyed her uncle, but there was nothing she could do. She was the one who had drawn Gray, and now Sofia, into this. She was the one who had put them in danger, and she would have to pay the price to release them. She closed her eyes. There was no other way. Irina was safe. And Sofia would be, too. Her sacrifice was a small cost.

Lana crossed the floor of the carriage to her sister, pulling her into her arms, her whisper soft against her ear. "If Lord Northridge is alive, find him and tell him everything. He will make sure you are safe. I love you, my sister."

"Lana, no, you can't do this!" Irina cried.

Lana wiped the tears from her sister's face, memorizing every curve and every hollow, and the way her soft dark hair curled into her cheeks. "I must."

She turned to her uncle, her chin high. "Once Irina is safe and Sofia is out of harm's way, you have my word."

Chapter Twenty-Five

Gray wasn't going to take any chances being seen or heard coming upon Ferndale. It was an overcast night, but the moon was high and bright behind the clouds. If he could easily see the bright swells and shadowy dips of Ferndale's meadows as he rode over them, then Zakorov and his comrades would be able to see a horse and rider streaking toward the main house.

They would be keeping watch on the main drive up to the manor, waiting either for the three brutish men he and Langlevit had dispatched, or for any signal that the three had failed in their task. So Gray had traveled through the woods he knew well, aided by the unusual gleam of moonlight, and approached the house around the rear, near the pagoda just outside his father's library. Langlevit, meanwhile, had taken the obvious main drive with a mission to distract Zakorov's cronies long enough for Gray to slip inside the manor through a rear entrance or window. The Russian had entered Hartstone with three men at his side, but he undoubtedly had more in the carriage in which he'd whisked Lana away in.

Gray was going to kill Zakorov. He held no qualms about

that. The man was a traitor and a threat to Lana—*Svetlanka*. His mind had still not grasped the truth. She wasn't the princesses' maid. She hadn't been cast aside, as she'd led Gray to believe. She was Russian *nobility*.

He had known, at some level, that she was no servant. Her poise and her stubborn pride, her elegance and educated mind, her skill at dancing and riding, and even her ability to read French, they had all spoken the truth, even if Gray's ears and eyes hadn't been listening or seeing at the time. He'd only been focused on one thing: his all-consuming attraction to her.

But now was not the time to focus on who Lana was. He only needed to focus on how to get her to safety. And then, how to make sure Zakorov and Lana's duplicitous uncle could not do any more harm.

Gray dismounted his horse and tied him off on the low-hanging branch of an apple tree near the pagoda. He took the pistol Langlevit had armed him with and listened. Any commotion at the front of the manor would signal Langlevit had been spotted. But nothing came. Pure silence. Gray entered his father's library through the pair of glass doors on a small, secluded terrace. The grand room was dark, the only noise the soft scuffing of his Hessians' soles over the Persian rug. When he reached the door that led into a dimly lit corridor, he paused—and knew.

They were not here.

Gray threw open the door and stormed down the corridor to the foyer, and at that same moment, the front door crashed open. Langlevit appeared, pistol in hand, a second holstered at his thigh.

"We are too late," he grit out.

"Or they were never here," Gray replied, annoyed and infuriated, but not with the earl.

"They must have been. Lana keeps the letters with her at all times, and if she had returned to Ferndale, they would be among her possessions—"

"Lord Langlevit!"

A wisp of a girl with long, untended dark hair darted from the front sitting room and collided with the earl. She threw her arms around him and buried her head in his chest. Gray had never set eyes upon her before, but at once, he knew who she was.

"Irina," Langlevit said, the hand not holding the pistol coming up to cup the back of her head. She wore a yellow day dress, creased with wrinkles, and when she pulled her face from Langlevit's waistcoat, Gray's breath left him in a rush. Though still young, the girl bore such a resemblance to Lana that he couldn't think for a minute. She had the same proud cheekbones and long, glossy hair, though her eyes were violet instead of green.

"Lana's sister," Langlevit said to Gray, bringing the girl's startled eyes to him. "Where is she? Where is Lana?"

Braxton's shoes tapped quickly into the foyer behind Gray, followed almost as quickly by those of his parents. They emerged from the sitting room cautiously, their eyes wide with alarm.

"Graham?" his mother said, her coloring high on her cheeks. She was upset and, if her lack of speech was any sign, utterly confused.

"What the devil is happening here?" Lord Dinsmore asked.

"I'd like to know the same thing," Gray replied, and then echoed Langlevit's question: "Where is Lana?"

Braxton spoke first.

"My lord, it is utterly preposterous what this girl is saying, but at least one thing is true—there was a carriage. It trundled up the drive with Lady Briannon's maid, who was accompanied by one of Lord Dinsmore's prior guests, Baron Zakorov."

Despite his usual stoic composure, the butler had trouble concealing his scandalized expression. Gray understood instantly what Braxton would be thinking having seen Lana arrive alone in such company.

"I've already told you, Braxton, you cannot possibly have it right," Lord Dinsmore grumbled. "What on earth would Zakorov be doing in Essex, and with Briannon's maid, no less?"

Gray ignored his father for the moment. There was no time to explain.

"What then?" he asked Braxton.

"Miss Volchek went to her room, accompanied by Lord Zakorov. They tarried but for a moment before bolting off again and leaving this waif—whom I can only assume is some relation—on the doorstep. I am deeply sorry, my lords. My lady," he said, bowing to them all. "I will have her sent to the kitchens at once."

"You will do no such thing," Gray said tiredly, scrubbing a palm through his hair. "This young lady is indeed Miss Volchek's sister, but she is Princess Irina Volkonsky, and you will accord her with the proper respect."

His mother's speech came roaring back to her. "*Princess?*" she shrieked.

Braxton's surprise flashed in his eyes as well, but he bowed quickly. "Of course, my lord. My apologies, Your Highness."

"How long ago did they leave in the carriage?" Gray asked, already anxious to find a fresh mount and follow.

"Less than ten minutes, my lord, at the most," Braxton answered.

"Graham!" his mother cried, coming forward. She stopped abruptly and made a small, perfunctory curtsy toward the young princess, still wrapped protectively under Langlevit's arm. "Please tell us what is happening!"

"Lana is in danger. I can't explain all of it right now, but

I will, I promise. Thank you, Braxton. Please have a footman fetch me some paper and a quill."

"If this young lady is a princess *and* Miss Volchek's sister," Lord Dinsmore began. Two seconds hadn't passed before Lady Dinsmore strangled a gasp and clapped her hands over her mouth.

"I see I don't need to explain after all," Gray said, knowing his mother had made the connection.

Braxton returned, and Gray scribbled a note on the piece of parchment and signaled to the waiting footman. "Send our fastest messenger to deliver this to Lord Thorndale at this address in London, and have James saddle two of the strongest mounts at once." He turned to the earl, who still held the girl cradled under one arm. "Our window is small even if we ride at a breakneck pace. We have no idea if they will go to where the count is staying or Zakorov's old apartments at the Stevens Hotel, or somewhere else altogether."

Langlevit held the girl out so he could peer down into her frightened face. "Did you hear anything? Do you know where they are going, Princess?"

She jutted her chin in a way that reminded Gray of Lana, though it wobbled slightly. "Back to London," she said. "They are planning to set sail for home, where Lana and the baron will be wed."

"Wed?" Langlevit choked. His eyes met Gray's, whose hands clenched into fists at his sides. The storm brewing in his veins hit full force at the thought of Zakorov anywhere near Lana.

"I thought Zakorov wanted the princesses for treason," Lord Dinsmore said at a near shout. "What is this about a marriage?"

Irina shook her head, her curls springing. "He is the treasonous one! And Uncle Ivan forced her to agree."

Gray frowned. "In exchange for the letters and your

freedom?" His eyes narrowed as the girl nodded. "And she went to her quarters here with Zakorov?"

"Yes."

Gray set off at a run, taking the stairs two at a time, the earl hot on his heels. He pushed open the door to her room for the second time that day, his heart in his throat. The spartan chamber wasn't empty. Mrs. Frommer, the housekeeper, stood near the bed, rifling through Lana's possessions, some articles of clothing already draped over one arm. The woman was worse than a bloody vulture. Gray's gaze narrowed as he made his presence known.

Mrs. Frommer paled. "My lord," she began with a guilty look. "That scheming little thief ran in here with a man who must be her lover to—"

"Get out," he snapped. "Or so help me, I'll remove you myself."

Paling further, she bobbed and fled from the room.

He entered the chamber and saw Lana's black cloak on the floor still. Only, this time, there was a suitcase open on her bed, and some strewn clothing around it. A nearby chest was open, but it offered no clues. Gray frowned, his eyes searching the room methodically. The Lana he knew would not have left without a sign of some sort…a trail of breadcrumbs. She was too smart not to know—not to trust—that he would be close behind.

Following the earl, Irina entered the small room tentatively, blinking back tears. Gray was about to give up his search when his eyes fell on the discarded clothes on the bed that hadn't been there earlier. It was a pair of Brynn's breeches—the ones Lana had worn when she'd taken it upon herself to break into Zakorov's rooms at the Stevens alone.

A breadcrumb, as it were. He almost sighed with relief.

"They're going to the Stevens Hotel," he said.

"Are you certain?" Langlevit asked.

"Yes. Let's go."

Gray's eyes moved to Irina, who stood near Lana's chest of drawers. She held a small, framed portrait. Tears were pouring down her face, and Gray felt the oddest inclination to comfort her. "All will be well again, Princess," he said. "I'll get her back."

The girl bit her lips, raising her bleak eyes to his. "She told me to find you. She said you would make sure that I was safe." Gray's heart hammered in his chest at her soft words. Lana had trusted him enough to want to put Irina in his care.

Irina fingered the gold frame of the portrait, and Gray frowned at it. Lana must have kept the portrait tucked away. Such a frame would be out of place in servants' quarters. It was made of heavy, ornate gold—easily worth two years' wages of any maid. Lana was younger in the portrait, likely the same age as Irina was now, standing and smiling with their parents.

"May I?" Gray asked, reaching for it at the same moment that she released it. The frame clattered to the wooden floor, the glass cracking and the backing coming loose. They both knelt at the same time, Irina uttering a sharp cry of disappointment as she reached for the portrait. A piece of thick parchment coming loose from the frame's backing caught Gray's attention.

"Langlevit," he said, his voice hoarse. "Is this what I think it is?"

The earl stooped beside him. His eyes met Gray's as he unfolded it. It was a rectangle of stiff parchment with odd cutouts at various intervals. "It's the key," Langlevit said, staring at it in shocked disbelief, as if expecting it to disappear at any moment. His triumphant gaze lifted to the young girl at his side, and he grabbed her in a jubilant embrace. "You did it, Irina!"

A blush suffused her cheeks as she gazed wide-eyed at

the earl. "Did what?"

"Found the cipher your father hid for safekeeping," Gray finished and rose to his feet. "Come, we have no time to waste."

They made their way back downstairs, where his parents were still standing in hushed conversation and a few more curious staff had gathered.

"Lord Dinsmore, Princess Irina will have to stay here, if that is fine by you," Langlevit said as they entered the foyer.

Gray's father and mother both nodded, Lady Dinsmore with a touch too much vigor.

"But of course! She is most welcome," his mother said, her eyes clouding over. "But, Graham, this all sounds so very dangerous—"

"It is. That is why I must go." Taking a breath, he added, "Lana—Princess Svetlanka—needs my help."

And he was losing time every second he stood still.

Langlevit peered down at Irina. "You will be quite safe here, Your Highness."

Gray kissed his mother's cheek. "Do not let her out of your sight, Mother." He turned back to Irina with a gentler tone. "Lady Dinsmore here will take lovely care of you. And Cook"—he pointed out Mrs. Braxton standing with the other servants—"makes the best raspberry puddings in England." Seeing the tears brewing in her eyes, he bent to kiss the back of Irina's hand. "I swear on my life that I will bring your sister back to you."

"And the little girl, too?"

Gray froze. "Which little girl?"

"In the carriage, they spoke of a child they had in London. A girl with blond hair. It made Lana upset." She blinked and bit her lip, as if trying to recall exactly what was said. "The baron said something about her looking like her father." Gray's blood turned to ice as her gaze fluttered to his hair.

"Oh, no. Is it you?"

He swallowed hard, his eyes going to his parents, who were both staring at him in stunned disbelief. "Yes. Sofia is my daughter."

Lady Dinsmore let out a scream—and promptly fainted. Gray's father caught her before she could crumple unceremoniously onto the foyer floor.

Irina stared at him, wide-eyed with determination. "Then you must save her."

Gray stood, forcing himself not to sprint to the stables. He met his father's eyes, which were looking at Gray with open shock. It was time he did the right thing for Sofia. The child was his, and everyone would know it.

"You have a granddaughter, my lord," he said to his father with a soft, rueful smile. "I promise I will explain everything later. But I must go."

Lord Dinsmore still crouched near the floor, supporting Gray's unconscious mother, and sealed his lips. He gave a short nod, and Gray and Langlevit exited through the front door.

They did not speak on the way to London, riding at a pace Gray normally would not have subjected his horses to, but lives were on the line. Lana's. Sofia's. Every moment lost was one closer to losing them. They stopped once to feed and water the horses, and even so, they managed to reach London in short order. Dawn was just breaking over the inky sky, streaks of gray seeping through the darkness.

The first stop was the Earl of Thorndale's home, where he'd sent his messenger. Sure enough, Thorn was in his stables readying mounts with the stable boys, his face grim. "Your messages barely preceded you, North. I'd hoped you were jesting, but I've done as you asked. The agents from Bow Street should be here any minute." He squinted in the gloom. "Who do you have with you?"

"No jest," Gray said, hoping to God the agents didn't tarry.

"Morning, Thorn," Langlevit said. It was all that was needed by way of introduction.

Thorndale nodded a greeting and handed over the rest of his task to a waiting stable boy. "So is someone going to tell me what the devil is going on?"

Gray explained in a few short sentences who Lana was and what had happened. To his credit, Thorndale didn't blink an eye at what Gray knew sounded like a ludicrous tale. And when the two agents arrived, their burly frames setting Gray at ease, Thorndale quickly repeated the specifics to them. The two men remained stern-faced, though their expressions grew agitated at the mention of Zakorov.

"Aye. We've heard of this one," one of them said.

"Then this is your chance to get to know him better," Gray replied, accepting a fresh mount from one of the stable boys. Langlevit did the same.

"Lead the way," Thorndale said, mounting his own horse. As they left the stables, Gray was overwhelmed with gratitude at the man's unflinching help. "Thank you, Thorn."

He merely nodded, and Gray knew he'd made the right choice in reaching out to him.

The ride to the Stevens Hotel was quick, largely due to the empty roads given the early time of day. Most men were still tucked abed, and the only ones on the streets were the young crossing sweepers, clearing horse manure and mud from the dusty streets. Dismounting, Gray strode into the foyer of the hotel, waking up a disgruntled and sleepy-eyed footman. "Is there a man called Baron Zakorov here?" he asked in a low tone.

"Who's asking?" Gray's lips pinched tight, and the man paled visibly at the sight of the pistol appearing in Gray's palm. "He's not here, milord. Not since yesterday."

His heart sinking in frustration, Gray went to the entrance where the others were waiting, and scanned the street. Where else could they have gone? Had Lana been wrong in her assumption that they were going to the hotel? Hell, they could be anywhere. Gray couldn't help the panic gathering in the pit of his stomach as he met Langlevit's eyes. He pounded the doorjamb with a closed fist. "They're not here. What if we misjudged them, and they are still in Essex?"

"No, they are close," the earl said. "Princess Irina mentioned they had your daughter in London."

Gray could feel the weight of Thorn's stare at Langlevit's careless statement, but explanations would have to wait. With a ragged breath, he calmed himself and considered what he knew of both men. If the count had stayed hidden in London, chances are he would have wanted to be close to Zakorov.

Walking back inside, he reached into his coat pocket and extracted a few coins. The silver riveted the footman's greedy gaze. "Where did he go when he stayed here? Did he visit any nearby lodgings?"

"Mayhap across the street, milord," the man said, reaching for the coins. "The Abigail. But I cannot be sure. There are many guests going back and forth."

Back on the front steps, Gray took a look at the Abigail's stone facade. It was a more rundown place, one distinguished foreign dignitaries staying at the Stevens Hotel would likely visit for paid—and private—pleasures. Langlevit nodded thoughtfully. "That would be a logical choice if the count wanted to stay out of sight."

"Especially if he wanted to keep an eye on Zakorov," Gray agreed. He met Thorn's determined look and flicked his gaze to the Bow Street agents. "You two can cover the front and the back. We may or may not have the advantage of surprise. Thorn, you stay in the rear. Langlevit and I will go first. The safety of the princess and the child is our priority."

Like the Stevens, the interior of the Abigail was hushed and quiet, though far less well maintained. It stank of stale ale, cigar smoke, and the musk of other unmentionables. The thought that Lana and his daughter had been brought here made Gray's temper double in measure. He approached the dour-faced man at the rear of the room, watching their approach will ill-concealed rancor.

Wasting no time, Gray displayed the pistol tucked into the waistband of his trousers. "There is a man staying here with a Russian accent. He would have arrived not long before now, with a woman and a child. Where is he?"

The man's eyes narrowed, clearly unimpressed by the threat of a weapon. Gray chose another avenue and thrust a fat velvet pouch across the counter. "First floor up," the man said, pocketing the pouch and disappearing behind a pair of faded curtains. "Last door."

Gray and the two men made their way up the stairs, wincing at every creak and every groan of the wood beneath their feet. There was a chance that the man had lied, but as they drew near to the door in question, the soft muffled sounds of a child crying caught Gray's attention. It hit him like a blow to the gut. He nodded tightly to Langlevit, who took up position on the other side of the door with a gun in each hand, and Thorn, who retreated to the top of the stairs in case any of the count's men came running at the sound of a commotion.

With a sharp grunt, Gray kicked the door in. His eyes took in the relieving sight of Lana and Sofia huddled on a sofa in the far corner of the room before falling on two figures standing at the center, piling items into a trunk.

"Don't move," Langlevit ordered, leveling one of his pistols at the count and the other at the unfamiliar man at his side. "I assure you that if you do, you will not draw a single breath more."

"Norry!" Sofia wailed at the sight of him, but Gray couldn't let himself become derailed by her cries. Or by the sight of Lana with her arms curled protectively around his daughter.

He frowned. "Where is Zakorov?"

Neither of the men answered. "I won't ask again," Gray seethed, his pistol locking onto the count's chest.

"I am here."

Gray inhaled a sharp breath as Zakorov materialized from behind the billowing drapes of the open windows behind the sofa, a pistol pointed at the back of Lana's head. His fingers wound into her hair, dragging her off the sofa and to his side. A whimpering Sofia followed, clutching at Lana's gown, unwilling to let her go.

Lana's fierce gaze met Gray's, and he immediately understood what those blazing eyes conveyed: she would not give in without a fight.

Gray was torn between admiring her courage and fearing for her life, but time was too short to dwell on either. He nodded imperceptibly. Feigning unsteadiness, Lana leaned heavily to one side, her body shielding Sofia's as clumps of her silky hair were left behind in Zakorov's ruthless grip. The baron was pulled off-kilter by her deliberate fall, giving Gray the barest sliver of opportunity. But that was all he needed. He exhaled and fired, the shot blasting through the confines of the room and catching the baron square in the chest.

Thorn appeared in the doorway, his eyes concerned as he took in the scene and Zakorov's dead body. Langlevit still had both his pistols on the other two men, who hadn't moved a muscle. The count's face had gone white with shock and anger.

"Fetch the Runners," Gray told Thorn. "It's over."

Thorn nodded, and Gray moved toward Lana and Sofia, wanting only to hold them. Touch them. Make certain neither of them had been injured. "Are you…are you both all right?"

"We are now," Lana said, her tears breaking free as Sofia flung her little body into his arms.

Gray dropped to his knees and kissed the child's head, the tension draining from his body. He'd just taken a man's life, but it was an act he felt no remorse over. He'd kill any man who threatened his daughter. As Thorn returned with the two Bow Street agents and set about securing the count and the other man, Gray got back to his feet, keeping Sofia firmly tucked against him. He drank in the sight of the woman standing beside them. The thought of losing Lana and Sofia had been a sobering one, and even if he hadn't already made the decision to declare his fatherhood, there was nothing in the world that would stop him from doing it now. His eyes met Lana's. Or from claiming the woman who had captured his heart.

Maid or princess, it didn't matter. She was his. He almost smiled at the next thought that entered his head. *If* she would have him. In the eyes of society and the *ton*, Lana was more than his peer. She was royalty. And there was a very real possibility that she could refuse him. Push him away again. Though he'd determined she had only done it that once to protect him, to be able to run from Zakorov if she needed to, he still wasn't completely certain. Gray supposed he could compromise her by taking her in his arms right then and there. Then again, Langlevit currently held two pistols, and he'd made it more than clear that the matter of Gray's intentions had yet to be settled. Ravishing the love of his life would have to wait until they were in private. Lana blushed as if she could read his thoughts, and he wisely moved away from the bright source of his temptation.

There was still the matter of the count and his treachery.

"This is an outrage," the count postured, his eyes darting to Gray's as he approached. "You have murdered one of the tsar's most trusted officers. You will rot in prison for such an unprovoked attack."

"Unprovoked?" Langlevit cleared his throat. "You kidnapped the child of an English lord. As peers of the realm, Thorndale and I will swear that Lord Northridge's shot was to protect his daughter." He smiled. "And I fear that it is you who will rot in prison, Count Volkonsky, for your assassination plot against the tsar and the cold-blooded murders of Grand Duke Grigori and Grand Duchess Katerina."

The count laughed loudly as Langlevit crouched to retrieve the papers from Zakorov's coat pocket. "What proof do you have? Letters to my French lover?" he scoffed. "Those prove nothing."

"On their own, you are correct," Gray interjected, his eyes flicking to Lana's and seeing the surprise there. He reached into his own pocket and produced the code breaker. "But with Grand Duke Grigori's key, you will have much to answer for."

"Where did you get that?" Lana whispered.

"Irina found it," Gray explained. "Hidden behind your family portrait."

Lana's uncle paled at the sight of the stiff parchment in his hand, his mouth thinning as Gray placed it upon the letters. Langlevit scanned the documents using the code breaker and smiled grimly. "It's no small wonder you and Zakorov wanted these letters back in your possession. Not only do they confirm yours and the baron's involvement in a plot against the tsar, it also implicates both of you in the murder of your brother after he discovered your plans."

The count's furious gaze flew to his niece. "You bloody bitch."

Gray stepped forward, his fist cracking into the man's face like the strike of a snake. "You do not get to address her," he bit out savagely. "You do not get to so much as look at her. You murdered her parents. Drove her from her home. She lowered herself to drudgery...to the life of a paltry servant to hide from you." He drew his arm back again, intent on pummeling him until his face was unrecognizable, but a light touch on his arm stalled him.

"Stop, Gray," she said. "It's over now." He turned, drawing her into his arms, and, uncaring of his audience, buried his face in her hair.

A small weight launched itself at their joined bodies, and Gray's arm curved down to hold Sofia close. Lana's lips touched his ear, her whisper for him alone. "And do not begrudge my time as a servant, my lord. For without it, I never would have met you."

Chapter Twenty-Six

Six weeks later, Lana watched Lord Langlevit's face carefully as their carriage drew alongside the masses of others in the courtyard at Worthington Abbey. His eyes were troubled, his lips pressed thin.

"You did not have to come," Lana said.

Irina twisted from her rapt gaze out the window to stare up at her older sister. "Of course he did. It is a wedding ball!"

Leave it to Irina to correct her, Lana thought with an uncontainable grin. It wasn't just any wedding ball either. It was Lady Briannon's and Lord Bradburne's. They had decided they couldn't live without each other after all. Lana was glad for the two of them, and she had never seen Brynn look so happy in the days that followed their second, and final, engagement.

"And the Duke of Bradburne insisted upon Henry's attendance," Irina added.

Lana glanced fondly at her sister. "You're right, of course."

Having her sister back at her side and under the same roof for the last month had only underscored just how nervous

Lana had felt with her being so far away, in some estate she had never set eyes upon. She had not even been able to properly picture her sister at the earl's estate, she realized, and that had made Irina seem ever more distant.

But now Irina was safe, as Lana had promised so many months before on the night they had fled Volkonsky Palace. She'd made a vow to win back everything they had lost, and finally, it had come to be. Lana still couldn't quite believe it.

Lord Langlevit adjusted his cravat, even though it was already perfectly knotted. "Princess Irina is correct—somewhat," he said with a jut of one brow. "I am not attending because His Grace insisted, but because, as your guardian, I could not have allowed the pair of you to attend alone."

Lana had not objected to his proposal that he be their public guardian after the fiasco at the Abigail lodgings, though she knew it was mostly for show—and for Irina. They could not have remained at Ferndale, Lana's position as lady's maid now entirely unnecessary. Staying as honored guests, as Lady Dinsmore had so warmly suggested, her cheeks still a brazen red from learning she had employed a *princess*, was also out of the question. Langlevit had eyed Gray across the front sitting room and jumped in to say guest rooms for the princesses were already being prepared at Hartstone. With the countess en route to Essex, the princesses would be more than properly chaperoned.

Before leaving Ferndale, Lana had gone to her room to gather the rest of her belongings, left behind when she and Irina had been taken. She'd stood in the small room and bade a silent farewell to the space that had kept her hidden safely for so long. She did not begrudge her time spent here. The last months had changed her. They had most certainly widened her view of the world—and the people living within it. Good, decent people, like Mrs. Braxton and Mary, Percy and James.

Taking her valises, Lana had gone next to the kitchens,

where she'd been greeted by alarmed expressions, hasty curtsies, and stiff bows. She had acknowledged their awkwardness with a warm smile as she'd directed herself toward the housekeeper's room. None of them had ever been rude or truly unkind to her. The only person undeserving of her forgiveness was Mrs. Frommer.

She knocked upon the door and then opened it before the woman could issue an invitation to do so. Mrs. Frommer did not appear as surprised as the other employees had and stood slowly from where she'd been seated at her desk. It was almost as if she'd expected Lana to come.

She closed the door behind her and set down her valise.

"Mrs. Frommer, I think you understand why I am here," Lana said, her hands clasped before her, her chin held high.

The housekeeper did not move. Nor did she speak, though a sickly shade of yellow tinted her cheeks. The domineering woman was nervous, and for good reason. However, Lana took no pleasure in torturing her. She simply wanted to retrieve her property.

"I suppose you now understand what a lowly servant was doing with such a fine piece of jewelry." Lana's voice was soft. "I should not have been made to come here and ask for its return."

Mrs. Frommer took a breath, her lips pressing thin, and went to a cabinet beside her desk. She inserted one of the many keys upon her key ring into a lock, twisted, and opened the door.

When she turned back around, the diamond bracelet was in her palm. She came forward and dropped it into Lana's waiting hand as if the jewels had been blazing hot. There was no hint of regret on her face, and her complete lack of remorse made Lana pause.

"No apology, Mrs. Frommer? For accusing me of being a thief? For ransacking my room?"

As she stared at the woman who had turned the last few weeks into a living purgatory, Lana felt only pity. It was sad that her life was so absent of joy that she took such pleasure in making others miserable. Lana picked up her valise and stood tall, looking at the housekeeper, who suddenly seemed about as fearsome as a soaked kitten. "I forgive you, Mrs. Frommer."

Lana slipped the diamonds into her reticule as the housekeeper flinched and moved back behind her desk, still silent.

"I can only hope that, in future, you will choose to be kinder to those who rank beneath you. That you do not use your power as a way to oppress and threaten."

And with that, Lana had swept out of the housekeeper's office.

Afterward, she and Irina had moved into the earl's home and had become celebrities practically overnight. No longer a servant, but the absolute story of the season. Not a scandal, but a *sensation*, or so Brynn had whispered to her in delight the last time Lana had paid a visit to Ferndale.

And, needless to say, everyone who was anyone in the *beau monde* wanted to meet the mysterious Princess Svetlanka, who had been hunted by a traitor to the tsar and driven into hiding—as a *maid*, of all things. They wanted to meet the woman Lord Northridge had been held at gunpoint trying to protect, the one who had been vetted by two of the most respectable men of their set—Lords Langlevit and Thorndale. The papers throughout London had run numerous stories and accounts of Baron Zakorov and Count Volkonsky's treachery, but it had been the scandal sheets with their opinion pieces on Lana and Irina that had stirred such fervor.

But Lana had not been ready for any of it.

The idea of such wild attention had made her ill with nerves. Brynn had claimed she and Irina were sensations, and the opinion pieces had only supported that, but what if the fickle *ton* changed their minds? What if she and Irina were met not with the kind curiosity the papers were printing, but with scorn?

What if she was still an undesirable and socially impossible match for Gray?

"We don't need to stay long," Lana said as the driver stopped the horses and a footman swung the door open.

She knew Langlevit did not enjoy such crushes and would have much rather been at home in his study. And though he had said next to nothing on the matter, the death of the duke's sister, Lady Eloise, had definitely affected him.

"Stay as long as you like, Princess. You needn't worry about me," he replied as she took the footman's proffered hand. "Besides…I have a feeling you're going to fill your dance card within seconds of your arrival."

Irina scooted forward on the bench. "And what of me?"

Lana laughed and descended the steps. Once her sister had followed, she took in the sight of her and breathed out in relief that Lord Langlevit was indeed their guardian. While Irina still had the stickish figure of a young girl, she had a countenance that would surely capture attention.

"You should count yourself lucky. All other fourteen-year-olds are far too young to attend such a ball, but Her Grace, Lady Bradburne, insisted on your presence," Lana said. "You can be certain to have a full dance card this evening."

It was something she knew her sister would revel in.

"Will you dance with me, my lord?" Irina asked Langlevit as he joined them. His discomfort seemed to increase as he considered his answer.

"Irina, you must allow the *gentlemen* to propose a dance," Lana said, laughing again.

"Well, that seems a risk. What if the gentleman I wish to dance with doesn't ask?"

This time, it was Langlevit who cracked a grin. "The lady has a point." He extended his right elbow to Irina and his left to Lana. "And I will certainly dance with you, though your toes may suffer for it."

Lana doubted he was a horrid dancer, though he did move with definite stiffness. Whether it was his fine breeding, his serious nature, or some old wound, she didn't know. And as they entered Worthington Abbey, her nerves decided it didn't truly matter at the moment.

The doorman took their wraps, and they were led toward the grand ballroom. The last time Lana had been at a ball, she had been a servant. She had been next to invisible. Now, as she walked the corridor, she saw as well as felt eyes falling upon her. The main crush would be in the ballroom, but there were plenty of guests and footmen moving through the halls, and the looks they cast Lana were of pure astonishment. At least, that is what they felt like. They did nothing to quell her nerves, either.

"They have been waiting for this for weeks," Langlevit said.

"For what?" she asked.

"To see you."

She and Irina had sequestered themselves at Hartstone, wanting only to be together after having been apart for so long. Not to mention that they had absolutely nothing to wear. Irina had taken one glance at Lana's lady's maid dresses and had doubled over in laughter. So they had paid Madame Despain a visit, and she and her assistants had been flushed with excitement to be the shop that would outfit the remarkable, and instantly popular, Russian princesses. They remembered her from Briannon's visits, and Madame Despain had gone so far as to say that Lana had, in her opinion, carried herself suspiciously well for a lady's maid.

Lana drew a sudden shaky breath as they arrived at the

ballroom entrance. She did not know why she was so nervous. She'd been to hundreds of balls in St. Petersburg, but for some reason her knees wobbled beneath the voluminous skirts of the gorgeous sapphire satin gown that rippled like liquid every time she moved. Silver thread shimmered through the material whenever it caught the light, creating the illusion that the fabric had a life of its own.

With a black lace overlay, the perfect foil for its vibrant color, it was undeniably one of the loveliest gowns she had ever worn. Diamond earbobs and a stunning matching sapphire-and-diamond teardrop necklace glittered at her ears and throat—a gift from Countess Langlevit. The crowning piece was the magnificent tiara that rested upon her upswept curls.

Lana knew she looked the part, but deep down, she felt like a sham. A *fake*. How could that be? For so long, she *had* been pretending. She'd been slowly forgetting what it was to be a princess. And now that she was restored to her true position, even that didn't feel right.

Her breaths shortened, and she grasped the earl's fingers as their names were announced by Heed, the duke's butler.

"Lord Henry Radcliffe, the Earl of Langlevit," he intoned. "Princess Svetlanka Volkonsky, Princess Irina Volkonsky."

Conversation winked into silence as every eye in the ballroom turned to fix on them. She caught Briannon's startled smile and the austere but approving expression of her new husband at her side, but Lana was only looking for one person.

Her heart felt as if it would burst as her eyes traveled the crowd, fluttering in her chest like a frightened bird. And then, as the trio descended the marble steps to the floor, she saw the object of her frazzled thoughts standing at the bottom. Dressed in raven black from head to toe, except for the crisp white of his shirt and cravat, Gray made her breath catch. If she hadn't kept firm hold of the earl's arm, she would have stumbled. Heat saturated every inch of her skin at the admiring look in those blue eyes. Eyes she had come to know so well. Eyes that had seen her in ways no one else ever had. As she reached him, everyone else ceased to exist.

Until Langlevit's voice drifted in between them. "Lord Northridge," he said, a laughing note tingeing his voice. "May I present Princess Svetlanka Volkonsky, and her sister, Princess Irina Volkonsky."

Gray first greeted Irina with a formal dip of his head and shoulders, and then winked surreptitiously at her, making her giggle. He then turned to Lana and took her hand. He bent over it and pressed his lips to the satin. Heat seared through her gloves, making her entire body burn. "Your Highness, it is a pleasure to meet so beautiful a princess."

"Thank you, my lord," she said, flushing not from his praise, but from his utterly possessive expression and the seductive way his lips had framed the word *pleasure*. It reminded her of things she had no business thinking of right at that moment.

"May I?" He extended his arm to act as her escort. Irina smiled up at her and remained at the earl's side. Lana was acutely aware of Gray's body beside hers as they walked toward Briannon, her new husband, and their surrounding family and friends. Though he held himself rigid and proper, she also felt a yearning. From his body or her own, she wasn't entirely sure. She only knew that beneath those crisply starched clothes was warm skin, hard muscle, and a man that had held her in the most intimate of ways.

She pushed the thoughts from her mind as Gray performed the introductions to the Duke and Duchess of Bradburne. Lana nearly laughed at the pretense, as if she hadn't existed before this moment, but it was the way of the *haute ton*. Men and women who came into fortunes and titles were greeted with pomp and circumstance as if no one had known them before.

"Congratulations, Your Grace," she said to the duke before meeting the amused gaze of his bride. "Your Grace."

"Good heavens, Your Highness, so formal," Briannon teased, rolling her eyes and drawing Lana in for a very unladylike hug. Lana hugged her friend back, grateful that some things, like Brynn's unaffected warmth, hadn't changed.

"Lord and Lady Dinsmore," Langlevit continued.

Lady Dinsmore's complexion took on its customary hue whenever Lana was present. It reminded her of a newly ripened tomato. Despite Lana's protests that the Findlays had made her feel more like family than a servant, Lady Dinsmore couldn't seem to get past her mortification of having had a princess for a maid in her household. She'd apologized countless times and, to Lana's relief, didn't have the chance to do so again now. The earl's mother had moved forward for her proper introduction.

"The Countess of Langlevit," he said, and with a coy grin whispered, "Mother." He bent to kiss his mother's cheek, and Irina, defying propriety, flung herself into the lady's arms.

To Lana's surprise, the countess only laughed and kissed her young ward on both cheeks, an adoring expression on her lined face. Irina had insisted that she and the countess had grown quite close during their time together, and now Lana could see it was so. She hadn't thought it possible to be any more grateful to the earl or his mother, but knowing Irina had been truly cared for and not just a duty brought a sheen of tears to Lana's eyes.

She blinked them away as the introductions went on, the earl leading her and Gray through the ballroom, announcing names and titles, most of which she already knew. Though it was exhausting, Lana bore it with as much grace as she could muster. Gray's firm arm beneath her fingers lent her strength. She couldn't help sneaking glances at his handsome profile as she and Irina were presented to those in attendance. She'd never imagined the day would come when she would be with him in public—on his arm as if she had every right in the world to be there. It was unsettling. And exhilarating.

"Lord Northridge," a woman said, bobbing into a curtsy. And as she rose, Lana recognized her. It was Lady Cooper, and the smile she wore shone brighter as she looked at Lana. "Miss Volchek—oh, heavens, my apologies. *Your Highness*, of course."

"How wonderful to see you again, Lady Cooper." Lana took Lady Cooper's hand and gave it a reassuring squeeze. She had increased since the last time Lana had seen her. Lana felt something stir in her own belly—a phantom desire to one day look as radiant as Lady Cooper did. A tiny, secret, and completely irrational part of her had hoped that something would have come out of what had happened between her and Gray, despite his precautions. But her monthly flux had come and gone, and Lana's common sense had been returned to her.

"Is Sofia in attendance, my lord?" Sir Cooper inquired as he joined his wife.

"She is with her governess," Gray answered, and Lana caught his prideful grin. "In the refreshment room."

Declaring Sofia's legitimacy as his daughter hadn't been as explosive as Gray had expected. Perhaps it had been eclipsed by the two Russian princesses in hiding that had taken London by storm, or by Gray's own heroic role in rescuing them. Either way, Lana was grateful for Gray's sake. As she had anticipated, after the initial shock, Lady Dinsmore absolutely doted on the child. Sofia's laughter at Ferndale had been a welcome arrival in the wake of so much tragedy—not just the culmination of what had occurred with her uncle but also the death of the duke's sister, Lady Eloise.

Claiming a daughter was a much-needed ray of sunshine

in a world so marked by cynicism and affectation. Although having little part in it, Lana couldn't help feeling pride for Gray's courage. Of course there were those who whispered of scandal, Briannon had imparted to her earlier, but that was all they were. Timid whispers.

"May we say hello?" Lady Cooper asked. For a moment, Gray seemed to become even more rigid than before. He took his arm from underneath Lana's, a gentle touch on her wrist as if to tell her he would return shortly. He took Lady Cooper's gloved hands in his.

"You need never ask for permission to see Sofia, my lady. You and Sir Cooper are our family, and always will be. I'm certain she will be delighted to see you both."

Lady Cooper's eyes brimmed with tears, but she smiled and dipped into a short curtsy before they could fall. As the Coopers took their leave to visit the refreshment room, the strains of violins filled the ballroom.

"That was kind of you," Lana said to Gray, grateful the guests' attention had started to transition away from she and Irina.

Gray took up her arm again, fulfilling his silent promise to return. "Not at all. They *are* family. They raised my daughter for three years and love her."

"Not all men would think in such a way," she said, knowing he was not, in any way, like most of the other men in his sphere.

He cut her a sly glance. "Are you finally admitting I am exceptional?"

She sealed her lips and made a show of not hearing him. He laughed but then quieted as the duke led his radiant duchess to the dance floor for the opening waltz.

Lana's heart melted at the sight of them. "Brynn could not look more beautiful," she murmured.

"Your Highness," Gray said, his voice husky instead of

playful now. "May I have the honor of this dance?" Her eyes flicked to Langlevit, who stood close by with Irina. He cleared his throat before escorting his young charge to the middle of the floor. Irina's expression was beatific.

"I would love to, my lord," Lana replied.

As Gray's hand slid around her waist, scorching through the layers of satin and drawing her close, Lana almost lost her footing. *Almost.* The joy of dancing—*real* dancing—made her feel buoyant with delight.

"This is much better, don't you think?" Gray said, his eyes alight with mischief. "Dancing in a proper ballroom."

"I don't know," Lana said, matching his playful gaze. "I rather enjoyed the thrill of dancing alone in a horse stall."

He looked askance at her. "Thrill?"

She leaned slightly closer and whispered, "The risk of discovery. Mrs. Frommer always searching for a reason to dismiss me. We did give her plenty of opportunity."

Something changed in Gray's expression. He started to glower. "Ah, yes, that horrible woman. I should tell you the news—she's been dismissed."

Lana gasped and pulled back, her feet faltering. "What?"

Gray tugged her back into place, closer against him, as he carried them both through the next few dance steps. "A footman found her stealing from the butler's pantry."

She gasped again and accidentally stepped on Gray's foot. "*Stealing?*"

"They found a few other things in her room. Small trinkets no one had bothered to miss. Including a few pieces of Lady Dinsmore's jewelry, put aside from past seasons."

Lana couldn't believe it. Why, that shameless hypocrite! Accusing her of stealing when she was off doing it for real. No wonder she'd seemed so unrepentant when she'd returned the bracelet—she was a hardened thief. Lana pursed her lips and frowned.

Gray looked down at her, curious. "Have I upset you?"

She recovered, shaking her head and trying not to smile. "Not at all. I do wish she'd been discovered earlier, of course." Lana considered a formal, suitable finish for her sentence, but it was not in her heart to do so. She grinned up at him. "If only to have given us a bit more privacy, that is. You see, I seem to have developed a distinct partiality for"—her voice was a provocative caress against his ear—"indecent outings in stables and gardens and gaming hells."

At her words, the amusement fled from his eyes. They darkened with immediate passion, and Lana couldn't help reveling in her ability to affect him as profoundly as he did her. "Lana," he whispered in a strained voice. "Do not say such things to me here in the middle of this room when all it does is make me want to kiss you until you are breathless and drag you off like a mindless brute to find a suitable linen closet."

"Linen closet?" she asked and then answered her own question at the hotly possessive look in his eyes. *Oh.* "It is what I wish, too," she admitted with a fiery blush. Gray's fingers flexed compulsively on her waist as he led her through another turn, almost stumbling himself.

She laughed, and he laughed, too. Lana caught Brynn's delighted smile as she danced with her duke two couples away and grinned back. A few weeks ago, she had never imagined she could be so happy...her sister safe, their identities restored, and dancing so openly in the arms of a man she cherished beyond belief. Their bodies moved in perfect unison to the tune of a magic that belonged only to them. Ballroom or stable, it didn't matter, as long as she was in his arms and he in hers. Even if it were only this dance, she would safeguard it in her heart forever.

"I have missed dancing," she said, her happiness suddenly tinged with melancholy as Gray twirled her expertly. "It was my favorite thing, and now it's my favorite thing to do with you."

His breath skimmed her ear. "I would agree, but dancing is only my *second* favorite thing to do with you."

The wicked timber of his voice made every part of her body tingle. "And what's the first, my lord?" she asked with a smile, the edge of her sadness fading.

"Gambling."

His low answer was a caress, and as Lana lifted her burning gaze to his, the rest of the world seemed to fizzle away. The way Gray was looking at her—like she was the only thing worth seeing—eclipsed the playfulness of his words. The dancers blurred, the music dimmed, and it was only his strong arms anchoring her to him. She never wanted to be anywhere else, not for a single second.

Her eyes drifted to her sister dancing with Lord Langlevit, and she thought of Irina's earlier innocent, childish comment about dancing partners. What if Gray did not know how she felt...at least now, as Princess Svetlanka, enough for him to pose the question? What if he thought she was no longer within his reach? Or worse...that she did not want *him* for more than what he had already given her? Attention and protection, and a handful of scattered, passionate interludes? She'd said such horrible things before, convinced him that she did not care, when the truth was the opposite.

She drew a determined breath. "My lord—"

"Lana—"

They'd spoken at the same time, and Lana lowered her eyes. "You first."

Gray stopped then, right in the middle of the waltz and in the middle of the room. Lana could feel gazes flutter to them as other couples adjusted their pacing and movements to avoid a collision. It was unheard of to halt so suddenly, uncivilized. Then again, neither of them had ever been advocates of convention. The sound of her heartbeat rushed in her ears like thunder as the ball faded away. The only thing left was the man standing in front of her, his heart on his sleeve.

"I wanted to wait," he whispered. "Court you properly as you deserve. But I cannot. I can't wait one more second to make you mine. Not for this waltz, not for this ball, not for this night." Gray's words were short, as if he couldn't formulate his thoughts properly, but she almost swooned at the look in his eyes as he drew one of her gloved hands to his lips. "Will you have me, love?"

Lana couldn't breathe. Her chest felt full and yet empty at the same time. "Have you?" she repeated, confused and hopeful and terrified that he didn't mean what she wanted him to mean.

"I want you as my wife, Lana."

She found she still couldn't take a breath, but not because she was delirious with joy. Rather, she couldn't breathe because she was suddenly afraid. Suddenly uncertain.

She pulled her hand from his, and the sounds of the ballroom returned. "Why?"

By the look in Gray's eyes, he hadn't expected the question any more than Lana had expected to pose it. But she needed to know.

"Why?" he echoed.

"Why do you want to marry me? Because I am a princess now?"

Hurt replaced his confused expression, and she realized how harsh she had sounded. Lana rushed to explain. "Before, when I was nothing more than a maid—"

"I loved you," he interrupted, louder than perhaps he'd intended. The words reached a few of the closest dancers twirling around them, drawing their shocked glances. "When you chastised me for endangering Brynn's health, I loved you. When you refused to tell me the truth about who you were, I loved you. When I saw you tend to Sofia through her illness, I loved you."

He reclaimed her hand and pressed it against the lapel of his jacket, over his heart. "I won't lie. My plan to take you as my wife is going to be a hell of a lot easier now than it was before, when I'd determined to marry my sister's stubborn maid, claim my illegitimate child, find my love's lost sister, and take you all somewhere, anywhere, we could live together in peace."

He took a breath and finally, *finally*, so did Lana. With it came a stone of emotion lodged right in the center of her throat.

"You were going to do that?" she whispered. "Leave your family?"

"I was going to do whatever I had to in order to be with you," he answered, and she saw that for him, the rest of the ballroom was still invisible.

"And Irina?"

He smiled, his blue eyes intense. "I come with a daughter, you come with a sister. Such a thing could not please me more."

"Oh, Gray." Her own eyes filled with tears.

Gray sunk down onto one knee, right there, in the center of the dance floor, and the couples waltzing around them all tripped to a halt and stared openly.

"Lana," he started, and then with a halting smile, finished, "That is, Princess Svetlanka Volkonsky...will you be my wife?"

There it was. The question she'd been desperate for... longed for. Lana's answer was already at the tip of her lips, pushed there by the blissful throb of her heart. "I am yours."

Chapter Twenty-Seven

The hour was late as Lana's betrothed escorted her to Hartstone after many more dances and congratulatory toasts at the ball. Briannon—soon to be Lana's sister-in-law—had been beside herself with joy. She'd witnessed her brother's public proposal from where she'd stood on the dance floor and had rushed to embrace both of them while the rest of the guests had clapped and cheered in utter astonishment, only a handful of the oldest and most stringent tut-tutting at the overt show of emotion.

Lady Dinsmore had been heartily congratulated for having pulled off two of the most brilliant matches that the *ton* had seen in recent years, which made Lana smile and Gray roll his eyes. But the most heartwarming had been Sofia's reaction when her governess had brought her into the ballroom to bid Gray good night. He'd lifted her into his arms and told the little girl that Lana had just agreed to marry him.

"Will *you* be my mama now?" she'd asked shyly.

Lana had felt as if her chest would not be able to contain her love. "Yes, if you'll have me."

"Can we have jam samidges with cream?"

She had laughed her answer through her tears. "Of course, sweetheart. Anything you like."

After so many months of uncertainty, Lana felt consumed by happiness. She and her sister were safe, and the man she loved had asked her to become his wife. She was still walking on air as Gray led her up the stone steps to the manor.

He bowed low, his mouth brushing her knuckles. "I shall pine away the hours until I see you again, my lovely bride-to-be."

Lana blushed, basking in the warmth of his gaze. She glanced up at the blanket of stars in the inky velvet sky. "I must admit that I am not quite ready to retire."

"Shall we indulge ourselves with a midnight stroll, then?"

"It is a lovely evening," she agreed. The June air was balmy against her skin, and a stroll in the earl's gardens sounded too romantic for words. And the plain truth was she wanted to extend their magical night for as long as possible.

They walked in silence, the pathways lit by the brilliant light of the moon riding high in the sky. All the flowers and leaves were gilded in silver, lending a mystical air to the gardens. After a while of strolling hand in hand, they chanced upon the start of a maze in the center of the lush gardens.

"Oh, lovely!" Lana exclaimed, staring at the immaculately groomed hedges looming above them. "It's like the one we have at Volkonsky Palace. When we were children, Irina and I would get lost for hours in it. There was a fountain at the center of ours!"

"Since it appears that you are a maze expert, I shall give you a five-minute head start," Gray said with a playful wink. As she turned to leave, he pulled her toward him, making her gasp at the feel of his hard body pressed against hers. "But first, we must discuss terms."

She licked her lips. "Terms?"

"For the winner."

Her limbs turned useless at the thought of their last bet at The Cock and the Crown. A muscle worked in his cheek at the memories that were obviously tormenting him as well.

"A kiss, perhaps?" he suggested.

Wrapping her arms around his neck, Lana pressed her mouth to his, her tongue darting in for one swift taste before retreating. "I have a better idea for the winner's prize." Gray's eyes widened in surprise, but she slid out of his grasp and disappeared around the first bend of the maze. "But you must be swift, Lord Northridge."

"Lana," he growled in amused frustration.

"You promised five minutes, my lord," she sang over her shoulder as she came to another opening.

It didn't take her long to work out the maze. Every maze had its own mathematical pattern, and this one seemed to be every third left and every second right. Lana smiled to herself as she peeled the glove from her left arm and left it in the pathway. A few paces later, she dropped the second. Her entire body was tingling with anticipation as she left her slippers behind, and then, at later intervals, each of her stockings. She knew it was utterly scandalous, but she didn't care. She felt free and unfettered, the cool, smooth stones under her feet exhilarating. The sublime glow of moonlight and the enchanted nature of the maze made her feel like a woodland sprite. It was an ethereal landscape, one that filled her mind with indecent fantasies.

A laughing gasp froze on her lips as she came to the center of the maze. It wasn't a fountain like the one at Volkonsky Palace or some Greek statue. Instead, the jewel of this maze was a gorgeous stained-glass greenhouse. She pushed open the door and smiled in delight. A circular cushioned bench dominated its center, while fragrant miniature roses of every hue ran its circumference.

She was so spellbound at the whimsical sight that she didn't hear Gray until his arms slid around her waist from behind, his lips nibbling at her ear. "You are a minx," he murmured, her discarded items of clothing falling to the floor.

Lana turned in his arms. "Have you ever seen anything so beautiful?"

"Yes." It was clear he wasn't referring to the greenhouse, and she blushed. His fingers caressed the sensitive skin inside her elbows with grazing touches that left tingles in their wake. Gray's gaze slid to the tips of her bare feet, peeping from the hem of her dress. "My barefoot princess," he whispered before his lips claimed hers in a tender kiss.

Lana pulled away before the kiss evolved into something more urgent. "Gray," she asked, her voice trembling. "Would you have truly wanted to marry me if I were still a maid?"

"I would have wanted you if you were an urchin on the street without a farthing to your name," he breathed. "You belong with me, Lana. I think I knew it when you gave me that dressing-down in the kitchen stairwell without a care for my station, just to protect my sister. I knew I had to have you, especially after that morning you were in my carriage along Ferndale's drive. Do you remember? You asked me if I liked what I saw." His smile turned wolfish. "I did, very much."

She bit her bottom lip. "That was bold of me."

"I love it when you're bold." His thumb slid over her lower lip, freeing it from where her teeth had it pinned. "I love everything about you."

"You do?" she asked, her voice thin with sudden nerves. Her feet were cold against the slate floor, but that wasn't why she'd started to shiver.

Gray's palms cupped her cheeks. "My sweet love, you have had my heart in your keeping for months."

He drew his mouth down to hers, and Lana's lips parted, welcoming the hot sweep of his tongue. He lifted her in a smooth motion, kicking the door shut with his heel and walking toward the center of the greenhouse. He set her on the round bench, the cushion soft beneath her.

He remained standing, gazing down at her. The moonlight caught the segments of jeweled glass and lit the inside of the greenhouse, as well as the two of them, in a kaleidoscope of colors. Gray turned to look at the small pile of her things he'd left on the floor near the greenhouse door. Her slippers lay underneath her silk stockings and gloves.

"Eager are we?" he asked, his attention coming back to her.

Lana drew her chilled feet up onto the cushion and felt the softness of her calves rubbing together under her gown. She flushed at her own audacity. "Call it incentive, my lord."

He lowered his chin and deepened his stare, the bright blue of his eyes a radiant ice color in the jeweled light. "You know I enjoy it when you are bold, but what I want to know," he said, one of his knees sinking onto the cushion beside her. "Is if you enjoy it when I am."

Leaning onto her elbows, Lana lifted her eyes and stared up at him. "How bold might that be?"

"Bold enough to tell you exactly what *I* want."

She felt an extra throb of her heart and a responding flutter of her pulse in her neck. "And what do you want?"

Gray gripped Lana's hips and with one swift motion rolled her onto her stomach. "Ooof!" she let out and tried to push up onto her elbows. He'd climbed higher, bracketing her upper legs and pinning her into place. "What are you *doing*?"

"I am planning a letter to Madame Despain in which I tell her to never design another dress for you that has laces up the back."

She felt him tugging at the intricately laced satin ribbon that wove up the back of her dress.

"Gray—"

"I told you I could not wait to make you mine," he said.

Her bodice became looser as he spoke, her front still pressed into the cushion of the bench. "But we are in Lord Langlevit's greenhouse! And I am already yours. We are betrothed."

"I now mean to make you mine in an entirely more carnal way."

She gaped at the creamy white cushion beneath her, her body igniting to flame at the mere spark of his words. Of course he had already done so. At The Cock and the Crown. And it would be a lie to say she had not dreamed of being underneath him again. *And again.*

But the earl could return to Hartstone at any time. And Irina! She had begged to stay at the ball to fulfill her dance card completely and perhaps have a little more cake, but Henry was no doubt growing restless. The countess, as well.

"We cannot," she whispered, as if someone might already be lurking just beyond the stained-glass exterior.

He slowed his tugging, but after a moment, Lana realized it wasn't because he was in agreement. Gray opened her bodice, the cool air touching her bare upper back.

A pair of warm lips followed. They were light, delicate nudges, but to her astonishment, each one elicited a reaction within her as deep and resonant as the strike of a bell. She gasped at the familiar prickles of desire between her legs.

He lifted his lips from her skin just long enough to murmur, "I want to strip this gorgeous gown from your body and lay you out before me."

Lana closed her eyes, allowing him to gently free each of her arms from their cap sleeves. She then stretched her bared arms before her and clutched the edge of the bench.

Gray began to pull at the unlaced bodice and stays. The layers slipped down her body, and she felt him shifting side to side to allow the voluminous skirts to ripple down onto the floor. Within moments, she was in her chemise and drawers, his knees still caging her legs.

"I want to see every inch of your delectable skin," he said, his breath hot against the low-backed cotton chemise. Lana shivered and felt his fingers pushing the cotton up over her head, his body reaching to pull the fabric from her arms.

"I want to taste every part of you," he said, and Lana's eyes snapped open.

"Wh—what?" she asked, her throat barely able to make sound.

Gray slid one palm in between her body and the cushion, and filled it with her breast. He kneaded her gently, and Lana tried once more to rise onto her elbows. She gasped, her other breast yearning for attention. But his free hand had traveled southward, to the final article of clothing she wore. His fingers dipped underneath the waistband of her drawers.

"I'm telling you what I want," he replied, lowering himself until she felt his weight against her back. He took her earlobe between his teeth and pushed the fabric down, exposing her backside. She swallowed a moan as his hand cupped one of her rounded cheeks.

"And what I want is for you to say yes," he said, his tongue swirling behind her ear.

Distracted by his caresses, she murmured, "I've already said yes."

"You said yes to being my wife," he corrected, her drawers now around her knees. Gray's hands caressed her from shoulder to thigh, his lips and teeth kissing and nipping her back in their wake. Lana wanted to turn over and wrap her arms and legs around him, pull him into her and feel every sublime sensation she had on that purple velvet sofa at The Cock and the Crown. "I want you to say yes to the things I've enumerated right here," he said. "Right now."

To see every inch of her.

To taste every inch of her.

Heat swamped her, her brain going utterly useless. What normal-blooded woman in her right mind would say no to the thoroughly wicked things this man was offering? She felt his lips trailing down the curve of her lower back and then along the rise of her buttock and promptly lost any and all care for where they were and who might chance upon them. She could not tell him to stop, not now, not when the hot, sweet ache in her core demanded otherwise.

"Yes," she admitted, blushing fiercely. "I want what you want."

His tongue stalled out on her rump, and she felt his smile against her skin. "Yes, you do."

The drawers sailed from her legs, and with one more roll, Gray had her on her back. The cool greenhouse air hit her breasts, and they tightened, gooseflesh firing up and down her arms and legs. Parts of her had been exposed to Gray before, but never *all* of her. And he'd never stood back, the way he was right then, and stared at her with such intrepid ardor. Lana felt the urge to cover herself, but she knew he would only coax her hands away. Besides, he liked it when she was bold. And so she lifted her chin and allowed his eyes to roam. A knowing grin pulled the corner of his mouth, and he lowered himself slowly in front of the bench. Lana tried to sit up, but he made a sound to stop her.

"But, what are you—*oh!* Gray—"

He'd run his hands up her inner thighs and nudged them apart, and slid her closer to the edge of the cushion. He kissed the inside of one thigh.

"I said I wanted to taste every inch of you," he murmured, kneading the sides of her stiffened limbs and moving forward until his lips were at her apex.

She went rigid with wild alarm at his warm breath fanning against her most private place—he couldn't possibly mean what she thought he meant. "But I—"

"Want me to? Yes, I know. I'm so glad we agree on this."

Before she could say another word, Lana felt one of his fingers enter her. She tensed, closing tightly around him and promptly losing all powers of speech or protest.

"Relax, my love," Gray whispered. "I promise you nothing but pleasure."

She had no doubt of Gray's skill or what he could give her, but the very picture of them in the greenhouse, with her splayed on the cushioned bench completely nude, his hands and mouth fulfilling those indecent promises—it should have made her worry. It should have shocked her. Instead, something else took her utterly by surprise: a sweep of pure, unadulterated lust.

Lana released the muscles in her legs and moaned as Gray stroked in and out of her. Sighing with pleasure, she stared at the stained-glass ceiling, bathed in the moonlight filtering through, and matched his rhythmic plunges with her hips. When he removed his finger, she whimpered—and then gasped loudly as something warm and wet replaced it. Lana arched her spine and dug her fingers into the cushion as Gray plunged his tongue into her core. She held her breath as he took long, deep licks, doing exactly as he'd intended. Tasting her. *Devouring* her.

Lana had never felt anything so divine—or as wicked. The wanton position, the sinful feel of his velvet tongue, and the return of his finger had Lana gasping for air. She cried out as pleasure built in swelling ripples, only knowing that the reward was there, right beyond her grasp, and she needed it. She worked her fingers into Gray's hair and held on, her body quivering and pulsing as each dive of his tongue, every teasing scrape of his teeth, pushed her toward the nameless, shapeless thing she craved.

And then she caught it, a trembling heat consuming her

from the very center of her body. Lana cried out again and again, embracing the heat as it started to flow away from her. And with it went her inexplicable yearning. Her muscles were slack, her fingers no longer tangled in Gray's hair. He lifted himself from her and kissed his way up her stomach, to her breasts, where he took a protracted moment to swirl his hot, talented tongue around each nipple.

"Gray," she sighed, unable to think. Unable to say anything more than that.

"Did you enjoy giving me what I wanted?" he asked, a teasing lilt to his voice.

It had felt more like Gray giving *her* something, but she couldn't do more than nod and smile.

He pulled back, standing once more beside the bench. Lana watched him through heavily lidded eyes as he stripped out of his jacket and began to unbutton his waistcoat. Somewhere, somehow, he'd already rid himself of his cravat.

"You cannot be serious," she whispered, beginning to rouse from the seductive web he'd woven around them. "What if we are discovered?"

Sobering, Lana immediately began to consider possible scenarios. Henry, Irina, and the countess, returning to Hartstone to be informed by the butler that, no, Princess Svetlanka had not arrived home on her newly betrothed's arm. The earl taking to the lawns in search of them. His eyes catching on the entrance to the maze, and then…

Gray pulled his shirt off in one overhead tug, and Lana stopped worrying. Stopped thinking. Stopped breathing. He was beautiful. The muscles of his chest and shoulders were broad and able, tapering into a narrow, sculpted torso that made her mouth go dry.

"Then I suppose we will simply have to marry," he replied, releasing the fall of his trousers and shucking off those next. With them went his smalls, and Lana shot to her elbows, her eyes riveted on his...oh, sweet heavens. She knew that part of him had already claimed her once before and had seen his impressive length between their bodies. But she had not viewed it like this.

"I think it only fair. I did get to see every inch of you, did I not?" he said, that teasing grin of his falling back into place.

"Gray. You're..." She didn't know how to finish without sounding absurd. *Perfect? Manly? Breathtaking?*

He crawled onto the bench and hovered over her. "Exactly where I want to be for the rest of my life."

She smiled up at him, suddenly giddy. "In Lord Langlevit's greenhouse?"

He remained sober, however, and she blinked in surprise at his seriousness. "With you, Lana. It doesn't matter where I am, so long as we're together. Like this."

Gray touched her, his palms coursing down her body, his serious gaze admiring her figure the way someone might admire a sculpture.

"You are the most beautiful woman I have ever seen."

Lana knew it couldn't be true. She had seen a number of women more beautiful than she at the ball tonight and many times before. But whether it was factual or not, in that moment, Gray was being honest. He thought she was beautiful. He wanted her. He loved her.

And she realized then that she had not yet told him how *she* felt. That she loved him, too. She loved him more than she'd ever imagined possible.

"I want one more thing," he said before she could speak. Maybe it was for the best. They were important words, and she wanted to say them when the timing was right.

"Yes?" she asked, half paying attention and half ogling the swollen length between his legs.

Gray didn't answer with words. Instead, he scooped his hands below her back and moved her again—this time on top of him—as he settled beneath her. He reclined on the cushion and positioned her legs so that she was straddling him. Her hair was somehow still swept up in pins except for a few tousled strands. She pushed them back, out of her eyes.

"I want to watch you come for me again, this way," he said, his voice husky. Lana went still, her heart skipping a beat and then throbbing hard to catch up.

She peered down at him, apprehension filling her. He wanted her to take control, and her immediate reaction was to say she couldn't. That she didn't know how.

But then she remembered that with every encounter she'd had with Gray so far, he'd shown her *how*. How to find pleasure, and how to give him the same thing. Each time, her body had learned, and swiftly.

Lana gathered the boldness she now knew he adored and shifted to put him at her entrance.

"Take your time, my love, I know your body is still new to—"

Lana rocked against him, feeling the smooth crown of his shaft nudging into her. Gray's sentence cut off with a groan at the intimate clutch of her body upon him, and he gripped her hips, his own rising in a thrust. She bit her lip as she met him halfway with an indelicate gasp, before fully seating herself and allowing her inner muscles to adjust to his girth. And then what had felt like a foreign body invading her began to feel like an extension of her own. She rocked forward again, the slick friction of their joining spiking her desire. With every decadent roll of her hips, Gray met her with a thrust, and soon their bodies were moving in a rhythm that made her breathless.

"Lana," he said, his own breath coming short. "Open your eyes. Look at me, love."

She hadn't realized how tightly shut her eyes had been until he bid her open them. When she did, the sight of his naked body underneath hers, of his dark, passion-filled eyes, made her feel a kind of power she had never experienced before. She was a princess, but she felt like a goddess. He belonged to her, and she to him, and she wanted to stay this way forever.

Maneuvering her legs around his hips, Gray sat forward and braced her back, giving her the freedom to lean back a little onto her arms. She didn't break her rhythm, or eye contact, and the change in positioning seemed to open something else up inside of her. An untethered euphoria swept from her core to the ends of her limbs, and as Gray's thrusts began to intensify, she knew he was feeling the same frenzied rush, that he was nearly to the edge of his own ecstasy. He kept his eyes firmly hinged on hers, and Lana became as intent to watch his pleasure break through him as he was to watch hers.

She could barely breathe, much less form actual words, but she had to tell him. *Now.* "I love you," she rasped. "I love you so much, Gray."

His eyes flared in immediate response, every muscle in his body tightening as if her declaration was the very thing to send him hurtling over the edge. Gray's fingers dug into her behind, urging her onto his length harder and faster than before, his only answer a grunt of pure satisfaction. With one tremendous surge he groaned his release, fastening his hips to hers. Within seconds she cried out, her inner passage convulsing around him as he continued to grind against her, their bodies cradled in intimate bliss. She clutched at him, wanting to stay in this moment, wanting only to prolong the last pulses of pleasure shuddering between them.

For a minute, Gray simply held her, their damp bodies still joined. He tried to even his breathing, and she did the same, her chest heaving.

Gray leaned forward and nuzzled her breasts, his lips then tracing just underneath the glittering necklace she'd forgotten all about, resting along her collarbone.

"Say it again," he said.

Lana tried to clear her head and determine what he meant, but then she remembered. "I love you."

He stayed rooted within her, and she realized then that he'd spilled his seed inside of her. He hadn't pulled free at the last moment to avoid unwanted consequences. Because whatever child they created together would never be unwanted. Or a mistake. Gray was going to be her husband, and she his wife. The mother of his children.

He kissed her lips, though softly. Unlike before. This was the kind of kiss that seemed to say they had plenty of time for other kisses.

"And I love you," he said, then heaved an affected sigh. "Though I do think one of these times I should get you into a real bed before defiling your luscious body."

She pressed her lips to his neck. "And why would you want to do that, my lord?"

"It seems like a more proper place for a man to ravish his wife."

Lana licked his earlobe and felt the responding rise of gooseflesh over his shoulders, where she'd wrapped her arms. "I think I prefer the inappropriate places more."

He captured her mouth with a less chaste kiss this time. "I'll take that as a challenge, Your Highness. Prepare yourself."

Lana laughed and kissed him again, quite certain that when it came to Gray, she would never be fully prepared. And she could not dream of having it any other way.

Epilogue

Gray glanced at Lana sitting opposite him in the carriage, cradling their eight-month-old son to her breast on one side and a sleeping five-year-old Sofia on the other. Now, finally on their way to Volkonsky Palace—their first visit there as a family—he felt a fullness rise in his chest. Sometimes, he still couldn't fathom that Lana was actually his. That she had married him. Accepted his daughter. Borne him a son. Some days, he half expected to awaken one morning to see everything had disappeared, as if part of some imagined fantasy. But it never did, and Gray had never been happier.

Experiencing St. Petersburg through his wife's eyes was like nothing Gray had ever imagined. Widely traveled, he had seen all manner of stunning architecture and breathtaking cathedrals across the continent, but Lana's natural exuberance and pride for her home transformed the visit into something magical. Whether it was her love for her city or the fact that she brought new light to anything they shared, Gray was in awe. He viewed the magnificent Winter Palace with fresh eyes, listening to her riveting accounts of the sumptuous balls she'd attended there with her parents. They visited the abandoned Mikhailovsky Castle together, and she regaled him with tales her father had told her of when Emperor Paul had lived there and was assassinated sixteen years before. Her anecdotal stories made the old city come alive.

Prior to their wedding in London, Lana and Irina had taken several trips back to Russia with the Earl of Langlevit to ensure that things were running smoothly at Volkonsky Palace. But Gray had remained in London to tend to his affairs. Lana's uncle was stripped of his title, along with his guardianship of his brother's daughters.

Alexander, the tsar himself, had attended their nuptials, causing quite a stir in London with his unplanned arrival, and had expressed his gratitude to both princesses as well as to Lord Langlevit and Gray for their assistance in unearthing the plot and the two traitors. The honor of Alexander's presence was noted by many in attendance, adding to Gray and Lana's startling rise in popularity among the *ton*, which of course meant little to either of them.

After their wedding, though Lana's visits to her ancestral home had grown shorter, Irina's had not. And on the last trip they took together, Irina had decided to stay in St. Petersburg for an extended period. Her absence had been tough on Lana, but Lana understood that her somewhat impetuous sister needed to find her own way. The Earl of Langlevit had secured a suitable chaperone who had met with Lana's approval. Gray knew that Lana was looking forward to a long overdue reunion with her younger sister at Volkonsky Palace.

Across from him in the coach, Lord Oliver Gregory Findlay cooed contentedly, snug in the capable arms of his mother. Although Lana had agreed to the occasional assistance of a night nurse, she adored taking care of their young son. As Gray watched her, his hooded gaze falling to her lush body, he felt something stir in his loins. Motherhood suited her, and his passion for her had not diminished in the least. Neither had hers, thankfully. His thoughts wandered to a few hours earlier, when she had screamed his name, her body arching beneath his as he brought her to fulfillment. He could never get enough of her, it seemed. And the ripe changes of motherhood had made her delectable body even more luscious, more irresistible. She drove him mad, and right then his desire for her drummed through him. He resettled himself in his seat, trying to think of something other than ravaging every inch of his radiant wife with his mouth. But it was an uphill battle.

Lana's laughing eyes met his as if she could read his thoughts, and he arched a lazy eyebrow in response. "*That*, my lord, is the reason I am with child yet again," she said softly.

"I cannot help it if you wish to seduce me at every turn."

Her low laughter filled the interior of the carriage. "Well, if that is your stance, I shall endeavor to be less…bold in the future." She paused, licking her lips and drawing his attention there. All attempt at controlling himself went out the window as the blood rushed to his nether regions, making him grimace. Her smile turned coy. "Which will be a pity, as there are so many inappropriate places to discover at Volkonsky Palace."

"Don't you dare," Gray growled with a laugh, taking her meaning and growing stiffer. He groaned and adjusted his position, fervently wishing that they'd let the children ride in the other carriage with the nurse and the governess. He'd have had his sweet wife's skirts over her head before she could blink. "And for the love of all things holy, can we talk about something else before I embarrass myself?"

Thankfully, she took pity on him. "I'm so looking forward to you seeing my home."

"I am, too."

"We're almost there," she said, leaning forward, her eyes lighting. "It's just beyond those hills. There's the village. And the old church!"

Desperate for any distraction, he peered obediently out the window, feeling his baser urges lessen at the sight of the picturesque landscape. It reminded him somewhat of Essex, although there were many differences.

"Look now, just past this bend." Lana's voice hummed with excitement as they neared Volkonsky Park, which she'd told him surrounded the palace.

But nothing had prepared him for the sight that greeted him as the carriage crested the hill...not Lana's stories or Langlevit's curt descriptions. The glittering curve of the Slavyanka River caught his attention first, and then his gaze lifted to the lush landscape crowned by a sprawling castle at least five times the size of Ferndale's manor house, resting like a jewel at the peak of a second rolling hill. He admired the long, sweeping lines of the architecture and the elegant neoclassical mix of Greek and Roman influences. His eyes drank in the aesthetically pleasing landscape park surrounding them, dotted with manicured gardens, shimmering lily ponds, and marble pavilions.

"What do you think?" Lana asked softly, watching him.

"It's beautiful. But I did not expect anything less."

The carriage ambled up the road and rolled to a stop in the courtyard, giving in to a flurry of activity as servants bustled out to welcome them, and the nurse came to take both still-drowsy children. But before Gray could descend to help Lana down from the carriage, she barred his way and closed the door.

"What are you doing?"

Lana moved to ensconce herself in his lap. "Before we go, there's one thing I wish to tell you."

"And what is that?" Gray said huskily, the firm press of her bottom against his thighs inflaming his senses. He nibbled her ear and dragged slow kisses along her jaw.

"Do you remember the maze I told you about?" Her voice shook as he kissed the corner of her mouth.

"Yes."

"You recall what I told you lay at its center?"

"A fountain. Why?"

His wicked wife raised a laughing gaze to him. "You should know that I used to sneak away to swim in there at night." She kissed him, her teasing tongue coaxing his to action. "Naked," she whispered into his mouth.

"Lana," he groaned, the combination of the erotic kiss and the thought of her frolicking like a water sprite beneath the spray of a fountain filling his brain with wanton desires. "I will not be responsible for what your servants think when I toss you over my shoulders and sprint for said labyrinth."

"My servants have learned to turn a blind eye to my antics."

"In that case." He moved to the edge of the bench, gathering her into his arms with an evil grin. "What are we waiting for?"

"That depends on how much you love me."

It was all in play of course. Gray would never embarrass her, even if her servants were used to their mistress's eccentricities. And there would be more than enough time for games later. In private. Either in said fountain or behind closed doors. It did not matter which…as long as she lay satiated in his arms.

He stared down at the woman who held his heart—the love of his life and the mother of his children—and wondered for the hundredth time how they'd managed to avert disaster at almost every turn. Their love had not been easily won, but now here they were…*together*, with a chance at true happiness. He would not waste a second of it.

Gray looked into his wife's eyes, his voice solemn as the day he'd given her his vows. "I will love you to my last breath, my darling."

Acknowledgments

Amalie Howard

Thanks always to my spectacular co-author, Angie Morgan, who astounds me with her talent. Seriously, I feel like I've won the co-author lottery! Huge thanks to our editor, Alethea Spiridon, and our publisher, Liz Pelletier, without whom you would not be reading this book. Props to the entire production, design, and publicity teams at Entangled, with special thanks to Curtis Svehlak, Holly Bryant-Simpson, Riki Cleveland, Melanie Smith, and Anita Orr, who make the book magic happen. A heartfelt thank you goes out to all my loyal readers, fans, and friends. I am so grateful for your support! Lastly, to my wonderful family—Cameron, Connor, Noah, and Olivia—I love you to pieces.

Angie Morgan

I have had a sinful amount of fun writing historical romance with my co-author, Amalie Howard! Amalie, I can't thank you enough for being my *other*, other half! We're a great team and I can't wait to write more books with you. Thank you to our amazing Entangled team, who've rallied behind our books and loved them as much as we do. Alethea Spiridon, Liz Pelletier, Curtis Svehlak, Holly Bryant-Simpson, Riki Cleveland, Melanie Smith, and Anita Orr—you're all the best! Our readers, fans, and friends are also the best! Thank you so much for your support. And of course to Chad, Alex, Joslin, and Willa – thanks for being the best family a girl could ask for!

About the Author

Amalie Howard's love of romance developed after she started pilfering her grandmother's novels in high school when she should have been studying. She has no regrets. A #1 Amazon bestseller and a national IPPY silver medalist, she is the author of *My Rogue, My Ruin*, the first in the Lords of Essex historical romance series, as well as several award-winning young adult novels critically acclaimed by Kirkus, Publishers Weekly, VOYA, School Library Journal, and Booklist, including *Waterfell*, *The Almost Girl*, and *Alpha Goddess*, a Kid's IndieNext pick. She currently resides in Colorado with her husband and three children. Visit her at www.amaliehoward.com.

Angie Morgan lives in New Hampshire with her husband, their three daughters, a menagerie of pets, and an extensive collection of paperback romance novels. She's the author of *My Rogue, My Ruin*, the first book in the Lords of Essex historical romance series, as well as several young adult books, including The Dispossessed series written under the name Page Morgan. Critically acclaimed by Booklist, Publisher's

Weekly, Kirkus, School Library Journal, VOYA, and The Bulletin, Angie's novels have been an *IndieNext* selection, a *Seventeen Magazine* Summer Book Club Read, and a #1 Amazon bestseller. Visit her at www.AngieMorganBooks. com.

Discover more historical romance...

ONCE A COURTESAN
a *Once Wicked* novel by Liana LeFey

Romance blossoms between Headmistress Jacqueline Trouvère and her mysterious new maths instructor, Mr. William Woodson, but both harbor deadly secrets. When danger jeopardizes the school, all will come to light, threatening to destroy their newfound love.

ONLY A DUKE WILL DO
a *To Marry a Rogue* novel by Tamara Gill

On the eve of Lady Isolde Worthingham's wedding to Merrick Mountshaw, the Duke of Moore, a scandal that rocked the ton leaves her perfectly planned future in a tangle of disgrace and heartbreak. The duke loathes the pitiful existence he hides from the *ton*. With a scandalous wife he never wanted, life is a never-ending parade of hell. When the one woman he loved and lost returns to London, he can no longer live without her. But vows and past hurts are not easily forgotten. Love may not win against the *ton* when a too proper Lord and Lady play by the rules.

One Step Behind
a novel by Brianna Labuskes

Lucas Stone, the Earl of Winchester, has a reputation for arrogance and a soft-spot for his sister, which is how he ends up in the predicament of hiding behind a curtain at midnight with the dreadfully dull Miss Imogen Lancaster. But he soon discovers appearances can be deceiving when the country mouse turns into a spitfire in front of his eyes. Now they must work together, which would be fine, if they could decide if they'd rather fall in love or kill one another.

The Madness of Lord Westfall
an *Order of the M.U.S.E.* novel by Mia Marlowe

Pierce Langdon, Viscount Westfall, is mad. So they say. But he actually has a psychic gift. He hears people's thoughts, and uses his ability in service to the Order of the M.U.S.E. Now he's investigating a plot against the Crown, and the Lady Nora Claremont, a sultry courtesan, seems to be at the center of it. If he wasn't mad before, Nora may drive him to it. Pierce knows just what she wants and what she's thinking. What Nora wants is Pierce...and what she's thinking could expose her as a traitor to the crown.